THE ALEWIFE
Curse *of* Obsession

Also from Jason T. Graves
www.jasontgraves.com

BLOOD ROSES
Book One of
THE NOCTIVAGAS CHRONICLE

MORNING STARS
Book Two of
THE NOCTIVAGAS CHRONICLE

MARS RISING
Book Three of
THE NOCTIVAGAS CHRONICLE
Coming Soon

GRETCHEN THYRD
ON THE BRIDGE
Book One of
THE TALES OF THYRD

Short Stories
Anthologized in

OFF THE BEATEN PATH I
EIGHT TALES OF THE PARANORMAL

BADASS AND THE BEAST
TEN "TAILS" ABOUT KICKASS HEROINES
AND THE BEASTS WHO LOVE THEM

The **ALEWIFE**
Curse *of* Obsession

JASON T. GRAVES

PROSPECTIVE PRESS
Winston-Salem

PROSPECTIVE PRESS

1959 Peace Haven Rd, #246, Winston-Salem, NC 27106 U.S.A.
www.prospectivepress.com

Published in the United States of America by PROSPECTIVE PRESS LLC

THE ALEWIFE: CURSE OF OBSESSION

Author photo copyright © Jason T. Graves, 2012

Cover and interior design by ARTE RAVE

ISBN 978-1-943419-27-2

Printed in the United States of America
First Prospective Press printing, January 2016
Second printing, October 2106
Expanded and Revised

3 5 7 9 10 8 6 4 2

The text of this book was typeset in Athelas
Accent text was typeset in DDC Ash

Previously published in 2014 under the same title.

PUBLISHER'S NOTE

Preface
to the Prospective Press edition

Thanks for taking a moment to read these few words about this new edition of *The Alewife: Curse of Obsession*. I'm very excited about the book you hold in your hands—even more excited than when it was first released two years ago—because this edition fixes several of the flaws that I felt existed in the previous edition. A few examples: first, the number of chapters has been reduced substantially, from 81 to 48, while the total word count has increased as passages were extended and greater detail added; second, in the process of expanding the chapters, several of the scenes were reordered to improve the story flow; and third, the language was returned to that found in the original manuscript, expletives and all. While some may find this offensive, I think it is important for the story, and its characters, to be true within and to itself.

Some readers have asked about certain elements in the story. If you, at any point, want more information about a *thing* that you discover in these pages, there is an epilogue with brief details of these *things*. Don't look now! Wait until you have questions. In the meantime, enjoy this newly and wonderfully re-imagined book; and, as always, happy reading.

Jason T. Graves
Winston-Salem, NC
October, 2015

Acknowledgments
from the original edition

While the craft of writing is predominantly a solitary process, the labor of re-writing is not. To that end, I want to give a thousand words of praise to my friends and companions who gather to dissect the mutterings I put to page and who, with graceful humor and handy blunt objects, coax me to make my stories better than I thought possible.

Special words of thanks to Darby, Stacy, Melissa, and Chris: I tip my hat to your insight and prowess, both with words and ideas.

With much appreciation, I acknowledge Suzanne, Mark, and Clare—three friends from the UK—for keeping Aiden sounding English.

And for *my* faithful "Jillian."

Even though my "Meeka" is made of words and dreams, silicon and code, I appreciate that you allow her—this writing thing I do—to occupy a place in our life.

Thank you

1

Doug's arms sliced through the water in powerful strokes, pulling him inexorably to his target. Old Soaker Island was only a deserted strip of rock, but today he would own it. He surged up through the surface and shook the Atlantic from his eyes. The smudge of island lay dead ahead—his bearing was right on.

Splashing drew his attention over his left shoulder. Thirty yards away, Brian was a machine, cleaving through the gray water. *Mighty... but off target as usual*, Doug thought and smirked. At this rate, Brian would miss Old Soaker by fifty yards or more. Without lane markings, Brian always had a hard time swimming a straight line.

"Swim with me."

Unexpected, the sound made Doug twitch, and then twist. The girl from the restaurant—*Meeka*—was pitching in the choppy waves a few body lengths away. *How'd she swim up without me hearing?* An enigmatic smile illuminated her face. He remembered those lips from last night, how cool and salty they were. How good they had felt on his.

His own lips curled a bit in response. "What're you doing out here?" A wince squeezed his features. *Oh, that was brilliant.*

Meeka's smile never wavered. "Swimming."

"Oh. Do you...do you swim here a lot?"

A wave hit him, flooding his nose with water. He hacked like an old smoker.

"Swim with me, Douglas."

An effusive smile cracked his face, twisted by a few straggling coughs. *She remembers my name.* "Was that you I saw out on the bay last night?"

"Yes. Why didn't you join me?"

Without thinking, he turned to check on Brian's progress. "Um, 'cause swimming in the ocean in the middle of the night isn't real safe, especially drunk." Brian was still far off course. Doug swiveled his attention back to Meeka.

Her gaze flicked out to Brian and back. "Yes, I can see how male companionship and beer was so much more alluring than spending the evening with me."

"Yeah, I, uh..." *Wrong choice, moron.* Instead of staying with Meeka, he had followed Brian down to the beach to drink beer with some college guys. Well into the binge, he thought he had seen her swimming off shore, waving at him.

"Douglas?"

But here she is now, why live in the past? "I'd like to make it up to you," he said in a stroke of budding maturity.

"Sure. I'd like that."

"Doug? Hey, Doug! Did you find a mermaid?" Brian's voice crested the waves, and he laughed. "Oh, it's just your mattress from last night."

Doug flinched, his cheeks warming. Brian was still sore from losing the prior evening's competition. *Why couldn't you have kept swimming?* "Sorry. He's kinda stupid."

"Who cares what he says." Meeka smiled. "And, I do want to make love to you."

What? "Um..."

"Swim with me." She beckoned him.

He smiled in response, pitched into the water, and reached her in a few strokes. Up close, he saw that his eyes had not lied to him last night—she was a beautiful girl. Their legs bumped as they tread water, and she laughed. She put her arms around his neck, drawing him in for another cool, salty kiss.

"Doug, come on man. What about our race?"

"You win," Doug called over his shoulder.

"No, you do," Meeka said, her smile dazzling. "Follow me." She lay back in the water in an elegant back stroke, and he gasped when he realized that she was not wearing a swimsuit.

"Seriously? Come on!" Brian called.

Doug was torn, but not terribly. "Sorry, man. Duty calls." He leaned into a breast stroke, matching Meeka's pace, while watching her lithe body glide through the water. Minutes of ocean slid by, before she popped out of the water, a look of irritation on her face. He looked away, flushed with guilt, thinking that she was mad at him for staring at her naked skin, but her glare went beyond him.

"Tell your friend to stop following us."

"Huh?"

Brian continued to churn up the water, more or less toward them.

"Go away, dude!" He felt Meeka move alongside him. Her breasts pressed into his back and biceps, and her lips skimmed his ear. Her breath tickled his wet skin. "Come, make love to me."

She shot away from him. He caught the tantalizing sight of more bare skin, and plunged after her. She was a good swimmer, but he was confident that he could catch her. He kept popping up to check, but she always remained slightly ahead of him. The fourth time up, Meeka was looking back at him, and he heard Brian call his name.

"Doug. Doug! Doug!" The last was a squeal of terror that he had never before heard his friend make. He saw Brian go under. *That was too fast...he's drowning!*

All thoughts of Meeka fled his mind as he swam back to where he thought he had seen Brian go under. He sucked in a lungful of air and dove. Without goggles, everything underwater looked distorted as he scanned the dimness, looking for anything pale. Seeing something moving, he swam towards it, and found Brian struggling with dark strands that tangled around his legs. He was doubled over, frantically wrestling with the ropy things. They looked like a squid's tentacles.

Doug's lungs burned, so he shot to the surface. Breaking it, he gulped air. "Help! Help! Help!" He flailed his arms. "Help! Swimmer down! Help!"

His chest ached from the size of the breath he drew, and he jack-knifed under the waves. Brian was nowhere to be seen. Doug cast around, his eyes bulging and heart pounding. He searched until his chest burned again. He went up, yelled, and returned so many times that he lost count. *I'll find you Brian. This time!*

He thought he saw something, down deeper, but some small part of his brain that still worked warned him away from such depths. He looked at the light colored smudge in the darkness, and his mind wailed. Around him, the sound of a motor made the water vibrate. He swam upwards, but stopped himself, his dilemma an abstraction as the carbon dioxide built up in his blood. If he surfaced now, he might get hit by the boat or its propeller. He tried to see where the boat was, but the water was too murky. Finally, the choice was made for him—either go up or pass out. He went up.

He gasped and inhaled some water as his face broke the surface.

"There, there!" Voices hammered his ears. "I see him."

Plop. Water splashed his face, and blaze orange filled his sight. Seized by coughing, he clutched at the life ring and felt it jerk under him.

"We got a hook?"

"No."

Splash.

He felt hands grab him and hoist him up.

"Brian," he said between coughs. More hands hauled him roughly over the boat's gunwale, and he collapsed. "Brian!" He choked.

"There's another swimmer?"

"Yes! He's still down there!"

One of the men who had hauled him aboard looked over the edge of the boat. "Don?"

"Hold on," said a voice.

A splash joined the slapping of waves against the hull. Doug coughed. A radio crackled. Seconds ticked away, until arms and a face rose over the gunwale, hands fumbling with a dive mask.

"Nothing," the man said. "I can't see a thing. How long has it been since the call?"

Silence settled on the water. Doug blinked the salt sting from his eyes and sat up. Three somber looking men stood in the boat.

"Ten minutes ago," said the man standing at the helm.

The oldest of the men, his face weathered from a lifetime of exposure to the sea, turned to Doug. "I'm sorry, son." He leaned against the gunwale and peered into the darkening Atlantic. "Chuck, call the Coast Guard and ask them to send a recovery team."

2

If silence was the death of conversation, then surely Jillian's expression held that, and the death of sex, too. Interstate-95 hummed under the Subaru's tires as Doug tried and failed, and tried again and failed again to come up with something to say to break her icy anger. A road sign loomed up:

Bar Harbor 32

Baby Harbor. That had been his apparently one-joke-too-many comment half an hour ago. Jillian had told him off, before lapsing into her moody silence. He had snapped his mouth shut and kept it that way since, musing instead on the purpose of their trip. Seven years of no pregnancy might be remedied—according to Jillian's gynecologist, Doctor Pauling—by a week of stress-free sex in a relaxing setting. It was a good place to begin, she had added, before starting fertility treatments.

Thanks, Doctor Gynecologist!

Seven weeks of intermittent planning, all by Doug, had gone into their present trip—seeing them arrive at their cozy, almost-waterfront hotel on the day before Jillian's peak of fertility. He had felt like a pimp travel agent by the time he had gotten it all set up.

He sighed and flexed his hands on the steering wheel. Now, all that coordinating was a cloud of greasy, black smoke, thanks to Jillian's emotional bobsled. Jokes about sex and pregnancy were apparently not on her menu du jour of approved comments.

"Bab—Bar Harbor..." His head resonated with a silent groan the size of Maine. *Why did I do that again?* "We'll be in Bar Harbor in half an hour."

She glared at him. "Stop mocking me!"

"It was an accident! I meant to say Bar Harbor."

"Isn't that convenient."

"Oh, please! Cut me some slack. A couple of sex jokes don't make me a monster."

Jillian rounded on him. "A couple? Try seventy-nine since we left home. Eighty, now.

"You've been counting?"

"Yes! Why can't you stop talking about it? You know this vacation isn't about that. It's about getting pregnant!"

He suppressed a chuckle. "Jill, you know those things are hand and glove. Sex makes babies."

Her face darkened. "You can be such a dolt."

"Why, because I state the obvious?"

"No, because you talk about it so much. You drag it out...drag it through the mud. Over and over again! Making love is like salt or chili powder...it adds spice to life, but you can't make a meal of it. It isn't living."

Speak for yourself. "Listen, I'm sorry. I'm not trying to make you mad. I just don't understand the fine distinctions that live in your head. You want to get pregnant, but you can't get pregnant without—"

"Drop it! I'm quite aware of that, so drop it, please! Talk about something else."

He exhaled sharply. "Sure. What do you want for dinner?"

She shrugged, her attention focused out the side window.

He did not want a return of the oppressive silence. "How 'bout baby back ribs, creamed baby corn, and birthday cake ice cream?"

She sighed. "Really? Did you really just say that?"

After a minute, she smirked and reached for his hand—par for the course with Jillian's roller coaster emotions. "You're still a dolt."

"I can live with that, so long as I'm the dolt you love. And you're not mad at me."

"Of course," she said, raising his hand to her lips. "I just don't want to talk about sex all week."

He grinned. "That's fine! I'm not a conversationalist. I'm much more a doer."

"For crying out loud," she said, rolling her eyes. "Shut up!"

Silence prevailed for several miles before she squeezed his hand. "I guess I'm just sensitive right now, okay? I really want this to work. I was talking to Mom last week, and it hit me all at once that my body is meant to do an amazing thing. My body is meant to work a miracle. I'm meant to give life to a new little human." She sniffed. "Lately though, I feel like I'm just a catcher's mitt for your nocturnal emissions."

Her words stung, but he grinned despite them and squeezed her hand in return. "I love you, no matter what happens."

She snorted. "Of course you do! You get your rocks off, regardless. That's why I was telling you to shut up about sex. I don't want to talk about it...you know *'it'*? I don't want to talk about *'it'* at all on this trip.

I want to talk about making our baby." She looked at him. "Do you understand the difference?"

"Yes. I do now." His smile fledged into a grin. "I will thoroughly enjoy helping you make a miracle."

She rolled her eyes again.

The Pequot Hotel stood at the top of small rise on West Street. An imposing Italianate structure of white clapboards, ornate purple trim, bay windows, and a tower, it overlooked the harbor and Bar Island. Gravel crunched under the tires as Doug pulled into the small, cherry tree-shaded lot behind the hotel. As Doug checked out the other cars, Jillian's gaze was drawn to the rest of the yard.

"Look! They've got a formal garden. That's beautiful." Her gaze wandered over the white gazebo, dripping with gingerbread trim and surrounded by tangerine daylilies, lavender clematis, and milky hostas. Crimson roses and purple sage bordered the yard.

"Oh, uh huh," Doug said. He felt too young to be impressed by gardens. *Men should be in their dotage before flowers fascinate them.* "I guess they wanted the backside guests to have a nice view, too." He made a flourish with his hands. "But, I booked us into the best room in the hotel—the second floor corner harbor view room. We can watch the boats, and see the sun rise out one window and watch the sun set from the other."

Jillian rubbed his leg, impressed with his acumen. "Sounds great! How'd you find this place?"

"Well, the internet, but I remembered it from an earlier trip."

His thoughts slipped back through almost half his lifetime to that fateful summer twelve years before. He and Brian had been best friends since forever, and they had been inseparable through their teen years. After high school, they had planned to take the summer between graduation and college to tour New England. The plan for the first leg had taken them to Maine, and they had spent a week in Acadia National Park, including a day and a night in Bar Harbor. They had eaten lobster at the Pequot and flirted baldly with the waitress—a contest that Doug had won when she chose him. His prize had been making out with the girl after her shift was over. He remembered her lips—

"It's nice."

Doug's reverie shattered. He glanced around, trying to clear the images of Brian and Meeka from his mind. "Yeah."

They toted their luggage to the small portico on the back of the building. An ancient wisteria vine wrapped the structure in a psychotic lover's embrace—a fierce and irreversible squeeze. The hotel was old and relatively well kept, but it was evident where changes had been made over the years, some more skillful than others. They passed a door to the dining room—the noise of eating swelling and receding—and located the small lobby. Scuffed marble tiles undergirded a soaring space rich in stained glass and intricate woodwork. Boston ferns, on delicate stands, flanked the front doors like leafy sentries. Doug rang the antique brass bell on the front desk.

"I love that it's got a kitchen," Jillian said. "We can eat in. Save time for other things." She bit her lower lip and smiled at him like that.

He felt himself responding. "Yeah, and the food is good."

"You've eaten here?"

"On the trip. I came up here with a friend after graduation."

Jillian shot him an odd look. "So this isn't such a chance find, after all? You've already romanced the Pequot?"

"It was a guy friend."

"Ah, so you bromanced the Pequot?"

"No! Don't be gross." He puffed out a breath.

She rubbed the back of his arm, making him shiver. "Relax. I'm just teasing you."

"Hello." A reedy voice floated over their shoulders. "Checking in?"

A man, scarecrow thin with neatly combed gray hair, came around the desk and smiled. "Mister and Missus Sandow?"

"Yes."

"Very good. We have you in room number four, overlooking Frenchman Bay. And you're staying with us for a week?" His gray, almost colorless, eyes surveyed them as they nodded. "Splendid. Dinner service begins at six and the kitchen closes at nine. The bar is open now and stays open until midnight, if you'd like to start off your evening with drinks."

"Not a bad idea." Doug winked at Jillian.

She shook her head. "Not yet. I want to get settled in first."

The man gazed at them, the skin of his face stretching over his bones as he smiled again. "Very well. My name is Charles. If you need anything, just let me know." He handed Doug a large brass key on an even larger plastic fob emblazoned with 'Pequot Hotel' and the number four.

Doug's eyes grew wide. "Check this out!" He dangled the fob for Jillian to see. "When was the last time you saw one of these? I remember them from when I was a kid. Dad would take us on vacation and we'd stay at these creepy, old, backwoods motels...the kind you see in horror movies."

Jillian's expression was bland. "You didn't really just jinx our trip, did you?"

Charles's smile stretched to artificial extremes. "The Pequot Hotel is as safe as houses. You'll be fine. Enjoy your stay."

"Thanks."

Climbing the grand, but creaky staircase, they arrived at the upper landing, which served as a small sitting room. Jillian cooed. "Look, they've got board games." She rifled through the collection. "I'll kick your butt at Scrabble after dinner, 'kay?"

"Whee."

They made their way to room number four, which proved to be larger than Doug had expected. *Always nice.* The room was white with dark-stained mahogany furniture and flooring. The *en suite* bathroom held an ancient, claw-footed bathtub.

"We should rent a sailboat and take it for a spin around the tub."

Jillian joined him and gasped at the size of the vessel. "Oh, I love you!" She hugged him, squealing in his ear. "This tub is amazing! This is the perfect place for...for our vacation. I'm gonna have a long bath right after dinner."

"Oh? I'll join you."

"Not for that. The secret weapon does not go in the tub."

He sighed. For the last two months he had shared his bed with a pelvic wedge—the butt pillow—a cushion designed to tilt a woman's hips to help her get pregnant. It had been a little fun at first, something different, but the novelty had quickly worn off. Now he found the necessary position uncomfortable, but she was convinced that the wedge was going to be the trick and used it religiously. It was a practice that cut into spontaneous sex—Doug's favorite kind.

He turned away. "Right."

"What?"

"Nothing."

"Something!"

"No, nothing. We're here to work a miracle, and the blessed butt pillow is going to help us make it happen."

"Don't mock me, Doug."

He rolled his shoulders in frustration. "I'm not mocking you! I love you. But I'm not having the easiest time navigating the new ways of doing stuff, okay? This all feels very rigid, and Doctor Pauling said to relax." He touched her. "So, let's relax."

She scowled. "We've done it your way the whole time we've been married, and we still don't have a baby. Will it kill you to do it my way for a couple of weeks?"

He bit his tongue, cutting off the remark he wanted to make. She had a point, but he was resenting the intrusion of their unconceived child. He wished she would just get pregnant already so life could get back to normal.

"No. I was just hoping that we could...can we just relax?" He leaned down and kissed her. She resisted him, but only for a few seconds. Their lips tangled and tongues were called into the fray. Hands caressed, and the protective barriers of clothing were violated. The large mattress of the four poster bed was comfortable, but they hardly noticed.

In the afterglow, she asked for the wedge, but he did not want to get out of bed and search through her luggage, so he grabbed one of the pillows from the headboard. "Up, up, up," he said, almost chanting, before lying down beside her again.

Silence ticked by. "Are you happy? With me?"

"Of course." He kissed her bare shoulder. "You?"

"Yes! I just wish that we didn't argue so much. I'm worried that it won't stop."

He traced his fingers across the gentle swell of her belly and the ridges and valleys of her ribs. "I've heard it's healthy for couples to argue."

"Says who?"

"It's true." He leaned down and kissed a breast.

She twitched away. "Doug!"

"What?"

"They're touchy!"

Always have been. He chuckled. "Let's hope you never have to nurse the baby right after sex."

"Ha! We won't be having sex after the baby is born. I'll be a mother."

He frowned in response. "Um...that's not funny."

She struggled to maintain a serious expression, but failed, and then laughed so hard she choked.

"I'm sorry," she said when she got her breath back. "I couldn't resist."

"Well, try harder next time." He ran his fingers along her cheek and into the dark blonde hair that draped her pillow. "That's every man's nightmare about having kids."

Her hand landed—a butterfly caress—on his forearm. "Don't worry. I know your love language."

"I hope so." His lips grazed hers.

He had heard the postpartum horror stories from his guy friends—tales of wives with cold shoulders and months-long headaches. He found it difficult to imagine such a turn of events with Jillian—she had always been agreeable to his passionate advances—but lately she had been increasingly uptight about sex. On top of that, he had turned thirty a few months earlier, and the realization that age was creeping up on him had been a blow. He was not as fast as he used to be, nor as strong. Things took more effort, it seemed, and activities such as workouts and yard work were punctuated by more resting than he liked. A dread floated, just beneath everyday thoughts, that his man plumbing might be next in this chain of changes. He feared a specter—the confluence of her diminished interest and his diminished ability.

On top of that, Jillian, facing that same birthday soon, had gotten baby crazy. It was no help, he was certain, that nearly all their married friends were on their second and even third child. Doug watched the expression on his wife's face now when she saw children—the longing. He could almost hear her ovarian timepiece, ticking away in her pelvis.

"Hey," he said, "it's almost seven. Do you want to eat here, or go find another restaurant?"

"I'm tired. Let's stay here. We can check out Bar Harbor's finest tomorrow." She wiggled. "I need another twenty minutes on the pillow, anyway."

When she felt she was done incubating, they dressed and went downstairs, hand-in-hand like the lovers they were. The elegant lobby was empty again, but they heard voices floating out of the dining room, enticing them to enter. Charles leaned on the small bar, talking to a woman whose red hair was laced with snow.

He looked up and beckoned them over. "Good evening. Mister and Missus Sandow, this is my wife, Susan."

Her smile drew them in. "Evening! Welcome to the Pequot Hotel. Are you getting settled?" They nodded. "Great! Well, sit anywhere you like. Meeka will be back in a minute."

Doug's eyebrows shot up. *Surely not. She still works here? Wow, this should be interesting.*

They surveyed the room. A dozen tables crowded into what had obviously once been an opulent dining room. Delicate mahogany woodwork cloaked the walls, while a detailed plaster ceiling crowned the space. However, the ceiling was in need of paint, the woodwork was in need of polish, and the bar—of maple and brass and mirrors—cut like a garish wound across the back of the room, partitioning it and detracting from its charm and grandeur.

They picked a petite table away from the other diners—an older couple, a group of college-aged kids, and a portly family of five wearing matching 'I ♥ Smitty Labs' tee shirts.

"Science nerd tourists. Go figure," Doug whispered to Jillian.

She offered him a tepid smile.

As a strength trainer for the Oldport University football program, he did not have a lot of space in his life for nerds. He started to say something further as his gaze wandered, but his vocal chords seized up. Walking around the bar was Meeka—not a woman approaching early middle age as she should be—but a young Meeka, no older than eighteen.

Reality shifted sideways. *What on earth?*

Black, pixie-cut hair topped her slender, olive face. She regarded him with twin pools of ink, her expression moving through stages of surprise. Her smile shouted happiness and her teeth flashed—a beacon against her darker complexion. She moved through the dining room like a model taking a runway, her long limbs swinging just so. She had the same swimmer's build. She moved like a predator. She—

Jillian kicked him under the table. "Close your mouth!"

"What?" He looked at his wife—short, blonde, and vanilla. He snapped his mouth shut. *I am so screwed.*

"Hey, there!" Meeka radiated excitement. "Welcome back!"

Not possible...this is not possible! She doesn't look a day older than she did when we kissed...not a day older.

"My name is—"

"Meeka..." Doug said, unintentionally interrupting her.

"Yeah! Thank you...for remembering. I'll be your server tonight. Wow...what can I get you to drink?"

Doug tripped through uttering scotch and soda, and it miraculously appeared by his elbow minutes later as he puzzled over how Meeka could look like his memories.

Jillian kicked him again. "Hey! Are you even hearing me?"

He looked up. "Sorry, what?"

"I'm telling you how freaking rude you're being! Who is she?" Her venomous expression was a klaxon, falling on his deafness.

"Sorry...I—I know her from—from before."

"Oh, that's comforting!"

Meeka appeared at their table and crouched down, just like an old friend. "Have you decided what you'd like?"

Jillian said something about cranberry chicken salad. Then, he felt the weight of those inky depths turn on him. "And for you?"

His head floated around to her. *She's so beautiful. And she smells nice.* "Uh...lobster, please."

"Good choice. That's what you had the last time you were here."

She started to turn away.

"Wait...please," he said.

Jillian's gaze was a thousand degrees of misery boring into his head.

"I—I haven't eaten here in years, but I recognize you. I don't understand. How can you be..."

"Be what?" Meeka asked.

"Be the same waitress as back then?"

"Alewife."

"Sorry?"

Meeka laughed. "I don't like the term waitress. I'm an alewife." She let the words hang in the air.

I've had this lecture before.

"I am the same person who took your order twelve years ago. I never forget a face, especially one as handsome as yours." Her gaze slid to Jillian. "You're a lucky lady!" She pivoted and walked away.

He made eye contact with his wife. "You're a lucky lady," he said in a weak echo.

Her expression was a desert of amusement.

"Listen, I'm sorry. That was just a big dose of cognitive dissonance."

"Stop using those stupid Freudianisms!" Her face was scrunched up, like she was smelling vomit. "I'm so thrilled you brought me to your girlfriend's hotel to conceive our child. Did you stay in room four with her, too? Did you fuck her on that bed?"

He felt his heart stutter. "No! It was nothing like that! Brian and I didn't stay here, we camped on the beach. We just ate here. I—I recognize her, but, seriously, this is not possible! She doesn't look a day older than she did!"

"Isn't that convenient," Jillian whispered.

"No, you don't understand."

Her face snapped up, its expression going from furious to nuclear. *Whoops, that was the wrong thing to say.* He took a gulp of scotch trying to keep his mouth busy doing anything other than talking him into a deeper hole.

"Hello."

Oh, what now?

"Hello," Jillian said. An old man had appeared at their tableside. She was all plastic charm now, Doug noticed—a thin veneer of civility covering her self-righteous anger. He surreptitiously glanced at the bar, hoping to see Meeka.

"...there's trust and fidelity. So much more to marriage than the marriage bed," the man was saying.

"Sure," Jillian said. She was talking to the man, but looking at Doug, her eyes narrowed.

"What?" Doug frowned, rejoining the conversation.

"Trust...in marriage," Jillian said.

The muscles in Doug's face twitched. "I'm entirely trustworthy!"

"Until now?" The man leaned down.

Doug glared at him. As he looked closer, he realized that the man was not as old as he had first thought. The man had white hair, but it must have been prematurely so, because his face was perhaps fifty. "Who the hell do you think you are? I'm trying to have a private conversation with my wife."

"Oh, I can hear that." The man thrust out a hand. "The name's Caul."

Doug regarded the proffered palm as if staring down a snake. His hands stayed on the table. "That's nice. Go away."

Caul nodded and dropped his hand, a knowing expression painted across his face. He turned to Jillian and raised a brow.

"You'll remember my words?"

"I will."

"And you," Caul glanced back at Doug and rapped his knuckles on the table. "Remember that there is more to life than sex—"

"No, really?"

"—so value your marriage."

"Man, shove off!" Doug vibrated. He forced his legs to stay relaxed, knowing that standing would lead to hitting, and hitting would lead to trouble he could not afford.

Caul's expression soured, but he walked away without another word.

"That was freaking rude!" Doug's hands ran across his face and short, sandy hair. "Where's that guy get off thinking—"

"Don't change the subject, Don Juan." Her plastic charm melted.

"Uh, huh." His gut churned the cheap Scotch. "What did he say you should remember?"

"Nothing," Jillian replied after a pause. She looked away and frowned. He followed her gaze to Meeka, making her way across the dining room. "I see you met old Caul." She laughed. "Just ignore him, he's harmless."

"Is our food ready?" Jillian's voice frosted the air.

"Oh, I doubt it. I had to go out to the bay and catch his lobster, after all." Meeka laughed again. "I'll go check with the kitchen, though."

She left. Jillian watched her back, before leaning across the table. "You're going to find me a new hotel to stay in."

He took a deep breath. "I prepaid the week here."

"Tough! I don't want to be around your girlfriend."

"She's not my girlfriend!" He looked away.

The college-aged kids were looking over at them and snickering.

Doug's neck felt tight. "Can we talk about this later?"

She waved her hand dismissively. The college kids guffawed. Even the portly nerd family looked at them.

Meeka glided across the room. Fortunately, she carried their dinner in her hands. "You want another one?"

Her teeth flashed as the plates hit the table like miniature bombs.

Doug's brows pinched. "What? A hotel?"

She laughed. "No. Another drink."

"Oh. No. Just some water, please."

"Well," she gestured toward the bay, "we've got plenty of that." She spun away. The scent of sandalwood teased his nose. He was hypnotized by her long limbs, sheathed in a loose black turtle neck and flowing black pants. He felt Jillian's gaze on him, so he looked elsewhere—anywhere but Meeka. Down seemed safe. Creamed spinach, rice pilaf, and a lobster stared back at him.

"Here're your four B's!" Meeka blew in with a storm of activity—Jillian's own personal black rain cloud. "Bucket, bib, butter, and breaker." She set a bucket, containing a plastic bib and a lobster cracker, and a dish of melted butter on the table. "I'll be right back with your water."

"Thanks." He restrained himself from looking at her.

"Is there anything else I can get for you?" Her hand lingered on the table near Doug's.

Jillian glared. "No! Go away, please."

Meeka retreated, leaving them to eat in silence—Jillian taking to her salad like a mower to grass. She finished well before Doug, and sat, glaring at him. The college students left, as well as the nerd family. The older couple worked on their seventh round of after dinner coffee.

The lobster cracked.

The butter congealed.

Mercifully, in some ways, Meeka did stay away from their table, allowing Jillian's anger to cool. "You ever gonna finish that lobster? I'm ready to kick your butt at Scrabble."

Doug felt a burden lift a bit from his mind. *Jillian's olive branch.* He sat back and glanced up. "I guess I've done as much damage as I can."

"Not hardly!" Meeka was at their tableside with no warning. "You want coffee? Dessert? The salted caramel brownie is to die for, and the kitchen's about to close."

Jillian's intake of breath was audible. "No, *thank you!* Just the check."

"Oh, we can charge it to your room, if you'd like. That's what most people do. You're in room four, right? I love the tub in that room! It's the only tub like that in the whole hotel. And that's the only King-sized bed we have. I nicknamed it Stephen. That was the master bedroom when this was a private house. You could fit three people in that bed, no problem."

Doug choked.

"All right, just the check it is," she continued. "If you change your minds and want something sweet, I'm here until tenish." She winked, as she pulled a slip of paper from her apron pocket and handed it to Doug. His gaze was drawn to it: salad, lobster, scotch and soda, thanks, Meeka, phone number.

His eyes bulged. *Oh, man!* "We—we'll charge it to the room, thanks." He dropped the bill into his lap, feeling excited by her interest and confused by its ramifications.

Meeka left them, and Doug pointedly looked the other way. "You ready to go lose that Scrabble game?" His voice sounded squeezed, like elephants sat on the words.

"I'm ready to go." Jillian's voice was flinty. As she stood and turned toward the door, Doug pushed the dinner bill into his pants pocket. They climbed the stairs and played a quiet game of Scrabble, which Doug lost badly. "Um, I'm sorry," he said at the end of the game.

"Why? You lost."

"Not that. I'm sorry about dinner."

The Scrabble box slipped from her fingers, and tiles—like large, pale fish scales—scattered across the low table. "Poop."

They lifted the little squares of wood in silence, until she looked up at him. "It's understandable, I guess. She's a pretty young woman."

He stopped picking up tiles and grabbed her hand. "She hasn't got anything on you, Jillie. I'm married to you. I love you."

She grimaced. "I know. It just pisses me off when slutty young things hit on married men—especially when you're the married man."

He gazed at her through narrowed eyes. "It's happened before?"

"Not this blatantly…'If you want something sweet, I'm here 'til ten!'" Jillian imitated Meeka's voice. "What a whore."

She leaned in, helping him pick up the rest of the tiles. "There've been a few times. After all, you're a handsome man, Doug Sandow. I'm not stupid. I wanted a good looking husband."

He chuckled without humor. *That's the reason you married me?* "Thanks. I think."

"Yes, thanks! Sheesh, don't dis my compliments. You're a hunk, but you're mine, not hers. Not anyone's." She popped up from her chair. "Come on. I'm ready for bed."

He put the game on a shelf. "I thought you wanted to try out the tub."

"I do, but I'll do that tomorrow. I'm ready for *bed*."

"Ah! Okay. Skip straight to the baby gravy, huh?"

She swatted his arm, before wrapping it with hers. "You're a jerk, but I love you."

3

Jillian woke and stretched luxuriantly under the covers. The smooth, warm sheets were an invitation to close her eyes again and return to slumber, but she felt an insistent fullness. She sighed and turned her head to look at the bathroom, wishing she did not have to get up. The secret weapon was a lump against her left hip, and Doug was a lump against her right hip. *Boxed in*, she thought. She moved the wedge and threw off the covers, exposing her nakedness to the cooler air. Normally, she wore pajamas to bed, but she and Doug had been so preoccupied last night that she had never put them on. Or brushed her teeth, she realized, and smacked her lips against the stale taste in her mouth. She looked around the room and saw that the morning sunlight was pouring through the curtains of one set of windows. *Just like he said it would*. She felt a surge of love for him—for his thoughtfulness.

After a quick visit to the bathroom, she climbed back under the covers and snuggled close to her husband's warmth. *We're here! We're really here.* She had been looking forward to this trip for weeks. She inhaled his musky scent and pulled herself tight against him. She had a visceral feeling of the rightness of this arrangement—she and he. Their babies would be awesome. She rubbed her hand along his chest, playing with the hair, and continued on down his flat belly. He stirred when she reached his happy trail.

"Mmm. Good morning," he said, his voice sounding scratchy from disuse. "What time is it?"

"Who cares?"

"My empty stomach."

Her slim, deft fingers found what they were searching for. Doug closed his eyes, his stomach apparently forgotten. She had not been this aggressive since they had been dating, preferring to let him be the mover and shaker in their love life, but she felt hot now, hotter than she had in a long time. She wanted him. She wanted their child.

Her voice was a whisper. "Do you love me?"

"Yes, of course."

She squeezed him, eliciting a yelp. "Then give me a baby," she said and straddled him.

They stayed in bed until eleven, dozing, before Jillian headed for the shower. Doug propped himself up on some pillows and flipped through the nonsense on TV, before getting bored and prowling around the room. The shower ended as he found a binder full of information about the hotel and the local attractions.

"Breakfast is over," Doug said, looking over the hotel information.

"That's okay," Jillian replied over the muted roar of the hair dryer. "We can go into town and get bagels and some stuff for lunch. I want to have a picnic."

He grinned. "That's a great idea. I know just the place."

"Oh?"

"Yeah, let's go to Acadia today."

"Sure. Some hiking would be fun."

Doug's mind wandered over the memories of the last time he had hiked in Acadia, as his feet wandered him into the bathroom. He surveyed Jillian's naked body as she ran the blow dryer over her hair. Hiking was not the most exciting activity he could think of. "Not as fun as staying in bed all day."

"Ha! Aren't you running low? Don't you need to go outside and do some sweaty guy things to recharge your sperm batteries?"

He wrapped his arms around her, pressing himself against her slightly damp skin. "No, sugar, I'm not running low."

She giggled. "So I feel. Well, I need to recover. I'm a little sore."

"Later it is." He kissed her neck, eliciting a sigh from her.

"Get ready, brute. I want to take home some non-bedroom memories of Maine."

He patted her cheek and hustled to the shower.

They found a harbor-front bakery café, and ordered bagels and strong coffee. As they exited the café, Jillian inhaled the steam from her cup and sighed. "Oh, yay! My body has been begging for coffee."

Doug sniffed his. "Huh."

"What?"

"Smells old."

"Stop it! It smells fine."

"Speaking of old coffee, did you know that Moses made coffee every morning?"

She eyed him skeptically. "No, I hadn't read that anywhere in the Bible."

"Yeah, before anyone else got up. Do you know how he made it, wandering out there in the desert with all those Israelites?"

"No clue."

His gaze strayed across the bay, his expression as placid as the water. "Hebrewed it."

Jillian groaned and walked away. From an outside table, they watched the ships move along Frenchman Bay. Seagulls paraded the quay, eyeing the bagels for any chance of an escapee crumb. On a lark, Doug tossed an entire chunk of bread to them, causing the birds to lunge and squabble.

Jillian made a sour face at him. "You shouldn't do that. It makes them dependent on us."

He snorted. "They're already dependent on us. Rats, pigeons, gulls...all of them dependent on mankind for their next meal. And god knows what other species out there look to us for a handout. We're all profligate SOBs, for sure."

"What's got you feeling so philosophical today?"

He leaned in and surprised her with a quick kiss on the lips. "I want to be a wise daddy."

She smiled, hopeful that his words would bear fruit.

They finished their breakfast, and glanced back at the café. Odd, life-sized carvings of fish-headed men flanked the door where a thickening horde of tourists queued—human omnivores, looking for lunch. Doug weighed their options, and Jillian seemed to read his mind. "This is probably still our best bet," she said. "Let's get some sandwiches and juice here, and have that picnic out in Acadia."

"Sure."

They stood in line for twenty minutes, so the sun stood overhead before they got started to the park. The traffic was light heading in, as most people had arrived hours earlier, being not so lazy as to sleep until eleven.

"What's the plan?"

A smile brightened his face. "We're getting a Cadillac."

He drove her to the top of a mountain and peeked at her as they got out of the car. "What do you think?"

"Wow!" She soaked in the panoramic view. "It's phenomenal! But where's my Cadillac?"

"You're standing on it." He grinned. "Cadillac Mountain."

She growled and poked him in the ribs. "Jerk."

"Sorry." He nuzzled her hair, making her laugh. "This is the tallest mountain in the park and, actually, on the entire Atlantic seaboard."

She took his hand and they walked, their boots kicking up the powdery dirt of the trail that looped around the crown of the mountain. Doug was her tour guide on the hike, pointing out all the various mountains, islands, and bodies of water. Jillian's photographer instinct took over, and she burned up capacity on their camera's memory card.

"We have a whole week here. Don't fill up the camera on the first day."

She scoffed. "Chill. There's still room for thousands of pics." She raised the camera and snapped another photo, just to prove her point.

"Did you just take a picture of the sky? That'll be a good one to put on social media. Ooh, look at this beautiful blue picture!"

"I was taking a picture of that cloud," she said in bluff and pointed. "It looks like a sheep."

"Huh. Looks more like a cottony turd."

"Spoken like a true philistine."

"Hey, why'd the sheep cross the road?"

"No idea, but I'm sure you're going to tell me."

"It had mutton else to do."

She smirked. "Oh, Doug."

Near the end of the trail, they found a warm boulder and sat, admiring the view of Frenchman Bay and Bar Harbor. "Thank you," she said and wrapped herself around his right arm. "This is a perfect vacation spot. A certain person excepted."

He felt chagrin worm through his gut. *Why did I pick Bar Harbor?* The details were fuzzy now—like the sheep-cloud—because he sometimes did things with the least amount of brainpower required. It had popped up when he had run a search on Maine vacation spots. He had fondly recalled the Pequot, which had vacancy—*click, click*— and their room was reserved. He certainly had not expected Meeka to still be working at the hotel. Even if she had, she should be a fisherman's wife by now, early middle-aged, with a brood of little Downeasters clutching her skirts.

"That won't be an issue," he said. "We'll just eat elsewhere."

"Sounds like a great solution."

"I know."

She leaned her head against his shoulder and squeezed his arm. "I love you."

"I know."

"Our baby's gonna be awesome."

"I know."

"Stop saying that!"

He kissed the top of her head. "I love you too. And, yes, he's gonna be an awesome football jock like his daddy."

"She'll be a ballerina."

"Yeah, he'll look great in blue and gold."

"She'll look great in whatever school colors she wants."

"He'll have rugged good looks, just like his mommy."

"She'll—you jerk!" She swatted his arm.

They retrieved the cooler and ate their lunch on the mountain. Afterwards, they drove along the shore of Eagle Lake, stopping at the park headquarters for a bathroom break. A fish-head sculpture stood guard over the facilities. Doug inspected it, noting that it was hand carved. "I wonder what's up with these. It looks like one of the Deep Ones in the Lovecraft books I used to read. There were some sculptures in Bar Harbor too. Which story was that...something about Innsmouth?"

Jillian shrugged, unnerved. "Dunno, but it creeps me out."

They took a few brochures, and spent the rest of the day kicking around the western part of the park, ending up in Bernard at dinner time. "Lobster?" She asked, looking at the choices.

"It is the Maine thing for dinner here."

She rolled her eyes. "Don't you ever stop?"

"Where'd be the fun in that?"

"Whatever. Lobster sounds good. I'm up for it tonight."

He glanced at her, a twinkle in his eye. "I can think of nothing butter to have for dinner."

She missed a step and a giggle escaped her. "Please stop."

"You should let me write the cheese ads for your agency."

Her eyes narrowed. "We don't have cheese ads."

"That's unfortunate. Cheese is a prestigious commodity to advertise. You should get a cheese maker as a client. I'm sure if you tried, it wouldn't be too high of a curdle."

"Doug!"

"What? I'm a dairy punny guy."

She laughed. "I know, I know, but after ten years...good heavens!"

"Aw, you'd miss it if I stopped."

Her hand rose to his cheek. "I'm sure I would, but I'm full of humor, okay? Can I have serious Doug for the rest of the evening?"

"Sure, sorry."

"Don't be sorry," she stretched up and kissed him, "just be serious."

They chose a waterfront restaurant, and stood in line while watching the boats return to harbor. As they got closer to the restaurant, they could see the nets and sea glass that festooned its walls. They finally made it in, and were approaching the counter, when Doug heard a familiar voice. "Meeka?" He turned and found her waving to them.

"Hey, guys! Welcome to Huston's! Pick your lobster, and I'll find you a table."

"This isn't happening," Jillian whispered, glaring at Meeka. "This is *not* happening."

"Yes, apparently it is."

"How can she work here, *too*?"

Doug shrugged. "Do you want to eat somewhere else?"

She glanced at her watch. "Not after standing in line for half an hour! Just ask for another waitress."

They chose their lobsters, and then Meeka came over and guided them to a table—her hand on Doug's back the entire time. "Did you guys enjoy your day in the park?"

Doug glanced at her, wondering how she knew that they had been to the park. "Uh, yeah, we did."

Jillian unclenched her teeth. "What are you doing here?" She ripped the words off like tearing cloth.

Meeka looked surprised. "Working...?"

"I thought you worked at the hotel?" Jillian stepped closer, her face changing from peach to plum.

A nervous laugh squeezed from the waitress. "I work all over the place...alewives don't get paid all that great, you know."

"Yes, I *do know*. But how the hotel and *here*?"

Meeka's smile was innocent. "Coincidence?"

"I'm not a big believer in coincidence."

Meeka shrugged and left to get their drinks. Jillian sat with a huff, while Doug pulled out his phone and dialed the Pequot. He could see how angry Jillian was. She glared at him, but her expression became puzzled. "Who are you calling?"

He held up a finger. "Hey, this is Doug Sandow, staying in room four...yeah, yeah, say could I speak to Meeka for a moment, please? Oh. Okay, sorry to hear that. Okay, bye."

"What?" Jillian asked, as he put his phone away.

"Meeka called in sick to the Pequot tonight."

Jillian's grin was evil. She pulled her own phone out, and snapped a picture of Meeka talking to a couple at a nearby table.

"Busted!"

"That's not nice."

"Sue me! The pixie-headed freak started this, not me." Her grin began to fall away.

"But you could get her fired."

She regarded him, the fine lines beside her eyes flexing and releasing. "Why do you care?"

"I don't...really. It's just mean-spirited. It doesn't seem like something you would do."

She leaned across the table, her eyes slitted now, and her voice dropping to a hissing whisper. "That slut offered to go to bed with you last night!"

Doug recoiled. "What? That's not what she said."

"Come on! How naïve are you? How naïve do you think I am?"

"Wow!" He rubbed his face. "Can we please stop talking about her?"

"I'd love to."

"Good!"

"Great!"

He pulled out his phone and accessed the Internet. "That's settled," he said after a few minutes.

"What?"

"We're eating in New Hampshire for the rest of the week."

Jillian looked puzzled for a beat then laughed. She grabbed the sides of his face and kissed him. "I love you!"

The grin he flashed her would not have looked out of place on a cat with a feather stuck in its mouth.

Not wanting the presence of Meeka to spoil another evening for her, she asked the manager if they could have a different waitress. He looked confused, but agreed, and a bubbly girl in a UMA tee shirt brought their dinner.

"Hey, there! My name is Jill and—"

"So is mine," Jillian said.

The girl's eye widened. "Seriously? OMG! That's amazing cool!"

She fist bumped Jillian.

Doug loosened up after a couple of beers, and they laughed a lot while they ate. Full of lobster and liquid, he excused himself to the men's room. He rubbed the belly of another grotesque fish-human sculpture as he passed—its stubby, webbed fingers were splayed and reaching, as if it wanted to return the favor. At the back of the restaurant and down a short hallway, he found the doors labeled 'Buoys' and 'Gulls.' He chuckled at the pun.

"It's pretty bad, right?" Meeka slid in beside him.

"Oh, hey! No, it's great. I love puns."

"Ah." She looked away. "Your wife...she, um, she doesn't like me, huh?"

He stifled a snort of disbelief. "Uh, yeah, well, you're kinda coming on to me. What do you think she's going to do?"

"Make way?" She said in a quiet voice and leaned toward him.

He gaped at her, acutely aware of how close she was, and then burst into laughter. "Really? Wow! You've got chutzpah!"

Her expression turned bitter, and her gaze strayed. "Not really. It's just that I've waited twelve years for you to return, and when you do, you've got...*her*. It isn't exactly fair."

The air was crystalline as he regarded her, and he found it hard to breathe as her words sunk into his mind. *She waited twelve years for me to return?* "I—I don't know what to say."

He saw tears gather in the corners of her eyes. In a sharpening of his perception, he noticed that she had a little scar near her left eye, high on her cheek. She sniffed and swiped at her face. "Don't say anything, okay? Let me pretend there's hope that you still want me."

She fled into the Gulls room.

...hope that you still want me. His breath hitched again. Shaking his head, he entered the Buoys room.

Jillian was frowning when he returned.

"Hey!" He grinned. "Miss me?"

She glared at him.

"What?"

"Why did Meeka follow you into the men's room?"

"Huh?"

"Don't play dumb! She went in right after you and followed you out, smiling like she'd won the lottery. What happened? Or should I guess?"

"Nothing happened! We talked for like thirty seconds, then she started crying and ran into the women's room. I peed. In the men's room. Alone. Nothing happened."

"That's so convenient." She snatched her tiny purse and left him at the table, storming across the restaurant and out the door.

"You're not making this any easier," he said quietly. He pulled out his wallet and waved to their waitress.

The ride back to the hotel was quiet, and they arrived back well after ten. Jillian looked into the bar area and found the proprietors. She hesitated.

Susan glanced at them. "Would you care for a nightcap?"

Doug stepped up to the bar. "Yes...bourbon. Make it a double?"

"I was curious about Meeka," Jillian said, approaching Charles.

"What about her?"

"Where else does she work?"

Doug made an irritated noise.

"Um," Charles said, glancing at Doug, "she works most mornings at a place on the mainland a ways west of here. Why?"

"So she doesn't work at a restaurant in Bernard?" Jillian forced a smile.

Charles and Susan exchanged a cryptic look. "Not that I'm aware of. Why are you asking?" Susan set the bourbon in front of Doug.

Jillian reached for her phone.

"We saw someone who looked a lot like her," Doug said, "but it probably wasn't her."

"Is that why you called, Mister Sandow?"

"Yeah. It was funny." He raised the drink and knocked it back, wincing afterwards. "I thought she might have a sister or something."

"No, she doesn't have a sister."

"Great, that settles it." Doug set the empty glass back on the bar. "Good night!" He turned, grabbed Jillian's arm, and started for the doorway.

Jillian yanked against his grip. "Doug!" She turned to Charles. "It was her. Here, I have a picture of her." She pulled against Doug's hold and showed the picture to Charles and Susan.

"Um...that could be her," Susan said. "It's hard to tell. The picture's pretty dark."

Doug cleared a baby hippo from his throat. "As I said, she was a look-alike. Good night!" He tugged Jillian toward the doorway. She made a sour face and followed, walking up to their room in silence.

The door closed with a thump.

"Why'd you do that?"

"Do what?" He opened the windows to relieve the stuffiness of the air.

"Say all that crap about it not being her, or trying to stop me even."

He understood her frustration, but he disagreed with her methods.

"Because I don't think it's right to try and get someone fired just because you don't like them."

"She lied to her employer."

A scowl crossed his face. "And that's any of your business *why*?"

"Because it's dishonest. I don't want to stay at a hotel where a dishonest person works. She might steal our stuff."

"Wow. That's a heck of a jump." He shook his head. "And pretty ironic coming from you."

Her body stiffened. "What's that supposed to mean?"

"You work in advertising." He smirked, feeling the bourbon kick in. "You'll be the first to cast a stone over dishonesty?"

She stalked away and slammed the door to the bathroom. He heard the lock click, followed by running water. *Great! Jillie and her emotions.* She was apparently going to have one of her marathon baths to cool off. He assessed the door, wondering how mad Charles would be if he broke it. His hatred over locked doors, and her proclivity for locking them during arguments, had resulted in four replaced doors in the early years of their marriage. Taking a deep breath, he strove to take the higher road. He was glad that he had peed before they left the restaurant, because he would not be getting into the bathroom for hours.

He undressed and climbed into bed, thinking that he would watch some TV. He turned the sound down, and was asleep in minutes. His dreams were chaotic, and he woke to the sensation of Jillian's lips on him—something he had not felt in years. *Nice apology.*

He groaned and looked down at the lump under the covers, before his head fell back and his eyes rolled up. As he neared release, the drain in the tub opened, and water swirled into the pipe.

What?

He heard Jillian humming in the bathroom.

What the hell!

He sat up and threw off the covers and came face to face with Meeka. Before he could say anything, he felt a stinging sensation on his right leg and she was gone—off the bed and out the window. He tried to follow, but he felt light headed. Flopping back on the bed, he knew nothing more.

4

Doug woke to a pounding head and sunlight streaming into his eyes. *Ugh! I shouldn't drink so much before bed.* He smacked his lips together—tasting the residue of beer and bourbon. *Wait...Meeka!* Memories of the previous night flooded his mind. He sat up and threw back the covers. There was nothing there, no evidence that anything had occurred.

What the hell? Was that real?

Jillian yanked the covers back over herself, as he stumbled to the bathroom to pee and give himself a once over. There was a small spot of dried blood on his calf, but nothing else. *I dreamt I was with Meeka while I had a wet dream that didn't happen, and I got bitten by a bug. That's gotta be the weirdest dream ever.* Going to the window, he pushed aside the curtains that his dream Meeka had dived through. A sheer drop of about fifteen feet stared back at him. The porch roof to his left was at least eight feet distant. *Not possible.* He closed the window and crawled back into bed with Jillian. He wrapped his arms around her, discovering that she was clad in her winter grammie jammies. *I thought she left those at home.*

He rubbed her hip.

"No, Doug."

"Um...why not?"

"You have to ask after last night? I'm not in the mood."

He wanted to make a smart comment about how babies required semen, but he realized that it was not a good time for flippancy. "Okay." He rolled onto his back.

He was just fuzzing out when she spoke. "You don't understand why I'm mad, do you?"

"No, not really."

She sat up and glared at him. "How can you be so stupid? You defended her. You defended *her!* I'm the one you should be defending! Not her. Seven years my husband and you're still not my hero."

Ouch! He put his hand on her back. "That wasn't really fair. And, I'm sorry. I just don't think it's great karma to get someone fired over—"

She smacked his leg through the coverlet. "That's not the point!"

"Then what is the point?"

She started crying. "You're supposed to love me!"

"Oh, for effing real? I do!" He embraced her and kissed the side of her head. "I will always go to bat for you."

"Words and actions!" It was an old argument from her, and one that did not really fit the moment.

"Come on," he said, coaxing her to look at him, "don't be mad at me." His fingers traced her jawline.

"Knock it off!" She pulled away from him and got out of bed. "I may never have sex with you again." She slammed the bathroom door. He glared at the paneled slab of wood. *Meeka wants me. She waited for me for twelve years!*

"She came on to me, not the other way around!"

"But you took her side!"

"No, I didn't! I just didn't want you making a crap storm over this girl's jobs. Vindictiveness doesn't suit you, Jillie."

"Oh, that's nicely self-serving!"

He dragged his fingers down his face. "Oh, wow! You boggle my mind," he replied, too quietly for her to hear. He flopped backwards on the bed, calculating how much money they would be out if they left the Pequot and finished their vacation somewhere else. *What about Meeka?*

"Ugh." There was no chance that he was going to leave before he talked to her again. There were too many unanswered questions clattering around his brain.

The shower started. "Seriously? You had an hours-long bath last night and you're taking a shower? No wonder the water bill at home is so high."

Over an hour had trickled away before they even walked into the dining room.

"Hey, guys!" Meeka called from across the room.

Jillian stopped, her expression noxious. "Oh, no," she whispered. "Not again. She's not even supposed to be here!"

"It's one meal."

"No!"

"Get over it."

"We're checking out," she said.

"No, we're not. We'd lose a lot of money if we did."

"I don't care."

He pulled out a chair and sat at the nearest table.

"I don't want to be here with her anymore," she said.

He picked up the menu.

"Doug!"

"We aren't having this conversation. The smoked salmon omelet sounds good."

She sat across from him, tense as a piano wire. "Yes, we are!"

"Jillian, I find it insulting that you don't trust me."

"What?"

"What what? You don't trust me! You seem to think that some chick can bat her lashes and make a provocative statement, and I will be all over her, and forget that I love you. That I'm committed to you. So, yeah...I find that insulting."

Her eyes thinned to slits, but she made no reply.

"Good morning," Meeka said as she approached their table. "Did you have a pleasant night?"

Doug glanced up at her, remembering the dream. She winked. He flinched and regarded her suspiciously. *Was that a dream?*

"What can I get you for breakfast?"

They ordered. Emotions simmered as they waited for their meal, which Meeka swiftly brought. She swirled away, leaving them to eat in relative silence. Doug was content to not be nagged as he pondered the memory of his dream, and Jillian was busy grinding axes. Meeka punctuated the silence with periodic intrusions to refill coffee cups and assess their satisfaction with the meal. She was clearing away the plates when Jillian spoke. "I thought you worked mornings at another place? How come you're here?"

"How...how'd you know that?"

Jillian arched her eyebrow.

Meeka shifted away from the table. "Um, yes, I do."

"Then what are you doing here?"

She hesitated. "They were slow this morning and didn't need me, so I came in to help out here."

"Isn't that convenient," Jillian said. "So, you live nearby?"

A nervous laugh slipped away from Meeka. "Yeah, up the street. My mom and I have a place."

"And a boyfriend or two, I imagine?" Jillian grimaced. "Pretty girl like you."

Meeka's face crumpled, as she retreated from the table. "No, I gave my heart away to the only boy I've ever loved, but he left and forgot about me." She looked at Doug, and then away, her eyes glossy. "I haven't loved anyone since. Will you excuse me, please?" She rushed away.

Jillian looked smug for a few seconds, before frowning. "Wait... she's not talking about you, is she?"

Doug flinched. "Uh, no. I knew her for like four hours."

"But you made an impression on her." Her nails scrapped white marks into the tablecloth as she watched Meeka's back. "She *is* talking about you!"

Caul appeared beside them. "Morning, folks." Uninvited, he sat and rested his elbows on the table. "Son, you need to be careful of that one." He stared at Doug.

"Would you two get outta my grill!" Doug returned Caul's stare. "I don't know who the hell you think you are, but you need to get lost. Now!"

"I'm just trying to warn you." Caul pushed back from the table.

"Warn us about what?" Jillian asked.

Caul glanced around. "You can't trust her," he whispered.

"I don't," Jillian whispered back.

Doug stood up, towering over Caul. "Listen, man...you need to take a hike!"

Caul abandoned his chair, raising his hands in surrender, and ambled to the bar.

Jillian grabbed Doug's arm. "Stop it! That was rude!"

"No more than giving uninvited advice and spouting weird comments about sex."

"Whatever. Let's go pack." She stood up.

"No."

She regarded him. "Excuse me?"

"We're not switching hotels. We'd lose over a thousand dollars just here if we changed hotels, and that's simply not happening."

Ugly crawled up her face and her voice erupted. "I don't want to be around her—"

"Stop! Just stop thinking about her!"

Doug realized that everyone in the dining room was staring at them. "Sorry," he said and left. Back in the room, he threw some essentials into a small daypack.

Jillian pushed into their room. "What are you doing?"

"I'm going for a hike. You're welcome to join me if you can ditch the bitch."

"Diplomatic lately? Don't be a dick!"

A growl of frustration escaped his throat. "You know what? I'm gonna go, and you can stay here and do whatever the hell you want to, okay? Go find another hotel, and have fun getting pregnant through immaculate conception or what-the-hell-ever. I'm tired of your drama queen bullshit, Jillian!"

The slamming door was an added exclamation point to his parting shot. He was backing the car out when she thumped on the passenger-side window. He lowered it part way.

"Open the door."

"Why? So you can get in and tell me how much of a dick I am? Whine about Meeka the whore? Whee, Jillian. That sounds like a thrilling way to spend the day."

"Open it!"

He puffed out a big breath, but unlocked the car.

She fell into the seat like a bag of wet sand and slammed her door. "Go." They were several miles down the road, before she spoke again. "This is what I was talking about. The fighting...the bickering. I hate this!"

"Then stop!"

She closed her eyes and inhaled deeply. "Would you please hear me out?"

He met her request with silence. She nodded, her hands fidgeting in her lap. "I worry. I worry that you're getting bored with me, okay? I worry that someone's going to take you away from me. Consider this from my perspective...you bring me up here to a hotel that you know, with a sexy, young waitress that you apparently had *something* with before you ever met me, who's whining about losing you and trying to get in your pants. She lies to her employers, so why wouldn't she lie to us? Lie to me?"

The sudden deceleration of the car caught her off guard. With wild eyes, her head snapped up, and she looked through the windshield as the Subaru left the road. She slammed back into the seat as Doug threw the shifter into park. Startled, she glanced over at him, but he was already gone—out the door. The car rocked and her door flew open.

"*I* wouldn't lie to you!" His face was inches from hers.

"I—I never said you would!"

He was gone again. She unbuckled and slid out of the car. Kicking gravel, he exercised his frustration farther down the shoulder.

"Doug? I never said you'd lie to me."

He spun and pinned her to the side of the car. "Then why are you freaking out about this? What are you worried about? It takes two to tango, Jillie, and I'm not interested!"

She was silent for a long time.

"Why are we doing this?" He broke the silence and stalked away.

"Doing what?"

"Wasting our time and money being snarky in Maine. We could have stayed home and done this for free."

"You know why we're here—"

"I know why you say we're here, but you getting stressed out and jealous over a flirty waitress and not having sex with me is kinda defeating the point of being here, isn't it?"

"You're missing *my* point."

"No, I'm not! Am I stupid?"

She sighed. "No."

"Do you trust that if I say I get your point that I truly get it?"

"Then what is it?"

He glanced at her. "You're mad that I got tongue-tied over Meeka."

"Of course."

"All right. But, if you'll listen to me...okay, she can't possibly look like that, because she looks just like she did twelve years ago. That's why I got freaked out, okay? The girl hasn't aged a day since I saw her last. She's still eighteen! Wouldn't that freak you out? Make you gawk if it was someone you'd known?"

"I guess."

"Then please stop riding my ass every time Meeka makes a stupid comment, okay? Just ignore her. That's what I'm doing."

She covered her eyes with her hand. "You know it's not that easy!"

"Yes, it is!" He returned and leaned against the car, putting his hands on either side of her.

"No, it's not!" She thumped the door panel. "Crap! I hate being mad at you!"

"The feeling's mutual." He kissed her forehead. "Come on. Get in, or we'll never make the park."

She watched him walk around the car and heard his door slam shut. "How can you do that?"

"Do what?"

Leaning down, she glared through her open door. "Turn off you emotions like that?"

He exhaled. "I didn't. I simply worked through being angry, okay? Please get in."

Resigned, she sat and clutched her head. They rode for miles in silence. Finally, she took his hand and squeezed it. "I'm sorry. I'm just on edge."

"I know."

She was lost in her thoughts for a while longer. "I trust you," she said at last.

"Thank you."

The remainder of the trip was relatively quiet. Neither of them was completely over the anger of the morning, but neither did they care to argue any longer. They were simply content to be with each other.

"Where are we headed?" Jillian asked after the tires had rolled many miles.

"Great Wass Island Preserve."

"Sounds...fun?"

"It's a great place for hot heads to cool off." He flourished the statement with a ghost of a smile.

Jillian nodded.

"And, there's a nature trail that winds around the island, with a bunch of rare native plants unique to the area. If we're lucky, we'll see seals. The island itself is owned by the Nature Conservancy."

"You sound like a travel brochure."

"I read up on a bunch of stuff. I wanted this to be an enjoyable trip."

She leaned across the arm rest and put her head on his arm. "It has been...it is."

They arrived and walked the island path, snapping pictures on their smartphones because Jillian had forgotten to grab their camera. They reached the southern-most tip of the island, and came upon an older couple watching seals. The sleek animals frolicked in the water and pulled themselves up on the rocks. Doug and Jillian stopped to watch for a few minutes.

The man glanced at them. "Would you mind taking our picture?"

"Not a problem," Doug said. He took the camera and listened to the man's ten second primer on how to use it. "I should let you do this," he said to Jillian, "since you're the better photographer."

She smiled. "Thanks. Sure."

She posed the couple several times, and moved around at different angles. She snapped over a dozen photos as she chatted with them. The wife was all smiles as she reviewed the pictures. "Oh, those are good! Are you a photographer?"

Jillian blushed. "No, I do advertising."

"Well, if you ever get bored of that, you should do photography!"

"Thank you."

"May we get a few of you?" The man looked pleased. "I can't promise to be as skilled, but you'll at least have something for your scrapbook."

Doug agreed and passed his phone to him.

Afterwards, the two couples walked together for a while, exchanging bits of life history. After half an hour, the others found a rock to sit on and said they were going to take a breather. Doug and Jillian walked on.

"How'd the pictures come out?"

Doug had given them only a cursory glance when the man had returned his phone. He pulled it out and handed it to Jillian. "Here you go."

She looked at the pictures of them standing hand in hand in front of the ocean, her leaning against him, them kissing. "What the...what is that?" She looked closer and swiped the screen to expand the image.

"What?" Doug tried to look over her shoulder.

"You've got to be kidding me!" Jillian said, her voice rising to a shout by the end.

She made a noise of disgust, and passed the phone to Doug. His attention was drawn to the expanded image of Jillian turning to him to receive the kiss. In the water, beyond her head, floated an off-white smudge with two inky spots and a pixie haircut.

5

They were halfway off the island before either of them spoke. "It had to be a seal or something. There's no way it could have been...the person we think it looks like. You know how people are programed from birth to recognize faces? I mean, people see faces in clouds and rock formations and all sorts of crazy places." He glanced at her. "That's gotta be it."

"Sure. Either that or she's haunting us."

"She's not a ghost!" Doug felt a slither of dread work its way up his spine at her words and the specter of Meeka that had haunted his dreams last night. *That seemed so real...but that was a second floor window.*

"Then what is she? How could she know that we'd be at the lobster place last night? How'd she even work in two of the three places we've eaten? That's freakish! And then she's there this morning—at the hotel. What the heck? She's stalking you." She glanced at Doug, worried that what she was saying was true.

The quiet roar of the tires and the wind filled their ears for a time. Finally rousing from her thoughts, Jillian shook her head.

"Interesting..."

"What's that?"

"I'm hungry, but I'm frightened of food."

Doug stifled a nervous laugh.

"I'm not kidding," she said. "I now really look forward to cooking in my own kitchen. I'm not sure I ever want to eat out again."

"Then you're not frightened by food, you're repelled by restaurants." He stepped out on a thin limb. "Or worried by waitresses...aggrieved by alewives?"

She waved her hand dismissively. "Semantics."

"I'm hungry too. Somehow we managed to forget about lunch today."

She checked the clock on the dashboard. "It's only three o'clock. Still lunchtime by some people's definition."

They rolled into Jonesport a few minutes later. "Let's find a grocery store and get some sandwich fixings and stuff."

Jillian nodded. "That sounds fine. It's a shame the room doesn't have a minifridge, we could take some food back with us. Maybe a different hotel would have minifridges."

Doug growled, but had a conciliatory idea. "How about we stock up the cooler with chocolate, red wine, and beer, and take it up to the room?"

Jillian purred. "Now you're talking. Well, at least with the wine and chocolate, anyway."

He grabbed her hand and kissed it. As he drove, she pulled their hands to her face and started nibbling his fingers. Jonesport rolled by, and he noticed that it seemed more blue collar in appearance than Bar Harbor. The houses were not as fancy, and the town had a rural feel, with more space between the buildings. It lacked some of the charm of Bar Harbor.

"Oh, that was a grocery store, I think," Jillian said.

"What? Where?"

"On the right. The big, green building."

"That looked like a barn."

"Preconceptions are a bitch."

He laughed. "Tell me about it!"

"Whatever. Hey, there's a pizza parlor. Turn in, turn in!"

He obliged her request. "I thought you were frightened by food... aren't you perturbed by pizza?"

"Funny. No, it's carbs and fat. Italian soul food...the motherhead of comfort."

"And beer. I bet it's not as good as The Kindest Slice," he said, referring to their favorite pizzeria in New Haven.

She made a non-committal sound and climbed out of the car. She looked around, then turned and walked backwards, giggling as she planted her feet awkwardly—toe to heel, toe to heel. "This is sooo dodgy! I hope we don't get food poisoning."

"You're so strange, lovely wife o' mine."

She put her arms around his neck, causing them to stumble as their legs entangled, and kissed him. He returned her kiss with enthusiasm. Breaking apart a bit, he stared into her eyes. *You're so beautiful. I just needed to see you anew.* "I love you!"

"I love you better!"

They entered the pizzeria arm-in-arm. The place was a narrow, but deep space, lined on either side with lacquered plywood booths. Small tables with rickety looking chairs ran down the center, and every horizontal surface was graced with thin red-and-white checked table cloths.

"It looks like a cowboy exploded in here," Doug whispered.

Jillian giggled.

"Hey, there! Welcome to Sal's! Sit wherever you'd like," a woman called from the back. Something banged in the kitchen. She made her way toward them, limping slightly. A flesh-colored eyepatch perched on her face.

"Thanks," Doug said. "What's the specialty? Lobster pizza?"

The woman grimaced. "Not from around here, are you?"

"No. Connecticut." Jillian suppressed the urge to ask about the patch. She and Doug slid into a booth, sitting side-by-side like they were dating.

The woman tilted her head. "Well, welcome to a little heaven on earth, then. I'm Pam. What can I get you to drink?"

Doug leaned on the table. "What kind of beer do you have?"

Pam clucked her tongue, grabbed a laminated sheet from her apron, and handed it to him. "Draft," she pointed to one side, "bottled," she pointed to the other.

"Great...I'll have a Shipyard."

Pam grunted. "You?"

"Oh, just water, please."

Pam limped away.

"Argh, matey!" Doug whispered in his best pirate voice. "I'll be fetching yer grog for ye now!"

Pam banged something in the kitchen.

Jillian giggled. "Shh! I think she heard you!"

Doug leaned in for a peck that turned into a long, sloppy kiss.

"You're beautiful," he whispered against her lips.

"Mmm. Thank you."

"And sexy." He slipped a hand down and gave her hip a gentle but meaningful squeeze.

"Mmm!"

"Will you have my baby?"

"Mmmhmm! I thought you'd never ask." Her lips slipped over his.

After a while, they heard footsteps. "Oh, hey guys! Did you have a good day exploring the island?"

They froze. "Tell me I just imagined Meeka's voice. That was Pam, right?" She gazed into his eyes.

"Pam, um hmm, has to be." He tilted his head a bit. "Just leave the drinks," he said to Pam and resumed kissing Jillian.

"Hey, um, I don't mean to be rude, but your beer's getting warm."

"This isn't happening," Jillian whispered.

Doug kissed her once more, like a gentle punch, and turned to find Meeka standing at the end of their table. He flinched.

"Sorry, but I wanted to get your drinks to you while they're still cold. Do you know what you'd like to eat?"

Doug glared toward the kitchen. "Where's Pam?"

"Oh, she's out back having a cigarette. She asked if I could take care of you."

His gaze slid back to her. "Bullshit. What are you really doing here?"

"I'm working."

"So...what? You expect us to believe that you work here, too?" Jillian pushed against Doug, trying to get out.

"Uh, yeah!" Meeka laughed. "As I said, I work all over."

Jillian stared her down. "It's awfully convenient that you work everywhere. Particularly everywhere we decide to eat, when we decide to eat. How exactly does that happen?"

Meeka shrugged. "Good timing?" A fleeting smile crossed her face.

"Not what I would call it," Jillian said, her voice rising. "More like you're stalking us."

"Stalking?"

Doug rapped the table with his knuckles. "How much is the beer?"

Meeka frowned. "Um, four."

Doug fished out his wallet and handed her a five dollar bill. "Merry Christmas. Get out of my way, please." She stepped back, and he slid from the booth, before helping Jillian out.

"But your beer," Meeka said. "Don't you want some pizza?"

Doug glared at her. "No." He started to turn away, but stopped and stuck a finger in her face. "Stay away from us."

They flew out of the pizzeria, and Jillian fell into a fit of giggles. "Did you see her expression? 'No!'" They were a mile down the road before she stopped laughing. "I love you!"

"Likewise." He kissed her hand. "Let's go have a relaxing meal in Bar Harbor, where we are now assured that Meeka is not."

"How does that happen? Seriously...this is beyond coincidence. She was just at the Pequot! I think she is stalking us. Well, you anyway."

A chill settled into the hollow of his gut. "How could she be if she works at each of those restaurants? That would be impossible to fake."

"How do we know she actually works at the pizzeria?" Horror, like clotting milk, welled at the back of her throat, while stress made her laugh. "We never saw them together. Maybe she tied up poor Pam and stuck her in a closet." She glanced at him. "You don't think that's possible, do you?"

Deceleration pushed her into her seatbelt. The Subaru rolled to an idle on the grassy shoulder.

"I—I don't think that's likely, but..." He checked traffic and whipped the car around.

"What're you doing?"

"Going back to check."

"That isn't safe! I mean, what if she *is* a psycho? We should call the police."

"No time," Doug said. *Could there really be a problem? If there is, why am I going back?* His mind returned to the dream of Meeka in his bed. *Was that really a dream?*

"I don't like this."

"I'm six-two and weigh two hundred and thirty-five pounds. What could she possibly do?"

"What if she has a gun?"

His eyes widened. "That's unlikely, don't you think?"

They pulled into the lot at the pizzeria and burst through the door. Pam was standing at their table looking at the untouched glasses and the five dollar bill. "Did you change your mind about lunch?"

"Maybe...where's Meeka?"

"Who?"

Doug felt the chill in his gut turn to ice. "The other waitress."

Pam barked a short laugh. "Look at this place." She gestured to the empty restaurant. "There is no other waitress. This time of day there is no other *anyone*. How'd you get drinks?"

"Meeka brought them, after you took our order," he said.

"But who's Meeka?"

"The other waitress!" The gears turned in his head about the potential for an endless conversation. "Where were you for the last few minutes?"

Pam looked irritated. "I was in the walk-in cooler, getting more chilled glasses, and the door got stuck. I just got out and came to check on you two." Her brow wrinkled. "But you've got drinks from some ghost waitress."

Doug felt the ice in his gut worm its way up his spine.

"Is she a ghost?" Jillian pulled out her phone. "This is what she looks like." She showed Pam the photo taken at Huston's.

"Never seen that girl before. She sure as hell's never worked here. You say she brought you your drinks? How could she know what you'd ordered? There was no one else here to hear your order." She scratched her jaw. "Do you want lunch?"

Doug looked around the restaurant. "Maybe we should check the place, first."

"There ain't anyone here," Pam said. "I'd know."

"And yet..." He turned to Jillian. "What do you think?"

She glanced around the restaurant. "I'm not really comfortable with this."

Pam's eyes narrowed. "What kinda game are you playin' here? You know, from where I sit, you went into my kitchen and ran my beer tap. That ain't friendly or legal."

"No, we didn't!" Jillian said. "It wasn't us. It was Meeka. She brought us the beer."

"There ain't any Meeka here! Look, I don't want any trouble, so perhaps you folks should leave."

"Are you kicking us out? Seriously?" Doug said.

"I'm asking you to leave, yeah."

"Whatever!" Jillian said. "We came back because we thought Meeka might have hurt you, and this is the thanks we get?"

"Out!"

They were back in the car before he spoke. "You saw her, right?"

"Yes!"

"She brought our drinks. What did she say?"

Jillian thought for a moment. "She asked if we had enjoyed exploring the island."

"So she knew we were on Great Wass...she is following us!"

"Where's her car?"

"Huh?"

"Her car!" Jillian felt close to hyperventilating. "How else could she be following us unless she's driving? Or she's a ghost."

He shook his head. "But ours was the only car in the parking lot, and no one came into the restaurant after us." He gunned the engine, and she squeaked.

"Where's the fire?"

"Bar Harbor. I think Meeka may have an accomplice...a driver."

Jillian frowned. "Who?"

"Caul."

"What? Why?"

"Why not? Those two seem to go together."

She shook her head. "I can't see that happening. Caul seems really frustrated with Meeka, like she's an errant child."

"Maybe she is."

6

The sun was low in the sky, and both of their stomachs were growling when they pulled into the parking lot at the Pequot. Jillian was feeling two hungers. On the long trip back to the hotel she had realized that nearly thirty-six hours had passed since they had last made love. "Dinner first, then upstairs, then we do some Hercule Poirot moves on the ghost chick," Jillian said as they entered the hotel. They ducked into the dining room, and she grabbed the closest table. She did not want a leisurely meal tonight.

Doug pulled out the chair across from hers. "Please don't go all Agatha Christie on me."

"I love Aggie. She was an awesome, strong, smart woman."

At the bar, Susan looked up from a magazine. She walked over, her expression wary. "Are we gonna have a quiet time tonight, folks?"

"Yeah, we are." Doug raised his hands in a placating gesture, before sitting down.

"Good. Have a pleasant meal." Susan returned to her post at the bar.

Jillian's lips pursed. "She didn't take our order."

"She's the bar tender. There's probably someone else working the wait staff...maybe Charles. At least we won't have to worry about—"

"Not even possible," Jillian said.

Doug swiveled, following her gaze, and found Meeka walking towards them.

"Hey, guys! How was Great Wass?"

"How?" Doug's vision narrowed to just her face as blood thudded in his ears. "How did you get here so fast? What'd you do at the pizzeria?"

Meeka looked puzzled. "Sorry, what?"

"How did you know we were on Great Wass?"

"You told me this morning where you were headed," Meeka said.

His brow furrowed as he regarded her. "No, I didn't!"

She shrugged.

"How did you get here so fast?" Jillian asked.

"I've been here for hours."

Doug stood up, leaning over the table toward her. "That's bullshit! You were in Jonesport an hour and a half ago. I saw you. I talked to you!"

Meeka backed away. "Excuse me."

She fast stepped across the dining room, and whispered something to Susan, who crossed the maroon carpet and returned to their table. "What seems to be the problem, Mister Sandow?"

"No problem, other than her strange behavior. We saw her ninety minutes ago in Jonesport, and now she refuses to acknowledge that we talked to her. That we told her to stay away from us."

The woman looked pained. "Meeka clocked back in over three hours ago, and she's been here ever since. I'm not sure what happened in Jonesport, but Meeka has been here the entire time. Is everything going to be okay?"

Doug's ears rang as he glared at Meeka, who crept closer. "But how?"

Susan stepped between them. "I don't know, Mister Sandow."

Everyone in the room was watching him. He finally relented and nodded. "Whatever."

"Can I bring you something from the bar?"

"Sure. Scotch, neat."

"Not right now," Jillian said. "I'm trying to get pregnant anyway."

Meeka made a small noise and retreated. Susan watched her go then she excused herself.

"What on earth is going on?" Jillian asked, pinching the bridge of her nose.

"We've stumbled into a horror novel?"

She gave a weak laugh. "Oh, horror!" Then her eyes widened and she looked up at him. "See...you did jinx us when we arrived! All that talk of creepy motels...what'd you check us into?"

"Psh! Do you want to go somewhere else for dinner?"

"Please."

After he downed his drink, they went downtown and found a quiet Italian restaurant. They were thrilled to have a waiter for a change. He suggested the salmon carpaccio, clams and capers in Alfredo sauce over linguine, and Chianti for Doug. By mutual consent, they talked about anything other than Meeka. They finished the meal with cranberry gelato, and returned to the hotel well after dark.

"Evening," Charles said. Caul was sitting with him.

Jillian nodded to the men and went straight upstairs, but Doug hesitated. He fixed Caul with a hard stare.

"Where were you this afternoon at around three thirty?"

"Sorry?"

"Don't 'Sorry' me, Caul. Where were you at three thirty?"

"I was at work."

"Let me guess, you work alone?"

Caul frowned. "No, I'm the director of research at Smithson Labs. I was there all day, until almost six."

Doug mimicked Caul's frown. "So you've got witnesses?"

Charles nodded. "He arrived a little after six. Shortly after you left."

"What's this all about?" Caul removed his glasses and polished them.

"Not sure," Doug said.

"Well, I don't like your tone. It's not your place to be interrogating me."

Doug cracked a few knuckles. "Maybe it is, if you've got some interest in my wife." He watched Caul's face. *If Caul is interested in Jillian, he may be using Meeka to drive a wedge between us.* "You related to Meeka?"

Caul jerked and started to reply but he choked and coughed instead. *Uh, huh.*

"Is there a problem, Mister Sandow?" Charles asked. "I heard that you were unhappy earlier. Something to do with Meeka?"

"When did she get here today?"

Charles glanced away. "Meeka arrived at work at 1:47 pm—I checked her punch card—and she did not leave the building. She's still here, in fact. Is there a problem?"

"Nothing I can't handle," Doug said. "I'm watching you, Caul."

Caul cleared his throat. "Well, then I'm flattered. Puzzled certainly, but flattered."

Doug checked himself from responding. His fists felt very close to hitting. Instead, he joined his wife at the top of the stairs. They made it to their room without a Meeka sighting, much to Jillian's delight. She spun and planted a deep, wet kiss on his mouth.

"What was all that downstairs?"

"Nothing. Just checking up on Meeka's accomplice. Nothing."

Her finger bridged his lips. "All right then. I demand your undivided attention now. Give me two minutes." She disappeared into the bathroom, closing the door behind her.

He sighed, shifting from one frustration to another. Sex was most often a ritual for Jillian. *Why can't it just be spontaneous? Why does every time have to be some secret, sacred event?* He stripped off his clothes and crawled into bed. It was still early, so he was not tired but he dozed, thinking back on the dream from the previous night. He felt his loins tingle.

Jillian exited the bathroom and moved across the hardwood floor. *Squeak, squeak.*

"What's this?"

Squeak, squeak.

"Doug...where did this come from?"

He opened his eyes and saw Jillian holding out a large, silver ring with a red stone. He blinked. The number 2001 was emblazoned on the sides. *That's not possible!* Moving tentatively, as if it might burn him, he took the ring from Jillian. The stone caught a stray beam of lamplight and flared like blood and fire. The ring was heavy—a burden in his hand. He turned it to look at the engraving inside the band and his breath stalled.

Brian Cole, Football God.

"Holy shit," he whispered. "Where was this?"

"Doug!"

"Where *was this*?"

"On the dresser. Whose is it?"

The ring blurred in Doug's hand. "It's my friend Brian's ring." He looked up at Jillian. "He was wearing it when he drowned."

"Wait, what? Your friend drowned?"

Doug nodded, his features slack. "We were swimming in Newport Cove. Something caught him and pulled him under. They searched for two days, but never found his body."

"Oh...but then...?" She pointed at the ring.

"I've no idea!" He slid out of bed and grabbed his clothes.

"What are you doing?"

"I've gotta go ask who was in our room."

"Can't it wait?" She rubbed his chest.

"No. I'm sorry, but I have to talk to whoever left this."

She grabbed his hand. "It can wait."

"Twelve years, Jillian! This isn't coincidence. Someone here knows what happened to Brian!" He searched her face. "I owe it to him, to his parents."

"It can wait an hour. Come on."

He sighed—torn—but followed her to bed. He was not gentle and finished quickly. She wanted to be held afterwards and talk, but he was tense. "I need to use the toilet."

When he returned, he began dressing.

Jillian frowned. "Is it really that important?"

Doug simply stared at her before he opened his mouth and pain gushed out. "He was my best friend. He drowned thirty feet away from me and I couldn't save him! I had to explain to his mom and dad—two people who were like my second parents—that their son was dead. That they wouldn't even have a body to mourn over and bury and visit. Do you know what that's like for an eighteen-year-old kid?" He stood, nostrils flaring. "Yeah, it is that important."

He quickly finished dressing and opened the door.

"I'm sorry," she whispered. Her hair hung like a veil around her face, closing her off from him.

All day, he had been looking forward to being intimate with her, but the revelation of the ring and his haste to get answers, had sullied their time together. He paused, clutching the knob. "Me too. I'll be back soon." He closed his eyes and rested his head against the edge of the door. "I've buried all of this for a decade. This," he held up the ring, "opened up a huge question. I need answers."

"I—I understand. Go. It's okay."

He managed a weak smile, before closing the door. Charles was still at his desk when Doug entered the lobby. Doug tapped his knuckles on the desk, causing the man to look up and blink. *Like a freaky owl.* "Hey, can you tell me who was in my room today?"

Apprehension marched across Charles's face. "Is there a problem?"

"Not exactly. I'd just like to talk to them."

"I'm sorry that your stay with us hasn't been to your satisfaction. Perhaps you'd like me to find you alternate lodging?"

Well that was unexpected. Doug blinked and rubbed his eyes, feeling fatigue catching up with him. "It's been...fine. Can you please just tell me who was in my room?"

Charles looked unconvinced, but after a few seconds he lifted a clipboard from a cubby in the desk. "Well, we share jobs around here, but Anne cleaned number four today."

"And she is?"

"At the moment, she's our cook."

"Was she the only one?"

Charles looked up. "Is there a problem?"

Slowly, his hand left its sheltering pocket. "I found this in my room a few minutes ago." Doug proffered the ring, but Charles's face remained blank.

"It's the ring my best friend was wearing when he drowned out by Old Soaker twelve years ago."

Owl eyes peered at Doug. "Sorry, we have a drowning or two every year. I don't remember—"

"His name was Brian."

Charles shook his head. "Maybe someone found it and wanted to get it to you?"

"He drowned wearing it. They never found his body."

"Oh." Charles pursed his lips.

"Yeah. Obviously, I'd like to know who put it in my room and how they got it."

"I understand. However, now isn't the best time to talk to Anne. I don't like to disturb her when she's in the kitchen, but I can introduce you in a little while."

Doug frowned. "Okay, then tell me about Caul. What's his story?"

"I'm not sure what you're getting at, Mister Sandow."

"Please, call me Doug," he said and held out his hand.

"All right, Doug. As I said, I'm Charles." They shook.

"Great. So, about Caul?"

"Again, I'm not sure where you're going with that question."

Doug scratched the stubble on his chin. "He seems to have some, um, thing about Meeka. He always wants to talk to us after she has. What's his deal?"

Charles shrugged. "He eats dinner here most evenings, and breakfast sometimes. Has for years. I mean, he's sweet on her, maybe...tips well, but he's mostly the same with her as he is with the rest of us. We've known him for years. You get used to having people around."

"So...that's it? They don't go out, hang out...conspire?"

Charles pushed back in his chair. "Not that I've ever noticed."

"Huh."

"Hmm?"

"Why would he warn us about Meeka then?"

Charles's expression became pained. "Warn you? About what?"

"He said we couldn't trust her."

Charles raised a hand, palm out. "Mister Sandow—Doug—Meeka's worked here longer than Susan and I have—"

"I know. She was here twelve years ago when Brian and I ate dinner...right there." He pointed into the dining room.

Charles's look was skeptical. "I really don't think you need be concerned." He paused and looked at the doorway Doug was still pointing at. "I just heard Anne. Come with me."

He led Doug into the dining room, where Susan and another woman were sitting at the bar, talking.

"Anne? This is Mister Sandow, from room four." Charles scuffed his foot across the carpet, leaving streaks of darker maroon. "Did you... put anything in his room today?"

The woman's ruddy face displayed a look of surprise that quickly shifted to irritation. "Toilet paper, soap, and clean linens." Her watery eyes snapped from one man to the other.

"Anything else?"

She straightened her back and shifted on the seat, her glare coming to rest on Doug. "What else would there be? We don't put mints on the pillows, though some could do with sweetening."

Doug frowned. "What's that supposed to mean?"

The woman shifted her bulk on the stool, hesitating. "You're being a bit hard on our Meeka, I think. She's come down to the kitchen and cried about it. She—"

"Anne," Charles said, holding up a hand. "That's enough."

Doug leaned away from her. "What are you talking about?"

"You! She cries about you. How you took advantage of her all those years ago, then stood her up. Now you come back and rub her nose in it with your trophy wife and your—your fancy car."

"Anne, *please*," Charles said, his face pinking up and voice rising a register. "That's not appropriate."

"Well, she has been."

Charles frowned. "That's not important."

Doug shook his head. "I never took advantage of her. We kissed a couple of times, but that was it." *And since when is a Subaru a fancy car?*

"Of course you'd say that." Anne sniffed.

"Seriously? She's lying! What the hell is going on around here?"

The atmosphere was leaden. The hotel workers looked at each other in discomfort. "Mister Sandow..." Charles cleared his throat. "Didn't you have a more...direct question for Anne?"

"I've got a lot of questions—"

"*Please*, Mister Sandow," Charles said, quietly.

Doug frowned, but held his tongue. He took the ring from his pocket and held it in front of Anne's nose. "Where did this come from? How did you get it?"

She crossed her eyes to see the ring. "That? It was in your tub."

Doug grimaced at her unexpected statement. "What do you mean?"

"In your tub." Her look of irritation deepened. "Right up by the drain. Fell off your finger, I reckon." She blinked. "You're lucky it didn't fall in. I put it on the dresser for safekeeping."

"But how did it get into our room? Where did you get it from?"

Anne looked sidelong at Susan. A fine slick of sweat shimmered on her lip.

"Just answer his question, please," Charles said.

"It's *your* ring! I found it in *your* tub. I picked it up, rinsed it in the sink, and put it on *your* dresser. End of story." Her expression dared him to gainsay her.

Doug felt his pulse pounding. "It's not my ring. You expect me to believe that you just found this in my tub? I showered there only hours before, and there was nothing in my tub. Where did it come from?"

Anne leaned close. "I don't know."

They glared at each other.

Susan tapped the bar. "Why did you rinse it in the sink?"

Anne broke the contest with Doug. "It was covered in slimy gunk." She glanced at Charles. "Are we done here? I need to go home."

"Yes," Charles said.

"Hold on! That doesn't make any sense," Doug said. "How can this ring just appear in my tub?"

Anne shrugged, bid Charles and Susan goodnight, and walked out.

"Who else was in my room today?"

Charles made a small noise of irritation. "Just Anne."

"Okay...who had access to my room?"

Susan's eyes narrowed. "What are you suggesting?"

She looks ready to pitch me out of her hotel...redheads! "I'm not suggesting anything. I'm just asking."

"All the staff have access to the rooms," Charles said. "Like I told you, we all share responsibility here."

"And the staff is?"

"Me, Susan, Karen, Anne, and Meeka. We have other people who come in part time, but none of them have been here these last few days."

"So Meeka had access to my room today?"

Susan and Charles shared a look of concern. "No, the rooms had been cleaned and the keys put away by the time she returned," Susan said. "And, she was with me or Anne the entire afternoon."

Doug looked at each of them in turn. "And yet, somehow, the ring of my dead friend mysteriously appears in my room...twelve years after he drowned?"

Susan turned away, her face marred by a look of exasperation, and Charles would not make eye contact. "I don't know what to tell you, Mister Sandow."

Something weird is going on. They know something and aren't saying.

7

Jillian was asleep when he returned to their room. His nervous fingers turned the ring over and over in his pocket as he leaned against the desk and stared at nothing. *Brian was wearing it the day he drowned, I remember!*

Jillian shifted on the bed and opened her eyes. "Hey, sexy. Find out anything?"

"No. Nothing. The woman who cleaned our room claims she found it in the bathtub."

"Claims?" She sat up, the sheet falling away from her torso. "You don't believe her?"

"How can I? How could it just show up in our tub?"

"Well, if I had to guess, I'd say that Meeka put it there."

He exhaled and slumped. "I thought about that already. Susan swears she was with her or the cook the entire afternoon."

"Yeah? She was also in Jonesport." Jillian raised her eyebrows. "If she can be in two places at once, why not three?"

He swallowed. "Okay, you know that's not possible?" His voice sounded tight and unnatural in his ears.

"What other explanation do you have?" She got out of bed, and he watched the muscles of her back and buttocks flex as she walked to the bathroom. He wanted her again—not rushed this time.

"They're lying to us?" *Or I booked us into a possessed hotel?* He had not read much fiction since he was a teenager, but the plots and images of the horror comics and mystery novels of his youth were rising up in the back of his mind like flotsam in a tide pool.

She leaned against the doorframe. "It's the only rational explanation."

"But it still doesn't make sense! Why lie to us about this?"

"Money? Revenge? The usual reasons."

They're psychos? They want to harvest our souls and eat our organs? He squeezed his eyes shut. "That makes no sense. At all. We're not rich, and no one..." His eyes widened. "Maybe Meeka's angry because I never came back?" *Is what Anne said credible? Could Meeka really believe that crap she told Anne? Everything seems to revolve around Meeka.*

"It makes as much sense as anything else that's happening. So, let's go investigate."

"Ouch!"

"Shhh!"

"A twig just poked me in the eye!"

"Shhh! You make a lousy detective."

Doug crouched in the shrubs, his eyes shedding tears like a water-fall. "I doubt Poirot ever slunk around in anyone's azaleas."

"You'd be amazed."

He shook his head. "This feels more like Scooby Doo."

A single lamp burned in the converted carriage house. The paint was weathered, peeling away from the window frames, and the curtains were cheap and thin. A battered Oldsmobile was quietly rusting by the front door.

"You're sure that's her house?"

"Yeah. You doubt my ability to use a computer?"

Doug grimaced. "It's a phone, but no, I don't. I'm just surprised, is all."

"Why? She's a waitress. Where would you expect her to live, the Taj Mahal?"

"Haha." He applied sarcasm and shifted his weight. "It's just real small."

"Single white female," Jillian whispered.

"What?"

"Nothing. I'm going to get a closer look." She crept away.

"Jillian! Seriously, not a good idea. People get arrested for stuff like this."

"Oh, lighten up. She'd never press charges." Her voice changed to a sing-song. "She loves you too much."

Doug groaned. "Please, shut up!"

Her laughter floated though the dark.

She ran across the dead-grass yard, crouched over like she had seen actors do in a hundred action movies. Doug looked around and followed. They peered over the window ledge, through dirty glass panes, into a small, spare living room.

Jillian wrinkled her nose. "Nice. Looks like discards from a thrift shop. Shabby without the chic."

Something about the room bothered Doug. An old, wicker rocking chair sat next to a circular table. A green, ceramic lamp with a stained, off-kilter shade rested on a doily on the table. A closed door at the back of the room was the only other feature. *There's no TV, no radio, no books, no magazines, no pictures, nothing.*

Jillian's whisper broke his reverie. "There's nothing here. Let's go look in the back."

"I think we should leave."

She made a dismissive noise and crept away in the dark.

"Seriously! Something's not right here."

He followed her, his eyes straining to see after exposure to the light in the front room. A solitary, darkened window marred the back wall of the building. The yard was a sea of pitch.

"Jillian?"

"Psst!"

He followed the sound and bumped into her in the dark.

"What do you make of that?"

"What?" he asked.

"Look down the hill."

He turned in the narrow space between the building and some low shrubs that climbed the steep slope behind it. A BMW, faintly illuminated by a distant street light, was parked on the road far down the slope. A figure sat in the driver's seat—a figure with white hair.

"Is that Caul?"

"Appears to be."

A surge of triumph flooded Doug's brain. "He is her accomplice!" *Or something.*

"Or he's a freaking creeper, watching her bedroom. Are those binoculars? Whatever. Looks suspicious, either way."

Light poured over them, and Doug felt his heart explode. He plowed into the shrubs, turning to look behind himself. He caught a glimpse of a figure with short hair, framed in the window, before the blinds snapped closed.

Jillian fell over in a fit of giggles as soon as the front door of the Pequot whumped shut behind them. They had run all the way back to the hotel, convinced that the police would appear at any second. She trembled as she threw her arms around Doug's neck.

"That was a blast!" She whispered in his ear. "I haven't felt that alive in a long time."

"I'm...glad. Are you going to make a habit of it?"

"Weenie! Come on, let's get a drink and go to bed."

She pulled him toward the dining room and bar, but Doug was rooted to the spot and refused to move. "Wait! I know what was bugging me about her house." He locked gazes with her. "Meeka said she lived with her mother."

"Yeah?"

"There was only one chair in the living room."

8

They rose early. After a quick dalliance and a shower, they walked hand-in-hand to the waterfront. Near Agamont Park, Doug found a coffee cart. He joined Jillian at the quayside with two tall Americanos and a large bag of pastries. A look of dismay crossed her face. "Heaven's, that's a lot!"

"Hey! I have to keep my energy up."

"That's not the only thing you have to keep up, stud muffin. What have you got in there?"

He opened the bag and then peered inside. "Nope."

Her eyebrows drew together. "Nope what?"

"No stud muffins. Bran or cran are your only choices."

She sighed. "Oh, Doug…if you were any cuter, I'd have to pickle you and put you in a little jar on the mantle."

"The hell! Like I'd fit in one jar."

"I'll mince you up into sweet, little Dougie morsels."

He snorted and tapped his head. "Bit of a problem with your dastardly scheme. This won't fit in a jar."

"I'll hire a headshrinker first. You would benefit from that, I think."

He smiled and tweaked her nose. "Oh? But there's one head you don't want to shrink, baby."

She turned away, but not before he saw the corners of her lips twitching higher upwards. She took a deep breath. "Oh, wow. Is it going to be one of those days? Conversation peppered with penis jokes?" She turned back and reached for the bag. "Really, what's in there?"

"Cinnamon rolls. One kiss apiece."

She planted one on him, long and sloppy. They parted with a smack, smiles gracing their faces.

"Mmm," he hummed. "For that, you can have the whole bag."

She giggled and took a pastry. "What's the plan, man? Why'd you get me up so early?"

He took a sip of coffee, and then pointed to a boat topped with a green and white striped awning on poles. "See that fair craft of the high seas?"

She nodded. "You bought it?"

"Hardly—although it would have been a hull of a deal."

She rolled her eyes, but chuckled, as he checked his phone for the time. "In exactly ten minutes, that vessel will be your exclusive chariot for a guided tour of Frenchman Bay and all the bitty and sundry islands thereabouts."

"You're in a rare mood." She glanced back at the coffee cart. "Did he put vodka in your Americano?"

"No, dear. That would make it a Russiacano."

She slapped her forehead. "I'm gonna step over there and stop talking to you for the rest of the day."

"Aww! Spoilsport."

They finished the pastries, and then strolled, arm-in-arm, to the pier. Several other people were lining up at the weathered ticket booth that stood beside the boat's moorage. She poked his ribs. "Thought you said it was exclusive."

"Oh...did I say that? I'm pretty sure I said executive. Aaaaand, the last time I checked, you're an executive."

"You know you lie terribly, right?"

"That wasn't a lie! It was a creative interpretation of reality."

"You're so bad."

They examined the boat from a distance before arriving at the booth on the pier. Hulking next to the petite structure was another abominable sculpture. Doug examined the thick body, stubby limbs, and wide, webbed hands and feet. *How grotesque.* The people ahead of them finished, so Doug stepped up and peered through the smallish window of the booth.

"Morning. Can I help you?" The glare on the glass rendered the person within faceless. Doug felt like he was being talked at by the Headless Woman.

"Yes, reservations for two. Sandow."

"Got you right here. If you'll both sign this waiver."

Doug scribbled his name and passed the clipboard to Jillian, who started reading the form. *Of course you would.* He peered at where he hoped the Headless Woman's eyes would be. *If she has any...*

"What's the story on these super attractive fish heads stuck all over the place?"

"Hmm? Super attractive...that's the first time I've heard someone say that. I think they're freaky."

"Yeah, I wasn't being serious. It looks kind of like a puffer fish mated with the Creature from the Black Lagoon."

The woman chuckled, but it was a sour sound. "I'm glad you weren't serious. I hate those things. They're supposed to be chotah, the fish people who haunt these islands. It's a local legend, depending on what you believe."

"Everyone seems to have one."

"Well, they're made by a local sculptor—old family on the island. The city bought a bunch of them. You know, civic pride and all. Here." She slid a limp, photocopied pamphlet through the window. "Here's his information. He's a bit of a nut, from what I've heard."

"Thanks." Doug pretended to look at the brochure, as Jillian read the waiver. Someone in line made a super fake cough, and Doug looked up. "Jillian, really. All it says is if the boat sinks, and we drown, we aren't going to sue them. Sign it already, please."

Her gaze was cool. "You know I don't work that way."

"Yup." He slipped the brochure into his pocket, before taking the clipboard and holding it for her. "But I want to be back before sunset. And so does everyone behind us." He raised his eyebrows.

She sighed and signed.

Boarding the craft provided minutes of entertainment as it rocked with each new passenger, causing everyone to pitch around in laughter. Once loaded, the boat rumbled out of the harbor, headed north. Out on the open water, a breeze kicked up, and Jillian snuggled close to Doug.

"You make a good windbreak."

"Good 'n' Hunky," he whispered, making her smile.

"And plenty," she whispered back, squeezing his thigh.

A college-aged man stepped to the bow and lifted a microphone. "Hey, good morning! Welcome to Clearwater Tours. I'm Clarence, your guide. In the back of our fair craft is the lovely Shelly, who will be our captain and pilot for our three hour tour."

Shelly waved from the stern.

Jillian put her elbow into Doug's ribs. "Three hours? Sheesh! You could have warned me, I'd've skipped the coffee."

"Sorry. If it gets too bad, you can pee over the gunwales."

"Not likely, buster."

Jillian pulled out their camera and snapped photos of everything that caught her eye. Towering conifers and idyllic inlets captivated them for a while, but even Jillian was tired of trees and water by the time the boat had circumnavigated Frenchman Bay and chugged its way to the Gulf of Maine. Clarence had run out of entertaining things to say by then, so no one protested when he set the microphone down and went to the stern to hit up the captain for a date.

Jillian snuggled against Doug.

"I've been thinking…you know what those people said, yesterday, about me going into photography? I'd actually been thinking about it. I think I'd like that."

"Oh, yeah? I could be your model." He nudged her.

"I'm being serious." She looked out across the water. "Your career is moving up, and we've got enough in savings. I think I'd like to slow down and work less."

Doug frowned. "Can you do that? I mean, won't that affect your promotion…your chances for promotion?"

"What promotion? Everyone above me at this point is a founding partner. Besides, I kind of want to do something different. I've slain my dragon. I'm ready for a new challenge." She kissed his cheek. "I want to do photography. The hours are more flexible."

"That would be a substantial hit to our income." He envisioned the austerity that such a change would cause—more salad, less steak.

"So?" She punched his arm. "Suck it up, you bum!"

Doug smiled ruefully. Jillian's income was over twice as much as his. "I'm not a bum."

"I know, but we can live on your salary and our savings…just until I get the photography business up and running."

"That's kind of abrupt, dumping this in my lap."

"Really? Did you think I was going to keep working seventy-hours a week? You're nuts if you did."

"Okay…well, no. Not really." He shook his head. "I hadn't actually thought about it at all."

"Well, think about it, okay?"

She looked away. He watched the wind tease her hair as it shimmered in the sunlight reflecting off the water. *I'm lucky to have you.* He leaned in and kissed her head. She fell against him, smiling, as the boat picked up speed. They cruised by Old Soaker and Great Head, and Doug looked at the very spot that he had last seen Brian alive. *I should go there.* He wrinkled his nose and shooed the memories away. "Clarence!"

"Sir?" The tour guide glanced up, his brown eyes reflecting the sea.

"What can you tell us about the chotah?"

Clarence smirked. "It's a tired, old legend."

"So, humor me."

"Humor you how? Fishfaced men coming out of the ocean to snatch people? That's the kind of stuff you tell little kids to make them behave."

Jillian looked at the water behind her and shivered.

"So pretend I'm a little kid and scare me," Doug said.

Clarence shook his head. "Ain't nothing to scare you with, man. It's a musty old myth." He went back to chatting with Shelly.

Doug looked away. "Fat lot of good that was."

"Better luck next time." Jillian rubbed his arm.

"They're not a myth." A woman on the center bench leaned closer to Doug. Her face was an old apple, dried in the sun. "I've lived in Bar Harbor ever since I was a girl, and I've seen them...the herringmen. They take things—food, tools, toys, rope, animals, even people! My friend Nettie Uhlebe went missing one summer...'31? Maybe '32. She was asleep on her back porch near her younger brother, Fred—bless his soul—he and I were married for sixty-two years before he passed, but he swore to his dying breath that the chotah stole his sister from the porch that very night. Bundled her up and carried her away to the sea. He was so frightened he couldn't speak for three weeks after. Imagine!"

She smoothed her purple windbreaker. "There are some who think it best not to mention the herringmen, but they don't frighten me. I've lived through a lot, young man. Seven babies...all boys! If that don't beat all, right? A platoon of rambunctious little men. What're we gonna do with all these boys, I used to ask Fred, and he'd say, 'Start a football team!'" She laughed. "You look like a happy couple."

"We are." Doug squeezed Jillian.

"Don't ever let go of each other. Hold on, keep up the good work," she winked, "and you'll have your own football team soon."

Jillian smiled wistfully.

The woman leaned forward. "Is it a boy or a girl?"

"Excuse me?"

"The baby...is it a boy or girl?"

Air refused to flow into Jillian's lungs.

Doug grinned. "She's not pregnant. Not yet, anyway."

"Truly? By your look you're either newlywed, pregnant, or you just robbed a train."

"None of those, but we're trying for the middle one."

"Trying? Don't you believe me?" The woman held up her left hand in a fist. "I have seven children—" she raised a finger "—twenty-three grandchildren—" another finger "—fifty-one great grandchildren—" finger "—and, um, I'm pretty sure thirteen great, great grandbabies—" finger. "I know a few things about pregnant women. How many times have you been pregnant, young man? How many babies have you delivered?" She slapped his knee.

"Ow!" He laughed in surprise. "Well, never, none."

"Exactly! Don't try to tell me my business. I'm eighty-eight years old. Have some respect."

Jillian felt a thrill of possibility, which heightened when the old woman locked gazes with her. "Oh, I knew there was a reason I felt the call to ride the water today," the woman said. "Your heart's desire will be yours, but there's something after you."

The boat hit the dock, jarring everyone sideways. The woman pushed herself back up. "Oh, my! That was exciting!" She stood up.

"Hold on!" Jillian grabbed the woman's elbow. "What did you say? About something being after me?"

The smile on her face was enigmatic. "What is your name, child?"

"Jillian."

The breeze dropped, and the air became still.

"What's your hidden name?"

Jillian frowned. "My hidden name? I don't understand...oh, you mean my middle name? It's Ruth."

"A sign." The woman beamed at her. "I'm also named Ruth...like the long-suffering and faithful woman in the Bible. She became a mother, too, thanks to her faith." She took a pendant from her neck, then turned Jillian's hand over and pressed it into her palm. Her hands held surprising strength as she folded Jillian's fingers around it. "I have a feeling you will be needing this more than I. Be strong on your voyage. Be strong for your unborn child. God bless you, Jillian Ruth."

Ruth released her hand, and Jillian opened it.

A small medallion and chain rested on her palm. She nudged it to get a better look at. Doug peered over her shoulder. "What is it?"

"It's a Saint Christopher medal. But, why?"

Jillian looked up. The old woman was gone. "Where is she?" She looked throughout the boat and up on the pier. "Where'd she go? She was just here!"

Doug stood on one of the bench seats, leaning out over the side of the boat to look around, but she was nowhere to be found. Jillian shook her head in disbelief. She fingered the medal as they exited the boat. Stopping at the quay, she fastened the necklace around her throat. "I haven't worn a religious emblem in years."

"No reason to."

She watched Doug walk away from her, along the waterfront. "I might like to change that," she whispered.

9

Doug and Jillian purchased some sandwiches, cold drinks, and ice, and returned to the hotel to get the car. Afternoon sunlight poured through the windshield as they headed into the park.

"I enjoyed the boat ride."

"Good. I'm glad you liked it."

"Where are we headed now?" Jillian asked.

"It's a surprise."

"Oooh, I like surprises!"

Me too, most of the time. Finding Brian's ring had raised the ghost of his memory, and seeing the spot where he had drowned had solidified the need for Doug to go pay his respects to his friend. Doug remembered the first time he had been to where they were headed. He and Brian had bummed around Acadia for several days, staying in the Blackwoods campground. They had used it as a base, and hiked all over Hunters Head, Ingram Point, Otter Point, and Great Head—a name that they had joked about until even they were sick of the dirty humor. They had climbed Cadillac Mountain, The Beehive, Gorham Mountain, Day Mountain, and The Triad. They had swum in Newport Cove, at a chilly fifty-five degrees, and Doug had challenged Brian to the ill-fated race out to Old Soaker.

"Well?"

Doug glanced at Jillian. "Well what?"

"I've waited the requisite thirty seconds. Now you'll tell me where we're going, right?"

"No."

She pouted, lip out. "You're no fun. I'm going to trade you in on a funner husband."

"Funner isn't a word."

"Well, it should be. My other husband is funner than you."

"My other wife is more fun than you are," he replied, not thinking.

"Psh!"

"Yeah."

"We should do that."

He frowned. "Do what?"

"Take a second wife. She could clean the house and cook and do laundry. I'd like having a wife."

He regarded the yawning pit that she had just opened at his feet. *What the hell?*

Jillian poked him. "What do you think? She could even take care of your needs when I have a headache or the baby has been too clingy and I don't want you touching me."

Guilty thoughts whelmed him and he swallowed hard. "That's not even funny."

Her laugh was strangled. "Nice, political answer. Yes, it was funny. You would have laughed at that before, because you'd have recognized it as absurdism. Now you take it more seriously than it deserves, and that makes me wonder why. Makes me worry."

"Well stop. Stop trying to trick me with questions, and stop worrying about me. I've told you all along: I love you and no one else."

She looked away, gazing out the window.

"But you'd bed her again, if you had the chance. Wouldn't you?"

He gaped at her. "I never bedded her in the first place! We kissed. That was it."

"But you would?"

"No!"

He drove on in silence, angry that she was trying to trap him with her words.

"I'm sorry," she said, after a while. "That wasn't very kind of me. Not sure what prompted it."

"I'd really like to stop talking about her."

"Yeah, me too."

"Then let's!"

She rubbed her face. "Meh. It's like a scab. I can't quit picking."

"Picking leaves scars."

"Hmm. Good point."

"Thank you."

"My pleasure."

After a few miles of silence, he pasted on a smile. "I love you."

"I love you more."

"I love you morer."

Her features scrunched up. "Morer's not a word!"

"It's as much a word as funner."

"Psh! I love you most."

"I love you mostest."

"Oh, for heaven's sake."

They parked at Sand Beach and hiked out on Otter Point, enjoying the view from the cliff-side trail. "That right there is Great Head—"

"That's what he said…"

He fixed her with a sidelong glance. "That's teenaged boy humor. Who are you, and what have you done with my wife?"

"Oh, haha. Like you wouldn't have said it."

"I have…but I'm a teenage boy underneath this hunky exterior."

She rolled her eyes. "I'm gonna regret saying that to you, I can tell."

"Nah. Just keep putting my hunky exterior to good use."

"Whatever." She started off down the trail.

"Wait! I didn't finish telling you my story."

She sighed facetiously and returned.

He turned and pointed over the water. "The little blob of land there—"

She stifled a snicker. His brow wrinkled. "What?"

"You said little blob…it's floating at the end of Great Head!" A fit of giggles swept over her. "It came!"

"Seriously? You're worse than a fourteen-year-old boy."

"No, no, not!" She fanned herself. "Just funny. Too funny!"

"Yeah, well. The last time I was here, I challenged Brian to a race out to Old Soaker, and—"

"Old Soaker?"

"The island."

"Oh, right."

"Yeah, so we swam out, it's only like a quarter mile, and we were swimming hard for a while." *And that was where I saw Meeka.* "But Brian had…trouble, in the water." *And that was when Meeka approached.* "And that was when…when…"

Her expression remained neutral as his pause lengthened.

"And that was when, what?" She finally prompted.

"Um…" Doug felt lost in juxtaposition.

She followed his gaze. Meeka stood on a bluff a few hundred feet distant. The ocean breeze carried the scent of jasmine. Doug was lost in a memory of Meeka, bobbing in the choppy water, speaking— singing—to him.

Coming closer.

"Swim with me, Douglas."

Treading water.

"Swim with me, Douglas."

Brian, yelling, distantly.

"Swim with me, Douglas."

The Meeka of the past and the Meeka of now were looking at him, with those same inky eyes.

"Swim with me, Douglas."

"Oh, this is too much!" Jillian's voice tore the air like a chainsaw.

Doug snapped out of his reverie and watched her thunder down the path toward Meeka. "What the hell are you doing here? Just what the hell are you doing here? Leave us alone, you little slut! Leave my husband alone! No, he doesn't want to swim with you!"

Meeka laughed.

"Leave him alone," Jillian yelled, "or I'll tear your stupid Tinkerbell hairdo off and stuff it down your throat!"

Meeka simply smiled. "Will you?"

"Yes, I will!" Jillian's emotional kettle was whistling.

"Have fun with that." Meeka stepped off the cliff edge.

Jillian stopped dead and screamed.

Doug was beyond her in seconds. He scrabbled to a stop, flopping on his belly, and peered over the edge. "Meeka!"

"What was she thinking?" Jillian's voice was tiny.

The cliff face was empty, and the ocean churned around the rocks at its base. The force of his hammering heart drowned out the roar from below.

"Do you see her?"

"No!" Doug said.

"What the hell was she thinking?"

"How should I know? Maybe she thought you were serious about tearing her hair off!"

"Well, I was, actually. But I didn't think she'd jump. I mean, that's stupid crazy!"

Doug scanned the rocky shoreline for over a minute. He saw nothing but water and boulders. He pushed himself up from the cliff edge. "She's not down there. She must have hit the ocean."

"I hope so! How far down is that? Could someone survive it?"

He turned to her. "I've no idea! I don't go jumping off things like that! I doubt it. Crap!"

"What're we gonna do?"

"Do? We're not going to do anything! We're gonna go down to the beach and eat our lunch and pretend this never happened!"

"But she might be hurt! We need to call—"

He slapped his head. "Seriously? Two minutes ago you wanted to kill her. Now you're worried she might be hurt?" He lowered his voice. "Look down there...it's nothing but jagged rocks and pounding waves. She's..." His voice caught. "She's dead. And we are not getting tied up in a police investigation!" He ran his fingers through his hair. "Okay...nothing happened. Nothing happened."

"But—"

He grabbed her arms and shook her. "Jillian! Listen to me! Nothing happened up here. You got that? Nothing!"

"But..."

"Come on."

He strode back down the trail, pulling her along. After a few seconds she shook his hand off her arm. "Okay...okay! I got it. You're gonna leave a bruise."

They walked in silence for several minutes. "Why do you think she did that?"

"Stop talking about it!" Doug yelled. An imagined scene was playing in his mind like a video on repeat: Meeka's body, smashed on an ocean boulder, and then torn away by a surging wave. *I'll never see her again!* He thought of the carefully folded bill that bore her phone number, tucked away in his wallet. The number for the phone that now tumbled in the salty foam, its electronics ruined—never to receive his calls, his questions never to have answers.

"But it makes no sense! I'm not that sc—"

He spun and she bounced off of him. "Jillian! I don't want to go to jail...do you? Several people saw you getting pissed off at her two nights in a row, and if you keep talking about her jumping, and she comes up dead, how much freight do you think your story is going to truck? Everyone—*everyone*—is going to assume that you pushed her, or I did, and there's not a damn bit of evidence to the contrary!"

His eyes were wild, and spit flew from his lips. She flinched and recoiled from him.

"Do you understand?" His nostrils flared. "Do you understand?"

She nodded.

"Good! Then shut up!"

As he stumbled along the trail, he could hear Jillian crying. He imagined her makeup running, providing an easy target for the gawking curious; something for them to remember in court six months from now. He stopped himself from yelling at her again, not wanting to make matters worse. He could not understand how she, who was normally so smart, could be so stupid in times of crisis.

Emotions.

Women suffered from feelings that Doug never understood. He was never one to have intense emotions, and he certainly never wanted to analyze the ones he did experience. Jillian's reliance on emotional validation and her scrutiny of every last little thing she felt were sources of stress for him that he had nevertheless learned not to criticize because the ensuing crap storm was never worth it. Better to grin and bear it.

He unzipped his pack and handed her a bandana without looking.

"Thank you." Her voice sounded as flat and icy as a pond in January.

They passed a few other hikers without incident, and reached the safety of their car. Doug had parked in a shady spot, but he still rolled the windows down to let in a breeze. They sat, not speaking, for several minutes.

Jillian sniffed then looked toward, but not quite at, him. "So... what now?"

He inhaled deeply. "Now we eat lunch, because that's what people normally do after a hike."

"What?" Her voice broke. "There's a dead woman out there—"

He slammed his palm against the steering wheel and ran the windows up. "Jillian!"

"No! I can't not talk about this, Doug! I can't turn my emotions on and off like you. We just watched her commit suicide, and you want to eat? What is the matter with you?" She buried her face in her hands. "How can you do that?"

He growled. "What part of going to jail did you not—"

"I got that! I don't want to go to freaking jail, but I don't want to act like nothing happened either! Lie to the police, but don't lie to me! And don't ever tell me to shut up again."

He pursed his lips and blew, feeling guilty for yelling at her. "I'm sorry, I just got freaked out by all that—that mess."

"Me too. I've never seen a suicide before."

"Well, please forget you saw it, okay?"

"Geez, Doug! Yes, I got it!"

"And yet you keep talking about it! Please, please, please, stop talking about it! I love you, Jillian! I don't want anyone suspecting us of anything, so let's go down to the beach and eat our lunch, okay?"

"Whatever...I still think you're wrong." She exited the car and retrieved the cooler from the back. They passed happy couples and frolicking children as they slogged down to the beach. The sun was out, but they each pulled a little gray cloud behind them. With a minimum of thought, they found a spot of sand and spread a blanket.

They sat in the sunlight, not touching. While Jillian was a mass of emotions, Doug felt hollow. "I'm hot. You wanna go swimming?"

"You can't be serious? She's out there—"

"Shhh!"

She glared at him. "I didn't bring a suit."

"Fine. I'm gonna go swim."

"Neither did you."

"So? I'll swim in my boxers."

"Doug!" She rolled close to him, propped herself on her arm, and whispered. "What do you think you're doing? Isn't this where Brian drowned? And now Meeka? That's freaking creepy!"

Her words only galvanized his resolve. "So?"

"So? So, I don't want you going out there. It's too dangerous."

"That's not dangerous. It's a cove!"

"What about Brian?"

He turned away from her and shucked off his polo shirt. "Don't do that to me, Jillian."

"What? Do what?"

"Question my manhood."

She rolled her eyes and flopped back on the blanket. "Oh, for crying out loud. I am not questioning your manhood. I just don't want you going out there."

He considered the slippery slope of giving in. "I'll be back." He removed his shorts and trotted out to the surf line. The water was cooler than he normally liked, but he would adapt quickly enough. He waded to a mid-thigh depth before diving in. The water felt like landing on an iceberg. He broke the surface and exhaled sharply. Muscling through it, he thrust his arms into the greenish wet before him. His memory of the cove was nowhere near this cold, but the rhythm of swimming numbed his mind. He focused on his stroke, his kicking, and his breathing. He had swum competitively in high school and college, and still hit the pool several times a week, so he was fit. Old Soaker would be his this time. *Is that why I'm really out here? Or am I searching for Brian's ghost?*

10

Jillian watched him run down the beach, angry that he had blown off her concerns, but not terribly surprised. He was bull-headed. She was used to it. Despite her simmering anger, she could not help but admire the breadth of his shoulders and the taper of his back. Even at thirty, Doug had no love handles. And, even after ten years of knowing him and seven years of marriage, she still found him absurdly sexy. She loved him, and not the comfortable love that their married friends had settled into, but the stupidly intense love of their courtship.

She hated to be away from him and he often made her crazy.

She watched his muscular legs as he waded into the surf, picturing the way they had looked a decade ago when she had first seen him, playing intramural football. Little had changed. He plunged into low waves and surfaced a few seconds later. His arms rose and fell as he swam away.

She lay back on the blanket, watching clouds scuttle overhead, thinking about what Ruth had said that morning. Jillian put her hands on her belly. *Please meet*, she thought a prayer to the tiny cells within her, *and make a miracle for me...for us.*

A transient thought sparked in her mind, making her wonder if a baby would change the way she felt about Doug. *Will we become comfortably in love like our friends?* The thought distressed her. She did not like the cavalier way that some of her besties talked about their husbands—how if their men wanted sex, they should go find a girlfriend. Jillian had never had a needy baby clinging to her for hours on end, so she could not appreciate exactly what her friends were talking about when they claimed aversion to being touched by their husbands. However, to even joke about sending Doug into the arms of another woman was unthinkable. *Before Meeka, that is.*

She had said those things to him a few hours ago because she had never seen him respond to a woman like he had responded to Meeka. She was feeling out this new experience, and it felt like probing a wound. The sense of peace that she had gotten from Ruth's gift sputtered out like a candle in a windstorm as she recalled that her first meeting with Doug had not even remotely affected him like Meeka had. Jillian remembered the day that she was sure that he loved her, but it had occurred months after they had met.

Meeka had him at a glance. Bitch.

Jillian felt the sympathy of the last hour fall away like an ill-fitting coat. *You deserve to be dead for trying to take my husband.* She let the full bitterness of the situation wash over her. *For being more attractive to him than I am.*

Hate curdled in her gut, cold and hard. *I'm glad you're dead.*

The chop increased as Doug pushed farther out into open water. He thought of Meeka's face on that day twelve years ago, and it superimposed with her face from earlier today. *Identical beauty.* It struck him that he was out here chasing a ghost, but not Brian's. Despite the trouble that Meeka had caused them over the past few days, he still found her amazingly attractive and interesting, and he could not believe that he would never see her again. She can't be dead. Her voice drifted in his memory: 'Swim with me.'

He stopped swimming and wiped water from his face—impossible to tell where the sea ended and tears began. "Don't be dead, Meeka."

"Why would I be?" A voice seemed to float over the water.

He spun. "Meeka?" *Did I imagine that?*

Only the slap of the waves on his chest and the cries of seagulls reached his ears. Around him, the ocean was empty. He was out in the open channel now, beyond Great Neck, and only a couple of dozen yards from Old Soaker. It was conceivable that someone on shore had spoken and he had heard it, but the nearest shoreline was a blank stretch of rock and trees. He had the impression that the voice had been Meeka's.

"Where are you?"

He heard laughter behind him, and spun again to survey the small splat of rock that comprised the island. "Meeka?" The smell of jasmine teased his nose. He pitched forward, and started swimming again. Visions of her surviving the fall and washing up on Old Soaker filled his mind. He felt his excitement and anticipation swell.

Something cold brushed his thigh.

He flinched and mistimed his breath, getting a mouthful of seawater. He came up coughing and treading water as he tried to clear his lungs. Each time he hacked, he slipped down in the water and got slapped in the face with a wave. Kicking up, he forced in a deep breath and coughed hard. *This is where Brian drowned,* he thought. An irrational fear that Brian was coming to settle things made his heart race. He had a wild vision of Brian's dead hand rising out of the drain to deposit his class ring in the tub—a lure that Doug would find impossible to resist. *Why didn't I listen to Jillian?*

Something touched his belly.

He struck out with his hands, but felt nothing. He kicked with vigor, launching himself at the island. Thoughts of sharks and squid raced in his mind, accompanied by memories of Brian struggling with whatever had gotten ahold of him that day. Now, corpses swam with the sharks in his imagination. *Great! What the hell was I thinking, swimming out here?*

Something brushed him again, and his brain was throttled with fear. He pictured cold, dead hands touching him, and he swam as one possessed. Something cold and ropy tangled around his torso and legs, and yanked him beneath the surface. Lashing out with his hands and feet, he finally connected with a lumpy, rubbery-feeling thing. He struggled to not inhale, as the slimy ropes tightened around his legs.

No, crap, crap, crap!

Opening his eyes, he could see a dark mass below him, clamped around his legs and hips. Striking it seemed to do nothing. He looked up in desperation, and vaguely understood that he was at least twenty feet down and sinking rapidly.

His lungs and ears were on fire, and his brain was melting with fear. *I don't want to die! Not like this!* Darkness bordered his vision, and hazy herringmen swam out of the depths, surrounding him. He thought he heard singing. Was that Meeka who swam up in the dim light? Her dark hair a tiny nimbus about her head. She smiled as she leaned in to kiss him, and her hands went to his belly and slid down. He felt her hands caressing him as her smiling face filled his sight, and then darkness took it.

Light. Warmth. Air.

He snapped his eyes open and gulped a breath. Something touched him, making him yell and slide back beneath the water. He scissor kicked, hit something, and popped back up, casting around madly in case the squid attacked him again.

Nothing came.

Within seconds, he pitched over on his back, completely spent, and did nothing for several minutes but float in the water, coughing periodically, and fuzzing in and out of consciousness. He felt as if he had run a marathon and been in a couple of fistfights. The squid did not return. With immense weariness, he opened his eyes to a blue sky that gazed down on his calm sea. He was close to Sand Beach, being carried in by the tide. A wave of gratitude swept through him—he was alive and close to the shore.

He rode the surf in until he felt the sandy bottom on his hanging toes. He rolled, pushed out with his legs, and stood unsteadily. The little waves bumped into him and threatened to knock him over. The sun was low, and the beach was nearly empty, but he could see Jillian lying on their blanket. She seemed to be sleeping.

He heard a gasp, and looked over at a couple wading in the water. Anger frothed on their faces. "This is a family beach! Put some clothes on!" The man's gray hair seemed to bristle from his scalp as he pulled his wife away. Doug looked down at himself and realized that his boxer shorts were gone. He dropped into the water.

"Jillian!" His voice came out as a scratchy croak. "Jill!" He looked at the retreating couple. "Can you help me get my wife? I almost drowned. I lost my shorts."

The man stopped and returned without his wife. "Really?" He wore skepticism like a brand. "Um, I guess. Where is she?"

Doug waved vaguely toward Jillian, before sitting on the sandy bottom and allowing his eyes to slip closed. He felt fatigue rise, as if his body were drawing it from the seawater. The man spoke to his wife, and Doug sensed that he came closer.

"Are you okay, buddy? Sorry for yelling at you. I had no idea you'd had trouble out there." He laughed with an edge of nervousness. "You got cuts all over you. Did you get tangled in a net or something?"

"I—I don't know. Something."

"Doug!"

He looked up in time to see Jillian hurtle through the shallow water and dive to her knees to embrace him. "Are you all right? She said you'd nearly drowned! Are you okay?" She pulled back and ran her fingers through his dripping hair. "Doug?"

"Yeah, I won." He managed a weak smile. "I'll be fine."

"I think he got caught in a loose fishing net," the man said. "He's got abrasions on his legs. Oh, hey, here, let's get you covered up."

Doug opened his eyes to find the man taking the beach blanket from his wife. "Let's get you out of the water. Can you stand?"

Jillian and the man helped him to stand up and wrapped the blanket around him. They walked out of the surf together. The dry sand between his toes felt like a blessing.

"Do you live nearby?" the wife asked. "You should go to the hospital and get checked out."

The woman's concern was touching, but Doug really just wanted the couple to go away now. "No." Doug's voice rasped. "I'll be fine. Thank you."

She took a half step closer. "Are you sure?"

"Yeah, I just need to sit for a few and rest."

The couple escorted Doug and Jillian back to their spot on the beach. Doug's clothes lay strewn on the sand from where they had fallen off the hastily retrieved blanket. He gestured to his shorts, and Jillian helped him pull them on while the man made a screen with the blanket. Afterwards, Jillian spread it back on the sand.

"Thank you," Doug said to the couple and sank down onto his back.

The couple hovered. "Do you need any help with anything?"

"No, thanks." Doug wanted only to lie there and sleep.

Jillian shook their hands. "Thank you so much!"

"It was nothing," the man said. "Sorry again about getting mad at you. You didn't tangle with that net willingly, I bet." He laughed. "You folks have a better evening!"

Doug let air flow in and out of his lungs as he listened to the couple's receding voices.

"What happened?" Jillian asked.

"I thought I got attacked by a squid, but maybe it was a net. I don't know." He rolled onto his side, as thoughts of Meeka flowed through his memory. She had been naked as she kissed him—as she touched him. *Best not mention the hallucinatory elements of my near drowning*, he decided. *That couldn't have been real.*

"It scared the life out of me when she came up yelling about you drowning. Are you sure you're okay?"

Meeka? Oh...the woman. "Yeah. I just need to rest."

"Shouldn't we go back to the hotel, then? I can drive."

"Yeah. Just give me a minute." His eyes slipped closed.

Jillian watched his face for a few seconds, before directing her attention to his torso and legs. His skin there bore a multitude of scratches and crescent-shaped welts. She was curious about what the rest of him looked like, but she was not going to be taking his shorts off here on the beach.

She redirected her curiosity to her phone.

"Doug...Doug, sweets?"

"Hmm?" His eyes snapped open, wild for an instant.

"Come on. I let you sleep for an hour." Jillian took her hand from his shoulder and looked around. "Everyone's left, and I'm hungry."

"An hour?" He rolled onto his back and rubbed his face, dislodging the salt that had dried in a rime on his skin and eyebrows. "Wow. I feel like crap."

"Should I take you to the hospital?"

"No, it's not that bad."

"May we go, please? This place is starting to creep me out."

He sat up and groaned. The walk from the beach was slow and silent, and they packed the car with a minimum of conversation. He headed for the driver's side of the car, but stopped when he felt her hand on his arm. "Are you okay to drive?"

"Sure, I'm fine."

"Okay...I was looking at a map while you slept and found a restaurant in Otter Creek. It's closer than Bar Harbor. Let's eat there."

"Hmm, no. I only want to drive once."

"I'll drive back."

He remained silent for a while, contemplating the nearness of death. Salt prickled his skin. "I really want a shower before I eat."

She frowned. "Okay, but let's eat somewhere else tonight."

"That's fine." He thought of the Pequot's dinner menu. "Not sure I want seafood anyway."

They drove up Schooner Head Road in silence, lost in their thoughts. When they passed a sign for The Smithson Laboratory, Doug glared at the brick and glass-walled buildings, trying to exclude thoughts of Caul. They finally returned to Bar Harbor, and the hotel was a welcome sight—a white beacon on its short hill. Doug went straight to the shower, allowing the warm water to sluice away the salt and pain. The shock of his misadventure swirled at his feet, before being lost to the drain. Once the heat had soaked into his muscles, he liberally applied soap and winced as it got into his cuts. He inspected his abdomen and each leg in turn. His skin was an idiot's map of scratches, small cuts, abrasions, and quarter-moon shaped bruises. Even his genitals were bruised, a discovery that sparked a snatch of memory. *Was Meeka really there? Did she really touch me during all that?*

"Hey, you feeling human again?" Jillian asked through the steam and plastic that surrounded him.

He startled, feeling guilty at the memory. "Yeah. All these cuts sting."

"Well, get out, and I'll help you dry off. That net certainly did a number on you."

"Um, sure." He was not sure he wanted Jillian seeing all of his injuries, especially the bruising on his genitals. He could not rationalize a net causing that injury. He also could not figure out how he had gotten clear of the net, if he had actually been caught in one. He turned off the water and stepped out in front of her. She stood with a sympathetic smile and a giant, fluffy towel.

She surveyed him as he stood dripping on the mat. Her gaze was drawn to his penis, and the ugly, bluish-purple bruise that marred it for over half its length. "Oh! How'd that happen?"

His discomfort filled the room. "I don't know. I can't figure how a net would cause that. Maybe it *was* a squid."

A shadow of doubt crossed her face. She shook her head. "Maybe it thought Little Doug was a fish, and was trying to eat it."

He flinched.

"If I remember correctly, from zoology, squid have sharp beaks…"

"Thanks, Jillie! As if nearly drowning wasn't bad enough, you have to pollute my mind with that."

She stepped forward and wrapped him in the towel. "Sorry. Not trying to traumatize you." She kissed him. "I just hope it still works," she whispered as their lips parted.

He made a strangled sound. "For crying out loud, woman! Shut it!"

She giggled and touched him. "We can always find out after dinner."

They entered the dining room a few minutes later, having changed their minds about going somewhere else. Charles was bustling around, wearing a short apron. "Hello! Welcome back." He looked at his watch. "The kitchen closes in an hour, just to let you know."

The older couple from the first evening and some other people were scattered around the room. Doug and Jillian sat at a window-side table and looked at the menus. Charles came over after a minute. "My apologies! I'm having to cover for Meeka this evening."

Jillian gloated. *She deserved it.* The weight of the pendant slid across the hollow of her throat, and she felt a bit sick at her sense of satisfaction from Meeka's death.

He continued. "Anyway, what can I get you to drink?"

They ordered drinks and dinner, and Charles bustled away.

"What do you want to do tomorrow," Jillian asked, fingering the medal.

Doug grimaced. "Sleep."

"Besides that."

"I'm not going to do anything more strenuous than sleep tomorrow."

The corners of her mouth fell. "Sorry? That doesn't sound like my husband, Mister Get Up and Shake It Off."

An odd expression worked the planes and angles of his face. His mind was poring over the new reality that he had perceived. "Jillie... you understand that I almost died today?"

She stared at him. "That seems a bit dramatic. I've never known you to be like that."

"I'm not being dramatic! I was pulled underwater, probably twenty or thirty feet down, and blacked out from lack of oxygen. I should be dead." He looked up at her face. "Somehow, I was spared. We came up here to get a miracle. What happened today...I think that constitutes a miracle."

"Well, good! Then I hope we got two!"

"Of course you'll get your miracle, but..." He shook his head. "What happened today...it was—"

"Here you go, Mister and Missus Sandow," Charles said, bringing their drinks. "We'll have your food out in a few minutes."

"Thanks." Doug rubbed the condensation on the glass as he watched Charles leave. "Anyway, I've never been that close to death before. It—it feels important. Huge! But, I'm still too close to the experience. I can't get my mind around it. I can't get perspective."

She smiled at him and took his hand. "Then don't try."

"You don't understand."

"No, I don't. I can't. But that's not important. You're alive, that's what's important. I'd die without you, but you're alive, so let's not dwell on the negatives. You had a profound experience today, I understand that, but don't go somewhere I can't, okay?"

He exhaled in frustration. "Whatever."

"Please don't be like that." She squeezed his fingers. "I love you."

The pad of his thumb rubbed her knuckles. "I love you, too. I'm sorry...I just don't want you to dismiss my experience."

"I'm not. I don't understand it, but I'm not dismissing your feelings."

He nodded. *Enough of that, I guess.* "Okay. What do you want to do tomorrow? No hiking!"

"I was...well, tomorrow's Sunday. I was kind of hoping we could find a church..."

Doug flinched. "We're already married. I've got the ring to prove it."

"Doug, please be serious. I want to go to church tomorrow."

"We don't have the clothes for it."

"I don't think that's going to be a problem." She had that look on her face that Doug found hard to resist.

"Um, okay. I said I wanted to sleep anyway."

"You're so bad." She smiled. "Thank you."

He smiled in return and froze. In his glass of water, he saw a refracted image—a miniature, pixie-haired woman. He looked up. Meeka stood by the bar tying on an apron. Her voice floated to them. "I'm so sorry, Susan! On top of working late, my car got a flat tire. Bad things always happen in threes! I'm afraid to think of what'll happen next. Listen, I'll stay late and make it up to you."

Susan said something to Meeka, and the girl laughed. "Thank you! You're a sweetheart!"

Doug glanced back at Jillian. Her face was a mask. "Please tell me that that woman is dead," she whispered.

He shook his head, as his heart hammered blood into his neck and groin.

"She couldn't have survived. It's not possible!"

"Possible." Doug felt a thrill, followed quickly by horror. *What if she's not alive?* He thought back to how cold her lips had been, all those years ago. *She's cold, she doesn't age, she can't be killed, she can fly, or manipulate time, or cloud minds, or something...crap! She's a vampire!*

Meeka was threading her way across the dining room toward them. "Hey, guys! Sorry I'm late. How was your swim?"

"Who do you think you are?" Jillian asked between gritted teeth.

Meeka's eyebrows drew together. "I'm sorry...what?"

"Jillian!" Doug whispered.

She ignored him. "What was that stunt on the trail today? Huh?"

"Stunt?"

"Don't play stupid with me. Leave my husband alone, you little whore!"

Meeka recoiled, as if Jillian had slapped her. "I'm...I'm sorry? Did I say something wrong?"

Jillian stood up—the top of her head barely reaching Meeka's chin. "I told you, don't play stupid with me! All that crap about sweets the other night and 'Swim with me, Douglas' today!" She pushed her finger into Meeka's chest. "Leave my husband alone!"

"Is there a problem?" Charles appeared beside his waitress.

"Um, I'm not sure," Meeka said, as tears fell from her eyelashes. "I don't think I should take care of her anymore. I'm sorry." She turned away and fled across the dining room.

There was a moment of held breaths as everyone watched her go. "I apologize for whatever happened," Charles said. "I'll take care of you tonight, okay?"

"She's been flirting with my husband! And she was following us this afternoon—"

"We don't know that for a fact, Jillie," Doug said and kicked her foot. He turned to Charles. "We saw someone who looked like Meeka, today, in Acadia. My wife got a little upset."

Charles struggled not to frown. "With all respect, that couldn't have been Meeka. She works the day job I told you about, in Blue Hill. That's an hour west of here. And, they kept her late today. I don't know what happened to you, but I don't think Meeka could have been in Acadia today."

"Then how could she have even known that Doug was swimming today?"

Charles lost his battle, and the corners of his mouth turned down.

"Oh...I don't know" he said. "I may have mentioned that you looked like you went to the beach? I don't know, but I hope we can put this behind us. Let me buy your dinner tonight, all right?"

"No," Doug said in protest, "you don't need to do that."

"To make amends," Charles said, "dinner is on the house."

"Really, that's not necessary."

"I insist. I want to make sure that you have a wonderful stay at the Pequot."

Doug raised his hands in surrender. "Do what you think is best."

"Very good," Charles said. "I'll go check on your meal."

Jillian watched him walk away, and caught sight of Meeka bringing out an order to another couple. She had on a brave face as she spoke to the other people. The husband said something to Meeka and looked pointedly at Jillian. The wife and Meeka both glanced over, but Meeka quickly turned away and spoke again to the couple. The woman patted Meeka's hand.

Jillian turned away, disgust etched on her face. "What is going on? That little tramp is trying to get into our bed and suddenly I'm the ogre for protecting my marriage? That's absurd! I was feeling so peaceful until she showed up."

"Jillie, you don't know that what she's trying to do, really. I mean, it may all be a misundersta—"

"Doug Sandow! You were on that trail—"

He shushed her.

"What? She's obviously not dead! Why does it matter if we were there or not?"

He thought about her question. "Principle," he said at length. He wanted to tell her about his deduction, about Meeka being a vampire, but he felt stupid saying the word out loud.

"What? What are you talking about?"

"Shhh! We still don't know what happened today...on the trail." Or in the ocean. "Until we do, we shouldn't be too talkative."

"Doug!"

He hushed her again. "Charles is coming."

She rolled her eyes. "Thanks for the head's up, Nancy Drew." She turned to Charles. "May I get mine to go please?"

He hesitated only a second. "Do you mean to leave the hotel?"

"No, just to go to my room."

Doug felt a trickle of anger. "Jillian..."

"Not a problem, Missus Sandow," Charles said. "I'll take it up for you, if you'd like."

"Jillian, what are you doing?"

"I'm getting a headache, and I want to eat in peace." She stood and walked out of the dining room. Charles looked at Doug and raised an eyebrow.

"Go," Doug said. "Thank you. I'm sorry. I don't know what's gotten into her."

Charles inclined his head and followed Jillian. Across the room, the man who had spoken to Meeka gave Doug a golf clap. Doug briefly considered introducing his fist to the man's face, but thought better of it. He glanced down at the steak he had ordered and pushed it away. His mind wandered.

"Is it okay?"

He smelled roses and looked up into inky pools. *How can a woman be so beautiful?* He smiled ruefully. *You're freaking me out and I still can't not like you.* "It will be once I get my appetite back."

"Sorry." She cast her gaze away, but only for a moment. "I can heat it up for you, if you'd like."

"Meeka, what happened out on Otter Point today?"

Her brow wrinkled. "Um, I was working all day today."

"Come on...you can tell Charles that, but I saw you. I heard you. You spoke to me!"

The air stilled.

"Um." She laughed, high and forced. "What'd I say?"

He squinted at her, at her little scar, feeling light-headed. "And how could you be the same waitress who served me lobster twelve years ago?"

"I said that?"

"No! That was a separate question."

"Okay, easiest first: why couldn't I be the same alewife?"

"You don't look a day older!"

"I age gracefully?"

"No one ages that gracefully."

She shrugged and gestured to herself. "I don't know what else to say."

He shook his head. "How old are you?"

"That's not a polite question to ask a woman."

"Please."

She looked around before settling into Jillian's vacated seat. She smelled like warm skin in sunshine. It was intoxicating.

"I'm thirty."

He gaped at her. "Shut up! You're not a day over eighteen."

"Listen, Mister Sandow—"

"Doug, I'm Doug. Remember?"

"—I...Douglas. I don't mean to seem rude, but I am telling you the truth. I was eighteen when you first met me, so I must be thirty now, right? That's only logical. You're just going to have to believe me."

Believe me. Turning her words over in his mind, he rested his arms on the table and leaned closer.

"What happened at Otter Point today?"

She mirrored his gesture until their foreheads nearly touched. "I don't know yet," she whispered.

"Yet?" The ocean filled his ears. "What's going on? How could you be in two places yesterday? Why are you everywhere we go to eat? Are you stalking us...me?" His eyes narrowed. "Are you a ghost?"

Meeka made a wounded noise.

"Or are you a vampire?"

Her eyes bulged. "What? Are you for real?"

"And where did you get this from?" Pulling Brian's ring from his pocket, he held it up to her face. For a split second, she froze, her eyes growing even larger, and then she recoiled. "How?"

"That's my question—"

"No, how did you get that?" Her gaze snapped from the ring to his face several times. "No. Oh, no, no, no!"

She pushed away from the table, her face a mask of shock. Doug smelled vinegar. "Meeka?"

"I—I've got to go talk to Mother." She fled.

11

Meeka did not return, leaving Doug to suffer through the visual recrimination of golf-clap man and his uptight wife. Charles approached the table after a few minutes to apologize about Meeka's sudden departure. "Something to do with her mom..."

When Doug had finished eating, he bid Charles goodnight and climbed the creaky stairs. He frowned when he found Jillian and Caul occupying adjacent upholstered chairs in the sitting room. Their conversation was animated, but quiet. The remains of Jillian's dinner rested on a small table in front of her.

"Hi," he said. "What's going on? Are you staying here, Caul?"

The man looked up and cast an unattractive smile at Doug. "I often take my meals here."

"Oh?" Doug looked around for dishes.

"I'm not eating now," Caul said. "I'm telling stories to your lovely wife."

Doug felt his anger rising at this lecherous, old-young looking man. "What kind of stories are you telling to *my* lovely wife?"

"Sit down, and we'll tell you," Jillian said, gesturing to a chair next to hers. "When you were asleep on the beach, I looked up information on sirens. They—"

"Sirens? Like ambulance sirens?"

Caul's face got uglier. "No, Mister Sandow, like the creatures that sang to sailors, and lured them to their deaths. Sound familiar?"

Doug laughed in derision. "You've been smoking too many blunts, Mister Caul."

"Saunders."

"Excuse me?"

"Caul Saunders. And, no, Mister Sandow, I don't smoke."

Doug laughed even louder. "What do you do, Mister Saunders? Tend mushroom gardens?"

"Doug!" Jillian said, chiding him. "Caul is a scientist at Smithson Labs, but he's also a folklorist, and he studies the history of New England, particularly Maine."

What about him being Meeka's accomplice? "Yeah, I knew that, about Smithson. That other stuff's important why?"

Caul dropped his voice. "Because, I think Meeka is a selkie or a havsrå."

"A what?"

Jillian practically bounced in her seat. "A seal woman, out of Scottish folklore. That's a selkie. The havsrå—" she stumbled over the pronunciation "—is a water spirit from Scandinavia."

"What?" Doug squinted at them. Their conversation sounded as if it was occurring at the other end of a pipe—their voices distorted and making little sense.

"A woman who is also a seal," Caul said.

"Yeah...like a wereseal?" Doug laughed. The sound was bright and overloud in his ears. "That's the stupidest thing I've heard all day." *Stupider than ghosts and vampires?*

"It's not stupid," Jillian said.

Doug was determined to have a go at Caul. "So...what? At the full moon, she turns into a seal?" He pulled his arms to his chest, clapped his hands together like flippers, and tilted his head back. "Arr, arr, arr!" He made fun of seals. "I'm a good boy, gimme a fish!"

Caul regarded him with an expression of disgust. "Very nice, Mister Sandow. You'd make an excellent selkie. It doesn't work like that, though. It's not tied to the moon."

"Great. Thanks for clearing that up. Hey, we saw a selkie the other day, didn't we, Jillie?" He looked meaningfully at her.

"Oh! That's right! Off of Great Wass! Do you have the picture?"

She showed the photo to Caul, who studied it for several minutes before handing back Doug's phone.

"Interesting," Caul said. "A pinniped legacy form, perhaps. Will you send me that picture?" He handed Doug one of his business cards. "My e-mail address is on there."

Doug smirked. *What a nerd.* "Seal woman! That's stupid. And so not scary."

"Well then pray she's a selkie and not a havsrå." Caul was unamused.

"Oooh, I'm frightened! It sounds like Danish cheese."

Jillian giggled. "That's Havarti."

"A havsrå is a preternaturally beautiful, supernatural woman who lures men to the water...to have sex with them. Similar to the huldra."

"Okay..."

Caul leaned closer. "She often drowns her partners, after they have provided their services."

Doug felt a chill, thinking of his recent experience. *Man, I'm getting sick of that feeling.* "Whatever! It's just fairy tales." *Except that there's definitely something weird about Meeka.* "Anyway, I'm going to the room now. You gonna join me?"

"In a minute," Jillian said and returned her attention to Caul.

Oh, so that's how it is. He looked at his watch. It was not even ten o'clock yet.

"Scratch that. I'm going to get a drink." He turned and started back down the stairs.

"Doug. *Doug!*"

He stopped. "What?"

"Please don't leave."

A sigh escaped through his teeth. "I don't want to talk about fairies or wereseals." *Or ghosts or vampires, for that matter.* "My legs feel stiff. I may go walk them out."

"I love you."

"I love you, too," he replied, but the words felt like acid on his tongue. *If you really loved me, you'd stop talking to that freak.* He continued down to the bar. Susan, usually cheery, appraised him with some reservation. "You've returned."

"Hi, yeah. Did Meeka ever come back? I wanted to apologize for my wife's behavior."

"No, she hasn't."

"Okay. How about a scotch and soda, please?"

She made the drink and set it before him. "Seven dollars."

"Can you charge it to my room?"

"Sure," she said. "And, I hope you don't think me rude, but what're you and your wife's issues with Meeka?"

Doug smiled and looked into his glass. He swirled the amber beverage around in a circle, before taking a long draw, wincing a bit as he swallowed. "My wife seems to think that Meeka is trying to seduce me...that she's stalking me."

Susan goggled at him for several seconds before laughing.

Doug's nostrils flared. "What's so funny?"

"Is that the problem? Oh, that's good. Well, Charles and I have been the managers here for eight years, and in all that time I've seen countless men try to woo our young lady, only to be shot down, one after the next. She might go out on a date or two, but it's never anything long term. She's got one love in her life—her mother. I don't reckon she's got a lot of time for extra stuff. Not enough to work two jobs, care for her mother, and have a man." She paused. "Tell your wife that Meeka's pretty safe. She hasn't got anything to worry about with that girl."

Doug's eyes narrowed. *They can't both live in that crappy little house.* "That's good to know." He knocked back the rest of his drink. "Thanks." He got up from the bar stool. "Say, uh, any of her dates end up as bloodless corpses?" *Maybe she has them stacked up somewhere, like cord wood...*

Susan blinked. "Excuse me?"

"Sorry...bad joke. Look, I need to go for a walk, to stretch out my legs. How late is the front door unlocked?"

"Your room key will open it."

Doug nodded. "Great. Hopefully, I can avoid more squid attacks... and, um, vampires."

Susan's eyes narrowed. "I certainly hope so." She peered at him. "Have a nice walk."

She must think we're freaking nuts. He gave her a charming smile and a small salute and left. The evening was pleasantly warm—a good night for a stroll. *Caul can't be Meeka's accomplice, not if he thinks she's a seal woman and watches her bedroom window at night. What a freaking creeper! Maybe he's her Renfield.*

Doug made his way up West Street, stretching his sore muscles as much as he could tolerate. With half-formed thoughts of Meeka, he realized that he was walking toward her house. *Not a great idea.* He was turning when his pocket vibrated. The number on his phone was not one he recognized.

"Hello?"

"...Douglas! D...wat...I...water!"

"Meeka?"

"...don't..." The connection failed.

He called the number, but got a busy signal. Pulling the dinner bill from his wallet, he checked the number. It was Meeka's. *How'd she get my number?*

He replaced the phone and continued walking. Night birds called in the darkness. And something else.

He froze.

Somewhere around, he heard a keening—a banshee's song—just at the edge of audibility. The small hairs on his body leapt up. *What is that?* He spun, aware of danger. Nightmares from his childhood were awakening.

The frantic slap of running feet reached him. Limned by the gray lights of the harbor, a figure broke across West Street, headed for the bay. *Meeka?*

"Meeka!"

His pursuit was slow—his muscles, pushed beyond their limits earlier, refused to be fast now. He turned left at Bridge Street, following her trajectory. The street ended at the partially submerged gravel bar that led across the bay to the eponymously named island. In the half-light that reached the swirling water, he saw her splashing across the narrow straight that separated the island from town. He swiveled. *Nothing's chasing her. Is something calling her?* The keening was no longer audible.

Cold gripped his sandaled feet as he stepped into water barely deeper than his ankles. He realized, halfway across, as water swirled around his calves and the ambient light of Bar Harbor finally petered out, that he should have brought a flashlight. He pulled out his phone, with the thought of using the camera light, when it rang.

"Hello?"

"Come to the north side of the island. Just follow the path and take the first left. Keep walking until you reach the water."

"Meeka?" Doug asked, before he realized that he was talking to a dead line. *What's up with that? Why am I chasing her?* He turned on the light and continued toward the wooded island. Missing the left turn, he wandered around until he found it. He kept on the narrow path until he reached a gently lapped stone and sand shoreline. The battery was low and the moon bright enough, so he turned off the light.

"Meeka?"

"It's about time." Her voice reached him from the darkness. "I've waited twelve years for this night."

"What?"

She laughed, but it held no humor. "I invited you to swim with me all those years ago, but you took your beautiful boy body and slept in a soggy tent instead of in my arms. Why did you spurn me? Why did you leave me? Why do you spurn me still?"

"I'm not...huh? Where are you?"

"Here," she said, rising out of the water before him. She was dusky and naked, and he sucked in a breath, immediately responding to the sight of her. Moonlight draped her curves and cascaded along lithe limbs, and he appreciated again how beautifully built she was.

"Hey, there!" His voice wavered. Besides Jillian, he had not been with a naked woman in over ten years. Thunder filled his chest. "What're you doing?"

"Swim with me." She opened her arms to him, and he stepped into the bay without thinking. The conversation about the havsrå briefly flicked across his mind, but she smelled of jasmine and sex, and the warning fled.

"You're so beautiful."

"Thank you." Her soft voice was a cat's purr in the moonlight. "But Douglas, I don't want to hold your clothes."

He stopped walking. "Um. This is a bad idea."

"I simply want to swim. Don't you want to swim with me?"

"I kinda don't, really. I had a bad time with that earlier."

She came to him, her steps gliding through the water with barely a ripple. "I'll keep you safe...if you're afraid."

He flinched at her words. *What's the matter with me? I'm acting like a total Nancy boy.* He stepped back onto the bank and shucked off his clothes, except his underwear, and hung them from a branch so he could easily find them later. A small splash marked his reentry to the water.

"Let's swim."

She reached for him with long, slender fingers that went around the back of his neck and into his hair, while her other hand sought the flap on his boxers. She drew his face down to hers, and their lips touched just as her hand found him. He gasped from the boldness of her behavior and the coolness of her fingers. She seized the opportunity to draw his lower lip into her mouth and suck on it.

He broke the kiss. "I'm sorry, we can't do this."

Her hand massaged him, withdrawing the pole from its tent. He felt himself responding. *Can't...*

She glanced down. "I was too hard on you earlier," she whispered. "I bruised you."

Again, an icy finger traced his spine. "I wasn't hallucinating? You were there? At Newport Cove?"

"In a manner of speaking."

"I was drowning..."

Their gazes locked. There was something different about her, something he could not figure out—something older and wilder than had been there only an hour ago when last they had spoken. He encircled both of her wrists in his hands and pulled, but she refused to surrender her hold on him.

"Meeka. We can't. I'm married."

She laughed.

"Doug?"

The word, distantly spoken as it was, still pierced the night—an alarm that made him jump like he had been hit with an electric prod. *What's Jillian doing out here?* He twitched away from Meeka, but she pulled insistently.

"Come away with me," she said in her purring voice. "Please, make love to me. I need you. I've wanted only you. I have forsaken all others, waiting for you to return. Please, Douglas, I need you inside me!"

"What? No! I can't! My wife is coming!"

"Leave her! She's ugly...rude and pale and sterile!" Meeka pressed in close to him, her cool belly trapping his turgor between them. "We will make exquisite love and beautiful children. I will make you cry out long into the night. Every night! But, you must swim with me, Douglas Sandow. Now...please!" She kissed him again, pressing her breasts against his skin.

"Doug?" Jillian's voice was closer.

Meeka pulled at him, but he would not move. His brain was throttled by the situation. He was not able to process what she was suggesting: to run away with her and completely abandon his wife of seven years. *For a vampire...*

"Please, Douglas!"

He smelled jasmine again and a trace of honeysuckle.

"No. I'm sorry. I can't just abandon my wife." He shook his head.

He smelled chocolate and cinnamon and hot iron.

"Oh?" She brought her face inches from his, her dark eyes flashing. "Why not let Caul have her?"

"Caul?" Doug was incensed by the thought of Caul touching Jillian. *He's trying to—*

"Doug? Please answer!"

"Mister Sandow? Are you out here?"

Doug stiffened in anger. *Caul? What the hell?* He turned his face toward shore, and Meeka pulled away from him. Within seconds, she was gone. He looked back to her, but the water barely rippled from her passing.

Damn!

He returned to the bank and pulled on his clothes. "What do you want?" He saw twin lights bobbing in the dark forest. "What the hell do you want? You're disturbing my walk!" He stomped, as best his sore muscles would allow, out to the main path and intercepted the two.

"Don't you mean your swim?" Caul said.

"No. I am taking a walk...see?" He gestured to his dry clothes. "To relax! And now, I am not relaxed!" His penis chaffed against the tightness of his cargo shorts. "Why are you here?"

Jillian regarded him in the wash of the flashlights, her eyes lingering on his wet legs and the bulge in his shorts. "Why are you so angry, honey? Did we interrupt something?"

He exhaled, letting go of his anger. "No. I'm sorry. I just wanted some time to think. Uninterrupted."

"We were worried about you, after what happened today, especially."

Doug noted her use of the plural pronoun. "We? Are you suddenly interested in my welfare too, Caul?"

"Yes, I am, although mostly for your wife's sake...at this point."

The barely suppressed anger roared back into Doug's mind. "What the hell is that supposed to mean?" He menaced the shorter, slighter man. "You taking a liking to my wife?"

Jillian sighed. "Doug!"

"I'll beat your ass into next week!" Doug leaned closer.

Caul's eyes widened and he stepped backwards, stumbling. "It's nothing like that! No, I don't like your wife. I mean, not like that. Get some perspective."

"Doug!" Jillian said. "Stop it! You're being a jerk, again."

He rounded on her. "Don't tell me what to do, woman!"

A strained silence settled among them as the trees creaked in the night. "Really, Doug...really?" Jillian asked at last. "You need to figure out where your priorities are." She turned and walked away.

"So do you! You're never gonna get pregnant acting like that!"

"And you're never going to prove you're a man acting like that!"

They watched her retreating back, before Caul took a few backwards steps, turned, and trotted after her. Doug stood in the dark forest, blowing out like a horse. He stood at a juncture in his life, physically and metaphorically. He had never had the thought to cheat on Jillian during the last ten years, because he had never met any woman who stirred his pot any more than she did—until this week. *Technically,* he reminded himself, *we met a dozen years ago.*

The simple point was that Meeka wanted him. She wanted him more intensely than any woman ever had, even Jillian, who had taken months to warm to the idea of dating him. It had taken years before they had married and fully consummated their relationship. He had waited, because it had been important to Jillian to wait. But here was Meeka—beautiful, mysterious, sexy, dangerous, intoxicating Meeka—begging him to have sex, begging him to run away and start a life with her. The combination was a powerful aphrodisiac that had Doug's mind staggering.

And if she's a vampire?

He shook away the thought and imagined what life would have been like had he not gotten drunk on the beach, if he had not taken that fateful swim the next day, but rather, if he had let Brian finish out the road trip alone, while he stayed in Bar Harbor for the summer to court Meeka.

Why didn't I?

He could have convinced her to return with him to Connecticut, or he might have stayed in Maine and gone to university in Orono or Augusta—both were close by. They could have gotten a small apartment overlooking the harbor, and spent Saturday mornings snuggled in bed. Later, she would have been pregnant and born him tall sons and inky-eyed daughters.

He yelled, inarticulately, into the darkness.

Life with Jillian had been fun, but life with Meeka would have been sublime. *Life with Meeka could still be sublime...*

In the tree-filtered moonlight, he evaluated both paths.

12

Jillian was shedding hot, angry tears when she reached the end of the woods and confronted the rising tide over the gravel bar. Caul had been following at a discreet distance, but he joined her now. They both stared in mute apprehension at the flooded passage back to town.

"I'm sorry, about what happened back there," Caul said.

She sniffed and swiped at the wetness on her cheeks. "Don't be. That's just Doug. He's stubborn, and frustrating! If he wants Meeka, then to hell with him! To hell with both of them." She felt a stab of regret at her words, but her anger flattened it.

After Doug had left the hotel, Meeka had called Caul's phone. He reported that she had said something about water, Doug, Bar Island, and love, before her terrible signal had been lost. Caul had prompted Jillian to go in search of Doug.

And when we came looking for you, we found you exactly where Meeka said we would, acting nervous and angry and guilty...and sporting an erection. She wounded the soil with her heel.

"Can we make it back across?"

Caul cleared his throat. "It's a couple feet at the deepest by now, but the tide is still coming in. If we wait any longer, we'll be camping on the island."

What about Doug? She looked over her shoulder, feeling creeping fingers of guilt. *He's made his choice.* She nodded, scattering the guilt like carrion birds from a carcass. "Let's go."

The chilly water flowed across their feet as they waded out, and it quickly reached Jillian's knees. "You'll need to empty your pockets," Caul said. "We're reaching the low spot. The water's going to be up to your thighs in a few seconds."

"How does the water rise so fast? It wasn't nearly this deep on the way out."

"Because the bay confines the water, amplifying the effect of the tide. The Bay of Fundy is the most extreme example. The tides there rise fifty feet within six hours. The tide in Frenchman is only eleven feet at its peak, but that's still a lot of water."

Jillian grimaced. "Especially when you're barely five feet tall."

He chuckled. "True. Also, the tide has been rising for several hours already. This bar is high and dry at low tide."

They heard a distant yell of anguish behind them, and Jillian froze. "Doug!" She turned and started back, but Caul grabbed her arm.

"Jillian, no! If you go back, you'll be stuck on the island until morning. You told me that Doug is a strong swimmer. He can make it back, if he chooses to."

Caul's final words hit her like a punch, and her vision blurred again. Now that her anger had slackened, she felt regret lodge high in her throat. *Doug! Please come home!*

She allowed Caul to turn her and get her walking again. She moved mechanically, imagining Doug lying down in a moon-drenched bed of ferns with Meeka. She pictured him hovering above her on his strong arms. She pictured him moving between Meeka's legs.

Bitch!

"Ouch!"

"What's the matter?" Caul asked.

"Something sharp just poked me. In the water. Ouch! Ow! Crap! Ow!" A hundred thick needles violated her flesh. She started running, pushing herself through the nearly hip-deep current.

"Jillian! Be careful or you'll trip."

Something was crawling on her legs now and climbing up the open legs of her shorts. She screamed and pushed at them with her free hand. They felt cold and hard, and they stung her—over and over.

"Help me!"

With his stronger, longer legs, Caul overtook her. "Wait! Let me carry you." He pulled her from the water, grunting with the effort. Small, crab-like animals, black against her pale skin, were crawling on her legs. She swatted at them, knocking them back into the bay.

"Save one of those! I'll want to get a look at it."

She was not listening to him, but shivered in disgust as she felt them scampering and sliding across her upper thighs. "Get them off me!"

"We're getting close." Something stung his leg. "Ow! That hurt!"

"Everything okay out there?"

They were impaled on a bright beam of light.

"Help us!" Caul yelled.

The light ducked and bobbed, followed by splashing. Two men in hip waders pushed through the water toward them. "Here! Give her to me," one of them said.

"Rolly! Thank goodness!" Caul gratefully surrendered her weight to the larger man, an employee of Smithson Labs. Another sting made him flinch. He felt himself hoisted out of the water by the second man, Jim. "Hang on, Doctor Saunders," he said.

Jim's broad shoulder pushed into Caul's bladder as they bounced forward. Caul's flashlight dangled from the lanyard around his wrist, making a crazy light show with the water as the beam alternately penetrated and reflected from the surface. In his rescuer's wake, he could see the small, black crustaceans boiling in the swirl. And, for one insane moment, he thought he saw Meeka's face beneath the surface, her eyes baleful and menacing.

Jillian was shivering by the time she felt herself laid down on a hard surface. By the feel of them, someone was going over her legs with a blowtorch.

"Well, damn! I've never seen anything like this. They're everywhere…even in your clothes. Lady, you've got crabs."

She flinched at the double entendre and opened her eyes to find the face of a man she didn't recognize staring down at her. "I know! Get them off me, please!"

The face retreated and rough hands swept over her. She was stung again. "Ouch!"

"I'm gonna have to take off your shorts."

"Fine! Ouch!"

She lifted her hips to allow the walking shorts to come off. She felt the rough hands again, touching her in places only Doug and her gynecologist were allowed to go. *At least I still have my panties on.*

"I think that's it." The man's hands retreated, and her face blazed along with her legs. She found her shorts and pulled them on with great care.

"That beats all."

Crunch. Crunch. Crunch.

"Wait," Caul said, "save some of them. I want to have a look later."

"That little bastard just bit me."

Crunch.

"Sorry, Caul."

Jillian tried to stand, but her legs spasmed uncontrollably. "My legs are on fire, and I can't walk! Can someone get me back to my hotel, please?"

The fishermen, led by Caul, carried her the few blocks to the hotel, and handed her off to Charles and Susan. Expressing concern, they got her upstairs and into her room. Susan drew a hot bath with Epsom salts, while Charles searched for ibuprofen and hydrocortisone cream. Caul waved off any offer of assistance. He had only been stung a few times, and the stings did not hurt all that much. He did ask Charles for a plastic bag.

"I'll be back in the morning to check on her," Caul said, and headed back down to the harbor.

Steam rose in mysterious curls into the air above the tub.

"You've caused quite a stir here," Susan said.

Jillian floated in the hot water, picturing the salt-laden liquid drawing the poison out of her violated skin. Large, livid boils had formed everywhere the black things had stung her, and her once shapely legs now looked like the limbs of a plague victim.

"I'm sorry about that," she said, trying to be diplomatic with the woman who was helping her. "I wasn't trying to cause problems. I just think Meeka's interest in my husband is inappropriate."

Susan chuckled. "Well, thank you. I'm not used to having such a lively dining room. And, to set your mind as ease, as I was telling your husband earlier, Meeka hasn't got time for a man. She shoots down every pining male who comes through here. Including your friend Caul."

"You're joking? Caul's interested in Meeka?"

"Interested? Oh, heavens, that man is obsessed with her! Has been since before we took over the hotel. That's why he's always here. Sure, he eats here occasionally, but he hangs around a lot longer than it takes most folks to eat. He's harmless, though, and Charles enjoys talking to him, so I don't mind him all that much. Charles doesn't believe that Caul's got a thing for her, but then, he's a man. What do men know about love?"

Jillian chuckled. *Huh...Caul's in love with Meeka.* She was surprised that she had never considered that possibility. She was not surprised that Meeka was not interested in Caul, but was interested in Doug. *Physically, he's twice the man that Caul is...but, he's also a lot of work. What would it be like to be with someone like Caul...dashing, considerate, articulate, talkative but not juvenile, not the object of so many other women's desire?*

There was a knock at the outer door, and Susan rose to answer it.

"Hey, babe," she said to Charles, and took the pain reliever and anti-histamine. "Thank you."

"How is she?"

"She'll survive, I reckon." She leaned in and whispered. "She's not as much a princess as I thought she was."

"That's good."

"Any sign of her husband?"

He shook his head.

"I guess we'll see him in the morning, then," Susan said.

"They really left him on Bar Island with the tide rising?"

"That's what she told me."

"Woof. Well, he won't be the first. Fortunately, it's early August and not late November."

"Ayup! I'd better get back to our mermaid." She gave him a kiss before closing the door.

13

As Doug stood, thinking about his years of marriage with Jillian, the allure of Meeka seemed to evaporate like a night mist. She was beautiful and so much more, but so was Jillian, and he could not throw away everything he had built with her over the last decade. He would not throw it all away. He started walking, shaking his head and wondering why he had even considered the prospect of running off with Meeka.

He could see the glow of Bar Harbor, when he became aware of movement in the woods around him. He stopped, his heart speeding up, and peered into the gloom. "Jillian?"

The tall, black trees swayed, while the boughs rippled and soughed. The woods abruptly felt wild and menacing, making him shiver. He took a step, but something large and dark moved onto the trail ahead of him, arresting his progress. He raised his phone just as the light went out. *Crap! The battery's dead.* The thing on the trail clicked and moved toward him. Other things in the brush moved as well.

In the distance, he heard Jillian scream. The sound jolted him into motion, and he ran toward it. He was preparing to vault over the thing in his path, when it reared up, sending insect-like legs into the air over his head. He slid to a stop, as an unearthly hiss erupted into his face. A yelp of panic filled his ears, and he fled the way he had come. The foliage of the island loomed in the darkness, pressing in, illuminated only sporadically by the moon. He heard skittering behind him. *Getting closer.*

He ran faster.

"Douglas, wait!"

He slid to a stop, grit and other debris in his sandals cutting into his feet. "Meeka? Is that you?"

"Yes."

She trotted, naked, out of the dark woods behind him. "Oh, Douglas," she said and wrapped her arms around him.

He pulled against her. "Meeka! We have to get off the island!"

"We can't, lover. The tide is coming in. You can leave in the morning."

"There's a creature on the island! We need to go! We can swim."

She laughed. "Don't be absurd. There's no creature." She kissed his unresponsive lips. "Come. I'll take you somewhere safe where we can rest."

He pulled against her again, scanning the darkness between the trees. "But I saw it!"

More laughter. "I spend a lot of time over here. I would know if there was a monster on this island. There isn't." She kissed him again and inhaled his scent. "You are the one. Come. I want to make love to you."

He gaped at her. "The monster!"

"There is no monster. Besides, even if there was, you'd be safe as long as you're with me."

Were those just branches in the dark, maybe? Just the wind?

"Come," Meeka said. "Don't you want me?"

She released him from her embrace, and slid her hand down his arm. He felt a small sting, like a mosquito bite, on the back of his arm, but she rubbed the spot and the pain disappeared. He shivered from her touch. So close to her, he smelled her perfume—orange blossom. The air was warm and dark. They were alone—thoughts of monsters fled his mind, and languor filled the void. "Yeah, sure." Her hand slid into his, and she led him into the darkness.

Susan got Jillian salved up with anti-histamine and put to bed. "Call me if you need anything, okay?"

"Thank you, Susan. You've been a godsend."

"You're welcome. Get some sleep." She closed the door to room four, and went to find Charles. He was at the front desk, with his legs stretched out from his leather chair, nursing a highball and staring at the wide, double doors that led to the front porch.

She slipped in beside him. "Do you really expect him back before tomorrow morning?"

Charles shrugged.

"It won't be the first time that someone has slept out on the island all night." Her hand went to his shoulder.

"Nope. How's Missus Sandow?"

"Settled into bed, medicated, and unswelling, as best I could tell." She pressed herself against him and ran her fingers over his hair. "This has been an interesting day."

"Ayup."

Her hand slipped down to the nape of his neck. "You ready for bed?"

"Ayup."

In a secluded area on the island, Meeka drew Doug into a small grove surrounded by a ring of hemlock trees that leaned in like a jury of spectators. A nest of blankets lay within, illuminated by moonlight. She turned and wrapped herself about him. "Come to me, lover." Her breath tickled his ear.

He frowned, his thoughts dull. "You planned this?"

"Of course."

She kissed him, her lips caressing his. Her hands pulled at his clothes, stripping off his shorts and drawing him closer to her. They broke their kiss long enough for him to pass his shirt over his head. Her fingers found him and coaxed him. She pressed herself against him, her skin cool to his heat.

We shouldn't be doing this. "Meeka—"

"Shh..." A slender digit imposed silence on his lips. "I've waited for this for so long." She locked her gaze with his, and he stared. Stars lived in those eyes—whole supernovas bloomed just for him. Entranced by the endless pools that regarded him, he followed as she tumbled backwards, pulling him on top of her. His gaze wandered over her face, taking in her smile and the dimples that formed at the corners of it, the shape of her face, and the wet mop of short, black hair that crowned her head. The scent of jasmine was borne on the wind.

"You're so beautiful." His voice was no more than a breath. "But, we shouldn't be—"

"Shh..." Her legs twined with his, pulling him closer. He resisted, wanting to... *What do I want? I want to see you. I want to hold this moment, not...not what?* He pushed himself up and allowed his gaze to slip down her long neck, the hollows made by her collarbones, her perfectly shaped breasts. He lowered his lips, and kissed her throat like a butterfly landing on a flower petal.

"Make love to me," she whispered.

He continued kissing, his lips sliding lower. *Why am I doing this? I need to stop.* Citrus mingled with the jasmine.

"Now, please!" Her voice husked out of her chest. She pulled insistently at his back and thighs, shifting herself, engulfing him. Her languid sigh evolved into a purr, while he gasped at the suddenness of his envelopment. Her enthusiasm drove him forward. When he tried to slow, she goaded him.

"I knew this would be wonderful," she whispered, and then kissed him, her lips caressing his.

He teetered on the edge—and fell into bliss.

"Oh, Meeka!"

He collapsed, wrapped around her upper body, and returned her kisses. His body shook. When the last of his tremors died, she planted her feet on his hips and pushed. A small whoop of shock followed him as he tumbled away.

"I'll be back." She disappeared through a gap in the trees.

"What the...?" He was not big into cuddling, but he had never before had a woman run away after sex. As he lay on the blankets, he felt wonderful, but cheated. He ran his hand over the spot where she had lain only seconds before. It was not warm like he had expected it to be.

Reality hit him like a punch to his teeth. *I just cheated on Jillian. I just broke my wedding vows.* A dull pain grew behind his eyes. He wanted to go back twenty minutes and make a different choice. He cast around for his clothes, pulling them on as he found each piece, covering his shame.

He peered into the darkness. "Meeka?"

Distantly, he heard someone calling his name.

"Meeka?" She was nowhere to be seen. *Where did she go? Oh, damn! What am I going to say to Jillian?* He heard the voice calling again, and now could make out the muted rumble of an outboard motor. He followed the sounds.

Caul stood in the prow of a Boston Whaler, playing a search light over the shore of Bar Island. Behind him, Rolly was piloting the small, shallow-drafted boat.

"Doug!" Caul called out. "Doug, come on! Jillian's been injured. She needs you."

"Maybe he's on the north side," Rolly said.

"It's worth a look."

Rolly gave the Mercury outboard some throttle and the boat nosed up. They rounded the eastern end of the island, slowing as Rolly dropped the throttle to a little over idle. Caul resumed yelling. They were about quarterway along the island when they heard a noise. Caul played the searchlight back along the shore, and picked out Doug standing in the shallows, waving his arms.

He was shaking and ashen-faced by the time they got him into the craft.

"You okay?" Caul asked.

Doug shook his head, staring off into the darkness. "What happened to Jillian? I heard her scream. I tried to come." He paused and swallowed. "I couldn't."

"I know, the tide was—"

"No," Doug's eyes were wide, "I mean I couldn't. There's something on the island. It wouldn't let me." He turned his face away.

Rolly dropped the throttle as they pulled into the harbor.

"What happened to Jillian?"

"A thing? What thing? Did you see Meeka?"

Doug's face burned. "Yeah."

"And?" Caul asked. He saw Doug's blush and anger clotted his throat.

"And what? Nothing! What happened to my wife?"

"Why couldn't you leave?"

He focused on Caul's face. Standing, he leaned over the smaller man. "Why do you care? What the hell happened to my wife?"

Caul's expression hardened. "We were attacked by crabs as we crossed the gravel bar. She got pretty badly stung."

"Stung by crabs? That's nuts! Is she okay?" Doug, his fists flexing and relaxing, crowded Caul.

"I don't know. We got her back to the hotel, and I came to find you."

Doug leapt out of the still moving boat and landed with a thud on the dock.

"Whoa! Hey, not cool!" Rolly yelled.

Doug ignored him and charged toward the quay. The streets were a blur. He wasted seconds fumbling with the lock on the hotel door and found the lobby deserted.

"Doug!"

He cast a glance over his shoulder at Caul, running up the street. *Back off, dude!* He closed and locked the door, before taking the stairs three at a time. Jillian was in bed.

"Hey, baby! I'm back," he said, stepping closer. "Jillie? I tried to follow you, but some...giant bugs stopped me. How are you feeling?"

The light from the bathroom fell across her face. Her skin looked red and her breathing was fast and shallow. He pulled back the covers and felt the heat rising from her.

"Jillie?"

He touched her cheek. She burned.

14

Strobing red lights illuminated the night. Doug watched the paramedics load Jillian into the ambulance, bouncing on the balls of his feet from anxiety and frustration. He could not understand how she had gotten so sick so fast. "Crabs?"

Caul was hanging back on the porch, talking to Charles. He glanced at Doug. "Yes, crabs."

"But, that's *stupid*! Crabs don't sting. What kinda weird crap do you people have up here?"

One of the paramedics gestured to Doug, so he crossed the lawn and got into the vehicle.

"Honestly? Crabs?" Charles asked.

Caul held up a plastic bag. Several of the crustaceans wiggled around inside. Charles looked closer and frowned.

"I've never seen anything like those before."

Caul chuckled. "Neither have I, and I smell a publication in these little fellas. If they really are new, I'll get to name them."

"Really?"

Susan poked at the bag. "I've never heard of a crab with a stinger."

"That's why it's a big deal." He grinned like a kid with a new bike.

"That's great, but is our guest going to be okay?"

Caul shrugged. "That, I don't know. I'm a geneticist, not a physician."

Doug watched the paramedic insert a needle into Jillian's arm and hook it up to a bag of fluid. The vehicle rocked its way through the narrow streets as the man took out a stethoscope and listened to her chest. He draped the scope over his neck and touched one of the angry red boils that covered her legs.

"Is your wife allergic to insect bites?"

"No, I don't think so. Why? She got stung by crabs."

"Yeah, but crabs—all crustaceans, really—and insects are related. They're all arthropods. I just wondered if her strong reaction was because she was already sensitive."

"No clue." He turned away from the disgusting, weeping boils. "She's going to be okay, though, right? Those'll clear up?"

"They should. The big problem now is she's really dehydrated—that's what the bag of saline is for—and I've given her something to bring her temperature down. She seems fine, other than being feverish and obtunded. They'll know more at the hospital." He glanced out the window. "And, we're here."

"Wow. That was fast."

"You probably could have carried her here almost as fast as we did," he said, and pushed open the back doors.

A nurse directed Doug to an intake clerk, who took Jillian's information and Doug's insurance card, while peppering him with questions and handing him a ream of papers to fill out. He struggled over it for a long time, his mind distracted by clashing thoughts of Jillian and Meeka. *How could I have had sex with her? What was I thinking?* The whole episode seemed surreal now.

"Mister Sandow? Good evening, I'm Doctor Powell, the ER physician. Your wife is in stable condition. She appears to be having an acute allergic reaction to the," she flipped through the file in her hands, "crab bites?"

"Stings."

She glanced at Doug over her glasses. "Crab stings. That's a new one."

"Tell me about it!"

"I don't expect any issues. We've got her temperature down, and she is showing signs of rousing. I suspect that she became obtunded from the fever. At this point, our challenge is to treat the allergic response and prevent any anaphylaxis. She will need to stay overnight for observation, at the least. I suggest that you go home and get some rest."

"Can I see her?"

"Certainly, although she isn't conscious, *per se*."

She led Doug into the ER, to a curtained alcove. He took Jillian's hand and kissed her forehead. "Hey, baby. The doc says you'll be fine." She did not respond. "I'm gonna head back to the hotel. I don't think they want me hanging around. But I'll be back first thing in the morning, okay? I love you!"

He kissed her again.

Charles was waiting up for him when he returned to the Pequot. "Did you walk?"

"Yeah," Doug said.

"You didn't have to do that. I'd have come and picked you up."

Doug waved him off. "Thanks, but it's close."

"How's your wife?"

"She's stable, whatever that means. The doctor thinks she's through the worst of it. Man, I'm tired." He rubbed his face. He had many unfamiliar emotions roiling his gut and did not want to think about any of them. "Did you know that crabs and insects are related?"

Charles nodded. "They're most closely related to spiders, mites, and scorpions, really. Not that that makes it any easier to stomach."

Doug thought about the lobsters he had eaten over the last several days. *Ugh! I ate a spider's cousin?*

"How do you know that?"

"I read."

"Great. I mean, so do I. Sports medicine journals and SI and such."

Charles smiled mildly, his wide mouth showing many teeth. "Is there anything I can get for you?"

"No, I'm good."

"Good. Then I'm going back to bed. Good night, Mister Sandow."

"Yeah. And it's Doug."

Charles nodded and left. Doug followed suit, climbing the stairs to his room. The bedclothes were on the floor. He vaguely remembered tossing them there while getting Jillian out of bed and downstairs to the ambulance. The bed looked incredibly inviting, and he was making his way to it when he heard water splashing in the bathroom.

"Hello?"

He pushed open the door and reached for the light switch, half expecting something to grab his hand. The glare from the fluorescent fixture revealed a tub full of water. *Jillian had a bath.* He was turning away when movement caught his eye. Stepping closer, he realized that there was someone in the tub...*Meeka.* She was not moving.

"What the hell!" He thrust his arms into the water and yanked her up. Water cascaded from her face and hair, as her eyes snapped open.

"You do care!"

"What are you doing in here? Are you crazy?"

"I love this tub! Come, make love to me again. I want you inside me all night."

"What? Get out! My wife is in the hospital."

"She didn't slow you down earlier."

Guilt flared. "That—that was a mistake. It can't happen again."

"That's not acceptable." She wrapped her arms around his head and kissed him. "Please make love to me! You were my eager buck, my stallion."

Eager buck? Stallion? He found her words stupid, but felt himself responding, regardless. He inhaled the scent of lilies from her wet skin.

"No."

"Yes!" She pouted. "Please?" She kissed him again, and her tongue invaded his mouth. He tasted salt and pulled away.

"What happened before was a mistake."

"Don't be like this, Douglas." She rubbed his back and he felt a sting.

"Ow! What are you doing, scratching me? You did that earlier."

"Nothing important. Come, lie down with me."

He felt light headed and stopped resisting her. *Jillian.* He returned her kisses, putting his hands tentatively on her wet back.

"Yes," she whispered against his neck. "Love me."

As earlier, she removed his shorts. He picked her up, her legs wrapped around his hips, and he carried her to the bed. She fell back against the fine sheets, and he stood over her, at the edge of the bed, taking in the beauty of her body and the electric sensation of her skin against his as he cleaved her. He ran his fingertips across the flare of her hipbones, and into the valley where her thigh joined her torso.

She shivered from his touch. "Yes, lover," she whispered.

Could we could make this work, Meeka and I? Fantasies of a life with her played out in his mind as he moved with the ebb and tide of her body. Her hands danced, teasing every part of him that she could reach, lingering in particular on his muscular abdomen. He leaned over the bed, bringing his face close and touching his lips to hers.

"I don't want you to leave," he whispered, thinking of the last time they were together. "Don't run away."

"I won't."

They kissed again—with tongues and at leisure—until a familiar release overtook him. She caressed his face as his tension escaped. "I love you," she whispered and landed fluttering kisses on his forehead, eyelids, and cheeks.

His throat closed up, but she did not appear to notice or care.

They shifted, after a time, and lay side by side on the bed. He gazed at her face. "How come you never told me how you felt about me? Back then."

She snuggled into the side of his body, molding hers to his, and rested her head on his shoulder. "I wasn't sure about you. Not until after you were gone. By then, it was too late."

"You could have come after me."

Her tiny laugh held sadness. "It's not that simple. I didn't know who you were, beyond your first name. I didn't know where you went."

"But there was a police report...wasn't Brian's accident in the newspaper? There should have been a trail you could've followed."

Her expression was enigmatic. "Not that I could find. And it's not really relevant now, is it? Besides, I couldn't leave my mother."

"Even for a couple of days?"

He felt her shaking her head. "Shh. No more questions, okay."

"Okay. I just can't help but think about what could have been."

"Don't regret your life. Simply think of the splendor ahead."

He felt a moment of panic. *What would happen now?* One time with Meeka was a fluke. A second time was something else entirely. As if sensing his thoughts, she slid her hand down his abdomen and took him gently in her hand. She squeezed, and he felt a pinch, but she kept moving, distracting his attention.

"Simply think of the splendor ahead," she said again. "I'll be right back." She rolled off the bed and fled to the bathroom, closing the door behind her. He heard water running, and other sounds that he could not identify. He began to doze, but awoke when he felt her hands on him again. She brought him back to attention and pulled him to her. The lights were off, but the scent of jasmine filled his nose.

"I missed you so much," she said. "I longed for you. I sang for you. I imagined the touch of your body on mine, the heat of your mouth on my breasts, the feel of your hands on my back, my thighs. I dreamt of the fullness of you inside me. Now, you make my dreams reality... and I am not disappointed."

"I'm glad," he said, his voice felt husky and congested.

"You are much better than my imagination. So much better than any of my dreams."

Later, as they lay tangled together in bliss, sleep swiftly overtook him, but he did not dream. He woke to early golden-orange sunlight slanting in through the northeast window. He was alone. *Crap...what am I doing?* He fell off the bed and stumbled to the bathroom. The window stood open, allowing a cool breeze to stir the lace curtains. As he relieved himself, he watched them flutter—the tatted wings of a bird that could never escape. Returning to the bedroom, he jerked to a stop. Meeka lay on the bed in a tight ball, her spine bent in a gentle arc and her long limbs tucked into her body. "I missed you."

He frowned. "Where were you?"

"By the window, watching you sleep."

He remembered back to when Jillian would do that. Thinking of Jillian made him panic again. In the cold light of morning, his fantasies of a life with Meeka were like puffs of dandelion seeds. He cleared his throat.

"About last night..."

"It was magnificent! Let's make love again." She unfolded herself on the bed, and it was like watching a flower bloom. He smelled lilacs. His pulse quickened as she ran her hands up his thighs. Something on her skin scratched him and he pulled away. She knelt on the bed, her knees dimpling the mattress, and tilted her head to the side. Her slender, olive hands traced the curves of her torso, and his will collapsed even as his desire swelled.

One more time can't matter.

He showered, regretting having to remove the scent of her. They parted with a kiss, and Doug made his way downstairs for breakfast. She assured him that she could get out of the room without being seen, but he still felt a surge of concern when he found Charles in the lobby, drinking coffee.

"Good morning. How did you sleep?"

"Okay."

"Any word about your wife?"

His thoughts were chaotic—two women trying to occupy the same space was stressful. "No, nothing. I'm going to get some breakfast and go down to the hospital."

"Fair enough. You've still got a couple of minutes for breakfast service."

A woman he had not seen before staffed the dining room. He ordered toast and eggs, and stared out the window after she left. He was having a difficult time comprehending how he had just cheated on Jillian, not once, but four times. *How had that happened? She's gotta be a vampire or a witch or something.* He had convinced himself earlier that he would ask Jillian for a divorce, only to reverse course within minutes of sitting down to eat. *I'm going to have to confess and beg her forgiveness.* He felt a migraine coming.

"Hey, would you like some company?" Meeka slipped into the chair across from his and winked.

He pushed back from her unexpected presence. "What are you doing here? I thought you had to go to work?"

"They didn't need me after all," she said and tousled her hair.

Gardenias? She looked cleaned up and fresh. He leaned close and whispered. "Did you shower in my room? That's dangerous!"

She looked confused. "Um, no...oh! I just ran some water over my head and face."

He sat, looking at her. The small scar by her left eye was gone. He shook his head. *Trick of the light.* "Okay, but you know there shouldn't be water running in an empty room?"

"Of course. Would you relax? It's not like Caul's around taking notes."

He frowned at her just as the waitress brought eggs and toast. "Hi, Meeka. I didn't expect to see you today. Would you like some breakfast?"

"No, thanks uh...Karen!"

The woman was slow to leave.

"Someone's covering my shift at The Pier."

"Oh." Karen finally left.

Meeka smiled. "What's the plan for the day?"

He felt a weight settle on his shoulders. "I'm going to the hospital."

"What are you going to tell her? About us?"

"I'm—I'm not sure." He took a bite of eggs.

"Does she make you happy?"

Doug looked up, stunned by her question. "Yes!"

"Pity," Meeka said quietly. She looked at the other diners. "This would be a lot easier if you didn't like her."

He did not disagree with her, but he was unhappy that she was talking about Jillian so flippantly. She was his wife and he loved her. *But I've cheated on her.* A hammer of regret smacked him between the eyes.

"You've gotta tell her something at some point." Meeka leaned across the small table, and the floral scent grew stronger. Gardenias always reminded Doug of funerals. "And the simple fact is, now that I have you, I won't let you go. I'll give you time, but not space. Understand? I need you."

He choked on his eggs. "What are you saying?"

"That you made love to me...you're mine now."

"Whoa! Don't you pull that possessive bullshit on me." He gazed into her eyes. *Funeral, sure—mine!*

"No, that's not what I mean. I'm just saying don't abandon me again. You can have us both, but I can't lose you again."

He considered her words and the secret they now shared. He remembered the way her body felt against his. "It's not that easy."

"It's super easy. Simply make love to me. Is that difficult?"

"No, but..." *Why am I even having this conversation?* "What happened...that can't happen again, all right? It should never have happened in the first place."

"So, you're just going to use me and toss me aside?"

He threw his fork down. "No! I—I'm sorry. I shouldn't have done that...with you. Sex, I mean."

"But, you did! You loved me. I accepted you into the heart of me. I might bear your child!" Her eyes were glossy. "Are you just going to walk away from that? From me?"

The migraine hit, flaming along his optic nerves. *How did this happen?*

Her hand crept across the table cloth. "We can't go back. You walked a bridge across a pretty deep river and you know what? That bridge is gone now. You've got me, whatever happens. I'm not leaving, and you've got to tell her that."

He rubbed his temples. "I can't just drop this on her. She's my wife. We have history. We have a life together." He felt his mind expand a fraction. "It would break her heart."

Meeka looked sad. "I was afraid you'd say something stupid like that." She tapped the fork against the table. "So, what will you do?"

He grimaced. "When she's better, we'll need to leave, to return home. We have jobs we can't neglect. I have to leave."

"What would make you stay?" She tapped harder.

He regarded her for a span of heartbeats. *She needs a concession...a bone to gnaw on until she gets over me.* "I'll come back...to visit."

"How often?"

"When I can."

"That's not often enough." *Her knuckles, clutching the fork, grew white.*

"I can't just abandon my marriage. I love Jillian. We have a life in New Haven. What happened last night...can't happen again."

Maybe. He remembered touching Meeka and how she moved with him. *Shut up!*

"I'll go down then."

He swallowed, misunderstanding her for a second. "Uh, I thought you couldn't leave your mother?"

"I'll make things work."

"I'm not sure that's a good idea." *Bigger bone.* "I'd need to get things resolved first. It'll take some time with Jillian—"

"Doug, you're not hearing me," she whispered and pointed the fork at his face. "I don't care about what you do with her, so long as you still make love to me. I can get an apartment in New Haven."

His heart stopped for a moment, either from the fork or the statement, he could not be sure. "Then you don't expect me to leave her? Or do you?"

"Not right away, no," she said. "Seven years is a lot to unravel, I get that. Just don't deprive me of you during the process."

Unravel. "I don't think leaving Jillian is really reasonable."

"Eventually."

"No, I don't think—"
She threw the fork down and seized his hand, squeezing hard.
"Ow!" He pulled his hand free and leaned back in his seat. "No!"
"Yes, Douglas!" She glared at him.
"I—" the room bent "—I'll see what I can do."

15

The walk to the hospital gave Doug time to think. He returned to the same thought repeatedly, and he hated himself for it. He could have both of them—Jillian at night, and Meeka whenever they could get away. Normally, he resented Jillian's trips to visit her parents in New Jersey—trips he always begged out of—but now he could see a benefit in her spending long weekends with mom and pop. *Maybe I can even convince her to visit them for a week.*

No doctor was available, but Doug got an update from one of the nurses. Jillian had regained consciousness early that morning, but they had her sedated at the moment. The fever was under control, and the allergic reaction appeared to be abating, as the swelling of her legs had gone down in the last eight hours. He sat at her bedside for about thirty minutes, getting increasingly antsy. Watching people sleep was not his thing.

His phone rang, but he did not recognize the number. *How do people keep getting my number?*

"Hello?"

"Hey, this is Caul Saunders."

Doug felt the migraine flare up again—needles of pain stabbing his eyes. "How'd you get my phone number?"

"I hacked the NSA servers and downloaded all your vital numbers."

"What? How?"

"I'm kidding. I got your number from Charles at the Pequot. I'd like you to come out to Smithson and have a look at something. I've already cleared you, just park in the visitor lot, and I'll come get you. Okay? It'll only take you three or four minutes to drive here from the hospital."

"How'd you know I was at the hospital?"

"Charles told me."

"Yeah, well, I'm with Jillian. What's so incredibly important?"

"I don't want to discuss it over the phone...NSA, remember? I'll expect you in ten minutes."

Doug frowned when the line went dead. Freaking rude. He was not exactly thrilled to spend time with Caul, but sitting with a sedated Jillian was as dull as dirt. *I should call Meeka...no, I shouldn't!* He glanced at Jillian and felt panic rise in his throat. *What have I done?*

His text message alert chirped, and he looked at the screen.

Nine minutes.

Suck it, Caul! He sat for another thirty seconds before he got up and left the hospital.

"You're late," Caul said as Doug pulled up to the visitor's lot.

"I'm aware of that. I had to go back to the hotel to get my car."

"Oh, you almost could have walked here faster."

Doug clenched the steering wheel. "I hear that a lot."

"Huh. Go ahead and park and we can head over to the labs. I've cleared you with the gate guard."

"Woohoo."

Doug took his time parking and sauntered back to where Caul waited.

"I know you don't like me, Doug, but I have your wife's best interest at heart. And yours, all right? There's no need to be arrogant and angry at me all the time. I don't have designs on your wife."

Doug simmered. "As if."

"Not every woman is impressed with big muscles."

"No," Doug replied, smirking, "just the attractive ones."

Caul grimaced. "You're a very unpleasant man."

"Okay, see ya." Doug turned back to his car.

"You'll want to see this, Mister Sandow."

"Not real likely."

"Especially considering your indiscretions last night with Meeka."

Doug stopped walking and suppressed the urge to vomit his meager breakfast on the sidewalk as a gallon of adrenaline poured into his bloodstream. *How...? How could he know? Did Meeka tell him?*

He pivoted on his heel and regarded the smaller man. "What the hell are you getting at, Mister Saunders? I don't appreciate your threat."

Caul lifted his chin in defiance. "Don't be coy with me, you cretin! You cheated on your wife with the woman I love!" He paused, breathing hard. "And it's *Doctor* Saunders! I didn't spend six years in graduate school to be talked down to by a knuckle-dragging mouth breather like you."

Doug inhaled sharply. "Wha...you love Meeka?"

"Any half-way intelligent and observant person would have noticed!" He made a strangled sound and kicked the air. Doug would have laughed under normal circumstances, but he was too shocked at the moment.

Caul glared. "Understand this...I hate you, Sandow. You've ruined everything by blowing into town...both times. However, your wife seems to be a decent person and an unwitting victim of your selfish stupidity, by and large, although why she stays with you is beyond mysterious. I don't think she should have to suffer any longer because of something that you unleashed."

Doug took another deep breath, thinking of Jillian. "Nothing happened between Meeka and me."

"Oh, please! Do you think I'd make baseless accusations against you? I've had this whole area, including the islands, under observation for years. I had drones deployed last night that caught your little tryst on the island and Meeka using your bathroom window like a revolving door. If I'd known at the time what you'd done on the island, I wouldn't have rescued your sorry butt last night."

Doug gasped, taking tiny sips of air, until he had calmed himself enough to talk. "Let me guess, you made a copy of the tape and mailed it to the police in the event I beat the piss out of you?"

Caul hesitated. He had not expected a threat. "That's so clichéd. No, the mpegs are saved in the cloud. Should anything happen to me—" he said in bluff "—they'll be e-mailed to your wife, your employer, the New Haven newspaper, and, sure, the Bar Harbor police."

Doug scowled. *What's his game?* "Okay sheriff, you got me. What now?"

Caul seemed to slump a bit. "Now, you come over to the lab and look at what I've discovered. Then, you can kiss my butt and tell me how smart I am."

"You're a sorry little freak."

"How'd you like me to show your wife the video of you on the island?"

"How 'bout I tell her first, and then introduce your sorry nose to the back of your skull?"

Caul gaped. "That would be supremely stupid. I think you'll appreciate what we're facing if you'll simply put a lid on your testosterone."

Doug smirked half-heartedly. *One of us has to have testosterone.*

Doug was looking through the eyepieces of a binocular dissecting microscope at a thing that resembled a giant, armored flea with claws and a pointy stinger. Caul was droning on about chitin and dodecapodia—"They shouldn't have that many legs!"—and the stinger, of course.

"I dissected several of them this morning and removed the toxin sacs. I'm running toxicology studies right now, but I can tell you that

E. coli won't thrive in any of the specimens. We'll see how the mice do. What I got hit with last night burned like you wouldn't believe, but I don't think it's acutely toxic. However, here's the funny thing... there were three toxin sacs, and it looks like each has a different toxin. I had one of my people run them on the gas chromatograph and we got different signatures from each one. Each sac was unique."

"So?" Doug was lost with all the geek speak.

Caul pushed his glasses up. "So, these guys can select which toxin they inject. They're like miniature biological inkjet printers...oh, hey, this time I need a little cyan...this time I need a little magenta. You get the idea?"

"I guess." Doug glanced around at the stark white and black lab. "Why is that such a big deal?"

Caul's expression betrayed his contempt. "You really don't see? There aren't many organisms that produce multiple toxins, let alone have the ability to choose which one they use—that I'm aware of anyway."

"Okay?"

"Okay? That's it? Science is wasted on you."

"Wow...I have a degree in science, so—"

"Which one?"

Doug frowned at the interruption. "Exercise science."

Caul's lip curled in disgust. "Like computer science, social science, and—God forbid—political science, any degree that ends in the word science is just faking at science. Ever heard anyone say chemistry science, physics science, biology science, or math science? No, you haven't! Because those are true sciences, and they don't need to have the word 'science' appended to make them look shinier than they truly are."

Doug pushed his chair back and laced his fingers behind his head. "Done with your period, Nancy?"

Caul looked askance at Doug. "My, you're a clever one. If you're so smart, tell me why all this is important." Caul thumped the crab.

Doug hated to admit it, but he really had no idea of where Caul was going with his diatribe, so he just shrugged. A smile split Caul's face, and he leaned forward.

"These blighters only stung Jillian...well, they stung me after I picked her up—"

"You touched my wife?" Doug rocked forward in his chair. "You've a lot of room to talk!"

Doug frowned, his concerns about Caul bearing fruit. "Don't you ever touch my wife again!"

"I am unlikely to ever need to, but at the time she was being stung, so I did what was best and carried her to safety. I kept her away from the crustaceans. Anyway, they only stung me after I started carrying her, and those stings were few and of minimal impact. Certainly not what Jillian was stung with."

"And?"

"And...the crustaceans appeared to be targeting your wife, both with their attention and a more potent toxin."

"You're saying they were more pissed at her?"

"Yes! So you see what that means?"

Doug shrugged. "They were more pissed at her?"

"No. I mean, yes, they were, but, more importantly, they can think!"

Doug laughed in Caul's face. "What? And you're talking smack about my degree? Even I know that crabs can't think. Eat, crap, and mate, that's about as much as a crab can do."

Caul removed his glasses and rubbed his eyes. "But these ones were showing a different behavior...a swarm behavior."

"What, like bees?"

"Exactly."

"So? Bees are stupid, too."

"Individually, sure, but hives are pretty smart. Bees dance to tell each other where food is, and ants communicate with chemical odors. Put a single ant in a room with a food source and its nest, and you will get crazy long trails from one to the other. However, if you then put ninety-nine more ants in the room, you'll find that the trail will get shorter. Why? Because the ants will deviate slightly, and the most successful deviations with be reinforced. Eventually, there will be a very direct trail from the food to the nest. And fish...fish will school, so exquisitely in synchrony that they appear to move as one organism. We see this in fact and in legend. The chotah, for example—"

"So what? How does that have anything to do with little, black crabs?"

"Synergism."

"Oh, for crying out loud! You know you sound like Sheldon on Big Bang Theory?"

"What?"

"The TV show."

"I don't watch TV. I have more important things to do."

"Like get crabs?"

Caul sighed.

Doug leaned forward, waving his arms for emphasis. "Oh, dude, I so agree! You're a total snooze-fest. I try my darnedest to be punny, and all you give me are snobbish sighs of the affected and imposed-upon, ineffectual pseudo-intellectual...yeah!" Doug pointed and gloated, responding to Caul's facial expression. "See, I know a few five-dollar words, too. You're not so freaking much smarter than me after all, huh?"

Caul sighed again. "Spouting a few words that you picked up from a pocket dictionary hardly suggests superior intelligence."

"Oh, do shut up! Why'd you drag me down here, anyway? To tell me stories about bumbly bees and freaking fake fishmen?"

Caul leapt into the breach. "Because the crabs only attacked Jillian."

"And?"

"They wanted to punish her for interrupting you and Meeka."

Doug's expression was toxic. He got up and walked away. Caul caught up with him just after he left the building. "Wait, will you?"

"No! You're a nutter. And a peeping Tom. And a blackmailer. And a know-it-all." Doug spun and stuck his finger in Caul's face. "Stay away from my wife. Stay away from me. And stay away from Meeka. If you have any sense, you'll destroy those videos, before I turn you over to the police for spying on people's bedrooms!"

Jillian heard voices. She opened her eyes to an empty room. The voices remained, so she turned her head and saw the TV on the wall. *Oh, how stupid of me.*

"You awake now?"

Jillian shifted on the bed, turning to look farther. Meeka stood near the headboard, playing with the IV pump.

"What are you doing in my room?"

"I asked you first."

"What?" Jillian blinked. It was Meeka, but she looked odd—older, somehow, and more wild.

"Doug wanted me to check on you, 'cause it kinda cramps his style to be seen with you," Meeka said and fanned herself with her hand. "So sorry!"

"Get out."

"Oh, and I wanted to tell you...he's awesome in bed—"

"*What*? Get out!"

"I love to watch the expressions that he makes when he's coming."

Anger seized Jillian's mind, and she struggled to sit up. Her heart raced. Much to Meeka's plan, it simply served to spread the poison that much faster.

16

The radio blathered something, but Doug was not really listening. He sat in the car, in the parking lot of Smithson Labs, his thoughts a flickering mosaic of guilt, erotic memories, insect behavior, and disdain for know-it-all dorks. Reaching for his phone, his hand closed around paper instead. Pulling the paper from his pocket, he saw that it was the brochure from the boat ride woman. He was starting to toss it on the floor when something caught his eye.

Sculptor Fred Uhlebe Jr.

He opened the brochure and read it. *Seriously? Is he be related to Ruth?* He found his phone in another pocket and mapped the address for Fred's studio.

On the western fringe of Bar Harbor, he found the studio, which really amounted to nothing more than a compact barn sitting in the yard of a sprawling, well-kept, 1950s-era ranch house set back from a narrow lane. He made his way to the barn and knocked, but he could see through the open door that no one was present. Glancing around, he assured himself that he was alone, prior to stepping inside.

The space was old and small, but not terribly cluttered. A workbench, surmounted by graying pegboard and an array of worn, oiled tools, spanned one wall. Along the back wall were open racks full of dusty boards. Light from a tiny, smudged window seeped through the stacked wood. Hanging from the rafter joists were dried flowers, jars of dark nails, and copious cobwebs. Above the joists, the head of a weathered plastic Santa poked from a holey cardboard box. An ancient riding mower moldered along the third wall, while the center of the space was dominated by a cedar log, as wide as his forearm was long and about as tall as he was. A snowdrift of chips and shavings lay heaped around the base—cellulose supplicants to the graven image. He turned a circuit of the sculpture, admiring the detail, but disenchanted with the subject.

"Like it?"

Doug jumped and twisted. A tall man stood in the doorway, leaning against the frame and watching him.

"That's the piker who tried to break into my house last week. I was all sorts of POed at that one. Nailed him but good, though. I put a double load of number four buckshot in him. So much for that fish."

Doug swallowed. "Mister Uhlebe?"

"Have some manners, son, my name is Fred." He stepped into the building, white hair windblown, a beer in one hand and the other stuck out for a shake. His grip was powerful. "What can I help you with? You interested in one of my piss ugly sculptures?"

Doug laughed. "That's quite a sales pitch. I'm Doug."

"Pleasure, Doug. And I don't make them—" he gestured to the statue "—for profit or art, as such." Fred took a slug of beer, smacking his lips afterward. "I make them as a warning. You want one?" He held up his can and shook it.

"Uh, sure. Thanks." *A little early for beer, but what the heck.*

Fred retrieved a can from a small, dingy refrigerator in the corner and passed it to Doug in a gnarled hand.

"What do you mean a warning?" Doug cracked the beer open and took a sip of foam.

Fred shrugged. "It's just a provocative thing to say; plays well with the tourists." He took another drink. "So, what can I do for you?"

"I've seen these—" he pointed to the carving "—around town and other places on the island, and I got your brochure. I wanted to find out what they're all about."

"You're not from around here."

Doug frowned at Fred. "No. What's that got to do with anything?"

"This isn't your fight."

The chill invaded Doug's spine again. "What if it was? What then?"

Fred looked out the door, before wandering to the workbench and perching on a battered steel stool. "Problems happen all over, right? Because people get blinded to reality over time. Grow up. Rationalize their fears." He glanced up. "That tightness in your gut? Your ass cinching up? That tingle at the base of your brain? Hey, that's a billion years of evolution telling you you're about to get fubarred. It's warning you to do something other than just stand there wearing a stupid smile, appreciating the art of it all." He glanced at the sculpture.

"Uh huh." Doug took a sip of beer.

"You get it?"

Doug looked at the sculpture, at the light that reflected from the places where a gouge had cut just so and polished the cedar. He ran his finger across one of these shiny spots. Ran it until it encountered the roughness where wood had given way by being torn instead of shorn. He shrugged.

"You ever been in combat?" Fred asked. "Iraq, Afghanistan?"

"No, I, uh, never joined the military. I wasn't interested."

Fred grunted. "Patriotism's going to shit." He spoke without rancor. "Just an observation, mind you. I did three tours in 'Nam. Not a draftee, I volunteered. Scariest time of my life, other than meeting my future mother-in-law for the first time." He took a pull from his beer and gestured to the sculpture. "And the first time one of these pikers came after me. Lawless pack of amoral SOBs. Parasites, really. They've always been a plague on us, for as long as I can remember, stealing stuff and harassing us. Kidnapping and killing. Sneaking around like thieves and assassins, keeping just out of sight, but they've changed over the years. Lately, they've started acting more like military. This one came with a group, precise, like a recon team. They're the ones that dragged the body away, while I was reloading."

The conversation had swerved into the gray area of disjoint that Doug had suffered through last night. "Are we still talking about wood carvings?"

Fred frowned and crushed the beer can in his hand. "Sure, son. I do all my carvings with a shotgun. Hear whatever you want to hear..." He glanced at Doug. "The enemy's at the gate. What're you going to do about it?"

"Um..."

Fred picked up a chisel from the work bench. "Take some advice? Get armed or get home. There's something after you."

Doug choked. "Ruth said that."

"Ruth? Ruth who? My mother?"

"Yes, I'm guessing. I met her yesterday, on a boat ride. She said that to my wife and gave her a pendant...a Saint Christopher medal."

With his free hand, Fred reached into the neck of his shirt and drew out an identical medal. "She does that for people." He tucked it away. "When'd you say?"

"Yesterday. Clearwater tours."

"Ayuh, I know about them." He rubbed fingers across his stubbly cheek. "That's interesting. My mother's an invalid. She hasn't walked for five years."

"Oh, sorry..." Doug's mind scrambled for something to say. "It must have been someone else, then. She said her husband was Fred Uhlebe and she had seven sons. I just assumed, when I saw your name, that..."

"Late eighties? Kinda short?"

Doug nodded.

"That's my mother. There are no other Uhlebes her age around here. It isn't a real common name, you know."

"Umm..." Doug's recalled the ticket taker's words about Fred Junior, *'He's a bit of a nut.'* "It can't be your mom. The woman on the boat stood up and walked."

Fred's expression clouded. He laid aside the chisel and stood. "Why don't you come in and say hello. Then, you'll understand." He gestured to the door. "You can bring your beer."

"Ah, I don't want to impose."

"You're not. Mother loves company."

Fred led the way, ascending a long, weathered ramp and entering the house through the front door. Doug always felt weird walking into other people's houses, like he was invading sacred space. The furnishings were old, but not shabby, giving off a comfortable, lived-in feeling. Fred pointed to the back door, with its large hole where glass and mullions used to be and plywood groused brown where sunshine should be. "That's where my visitor was trying to get in, before I popped him at two a.m. Good thing Mother is hard of hearing."

"I am not! Who are you talking to, Freddy?"

"A visitor. Doug." He went down a hallway in need of a fresh coat of paint.

"Do I know a Doug?"

They entered the first room on the right. Ruth sat up in a hospital-style bed, gazing at the doorway. Sunlight poured through the window creating a halo out of her white hair. Within it, her face wore a bright smile, and she raised her hands in greeting, seeking his.

"Ah, yes, Jillian Ruth's mister man. I dreamt of you yesterday."

Doug hesitated. "You..." He looked back to Fred in the doorway. A well-used wheelchair sat in the corner. "How were you on the boat yesterday? I saw you stand."

Her eyebrows lofted. "I wander many places while I dream...don't you?"

A surge of the absurd clogged his thoughts and he laughed. "Not like that! What's going on? You really can't walk?"

"I walk now only in my dreams."

"But, I wasn't dreaming yesterday!"

"There are more things in heaven and earth, Horatio, than are dreamt of in your philosophy..."

Doug swallowed. "Meaning?"

"Meaning, if Shakespeare saw ghosts, why can't you?"

"Because they aren't possible...they aren't real."

With tilted head, she regarded him. "What would be the purpose of a masquerade? Where would be the profit in a lie? My life's hour-glass is nearly at its end. The way you see me is how I've been for half a decade's sand now." Her expression became enigmatic. "Ah, I'm very close, aren't I? Sand now..."

"Close? I'm sorry, I don't understand."

"Quickly, Doug, take my hand."

Soft and cool, her hands enveloped his with surprising strength. "Hmm. Sandow, yes?"

"Yes."

"I was right."

"So? Jillian told you yesterday."

"Did she?"

He tried to remember exactly what Jillian had said, but could not. He shrugged. "It's not important."

"Oh, but it is! There is power in names, Douglas Reed Sandow. Knowledge of a name provides knowledge of a thing. Knowledge provides power. And power...well, power means you're half-way blessed or half-way damned, doesn't it? There was a time when your foe didn't know your name, but that time is over." Ruth's eyes widened, followed by a ragged inhalation. "Your nemesis knows you, Doug...she knows you...far more than just your name! Oh, what have you done?"

Doug's heart was thundering as she released his hands and reached for her neck. "My medallion?" She looked a bit bemused.

He tried to speak, but his voice died. *What does she know? How does she know? How did she know my middle name?*

Fred cleared his throat. "He told me you gave it to his wife yesterday."

"Yes, that's right. Her need for it was greater than mine, just as your need is even greater. Freddy, be a dear and get my jewelry box. Doug," she gazed into his eyes, "be a dear and help me dangle."

He nodded. Reaching back to memories and knowledge from his student days, he pulled her up, as she pulled the covers off her legs. Thin sticks of sagging skin—the emaciated remains of her legs—protruded from her nightgown and terminated in fuzzy pink socks. His doubt about her injury shriveled as surely as her muscles had, as he helped her turn on the sheepskin pad and dangled her legs over the bed's edge.

"Lumbar spinal transection. A lasting reminder of the automobile accident that stole my Fred from me. Pelvis broken in four places. Legs fractured. But I survive." She grabbed ahold of his arm and locked gazes with him again. "As must you, Douglas."

She released him and he backed away without hesitation.

"Thank you, Freddy." She took a blood-red cherry wood box from her son and rested it in her withered lap. "You are familiar with Saint Christopher?"

Doug shook his head. "No, I'm not Catholic."

"Oh? What are you?"

He looked at Fred, but got no help from that quarter; neither of them was looking at him.

"I'm—" he shrugged "—agnostic, I guess. I used to be Episcopalian."

"Used to be?" Her face rose, eyes of palest blue searching his. "God is not one to be *trifled* with."

"I—I don't..."

"Wear this." Her hand trembled as she held it out to him. A medal, identical to Jillian's, rested on her palm. "Saint Christopher is the patron saint of mariners and travelers. Wear it on your journey."

"I can't take it."

"I insist. I have others."

The medal felt cool to his fingers. He looked at her shrunken legs and considered the fate of Fred Senior. *It doesn't seem to have helped you much.* "Thank you."

Her skin around her eyes crinkled. "Doubt is natural. God never asked us to follow him blindly."

"Um, sure. Thanks...for this," he shook the fist that loosely clasped the medal, "and the beer. I need to go. It was a pleasure. I'll, uh, see myself out." He started for the door.

"Doug?" Ruth's face was radiant.

He hesitated. "Yeah?"

"Thank you."

He stood, shaking, framed in the doorway. "For what?"

"For visiting an old lady."

He nodded and fled.

Sitting in his car, he took several deep breaths. *What just happened?* He rubbed his eyes. *Screw the prepayment on the hotel, it's time to go home. Maine is freaking me out.* He looked at the medal for several seconds before dropping it into the storage bin between the seats.

Doug drove to the hospital, not actually looking forward to doing nothing but sit next to a sleeping Jillian for hours, but the day yawned ahead of him, featureless. Until she was better, it would be unreasonable of him to do anything other than eat, sleep, or sit with her. *Propriety must be observed. But, as soon as she's awake, I'll check her out and we can go home.*

The noise was his first tip that something was wrong. There was a flurry of activity around the door to her room—people rushing and shouting. He intercepted one of the nurses. "What's going on?"

She skirted him.

He barged into the room. "What's going on?" People were milling around Jillian's bed. He caught sight of her, and felt a beat of concern. She was pale and gasping. "What the hell is going on?"

A doctor looked at him. "Who's this?"

"Husband."

"Get him out of here."

"Mister Sandow, you need to wait outside."

"What's happening?"

"We'll come talk to you when she's stable," the nurse said.

He paced along the hallway for half an hour, before the doctor exited the room. "Mister Sandow? I'm Chuck Kegall." They shook hands.

"What's going on with Jillian?"

"She appears to have suffered a relapse. Her temperature started climbing, and she had arrhythmias and convulsions. We've got her stabilized, but we need to figure out what caused this worsening of her condition."

"Can I see her?"

"Not right now. They're getting ready to move her up to ICU where we can keep a closer eye on her. You look pretty strung out. Why don't you go home and try to get some rest. ICU visiting hours are from six to eight."

He left the hospital on autopilot and the short drive back to the hotel was agonized by nebulous worry. He sat at stop signs struggling with the future and his eyelids. *Not much sleep last night thanks to Meeka. Not much peace, either.*

Charles waved from the dining room as Doug entered the lobby. Glancing at the clock behind the desk, he was shocked to see that it was not even noon. "How's Jillian?" Charles asked.

"Worse."

Charles looked like a scolded puppy. "I'm sorry. Is there something we can do? Anyone you'd like us to call?"

Doug realized that he should tell Jillian's parents, but the thought of having them descend on Bar Harbor did not bear thinking about. They never had approved of him, especially Jillian's father. "No. Thank you, but I'll take care of it." He pointed upstairs. "I need a nap."

"Sleep well. I'll see to it that you're not disturbed."

Doug mumbled his thanks and climbed the stairs. The room had been freshened in his absence, and the windows all stood open. *Gods, this place must have smelled like a whorehouse after last night*, he thought. *That'd be hard to explain.* He flopped onto the quilt fully clothed and threw his arm over his eyes. He was asleep in seconds.

And it felt like only seconds later when he awoke to hands on him. He sat up and found Meeka removing his shorts with one hand and pushing his shirt up with the other. "Ouch! For crying out loud! What are you doing? How did you get in here?"

She seized him. "I don't really have to answer your first question, do I?" She put her lips on him, and he dropped his head back on the bed.

After a minute, she stood up, peeled off her clothes, and crawled past him, diving under the quilt and top sheet. "As to your second question, I work here, and you didn't seat the deadbolt."

He looked across the room at the door.

"Don't worry," she said, her words clipped and brow creased, "I did when I came in. Now, come over here, please."

"Jillian..." he shook his head, "Sorry, I mean Meeka. Listen, I'm really tired."

"Too tired to make love to me?"

He considered the question, considered Jillian and how she had looked at the hospital—how vulnerable she had seemed. In the light of day, he felt awful about what had happened and about what Meeka was asking him to do.

"Yes."

"Come here. I'll do the work."

"No. Please, just go. I need to sleep."

He felt the bed shift and her arms wrapping around his chest.

"Please? We have so much time to make up for."

"Sorry, what?"

She kissed his neck. "Please?"

"No! I went to the hospital. Jillian's sicker. Some kind of relapse or something. She was moved to the ICU."

"That means I can stay with you again tonight." Meeka's voice held a smile.

Doug frowned. "She could die!"

"I know that would be hard on you."

"That's putting it mildly!" He pulled against her arms, but she squeezed him, almost painfully.

"You'd still have me."

He considered her words, trying to rub the sore spots under her hands. *What are you doing to me?* The scent of lilies filled the air, almost choking him.

"If you still want me," she added in a whisper. She pulled away from him and lay back on the bed.

He turned, his head spinning and breath coming irregularly, and fell beside her on the bed. He watched, helplessly, as she moved in like a hungry animal. His eyelids fluttered and sleep took him.

Consciousness returned hours later, finding him tangled in the sheets. Meeka was gone. He stretched out on his belly, pressing his face into a pillow. *What is she doing to me? What the hell am I doing? She's...I shouldn't be doing this. It can't keep happening. Crap! What if she really moves down to New Haven?*

In his ear, a demon spoke: "If Jill dies, you won't have to stop..."

In his heart, a glacier split, and the emotions of the last several days gushed out like a hidden lake. The very real fear of losing Jillian flowed over him in an icy wave. He gasped and bit the edge of a pillow. Hot shame leaked from his eyes as the gravitas of ten years of their joined lives weighed on his soul. *How could I have done this to you, Jillie?* But Meeka's was the face that filled his mind. He knew he was lost.

The bed moved, and fingers brushed lightly through his hair. "What's the matter, love?" Meeka's voice was quiet. A hint of orange blossom perfume lingered on her wrists.

He jerked away and twisted his face on the wet pillow to look at her. "Please don't."

"I want you." She continued to stroke his hair.

"I know."

"Don't you want me?"

His eyes slipped shut. *That's the question at the heart of this. I can go one way or the other...or I can split the center. She smells so good.*

Her whisper stirred the air. "I told you—you can have us both."

He shifted on the bed and laid his head on her thigh. "I can see that going wrong in so many ways." *How can I even be thinking this?*

Her fingers traced patterns on his scalp. "I want you. Forever."

"I don't know...we'll see."

She sighed. "So, what now?"

"I don't know. I'm operating hour to hour." He rubbed his face, scrubbing away the dried tears. "Lunch."

"Sex first."

"Seriously? We just did like two hours ago."

"Are you complaining?"

He got lost in her smile and her eyes. *Don't do that!* "I don't know."

Leaning down, she kissed him.

There was a knock at the door. Meeka glared at it and growled.

"Doug? It's Charles," his voice came through the wood. "Sorry to bother you, but the hospital called. They need to talk to you."

"Thank you. I'll be down in a minute," Doug called out. "Sorry," he whispered, "I have to go see about Jillian."

Meeka turned away. "I'll miss you."

Caul was waiting for him at the ICU.

"Why are you here?" Doug's guilt simmered and Caul was not making it any easier to take.

"I made a preliminary identification of the toxins from the Saunders Crab."

"You named it after yourself?"

"I discovered it. I have the right to name it."

"Turdblossom."

"Excuse me?"

"Nothing, please go on. You were talking about toxins."

"Doug, you're a real boor."

"So you've told me."

The physician from earlier joined them. "Mister Sandow! Glad you could join us." He turned his attention to Caul. "Did you tell him about the toxin?"

"I was trying to," Caul said. He glared at Doug, daring him to interrupt. "The toxins we isolated appear to be from various marine animals. All of them are proteinaceous venoms—"

"Which means we can denature them," Chuck said.

"Correct," Caul's expression soured as the physician stole his thunder. "I determined that the toxins' optimal temperatures are lower than human body temperature, and hyperthermia should render them non-functional or at least impair them sufficiently to allow the immune system time to neutralize them."

"Okay?"

"We're treating your wife with sulfazine and hyperthermia pads to try to denature the toxins. We're also dialyzing her and administering diuretics to stimulate her kidneys."

Doug raised his hands in surrender. "Is she going to get better?"

"We think so."

"Good, then that's all I need to know. I want to see her."

"I'm sorry, no. It's not visiting hours yet, and there've already been too many unauthorized people tramping through my hospital today." Chuck glanced at Caul.

Doug frowned. "You?"

"I was collecting samples—"

Chuck's expression soured. "And you know better!"

"I'm sure I do."

"Were you in Jillian's room?" Doug stood up as Caul nodded. "Why? Why were you in my wife's room?"

"I said, I was collecting samples."

"What kind of samples?" Doug's hands collapsed into fists. "Why?"

"Because," Caul said, "something doesn't add up. Your wife shouldn't have gotten more ill, unless she was re-exposed to the toxin. Now... how could that have happened?"

"No clue."

Caul tsked. "Well, I might have one, which is why I'm looking. Who was with her today? For a long block of unsupervised time, hmm?" His eyebrows did a slow climb up his forehead. "See that, Doug? I'm thinking and doing something productive. Not standing around clenching my fists at the universe like some hormone-fueled felon. I suggest you cool your testosterone before you do something stupid. Something else, that is."

"What? What are you suggesting?"

Caul leaned close and whispered. "I'm simply pointing out that you were in her room today. And you might have reason to want a little freedom?"

Doug glared at him. *If I don't leave now, you will die.* Without a word, he turned and left.

The Subaru wandered aimlessly through Bar Harbor as his thoughts ambushed his attention. He found himself at the waterfront, just as a parking space was opening up. He nosed the car into the space and killed the engine. He sat and watched the boats on the water, allowing time to get away from him. *How did this happen?* He returned to the present and returned to the hotel. He ran into Charles in the back hallway and they walked through to the lobby.

"How is she?"

Doug sighed. "Worse, but then better. This is turning into a freaking nightmare."

"You'll get through it." Charles sat in his chair. "Susan had breast cancer several years ago. I spent a lot of time in that hospital and others. It's rough, but you'll get through it."

Doug regarded the older man, really looking at him for the first time in days. *He really seems to care.* "Thanks."

Charles waved away the word. "Just speaking my truth." His hand dropped back to a skinny thigh. "Why don't you get some sleep? Forgive me for saying so, but you look like hell."

Chuckling half-heartedly, Doug nodded. He climbed the stairs, expecting to find Meeka, but his room was empty. He sat on the edge of the bed and put his face in his hands. *What am I going to do? If Jillian dies...* He tried to block out Caul's words. Losing Jillian would be bad enough in itself. Getting charged with poisoning her was beyond his capacity to consider at the moment.

He heard a small noise and looked up. Meeka was standing in the bathroom doorway.

"Don't you ever knock?" He put his face back in his hands. The light was beginning to hurt his eyes again and they were watering.

"I'm sorry." Her voice was a rustling mouse.

He exhaled in a rush.

"She had a good life," Meeka whispered.

Doug frowned, his throat constricting. He glanced up at her through narrowed lids. "What? What do you mean?"

"Jillian. She had a good life. You were a good husband to her."

He felt nauseated. "Huh? Why did you say that? What do you know about Jillian?"

"Not much...she was a good woman. I'm sure she went peacefully."

"What the hell? Why do you keep talking about her in the past tense? She's recovering!"

Meeka looked shocked for a second, before a bland expression seized her face. "I—I assumed that she had died."

The tension in Doug's chest swelled.

"Why? Why would you assume something like that?" *She and Caul are freaking setting me up!*

She looked away. "Her illness. Your face. I thought you looked sad."

"I am, but not because of that. And, I am stressed the hell out. I don't know how I'm going to reconcile this," he waved his hands, "with the rest of my life."

"I told you—"

"Yes, I know what you've said! But, I can see that going wrong in so many ways. I'm not one to lie and skulk around! I can't do this."

She crossed the distance between them and leaned down to kiss his head. "Then make love to me in the open."

He held her loosely, pushing against her and holding her back. "I can't. Not right now."

A sound of frustration escaped her throat.

"I'm exhausted, Meeka! I can't think straight. I need to sleep. Alone!"

She stroked his hair. "All right, sleep. Dream of me."

The sunlight slanted along the walls when he woke. He still felt like crap, but he went down to eat, regardless. The dining room was crowded. Meeka bustled around, dispensing smiles and food. *She's a waitress*, he thought, *I've never been involved with a waitress.* He thought of Jillian and her ambition—climbing to a vice-presidency of her mid-sized advertising agency in eight years. Hard work and persistence had served her well, perhaps even better than intelligence. *How much ambition does Meeka have? Other than trying to break up my marriage...*

The devil returned to his shoulder. *But she's hot, and amazing in bed.*

Doug experienced a stab of remorse, followed by a pang of longing for Jillian. His stomach roiled. *I've been making some crappy decisions lately.* He sighed and watched Meeka. He felt a shiver of lust for her. *That's really all I feel with her...lust and possibility. Jillian's my wife. I've shared a third of my life with her. We've built something good together.*

He ordered dinner on autopilot, not engaging Meeka beyond the minimum necessary to get food. If that bothered her, he neither noticed nor cared. His skull felt too small and the lights were too bright. *Damn migraine.* A plate slipped in front of him.

"Should I bring you some acetaminophen?"

He looked up at Meeka and was caught again by her beautiful face, by her piercing, dark eyes. He nodded, wondering if he was being too rash. He hated himself for feeling tempted, but her wild beauty and raw sexuality overwhelmed him. She brought the pain reliever and ran her hand across his cheek, then left him alone to eat in misery. He picked at his food until his phone chirped a text message notification.

> **Doug, too busy to come talk to you (and you're a cretin), but thought you should know that Chuck says Jillian is improving. Also, the DNA sequence from my crabs is amazing! Too bad you wouldn't understand the results. Caul.**

Anger flared behind Doug's eyes. *Why's he telling me how my wife is doing?* Thoughts of hurting Caul marched through his mind as he jammed the phone in his pocket. *Jillian dying would have solved a lot of problems.* He threw his fork across the table as a tsunami of guilt and grief flooded his heart. *It's all falling apart. I'm not going to be able to keep what happened with Meeka a secret...and Jillian will kill me for it.*

"Hey, don't look so glum!" Meeka said, sidling up to his table. "Who messaged you?"

He glanced up at her. "You don't miss much, do you?" His throat was tight.

"Years of practice. Alewifery is all about being aware of your people. There are golden moments for things, like refilling glasses. You don't want to swoop in too early or you'll seem hovering, but if you wait too long, the glass will be empty and the customer will be upset. I've got the eye."

His own eyes unfocused. He was already half gone. "Huh. I'd never thought about it like that."

She smiled. "So, who was texting you?"

"Caul."

"About Jillian?"

He frowned. "Yeah."

"And?"

"And she's getting better."

A moment of consternation crossed her face. "That's, um, great. That's great," she whispered. "We can all be one big happy family: husband, wife, and mistress."

What did you say? "Oh, wow. Please don't ever say that again."

She scanned the dining room, before locking eyes with him. "Don't go see her tonight."

"Um, I kinda have to. I'd be an utter piece of crap if I didn't."

"Then be an utter piece of crap...with me."

"No. I'll be back."

Her eyes glossed. "Okay." She wandered away.

She would not handle being a...mistress, he thought. *This isn't going to end well.* He pushed the plate away and left.

17

Hey, sunshine!"

Doug tried to be upbeat, despite the pounding headache. He stepped into Jillian's room in the ICU and jerked to a stop. He barely recognized his wife. Her limbs and face were puffy—her eyes seemed lost in a sea of peach marshmallow. Doctor Kegall had warned him that the medicines had caused her face to swell, while the constant push of IV fluids and the dialysis were making the rest of her swell. It still did not prepare him for how she looked.

"Doug!" The sound was a reedy whisper. "Thank God you're here!"

"How are you feeling? You look great."

"Stop lying. You suck at it." He stepped closer to hear her, and she reached for him. "Have they arrested Meeka yet?"

Doug jerked again. "What?"

"Meeka tried to kill me! She was in here messing with my IV today. She gave me something. I told the nurses and that doctor. I'm not sure they believed me."

"I'm...could you have been mistaken? You were running an awfully high temperature. And, they had you sedated—"

"You're doing it again," she whispered louder.

"Sorry?"

"You're siding with her! No, I did not hallucinate her being here!"

Doug finally went to her bedside and took her outstretched hand. "No...no, I'm sorry. Please tell me what happened."

"She was in my room, this morning, doing something to my IV tubing. A few minutes later, I thought I was going to die!" She blinked. "I am going to die unless someone stops her. You haven't seen her, have you?"

His gut clenched. "Uh, yeah, she's working right now. At the hotel."

Her eyes widened as far as the swelling allowed, and her heart rate monitor beeped up tempo. "Go get the police and have her arrested!"

"And tell them what?"

"That she put something in my IV! Aren't you listening to me?"

He swallowed, wondering if what she said was credible. "I am...but that's kind of extreme."

"Please, Doug! I thought of all people...of all people, you would believe me!"

"I do! But that's a serious charge." *And the ensuing crap storm would surely reveal my infidelity.*

"You don't believe me!"

Doug grimaced. "Yes, I do. It's just...a bit over the top." *Is it really?* He tried to picture Meeka being so psycho that she would kill Jillian just to have him. *Oh, hell...*

"Give me my phone, please."

He was surprised by her request. "Why?"

"Because I want to call my parents and my brother."

"Your phone is back at the hotel."

"Then give me yours!"

"Jillian, listen, I'll go talk to Doctor Kegall and the police. We'll get this sorted out, okay? There's got to be a reasonable answer for her being here. I'm sure she didn't..."

Jillian frowned. "Why are you talking like that? Why are you trying to play this down? She's gotten to you, hasn't she?"

Panic flared in his chest. "W—what?"

"She's gotten to you. She was on the island that night..."

He felt heat pour from his cheeks. "She was, but it wasn't...like what...you..."

She pulled in a ragged breath. "Tell me you didn't have sex with her!"

His face glowed. "Jillian...I..."

"Please tell me you didn't! Doug...?"

He looked away, his face throbbing with blood. "I'm sorry."

"My God! Oh, my God!" She pulled her hand from his and covered her mouth.

Doug stood, petrified, as the bed shook. The monitor squalled and the IV pump beeped. He was assaulted by the sounds of Jillian's pain.

"How could you? You bastard! How *could* you?"

"Jillie..." His voice was a croak. "I'm sorry!"

She dropped her hands and glared at him through a stream of tears. "Sorry?" Her voice hitched. "You're *sorry*? You're my husband! You *promised*!" She sobbed and slapped at him. "How could you?" Her IV pulled out, spraying the blanket with blood and saline.

"Jillian, stop! You'll hurt yourself."

He reached for her arms, but she evaded him and slapped his face. "You bastard!"

Several nurses ran into the room. "What's going on? I'm sorry, but you're going to have to leave, sir!" They grappled with Jillian, restraining her arms. The fight went out of her like a balloon popping. She turned her face away, sobbing.

"You bastard! I hate you!"

He fled.

Mercifully, the lobby was empty when he returned to the hotel. Voices and laughter leaked from the dining room, but he shunned the happy sounds. He was halfway across the lobby when he caught sight of Meeka in the dining room. She waved, but he ignored her and ran upstairs. He locked the door and fell into the big, empty bed, his mind on fire with confusion. *My life is crap*, he thought before succumbing to fatigue.

He woke to feather-light touches. "Sorry, I was trying not to wake you up." He felt her cool hands envelope him, teasing him awake. He struggled with his emotions, gripped by an overwhelming melancholy. He was not sure how to approach his problem.

"Meeka."

"Um, hmm."

He felt her lips on him. "Jillian woke up."

She stopped moving, and the lips departed. "That's nice. Could we not talk?"

He took a deep breath. "She said you were in her room."

Silence.

"That you were messing with her IV." He heard his text alert chirp.

She laughed, but Doug thought it sounded forced. "Why would I do that? She must be imagining it, I mean, she's sick and all. Besides, I don't even like hospitals." She laughed again. "Please, let's not talk."

Her hand moved again. He looked down. She hovered over his legs, crouched like a predator. She saw him looking and smiled. Sinuously, she crawled up his body.

"I missed you." She kissed him.

Half of him wanted to push her away, while the other half wished to forget that he was married. *Jillian hates me now.* She rubbed against him and descended before he could make a decision. A purr resonated through her chest as she impaled herself on him.

"I missed you so much."

She moved slowly, while he lay paralyzed. He tried to block out everything, but thoughts of Jillian—bloated and bruised and weeping—flowed into his mind like a rising flood, turning his steel to ruin.

Meeka cried out. "What's the matter? You have to finish!"

She moved across him, attempting to elicit a response, but he withered. "Douglas, please! We had so few times today. I need you!"

"I can't. Jillian knows."

"Forget her! I'm here now! Aren't I better than her? Don't I make you happy? Don't I bring you pleasure? I will love you like this forever. Forever, lover!"

Loathing, like a gorge of bile—for himself and the woman who straddled him—rose in his throat, threatening to choke him. In his heart, he believed Jillian. He loved her and always had. Even if she never forgave him, he would still love her. Lust and desire for Meeka had clouded his judgment, but now that cloud blew away in shreds before the wind of rationality and regret.

He pushed her away, even as she tried to kiss him. Sliding from the bed, he grabbed his shorts and slipped back into them. "Why did you try to poison my wife?" He frowned. "And how did you even get in here? I locked the bolt. You're some kind of vampire or freaking succubus!"

She lay on the bed, dumbfounded and draped in a sad expression. She reached for him. "Douglas, please. I need you."

He pushed her hand away. "Why did you try to poison my wife?"

"It—it's really not important." She slumped to the mattress. "Please come back."

"The hell it's not! You tried to kill her!"

"Yes...I do things beyond my control." She gazed up at him, her eyes glistening. "I'm sorry. I tried to protect you. I love you."

"What? Why? What are you talking about?"

Her face went slack for a second and she twitched. "But you're a slow learner, aren't you, Sandow?" A guttural voice spewed from a face marred with malice. "So, what was this, then...one last fuck before you drag me off to jail? You're a piece of work."

His phone rang.

"I can't believe you'd use me like that!" She glared at him. "Dragging me in here and raping me, all the while accusing me of trying to kill your wife."

A confounding white explosion popped in Doug's mind. "Raping you? What the hell?"

"Yes! I went to Jillian to tell her about your inappropriate advances with me, but she got confused and thought I was trying to hurt her. And then, you viciously attacked and raped me! I should scream right now."

"Wha...what are you trying to prove?"

She glared at him. "That truth is subjective, Sandow. And it hurts me that you believe your wife's fever and drug-induced hallucination over me!"

His voice mail alert chirped.

Her expression changed again, going slack for a moment, and then light returned to her eyes. "I love you!" Her voice sounded normal once more. She sat up and wiped her eyes. "Douglas, run!"

"Uh...why?" He backed up, while his heart hammered. His text alert chirped again. He pulled out his phone and glanced at the screen.

Meeka on security DVR @ hospital when Jillian sick. Recovered traces of crab toxin 2 from IV tubing. Police on the way to you. Caul

He looked up to find her glaring at him. "What is it?" The guttural voice had returned and her eyes were dead.

"Nothing."

She frowned. "You lie badly, Sandow."

"Yeah, I've been told that."

Meeka rose from the bed, and he stepped back. *Wait, what am I doing? I outweigh her like two to one.* He watched her sinuous progress. The scar beside her eye was gone. *How's that?*

"I need you, Sandow. You must lie with me and not lie to me." Her black eyes locked on to his, but subtle movement near her navel drew his gaze. A tiny slit had opened on her belly and an appendage like a thorn extruded four inches from her body.

"What is *that*?"

"My insurance policy."

She stepped close, reaching for him, tilting her head for a kiss, bringing the thorn ever closer to—

He walloped her across the head with the desk telephone.

"Ow!" She spun away from him, falling to one knee. Her head rotated around like a gun turret, and he gazed down the twin barrels of her baleful glare. "You hit me. You piece of shit! How stupid are you?"

He heard her words distantly, for his attention was fixed on the nasty gash that the phone casing had laid open across her cheek. Where red blood should be flowing, he saw only clear fluid. As he watched, it began turning blue.

The world narrowed and he gasped. "What—what *are* you?"

She ran her fingers through the liquid on her cheek, grimaced, and laughed bitterly. "I am my mother's daughter." She stood up. "I would have made you so happy, Sandow...if only you had let me."

Downstairs, he heard a door open and loud voices. Blue light played behind the curtains of the harbor-side windows. Meeka heard the commotion too.

Doug turned toward the door. "The cops are here for you."

She uttered a withering laugh. "Pity they won't find anyone up here. You're coming with me, lover."

Moving like a cobra strike, she stepped close to him, three limbs sweeping the air. He swung the phone again, but she was prepared this time and blocked his arm. Pain shot up from his wrist, making him lose control of the old, heavy device, which shot across the floor until it was fetched short on its cord.

Her hands clutched his wrists, and her left leg snaked around his right leg. He tried to pull away from her, but she fell against him. Already off balance, his leg buckled as her weight bore on him. Her thorn brushed the fabric of his shorts as he tried to shift his body away from hers.

She grunted, straining against him. "Stop fighting me!"

"Let go!"

Heavy footsteps in the hall.

"Never, my love. My mother approves of my harvest. But she needs more. Much more."

"What are you talking about?"

She kicked herself forward, and he felt the thorn pierce his thigh. "Hey! Damn it!" Fire accompanied the thorn's withdrawal.

Her smile was feral. "Caul told me about his discovery, his crabs. Amazing, right? Am I not even more amazing? For I have many more than three glands."

Fists pounded on the door. Voices called.

Doug gasped at the pain invading his flesh. "You're...?" He stumbled—his legs absurdly weak.

"Goodnight, lover," she said, as he pitched face first into darkness.

18

A meeting rapidly convened outside room number four.

"You're sure he's in there?"

"Well, someone is...the night bolt is on. It can only be operated from inside the room."

"Step back."

"Don't break my door!"

They heard the sound of struggle from within and the words "Damn it" filtered through the panels. Charles pounded on the door.

"Step back!"

"You're going to pay for the damages, Troxell!"

The burly sergeant raised his foot and kicked the sole of his boot against the stout, wooden stile. Nothing happened. A second kick resulted in a satisfying cracking sound. The door gave way with a bang on the fourth kick, and three officers from the Bar Harbor police department flooded the room, along with Caul. Charles and Susan hung back in the hallway.

The room and bathroom were empty.

"I heard voices in here," one of the officers said.

"Ayup, they were in here," Troxell said.

Charles surveyed the damage to the door frame. "Then where are they now?"

Caul went to the open window. "There!" He pointed down the street.

A lone, hunch-backed figure trotted toward the harbor. As it passed under a street light, the figure resolved into a person carrying another over their shoulders, fireman style. Caul raced downstairs, followed closely by the police officers. By the time they reached the end of Bridge Street, they could barely make out the figure halfway across the gravel bar.

Caul gave pursuit until a hand on his shoulder stalled his advance.

"Whoa, cowboy. Where do you think you're going?" Troxell asked. "You're staying right here."

He pulled away from Troxell. "Why? Come on! They're getting away!"

"Because, Bar Island is part of Gouldsboro. We have no jurisdiction over there, but we're pursuing a suspect from a Bar Harbor crime."

"And?"

Troxell squinted. "And we can pursue, but I don't want to be responsible for your safety, so you're staying here. You'll have to wait for someone from the Gouldsboro PD, or a Hancock county deputy. I'll get calls going out to both agencies."

Caul remembered the pesky detail that the distant town of Gouldsboro had an old and creaky claim on Bar Island and the Porcupine islands. *Stupid! I can't let them get away.* He had done his level best to steer Doug away from Meeka, but it had not worked. He could not understand what sway Doug held over the girl to make her poison Jillian, but he was thinking furiously on strategies to exculpate her. He had texted and called Doug in the hopes of getting him to surrender, or at least not do anything stupid. Kidnapping Meeka counted as stupid.

Caul bounced from foot to foot, as he watched Troxell and the other officers ford the channel. "Okay, can you call me when they get here? I don't have time to wait around." He trotted away, turning left on West Street, heading toward the harbor. With his phone, he accessed his drone app, aiming the camera to the gravel bar. He found the figures with the infrared camera and zoomed in on Doug, and frowned. *The heat signatures are wrong...someone with a small signature is carrying someone with a big signature. The only way that could be...*

He was struggling with what it meant to see Meeka carrying an inert Doug. He felt the fear of having been wrong stirring in his mind. *What if Meeka poisoned Jillian on her own?* He shook the thought from his head. She was clearly afflicted with some kind of Stockholm Syndrome. *But why would she be carrying him? How could she be carrying him?*

He shook his head again.

He found the pier he was looking for and walked out on the floating planks. He slid down into Rolly's boat and felt under the seat for the ignition key that had been stuck there for all the time that he had known the man. He was happy to have some consistent people in his life.

He slipped the launch out of the harbor on its electric trolling motor to avoid drawing attention, keeping an eye on Meeka and Doug on the live feed. Meeka was moving unbelievably fast for carrying a two-hundred-plus pound man. *How is she even able to pick him up?* She carried him to the bower and left, running east along the island. Zooming the camera out, he kept an eye on both of them, until she reached the bay and dove in. She never surfaced. *Wait...someone else.* He watched the third figure trot from the west—the direction of the gravel bar over to the island. *Who is that?* He switched the drone feed over to a regular camera, zooming in on the person as they entered the open area at the middle of the island. It was a woman. She glanced up. *Meeka! But, then who was carrying Doug?*

He pulled the launch up to shore and fastened the bowline to a tree. Using a flashlight from the boat, he ran inland to the bower. Doug was stretched out on a thick layer of hemlock sprillans, snoring away like an outboard motor on a rough sea. A prominent smear of blood stained the right leg of his shorts.

"Doug," Caul said and kicked Doug's bare foot. "Hey!"

The larger man did not awaken.

Caul leaned over him, and shouted in his ear. Doug flinched, but remained asleep. Caul slapped him.

"Whada," Doug mumbled and swung his arms out.

"Doug!"

"Wha..."

Caul got his arm under Doug and lifted, grunting from the effort. "You need to eat less."

"Cau...?"

"Yes, I'm here."

"Careful...Meeka."

"Why?"

"Stinger...belly."

Caul frowned and looked more closely at Doug's leg. "Is that what happened here?" *Not quite your belly, Doug, but then you are ignorant.*

Doug nodded stupidly.

"Why did she stab you, Doug? Were you trying to harm her? Where did she get a crab?"

"No...tried to kill Jillian."

"I figured that out. You should probably hire a lawyer."

"No!" Doug struggled to stand. "Meeka!"

Yes, Meeka, Caul thought, *I'm trying to keep her out of this.* "Come on, there. Let's get you back to the hotel, all right?" *And the police.*

Doug got to his feet, swaying as if buffeted by strong winds. "Where'd she go?"

Caul helped Doug out of the grove of hemlocks. "For a swim, I guess." *But how'd she get back up the island so quickly? Or was someone else carrying Doug? Who? It'd have to be someone small but strong...or big and cold.* Caul frowned at the thought and its possible answers. *No, that's...unlikely. It was Meeka. Had to be. And Doug. It's his fault.* "Listen, you should leave Meeka out of this, all right? She's an innocent girl. Just confess what you did."

"What...you talking about?" Doug asked. The dark fuzziness was beginning to lift from his mind.

"We know what you did with your wife's IV. I'm just asking that you clear Meeka of any wrong doing. Tell them that you were threatening her. Be a man."

Doug stopped stumbling forward. "Wait...you think...I poisoned Jillian?" He laughed in a weird warble. "You're...an idiot, Caul."

"You're hardly in a position to be insulting me—"

"She isn't...innocent!"

"I fail to see how you can say that. You're the one having the affair—"

"Not Jillian! Meeka!" Doug swayed in the darkness. "She tried...to kill Jillian. Tried to frame me...for rape. Poisoned me with...her belly thorn."

"Caul?" Naked, Meeka emerged from the night. "Why are you here?"

Caul felt his cheeks warming.

"I—I saw you two...crossing the bar. You don't have to listen to him. I'll keep you safe, all right? We'll just go tell the police what happened."

He smelled sandalwood.

Meeka twitched. "Oh. I'm glad you're here." Her voice dropped through the registers, ending low and rough. "He tried to rape me. Then he carried me out here, but I got away from him."

Caul's face scrunched in thought. "Are you all right?" He went to her side, leaving Doug to stumble on his own. "Did he hurt you?"

"No, but I'm happy to see you." She held out her arms to him. In spite of his misgivings, excitement welled in his chest.

"Caul! Watch out!" Doug yelled.

Jealous? In the half-light, Caul gazed at Meeka. *Thirty-four years since I last held you—really held you.* He stepped into her embrace. *The worm turns.*

She drew her arms around him and clutched him close to her. He felt pressure against his waist. She made a sound of frustration and pulled away before forcing herself back against him. Again, he felt the pressure, and again the sound of frustration. She pulled away a second time.

"Stay away from her belly."

Doug's odd comment made Caul look down. A stinger extended from Meeka's abdomen. "What on earth?" He leaned down for a closer look just as she lunged forward. She missed him.

"Come here, you meddlesome runt." Her voice rasped in his ears as she grappled him closer.

There was a sickening thud, and she was torn from Caul's grasp.

In the dancing shadows made by the flashlight, Doug stood before him, holding a large rock.

"Let's go!" Doug said.

Caul gazed down at Meeka, crumpled on the forest floor. "Why...?"

"She just tried to kill you, that's why."

Heat flowed into Caul's chest. The word kill sank into his mind, but he stared only at the rock clutched in Doug's white-knuckled hand. "You murderer!" Caul started to step around her, but stopped when she stirred. "Meeka! Say something."

Doug moved closer, but Caul drew a gun from his pocket. "Back up! I should shoot you right now."

"She's trying to kill you." Doug dropped the rock and stepped back.

Caul looked down at Meeka, at the blue blood that dripped from her hair. He shook his head. *Blue blood? No! Not you, too.*

"Hey!" Doug knelt and looked at Meeka's head. "Shine that on her face. Here. What the heck? The cut on her face is gone. That's freaking impossible."

And she looks older. As Caul watched, the stinger retracted into her abdomen. *But why? Why you?*

Meeka stirred, her eyes opening to slits. Doug straightened up, backing away. Her gaze followed him. "I'm going to have a hard time forgiving you for that, lover." Her voice growled like millstones. She glanced at Caul. "Get that stupid light out of my face." She opened her eyes fully and extended her fingers tentatively into her wet hair. "That really hurts."

"Just lie still." Caul leaned down, raising his palm to her. "I'll get you to the hospital as quickly as I can."

"Aren't you sweet." She grimaced. "I should have eaten you years ago."

Caul frowned as she sat up. "Be careful. You have a head injury."

She punched him in the groin.

The world collapsed as Caul felt his testicles explode with pain—a hint of fume—burning metal—high in his sinuses—his hand rising—too late—to his flaring orchids—teeth jarring, as knees hit the ground.

Meeka vaulted to her feet, spinning around to menace Doug. "Why'd you hit me?"

He thrust out his hands in a placating gesture, and she grabbed his wrists—her grasp impressively strong—and wrenched his arms around. She whipped forward, her face inches from his, her voice a hiss in the gloom. "Stupid Sandow. Just so you know, lover, you don't need these—" she twisted his arms tighter "—for what I seek from you."

"Ow! Let go!" The torsion on his limbs burned from wrist to shoulder.

"Why should I? I offered you the world, and you hit me in the head—twice! I'll get what I need from you, regardless." Her face, once beautiful, now bore a hard, maniacal edge. "There's nothing you can do to stop that."

"Let him go." A strained voice rose from the forest floor.

"Or what?"

The sound of the revolver being cocked was loud in the night.

"You wouldn't."

"Let him go," Caul said again.

From up the island came voices. Doug shouted to them. Meeka peered into his eyes and licked her teeth. "You should have said yes," She whispered. Her lips touched his, and then she was gone.

Sergeant Troxell and Officer Bass escorted them back to the tiny police station on Firefly Lane, while the other Bar Harbor officer took Rolly's boat back to the dock. Several Hancock County deputies and a lone Gouldsboro officer continued the search on the island.

Troxell had not been amused by Caul's end run with the boat, and he sat in quiet judgment as Doug and Caul gave their accounts of what had occurred. Caul was unrepentant, but grudgingly acknowledged that Meeka was the person responsible for Jillian's poisoning, not Doug.

"Not surprising...women." Troxell scowled at Doug. "All right, don't leave town. I'll station a man outside your hotel, and I've already got one at the hospital. We've put out an APB on Miss Saury. We'll catch her soon enough."

Bass walked them out of the station and loaded them into his cruiser for the short trip back to the Pequot.

"Miss Saury? Did he mean Meeka?" Doug asked.

"Yes." Caul frowned. "You never knew her last name?" He turned away. "You're such a knave."

Doug was embarrassed to admit that he had not. He thought of how many times they had been intimate, and not once did he think to ask her about a surname. He just let her take him, over and over again. He felt like a man-whore.

They arrived, and Charles met them at the door. "I'm terribly sorry about what Meeka's done," Charles said to Doug. "If there is anything we can do to make this up to you, please don't hesitate to ask!"

"It's not your fault," Doug said. "I just want to sleep."

"I'd like to offer you a different room—"

"Have you cleaned his already?" Caul asked.

"Uh, no…" Charles said, feeling guilty that it had not even occurred to him. He had been preoccupied by fixing the door and casing, while Susan had been busy placating the other guests. "We'll go do that immediately."

"No!" Caul charged up the stairs.

Doug shrugged. "It's fine. We'll worry about it tomorrow."

He followed Caul up the stairs. The scientist was jittery. "Why do you want in my room?"

Caul looked uncomfortable. "I want to search for biological samples from Meeka."

"Whatever. You have five minutes." Doug rubbed his face, reviewing the events of the last few hours. "Hey, um, what is Meeka?"

"What do you mean?"

"Is she a sealwoman, like you guys talked about? I mean…a seal! Or a vampire? I mean, blue blood? What the heck! That is…what just happened?"

"No, I don't really think that. Jillian started talking about sirens, so I told her stories about selkies and havsrå. I study folk tales for enjoyment, but I don't believe them. I was mainly trying to keep her talking…to get information about you." He sucked air through his teeth. "You're very disruptive of my routines."

Doug exhaled the breath he had not realized he had been holding. "Great. So she's not a seal, just a normal woman. I haven't been… getting busy with a seal? That'd be weird."

Caul suppressed his anger at Doug. "No, but I'd hardly call her a normal woman."

Doug nodded slowly. "Yeah…maybe a vampire?"

"What?"

"Um, I've kind of wondered if she was a vampire. I mean, she doesn't age, she can move faster than my car, or she can be in two places at once, or she can hypnotize people. Dang, maybe that's what she was doing to me?"

Under other circumstances, Doug would have been the recipient of Caul's scorn, but this evening had hurt him too much. He wanted to gather his evidence and go. "There's no such thing as vampires."

"Yeah…I'm so swayed by your argument."

While Doug inspected the ghetto fix to the door and jamb, Caul scoured the room, locating several black hairs that were obviously not from the fair-haired Sandows. He put them into a small plastic bag.

"That enough?" Doug asked.

"That's what I have to work with, unless you have a blood sample lying around."

Doug snatched up the telephone, and presented the crusting, blue stain to Caul. "Voilà!"

"That's her blood?" Caul shook his head, recalling the bluish fluid that had dripped from Meeka's scalp injury.

"Yes. That should've been a wound across her cheek."

Caul stiffened, glaring at Doug. "You hit her with a phone, too?"

Doug nodded. Hitting her had been a reflexive reaction.

"Does that make you feel like a man?"

"What?"

"Do you make a habit of hitting women?"

Doug's face bore a bitter expression. He was sick of people challenging his masculinity, but the act of hitting a woman had felt like a sissy thing to have done. "No. I've never hit a woman before. Only the one who was trying to spear me...or you, I guess. Maybe next time, I'll let her stab you."

Caul exhaled sharply, considered recent events, and surrendered his anger. "No, I appreciate what you did."

Doug nodded. "How did you avoid getting stabbed, anyway?"

"I'm Ironman?" Caul looked down at himself and discovered two punctures in his belt. "Saved by the bell—t. Looks like being short has some advantages after all."

"You suck at comedy."

"Thanks."

"Yeah, well, the next time I tell you to back away..."

The two men exchanged a glance of grudging respect.

"I'll listen."

After Caul left, Doug locked the door, including the night bolt. He double checked the windows, pulled the drapes closed, and searched the entire room. Finally, he lay on the bed and wondered if Jillian would ever forgive him.

After half a night of chaotic dreams, Doug woke to a clicking sound and a strange smell, like burning sugar. He blinked several times. *Meeka!* His gaze swept the room.

"Hello?"

He heard scratching from the bathroom.

"Hello?"

A yelp of surprise escaped his mouth as he shifted on the bed and pain shot through the leg that Meeka had stung earlier. *As if wrestling with the net wasn't bad enough. I haven't hurt this much in years.* He pulled himself up and sat as still as possible, meditating on the pain.

The scratching noise in the bathroom resumed.

"Meeka?"

A clattering sound, like a plastic toy dropped on a sidewalk, was the sole reply.

Getting out of bed induced a whole body flinch. The sound again, and more scratching. He turned the switch on the bedside lamp. Nothing happened. He reached for his phone, but it was dead. *Damn, I forgot to charge it.* The bathroom window rasped in its frame, and he jerked his head up. *I locked that window!*

His heart thundered.

"Meeka! I know you're here. Look, this doesn't have to end badly, okay? Just give yourself up."

More scratching. *What is she doing in there?*

He rose and his feet slid reluctantly over the smooth wood. Sounds came to him now, in the room, all around—clicking, shuffling. He scanned the floor, but the dark boards revealed next to nothing— only vague impressions of variation. A thin band of pale gray light marked where the bathroom door stood, mostly closed. It felt cool under his palm as he pushed against it, the hinges squealing faintly. Scratching again, louder now, rose from the floor—the floor that moved.

Doug sprang back, falling against the bed. The white tile of the bathroom had changed into a shifting mosaic of black and gray.

Click. Shuffle. Scratch.

The floor flowed—a demonic fog pouring into the bedroom.

He pulled his legs up onto the bed and reached for the bedside phone. The clicking around the bed grew louder. Lifting the handset, he heard nothing. He felt the back of the phone and pulled the cord. It ended after a few feet, crudely cut through.

Great!

He surveyed the room again. An anemic shaft of moonlight fell across the floor. Small shards of black fog moved therein. Getting to the door or phone on the desk was out of the question. The fog crept over the end of the bed, a dark stain flowing across the white quilt. Swinging the handset, he knocked a swath of fog clear, and again heard the sound of plastic toys falling.

Crabs! It's not fog, it's Saunder's Crabs!

Snapping the quilt, he made a rain shower of crabs across the room, but still they came. He reached behind himself for a pillow.

"Ouch!"

A smudge of black stood out against the pale skin of his hand. The smudge stung him again. He flung out his arm, launching the crab across the room. It hit the far wall with a satisfying crunch. He twisted in the bed. The pillows were black.

He opened his mouth to yell, just as the fog of crabs flowed over him, stinging with abandon. The yell tapered off to a squeak, and he fell over backwards. The bed under him felt alive with crabs. He tried to roll off them, but his body no longer heard his brain.

The reek of rotting eggs assaulted his sinuses.

Light from the bathroom stabbed his eyes.

A shadow fell across him. His heart felt leaden, threatening to stop. A head blocked his view of the ceiling, but his eyes refused to focus on it.

"Hello, lover."

"Eeka?" His voice was a sigh.

"In a manner of speaking."

19

Caul had data—interesting data. And the person he, oddly, most wanted to share it with was not answering the phone. He had stayed up all night amplifying the DNA from the samples, before running it on the strand sequencers. The results, clutched in a manila folder, were still making him breathe funny.

"Chuck! Hey, I need to ask a favor."

The physician glanced up from the chart in his lap. "You look like crap, man."

"It's been a busy twenty-six hours."

"Sleep is important, even at your age."

Caul chuckled. "Your envy is noted." He lowered his voice and leaned across the counter at the nurse's station. "I need to speak to the Sandows...alone."

Chuck frowned. "Mister Sandow isn't here. Hasn't been here at all today, actually. Not surprising after yesterday."

Caul's eyebrows leapt up. "Oh?"

"Not really your concern."

"Don't be like that."

"You can ask them. If they want to share..." He shrugged.

"Okay." Caul tapped the manila folder on the counter, and then strode away to the ICU entrance.

"Hey. *Hey*! Not now. It's not visiting hours."

Caul ignored him and pushed through the double doors. One thing he had learned long ago was that ninety percent of getting something done was to just do it. Another thing that he had learned long ago was that if you looked like you knew what you were doing, most people assumed that you did and left you alone to do it. He marched through the ICU and went straight to Jillian's room. Her police guard was absent. "Must be in the restroom." He pushed through the curtain at the doorway. "Jillian?"

Her glare inspired his first feelings of hesitation.

"What do you want?"

"Hey! You look better. The swelling's gone down considerably."

"What do you want?"

"Well, the cheery approach didn't work." He smiled. She did not. "All right...I have some results I wanted to show to you and Doug."

She turned away. "Doug's not here."

Caul stepped farther into the room. "What happened yesterday?"

"Go away."

"Jillian...what happened?"

"None of your business!"

"Is it something to do with Doug? He's not answering his—"

Her head snapped around. "What do you *want*?"

He held up the folder like a shield. "I have sequencing results from Meeka. Her blood sample."

Jillian squeezed her eyes shut. "I don't even know what you're talking about, and I don't care. Go away."

"But I now know Meeka's genome, her entire genetic makeup. It's like having her blueprints, okay?"

"I don't care. I hate her!" Quieter. "She ruined my life."

So you know. He swallowed and chose his next words with care. "I know what happened...between Meeka and Doug." Jillian's gaze bored into him. "It may not have been entirely his fault. He may not have had a choice."

"Don't." She pulled at her restraints, hyperventilating. "Don't you dare! He hurt me...*he hurt me*! He lied to me, and cheated on me. He screwed that whore!"

"Jillian—"

"I hope she rots in jail!"

Caul's thoughts derailed. "What?"

"I hate her."

"Jillian, what happened? What did you say about jail?"

Her head fell back on the pillow. "They caught her. Does Maine have the death penalty?"

"When? How?"

"This morning." Chuck stepped into the room, sliding the glass door and the curtain closed behind him. "I told you it wasn't visiting time, Caul. You're upsetting my nurses."

"What happened with Meeka?"

Chuck shrugged. "The officer said they'd apprehended her early this morning, then he left." He turned to Jillian. "How are you, Missus Sandow? I'm sorry for the disturbance."

She shrugged, turning her head away.

Seizing Caul's upper arm, Chuck pulled him toward the door. "What was so important?" He whispered.

"Wait!"

Both men turned to find Jillian staring at them.

"Tell me." She swallowed. "Tell me she poisoned him, or cast a spell on him, or gave him a love potion. Tell me he's still my husband. Tell me he still loves me."

Caul pulled against the hand on his arm. "May I?"

Chuck relented. "Yes, all right. But quickly! I need to get back to rounds."

"Sure. You're welcome to leave." Caul pulled a chair to Jillian's bedside. "I'm sorry about what happened."

Susan's words flashed in Jillian's mind and her breath caught. "I probably shouldn't be so harsh with you. Susan told me about your feelings for Meeka."

He looked away, blinking. "I guess I haven't hidden that very well." He laughed without humor. "It's not important anymore. It never was. Love by proxy is a terribly unfulfilling prospect."

"Sorry?"

"Never mind. Here..." He opened the folder and held up two sheets. "What do you know of genetics?"

"Nothing. Why does that matter? Tell me why Doug didn't have a choice. What did she do to him?"

"Well, look here." He pointed to one of the sheets. "Do you see this region...the colors? They don't correspond. Do you see it?"

Jillian glanced at the papers. "What am I looking at?"

"Meeka's genetic analysis."

She looked back to him. "Great. Why didn't he have a choice?"

"I'm getting to that." He pulled out more papers. "Look, see this here? These regions and those, they're clearly not primate—"

"Which means?"

"Meeka isn't entirely human."

Jillian's eyes narrowed. "So, she's what, a selkie?"

"What's a selkie?" Chuck asked. "And how could she not be human? I've seen her. She looks pretty human to me."

"She isn't entirely human." Caul's smile was eager, but the others remained silent. "As far as her genetic identity with you or me, Meeka shares 99 percent of her genome with us."

"Okay..."

Caul raised his eyebrows. "And you and I are 99.98 percent identical."

"So what?"

"So? Chimpanzes—our closest living relatives—are only 98.5 percent identical to us."

Chuck nodded. "So you're saying Meeka's a chimpanzee?"

"Ah, no. Seriously? Don't be ignorant. Meeka isn't a chimpanzee, but she's almost as different from us as a chimpanzee. Humans can't breed with chimpanzees...neither do I think a human could breed with Meeka. She has lobster blood, after all."

Chuck scowled at Caul's insult, then shook his head. "What?"

"It's true. It's blue when it oxidizes. I saw it, and I can tell you, it isn't compatible. A human male could mate with her, but the union would never generate a viable offspring."

Jillian sat up, as much as her restraints allowed, her face red. "TMI, Caul! That's not helping! How did he not have a choice?" She shifted her attention to Chuck. "And when do I get these stupid restraints off?"

"As soon as you aren't going to pull out your IV."

"That was an accident." She shifted her glare to Caul. "Well?"

"Yes, I'm getting there."

"Very slowly."

Caul sorted through more papers, though he hardly needed them. "All right, here, she has genes from completely other groups of animals, such as lobster, herring—"

Chuck scoffed. "What? Lobsters and herring?"

"American lobster and alewife, to be specific. Common enough off the coast of Maine."

Jillian's eyes narrowed. "Alewife? She called herself an alewife—"

"That's where the name for the fish came from," Chuck said.

"But Meeka really is a fish? In reality, not just name?"

Caul's expression was triumphant. "Yes, in part, at least. Her genome doesn't lie."

She fell back against the bed, closing her eyes. "Oh, wow. So, she could be a selkie-like thing...I mean, that's crazy. People can't really be part fish or seal, can they?"

"Under normal circumstances, I'd say no, it's just folklore, but these data don't lie—"

"Wow. It was one thing to talk about them as an abstract, but...wow." Tears leaked through her lids.

Chuck chuckled. "It is still pretty far-fetched." He paused. "No, you know what? Really, that's just stupid, Caul, even for you."

"Do you mind?" Caul glared at the physician. "I never asked for your uninformed opinion. I know that this is hard to believe, but the facts simply cannot be refuted."

Jillian's nostrils flared. "Great, but that still doesn't explain how Doug had no choice."

"Yes, yes, getting to that. Look, these sections here, here, and here. These all code for proteins that aren't human, they're toxins. These sections here, here, here, and probably here and here...these code for enzymes critical in the production of chemicals and odorants. Pheromones and other things I'm not even sure of yet." He paused. "Meeka is, quite literally, a walking chemical factory."

Jillian's expression was blank. "So?"

"Pheromones! She may be making herself irresistible to men by the way she smells. She certainly smells good to me."

"Are men really that shallow?"

Caul's thoughts were derailed by her comment. "This has nothing to do with our character. It's biology, pure and simple. If all the other factors of attraction are there, the right odor can push us over the brink."

Her anger mounted at the thought of the other factors of attraction. Somehow, Meeka was to blame for everything. Jillian wanted to hold onto her anger, focus it, and use it as a weapon, but thinking of Doug made her tear up. Caul's explanation did not do much to absolve Doug's actual sin, but she grasped at the explanation that he was not at fault. That left only Meeka to deal with. "So, how is she doing it? How could she be part fish, and not entirely human? How could she have all that other DNA?"

"I have a theory about that—"

Chuck tapped Caul's shoulder. "But you need to stop talking now. It's time to go." Outside the room, he caught one of the nurses. "Give Missus Sandow her PRN diazepam." He turned to Caul, leaning in, his finger raised and face flushing. "You are forbidden from entering this hospital without my permission."

"Oh, get off your horse."

"I'm serious, Caul. You're riding roughshod over our policies. Call ahead next time. Just because we're poker buddies doesn't mean you get special privileges here."

Caul wasted no time in returning to his car. The drive over to the small, brick police station only served to sharpen his sense of righteous pique. He found Jamie McAllister working the front desk, which he rapped his knuckles on.

"Oh, hey, doc!"

"Hello, Jamie. I understand that you apprehended Meeka Saury last night, yes?"

"If you wanna call it that. Apparently, she walked right in front of John's Charger and literally froze like a deer in the headlights. Just between you and me? Seems like she's as numb as a hake! Real pretty, though."

Caul heard rushing in his ears. *Blood pressure.* "That's no way to talk about your...guest."

Jamie twitched, and then looked around. "Probably not." He leaned across the desk. "Thanks for not saying anything, okay?"

"We'll call it even if I can speak with Miss Saury."

"Oh, man! You just missed her. Andrew's taking her over ta Ellsworth...'bout fifteen minutes ago."

"Why?"

"County lock up, doc. We ain't got room ta house her here. Besides... attempted murder! The DA wants her in the county facility, so he can keep an eye on her."

"Ellsworth..."

"Ayuh."

"What are visiting hours today?"

Jamie laughed. "Ain't any way you're gonna get in ta see her today. They'll have to book her in and figure out her housing. Maybe tomorrow? Maybe never, since you're not family or her lawyer."

"Fine. Great. Thanks." Caul's day was going from bad to worse.

He was turning to leave when the radio crackled to life. "One Tango Niner requesting immediate back up. Route Three at Thompson Island. Escaped—no, no! Get off that rail—"

Jamie sat up. "One Tango Niner is Andrew's car!"

He turned, but Caul was gone.

20

Officer Andrew Wiggen had an eye for the road and an eye for the pretty, young woman in the backseat of his cruiser. He had seen her around town for years, so he was surprised as anyone that the chief had put out an APB for her arrest last night. She was charged with attempted murder and felony assault, but she had been perfectly docile as he had processed her for transport to Ellsworth. At the moment, though, she was pale and clammy, and breathing through her mouth.

"Are you all right?"

She opened her eyes briefly. "I'm fine." She put her head back on the seat. "Can you open the windows, please?"

"I've got the AC on."

"I'd like some fresh air, please."

He cracked the windows, just as she started panting. He kept an eye out for places to pull off—he knew the signs of motion sickness. The cruiser had just been assigned to him and it was nearly pristine. If she vomited, it would be a nasty clean up and it would take weeks to get the stench out of the carpet.

Another mile passed.

She moaned.

"Miss?"

"Oh! I'm gonna be sick!"

"Aw, hell! Right on the causeway." With no shoulder to pull onto, he just hit the lights and pulled the cruiser over at an angle, putting the corner of the bumper snug to the guardrail. "Out the left side," he said over his shoulder. He jumped out and opened the back door just as she flopped over and vomited on the road and his feet.

"Aw, no!" He skipped backwards and stamped his shoes, examining the sludge that now covered the freshly polished leather. He caught a blur of motion in the corner of his eye. He looked up. She was not in the cruiser. He spun and saw her running toward Trenton, hugging the right-hand railing.

Pursuit was an automatic response—he was watching his job run away, after all. She was farther ahead than seemed reasonable, so he put on a burst of speed and tilted his head to the mike on his shoulder.

"One Tango Niner requesting immediate back up. Route Three at Thompson Island. Escaped—no, no!"

She vaulted up to the top of the bridge railing, her cuffed hands useless in helping her balance.

"Get off that rail! Miss Saury, get off that rail!"

Like a toy spinning top losing momentum, she teetered for a moment before plunging over the edge.

"No!"

The M3 growled to a halt at the southern approach to the bridge on Route Three. Caul had made the trip in just over ten minutes. Lucky for him the police were busy looking for Meeka, not speeders. He could see the strobing blue lights ahead, but they looked agonizingly distant. A long line of unmoving vehicles stood between him and the place he wanted to be.

Why am I here? To witness Meeka's suicide location? This is stupid, I should go home and go to bed. He had already told his lab managers not to expect him to return today. Ahead of him, a car waited to turn left out of the picnic area across from the welcome center. Caul had a crazy idea and turned in. He parked facing the Narrows and retrieved his binoculars from the glove compartment. A broad sweep of lawn led him down to the muddy, rock-strewn tidal flats. Turing the binoculars northward, he surveyed the short bridge that spanned the navigation channel and found it swarming with officers—Trenton, Bar Harbor, Hancock County, and Maine State police stood talking and occasionally gesturing at the water. *She jumped.*

The drop from the bridge was not far. *Survivable.* He scanned the shoreline, not finding anyone visible who resembled her. *She may have swum west, but there'll be no finding her if that's the case.* He switched to scanning the water, working systematically away from the bridge in arcs. A Coast Guard rescue boat passed through his search pattern, but Meeka was not onboard, so he kept sweeping. He was rewarded two minutes later by the sight of a dark head intermittently popping up from the water near the north end of Thomas Island. With his phone, he repurposed the closest drone to an intercept course, sent an e-mail to the observer at Smithson, and sat on the warm grass to wait.

If it is her, what then? He rubbed his face. Up until a few days ago, he had been satisfied to eat at the Pequot Hotel, and the other restaurants Meeka worked at, for the opportunity to see and speak with her. Then Doug had returned to town—the prodigal bad penny—and thrown everything into disarray. *And shattered my bubble.* Doug's presence had raised the specter that Meeka was a legacy creation, as Caul had long feared but refused to believe. *How can you be related to the chotah?* He felt the toxic possibility invade the fantasy world in his mind. *Seventeen years I've watched you, Meeka Saury, and dreamed... but now I have to wake up.* The words he had spoken to Jillian at the hospital rang in his head: 'Love by proxy is a terribly unfulfilling prospect.' He stood up and flattened the grass with his passing. *You're not Evelyn.*

The M3 fired up with a muted, tinny roar. He imagined the car was anxious. *Spleeny. I certainly am. If Meeka's in the bay, then it's time I finally pay a visit to mommy.* As miles rolled beneath the car's wheels, he tried to talk himself out of actually carrying through on a plan that had rattled in his head for years.

The Pequot was quiet as he pulled into the lot. He noted that the Sandows' Subaru was still there, so he parked the M3 alongside it. *Best to park here and walk, then come back and talk to Doug.* Fifteen minutes saw him to Meeka's dilapidated carriage house—the same one he watched more often than he liked to admit. The overgrown lawn and hedges provided a wealth of privacy as he skirted the Olds in the dooryard and banged on the weathered entrance to the house.

"Meeka's mom. Open up, Meeka's mom." *I've checked every public database I can think of and you don't exist.* He waited a minute—long enough for someone to respond—before sweet talking the locks with an L rake pick. The door opened with a faint squeal, as a gush of stale air—carrying an odd scent—flowed past him. Decades of working around chemicals made him cautious, so he stuck his head over the threshold and gave the room a small sniff. The air was old, but breathable. He shook his head and entered the house. The front room was spartan, as he knew it would be, having peered through the windows long before Doug and Jillian thought to have a crack. Caul's first thought, upon seeing it years ago, was that it was a stage, dressed with just enough things to allay the suspicions of the inobservant or simple minded. *Like Doug.* He smiled a bitter smile—wormwood smiles, his grandmother had called them.

Nothing but bare walls and bare floor, save the chair, table, and lamp. *Who doesn't have something to read?* The lamp was plugged into a timer under the window apron. A clear bicycle reflector was screwed at a perpendicular angle to the wall next to the timer. *What's this for?* He scratched his jaw before turning and shutting the front door. A small plastic box with two lenses was attached to the wall behind the door. *Burglar alarm...but I don't hear anything.* He knelt down and inspected the wires attached to the device. One led to a power pack in a nearby outlet, while the other led through a hole in the floor boards. He was standing when he caught a whiff of the odd scent again. *What is that smell? Hydrogen sulfide...is there a gas leak? There can't be, the house doesn't have gas service. Rotten eggs?*

He inspected the chair, lamp, and table, finding only a fine settling of dust. Satisfied that the front room held nothing of interest, he went to the inner door. He tried the knob. *Locked. Great...and it needs a skeleton key. Just my luck.* He had other picks, but mortise locks were a different breed to pick open. He knelt down to peek through the hole, but it was dark.

He leaned closer and had impressions—*shiny, black...Pain!*

"Sweet mother of Peter!" He jerked away from the door.

Something dark and stringy snaked from the side of his face to the key hole. His right eye watered in sympathy, and the side of his head felt afire. He clutched at the thing and pulled it from his skin. It parted with a tactile ripping, which brought a scream tumbling from his lips. He flung the thing away, and his butt thudded to the floor. Warm blood flowed into his ear, as his head vibrated in agony. The stringy thing pulled back through the key hole, a bit of his flesh clinging wet and red to its barbed end. It passed through the hole with a *shlup*.

Then, with the loudest click he had ever heard, the door unlocked.

The nurse was cheery. *Too cheery.* As she headed for the IV pump, Jillian sat up. "What is that?"

"Hmm?"

"What's in that syringe?"

"Just something to help you relax."

"No."

The nurse smiled.

"No!" Jillian said, repeating her protest.

"It'll only take a minute."

"I am specifically refusing that drug."

"Doctor's orders, Missus Sandow."

"Is that what you'll tell my lawyer?"

The nurse's head tilted back, as if she smelled something objectionable. "Very well, patient refused medication."

She slipped the syringe into a pocket and turned to leave.

"And I want these restraints off. Now."

"Those are also by doctor's orders."

"Then perhaps you should run along and *fetch* him."

Scowling now, the nurse turned and left, thudding the glass door into its frame as she did. She found Doctor Kegall charting.

"Missus Satan would like a word with you."

Chuck frowned and peered over the edge of the chart. "Kathy, that's unprofessional."

"Sorry, doctor. Missus Sandow would like to speak to you. She refused her diazepam and she wants her restraints off."

"Yes, fine. I'll go talk to her in a minute. You can remove the restraints."

Kathy's scowl deepened to a snarl. She hated to lose face with her patients, so she took her time getting back to her. A quarter hour had passed before she breezed back into Jillian's room.

"Where's the doctor?"

"He's busy. We're all busy. He'll be here as soon as he's able." Kathy removed one of the wrist restraints. "Oh, and he ordered these off. You'll be happy, I'm sure."

"You need to take the IV out, too."

Kathy hesitated with the final restraint. "Why?"

"Because I'm leaving."

"You can't. Your doctor—"

"AMA. My brother's a nurse. I've heard all of his boring stories at every family gathering since 2003. I know all about leaving against medical advice."

Kathy finished. "Your insurance won't pay the bill if you leave AMA."

"That's not true and you know it." *I lie professionally, as Doug would say. I know my stuff.* "Your marketing strategies won't work on me. I do it for a living."

"Fine." Kathy's expression belied her tone. "I'll notify Doctor Kegall. We won't be responsible if you have a relapse."

"Oh, I don't intend on letting that fishy bitch get anywhere near me, ever again."

21

The door opened. On squealing hinges, it swung inward. The room beyond was enveloped in darkness. Caul's heart was trying to break a rib. "Hello?"

The room remained silent.

"Biological harpoon. Nice trick. Cone snail?" His voice was thin and warbled, and his face throbbed.

"Why did you come here, Saunders?" The whisper floated to his ears like gravel in a chute.

He swallowed dust. "How do you know my name?"

Motes and his question floated in the solitary sunbeam drifting through the window. "Okay, not important. I wanted to meet you, Meeka's Mom. Frankly, I didn't really think you existed. There's no record of you, and considering there's no real record of Meeka, let's just say that curiosity got the better of me."

"Curiosity? Why would anyone want such a thing?" The voice rasped.

How old is she? He turned his head, and flinched. "Why wouldn't you? Curiosity was my life, exploring the world...until you came along. Until you ruined everything." *Until you took Evelyn.*

"The world is darkness. The world is pain. The world is want and cold and misery. Who are you to condemn me?"

"I'm the man whose future you stole!" His tongue felt clumsy.

Guttural and hollow, a broken bass drum of a laugh made his hair rise. "You have such nerve to talk to me of stolen futures? My life was stolen before it began. And now I sit in the dark and collect knowledge. Yes, curiosity brings knowledge. Knowledge brings pain." The last word was drawn out and screeching, and Caul felt his head resonate as the screech continued. "My life is hell!"

Something hit the floor, making the house shake. He jumped.

"I want you to join me," the gravel said. "Come see my life."

Something moved in the gloom. Something large. Something wet.

"No, thanks." He fingered the gun in his pocket.

"Your behavior belies your words. Always, always, always, you are watching me. At the restaurants. From your stupid flying machines. From your pretty car behind my house."

He twitched. *She knows about the drones? My car?* "Um."

Mirth bubbled wetly. "Did you think I hadn't noticed? Did you think I hadn't seen? The way you fawn over me." Her chuckle sounded like a pot of boiling mud. "Come, Caul Saunders, come here and fawn over me now. I will take you to my bed and satisfy every fantasy you've ever held in you little, runty heart. Come."

What is she talking about? Fawn over her? "I'd rather not."

"It wasn't a request."

A figure moved in the darkness.

"Who are you?" Caul got his legs under himself. The numbness had spread across his face and down his neck. *What happens when it hits something important?* He backed up to the door, even as the figure in the bedroom advanced.

"Why do you run, Saunders?"

A gust of hydrogen sulfide made Caul's eyes sting. "I like to be conscious when I meet new, um, people." He ended with a cough.

"Ever the smartass."

"Beats the alternative."

"True. But you've met me...oh, you've met me."

A figure stepped into the room. It smiled as Caul gasped. He drew the pistol from his pocket and fired.

Doctor Kegall had tried, unsuccessfully, to talk her out of leaving. And when the nurse had told her that she would not be allowed to leave without a ride, Jillian had simply walked away. Walking through Bar Harbor in her pajamas was awkward, but it could not be helped.

Twenty minutes later, she was at the hotel. Charles stepped out of the dining room and did a double take. "Missus Sandow! We weren't expecting you so soon. How are you?"

"Not great, but that place was driving me nuts! Where's Doug?"

"Up in your room...we...is it true, what we've heard about Meeka? Did she really try to hurt you?"

Jillian's face became a landslide of disgust. "I'd rather not talk about it."

"No problem! Sorry if I offended you."

She waved off his apology and started up the stairs. She stopped halfway up and glanced back at him. "This isn't going to cause a problem, is it? With us staying here?"

His expression was blank. "How so?"

"Because Meeka was your coworker."

"No! Absolutely not!"

"Good. Because I didn't ask for any of this. I don't want anyone holding it against me. Or Doug."

"No! Heaven's, no! I'm sincerely sorry that any of this happened. Meeka's behavior was absolutely unacceptable. Please know that we want to make it up to you in any way possible. Don't hesitate to ask."

She nodded and continued up the stairs. She rapped on the door, noting the boot scuffs and cracked frame. *Hmm.* She knocked again.

"Doug? It's me. We need to talk." *Understatement of the century.*

She knocked four more times, before returning to the head of the stairs. Charles looked up from his desk, raising his eyebrows. She cleared her throat. "Will you, um, help me get in the room, please?"

"Of course."

He joined her upstairs and unlocked the door. The night bolt caught. "Mister Sandow? Doug? It's Charles. Your wife is here. Can you open the door?"

He glanced at her. "He's here. Otherwise the night bolt wouldn't be on." He thought about what had happened the night before, but he did not want to kick the door open again. "Um, I may need a ladder. Go in through the window." He had seen one of them open earlier in the day.

She waited in the hall, while her fears that Doug might have done something even stupider than infidelity ratcheted in her chest. Several minutes later, she heard cussing through the door. The bolt slid back, and Charles stood framed in the opening, his expression shifting between shock and outrage.

Her hands went to her lips. *Heaven help me! Please, no, Doug!*

He pushed past her. "It happened again. What a horrid mess." He continued down the hallway.

"W—what happened again?"

"I'll be right back!"

With nervous hesitation, she pushed the door open the rest of the way and stepped into the room. Instead of a suicide, she found an empty bed. Dirty, dried-mud marks covered everything on it and the floor. She was not sure what she was looking at. The phone lay on the bed, the handset off, and the wall cord disconnected. The floor got dirtier the closer she got to the bathroom.

"Doug?"

She pushed the bathroom door open all the way, revealing a gray, muddy floor where once was immaculate white tile. The antique tub was similarly afflicted, being coated with slimy sludge. She looked closer. There were several bare, human hand prints in the sludge, hardly visible, as it seemed that someone had tried to brush them out of existence.

Not someone...something.

She returned to the bedroom and was headed for the door, when she saw the mark on the wall. Two feet below, on the desk, lay a dead crab. *Of course. You're one of those bastards that stung me. You attacked Doug too, didn't you?*

She heard voices in the hall.

Going to the crab, she poked it with a pen from the desk. It did not move. Charles, Susan, and another woman pushed into the room, and the women gasped. "What on earth?"

Charles was talking on a cordless phone. "Yes, I know...what? She escaped? And no one thought to call us? Ayup...see you in a minute." He turned the phone off and glanced at his wife, who seemed to be in shock.

Jillian looked up. "Where's my husband?"

Caul's gaze flicked from the bullet hole in a floorboard to the thing that filled the doorframe. His ears rang from the report. "That is absolutely far enough." The gun shook in his hand.

Walleyes, like pale tea saucers, stared out from an ichthyic face on a bulbous head. Caul laughed nervously, sounding vaguely girlish by the end. It was stunning how closely the statues around town matched the creature that stood before him, rasping in breaths.

"Chotah...a real, living chotah!"

Two more of the monstrosities slipped into the room. They moved quietly, a placid flow of slimy silver scales, clenched fin-hands on muscular arms, and fin-feet that shuffled across the floor. *This has got to be a setup! This can't be real!* He rubbed at his left eye, clutching the gun in his right hand, realizing almost too late that the creatures moving along the walls were heading into flanking positions.

"Whoa!" Caul swiveled, failing to cover the three beasts with one gun. By some unseen signal, the chotah, in unison, bared long, slender teeth. "Ah, nuts!" *It's real.*

The gun barked, and the fishman on the right went down, a spray of gore marking the wall behind. Caul jinked right, and brought the muzzle around to the other two chotah. "Stop! I don't want to hurt you!"

"But they want to hurt you, Saunders." The gravelly voice spoke again, still in the bedroom.

The chotah were not placid now. Their muscular legs barreled them like missiles across the room, seeking him. The revolver barked a second time, the magnum round finding a very temporary home in the second beast's chest. It stumbled, but the third was there, towering over him, tackling him. Limbs flailed, and the gun bucked in his hands before it was knocked away. Silver shimmers and a hundred teeth, like a mouthful of stout sewing needles, filled his vision. Momentum carried them further across the room, crashing them into the rocking chair, which disintegrated with the sound of river ice in the spring.

Caul's head bounced off the bare, wooden floor. There was noise and things were falling. He reached out, blind to the world save the wide mouth that bore down on his face, with its strings of watery slime leading the way for fangs. The stench was intense.

Grasping something, anything, he swung. A satisfying crunch removed the nightmare face from his, while fragments of something rained down. He twisted, feeling the cold, oppressive weight above him shift. He heaved against it, pushing it to the side. Then, he managed a slide, a shimmy, a struggle—anything to get away. Claws raked his chest. A piece of wood came to his hand and he swung again, almost without thought, connecting with a dull smack that vibrated up his arm.

He was on his feet. *Where's my gun?* The dazed chotah was lying on the floor amidst a broken lamp. Caul spied the dull gleam of the revolver over by the wall. He regarded the broken chair leg in his hand before casting it away and vaulting for the gun. With a growl, the fishman rose up and tackled his legs in midair. The world shifted, the floor seeming to become a wall, a wall that grew huge and close, smacking him in the face.

Stars exploded, bells rang, and cold hands clutched. "Augh! Get off me!" He tried to kick the beast, with little success. He turned, looking at the crease where floor met wall. In the dust was something he wanted. Something glowing like a pearl. *Gun.* His fingers were already stretching for it. *Six more inches.* He kicked again, to gain leverage, and clawed the floor with his fingernails just as he felt claws sink into the meaty part of his thigh. Pain speared up his leg as he folded and twisted, seeing the fishman's mouth poised to bite him, and fired a round through the thing's head. Fish gore sprayed the window panes that survived the bullet's passage.

He pulled himself away from the corpse, shaking so much that standing was not an option. He slotted himself into a corner, sucking in shuddering breaths. *Think, think, think!* He rubbed his head. It was coming back to him. *Bullets...yes! Five shots, yes?* He opened the revolver and spun the cylinder, looking for the telltale dimple, a hammer strike on the primer. *Yes, five. Three rounds left.* He had a speedloader in his pocket, but his hands were like leaves in a windstorm. *Not a great time to reload.*

His gaze strayed to the three pale corpses. "Real." He laughed, but it escaped his lips as a giggle. "Chotah are real!" *Real dead.*

"Of course."

His head and hand snapped up. Something stood in the inner doorway. *Not a chotah...* Disgust mingled with fear. "Who—what are you? Heavens, you're ugly!"

The stench of hydrogen sulfide flooded the room, making him blink and cough.

"You talk too much, Saunders." The voice rasped from a wet hole in what passed for a face.

"What are you?"

"You always talk too much." It crept forward, muscular tentacles gripping the worn boards of the floor.

The wall was hard and unyielding against his back. "What are you?" Again, the girlish squeak.

The creature did something with the gash on its face. Perhaps it smiled. "I'm Meeka."

Even as the words filled his ears, he saw it—the shape of the face above the mass of tentacles, the black eyes, and the fringe of dark hair, even long and matted as it was. His heart pounded, but curiosity crowded in with the fear and loathing. "How?"

"Am I not amazing?" Her voice erupted, thick and wet.

"You're disgusting!"

She rankled, rocking on her thick lower limbs as if she wanted to pounce. "You're nothing special, Saunders. Don't look at me like I'm a freak. I'm the first of my kind. I'm the first Meeka! The Eldest."

Caul's eyes narrowed behind his glasses. "First Meeka?" *Meeka's not a name, but a thing?* "I guess you could be related to her. You're damn ugly, though."

She growled and flexed her long, clawed fingers. "Insult me, runt, but in a few minutes you'll be paralyzed and I will feed on you. Slowly. While you watch and suffer." A slimy appendage escaped the gash and licked rudimentary lips. "Humans *are* delicious."

He considered putting a bullet in her head right then. "No, I'm not going to be immobile anytime soon." He fished into a pocket with his left hand and held up a syringe of sulfazine. "I'm running an artificial fever from this chemical. Your marine venoms are getting melted by my hot blood." Sliding his legs under him, he managed to stand.

She did something with her face that made it even uglier. "I have many others—"

"And if you try, I'll punch a hole in you big enough for a pike to swim through." He cocked the hammer on the revolver to emphasize his point. "Now, tell me what you are."

"I will not help you—"

"Call it compensation then! There's a monkey beating a pipe on the side of my head. You owe me, squid witch!" He took a step forward.

"I have Doug. And he is quite...tasty."

Caul froze, his eyes narrowing. "Is he here? Doug!"

She laughed and slithered backwards on her four tentacles. "Why don't you come have a look for yourself?"

"You're bluffing." His mind rebelled at getting closer, but he forced himself to take another step.

"Come. Find out." She slithered back farther, her hand snaking out for the door handle.

"Stop moving!"

The revolver bucked as the reflected light on the door shifted. The slam of the heavy slab echoed the report of the gun. The magnum round had blasted a slanting hole through the wood, and Caul eyed it warily. "Fine, do it your way."

He glanced back at the dead chotah. "Real."

22

Jillian's question hung in the air like an awkward balloon.

"Your guess is as good as any of ours." Charles rubbed his eyes. "Troxell's on his way over. Meeka escaped." The women gasped again. "I told him that Doug has disappeared, like last time."

"What do you mean, disappeared like last time?"

Charles filled her in on recent events. She felt her breaths coming too quickly, so she went to the window for some fresh air. She leaned into the breeze and closed her eyes. "Who's Troxell?"

"Sergeant Troxell. Bar Harbor Police. I think he's going to take you into protective custody." He glanced at Jillian.

"Oh no he's not! I just got out of one lock up. I'm not going into another."

"I heard my name." Sergeant Troxell stepped into the room. "Missus Sandow, I'm surprised to see you up and about."

"I don't like hospitals."

Troxell nodded. "What happened here?" He looked at the dirty smears everywhere.

Jillian turned and sat on the window sill. She put her hands together and tapped her lips with her index fingers. "I'm guessing these crabs came out of the drain—that's where the mud came from—"

"And the slime on the ring," Susan said. "Of course! It was in the drain! It got caught on a crab, which carried it up here. It all makes perfect sense now."

The two women shared a glance. "Or the crab brought the ring here and left it for us to find."

"That seems pretty unlikely." Charles's expression was skeptical.

"Any less likely than a bunch of them coming out and carrying away a grown man?"

Charles colored. "Perhaps not."

"Sergeant, what can we do about finding my husband?"

As she watched, his spine straightened as if someone pulled on an invisible string tied to his head. "Are we sure he's missing? Sounds like there may have been some, hmm, issues?"

"Issues?" Jillian glared at him. "Perhaps you'd like to elaborate?"

"All I'm saying is that there's no evidence of foul play, just a lot of mud. And—"

"What about what happened yesterday? With Meeka?"

"Miss Saury was in our custody all night and most of today. What-ever happened here occurred hours ago. Long before she escaped."

"Okay...so, after all the exceptionally odd things that have occurred in the past two days, you don't consider it strange that my husband isn't here?"

Troxell frowned. "It's not my business, but I did hear what hap-pened between you two at the hospital. Based on that, I have every reason to believe that your husband wrecked this room and high-tailed it back home."

"Do you?"

"Until I have evidence to the contrary, that is what I think, yes."

"Then why are his clothes, wallet, car keys, and car still here?"

Troxell's eyes widened, and then narrowed.

"Uh, huh," Jillian said. "I think it was definitely crabs. Take a look at what's on the desk." She saw motion from the corner of her eye and turned to look. A man was running down West Street.

In the room, feet shuffled and voices exclaimed about the dead crab.

"I'm guessing that Doug fought them off, but there were probably hundreds or even thousands of them in here. Look at all this drain sludge. I think if you look, you'll find more dead crabs in the room."

The man on the street was old, and he clutched the side of his head like he could hear things that he would rather not. He looked straight at the hotel, and sunlight glinted from his glasses. *Caul!* She turned back to the room. "So, sergeant, please consider that my husband was poisoned and kidnapped. And act accordingly." She stepped to the door. "I'll be back."

"Missus Sandow?"

"I'll be right back."

She flew down the stairs, glimpsing Caul through the dining room windows. She charged out the back door and intercepted him in the parking lot. "Caul!"

He looked up, his expression wild and glasses askew. A bloody hand-kerchief hung from his right hand like some small, dead creature.

"Jillian! Why aren't you at the hospital?" He glanced over his shoulder.

"I checked myself out." She crossed the distance between them. "What's the matter? What happened to your head?"

"I—uh—an animal attacked me."

Her fingers pushed the matted hair away from the wound. "That's awful, and you're burning up. You need to get to a doctor!"

"Yeah, I was headed to the hospital. Maybe. So much to do." His brow wrinkled. "Why aren't you there?"

"I said, I checked myself out. I hate hospitals, and I need to find Doug."

His eyes grew round. "Doug? Why? What are you thinking?"

Her concern shifted to annoyance. "That he's my husband. That I love him. That I hate what Doug did, but I'll do anything to get him back where he belongs. I don't know that I can ever forgive him, but I still love him."

His head shook. "I meant is he missing? He's really not here?"

She took a ragged breath. "No! There're crab tracks all over the room. Charles told me that Meeka took him before...is that true? Maybe she took him again. That bitch! I wish I'd killed her the first time I'd laid eyes on her."

"Nuts! That complicates things." Caul had a momentary flashback. *Maybe Meeka's mom wasn't lying about Doug. Did I hit her?* "And, killing is wrong. You shouldn't say things like that."

"Yeah, sorry. I'm feeling kinda reckless at the moment. Do you know where Doug is?"

"Not exactly. Although Meeka's mom claims to have him."

Her head snapped up. "What'd you say?"

Leaning closer, he whispered and pointed to the gash on his face. "This wasn't caused by just any animal. I paid a visit to Meeka's house and met her mother. She—she's hideous!"

"Really?"

He shuddered. "Part human, part squid, part..." He shook his head. "I've honestly no idea. She looks like a madman's plaything, and she stinks like rotten eggs."

"What about Doug?"

"She claimed to have him. I don't know if she was telling the truth or not. I shot at her. I shot the chotah too. They're dead."

Her heart thundered. "Chotah? What? Where?"

"At Meeka's house."

Jillian flushed. "He's there? Are you sure?"

"I don't know. She said she had him, but I never saw him. She closed the door...I don't know."

She gaped. "She's still there with him? Unguarded?"

"Yes. I had no other choice. But I did trap her. The windows are both nailed shut from years ago, and I tied the seatbelt of Meeka's car to the doorknob. Mommy dearest can't get out of the house unless she breaks a window."

"Why are we just standing here? Let's get Troxell and rescue Doug!"

Caul grabbed her shoulders—it was like grabbing the rail of a ship on rough water. "No! I went in there half-cocked, thinking that she didn't exist, and nearly got my butt handed to me in pieces. We need to know more before we do anything. We don't know if Doug is even in there. It might be a trap, for all we know. I need to check my recordings. I need to call the lab. I need to call in reinforcements, before I start calling in favors with the police." He leaned closer. "This is bigger, and much weirder, than I could have imagined even a day ago. Sharon's talked about this, and I've suspected things—there are too many odd legends around here and missing people and peoples' stories. Heavens!" His eyes widened. "The chotah are real. What if it's all true?"

He turned abruptly.

"Come with me. I can use your help in reviewing the drone footage." He started toward his car.

"No."

He turned and peered at her.

"I need to go find Doug."

"You'll find him if you help me with the footage."

"No! No more talking and sciencing. I need to go look! Here. Now!"

A shadow crossed his face. "Do you have your phone?"

She nodded.

"Good. Stay safe. Stay in public areas, but be careful even there. If my suspicions are correct, this is potentially a whole lot bigger than just Meeka." He started to turn away. "And don't go to her house!"

"That would be foolish."

He grimaced. "Yes, it would! Listen," he looked at his watch, "let's meet back here in two hours, all right?"

"Sure."

She stood by as he drove away, and then returned to the hotel. Upstairs, Troxell and Charles were still standing in the room. The manager stepped over to her. "I'm going to put you into a clean room, if that's all right?"

She nodded. "Yes, thank you. I need a shower and some real clothes."

Susan returned with a housekeeping cart. She looked at Troxell. "Mind if I clean up?"

"Not in here." He stuck his thumbs in his belt.

"Why not?"

"In case this becomes a crime scene."

Jillian's eyes crossed at his response. "But, you just said no crime had been committed!"

"Uh, huh."

His mockery was irritating, but she chose not to argue.

"Let me get you to a new room," Charles said to Jillian, before he left.
Jillian glanced at Troxell. "Can I get some clean underwear, at least?"
He nodded. "I'd like to take you to the station."
"No." She pushed clean clothes into her suitcase.
"For your protection...until Miss Saury is apprehended."
"No." Bag in hand, she stared at him. "Instead of worrying about me, please find my husband. What happened at the hospital doesn't matter. Doug would never run out on me. That's not who he is."
His eyes narrowed as he poked at the dead crab.
"Please?"
He nodded again. "All right, Missus Sandow, I'll take your word for it. I'll consider your husband a missing person."

Jillian found the house and the car exactly as Caul had described them. She pushed her still damp hair from her eyes as she evaluated his handiwork. Trying to untie his knot proved futile, but the thick strap parted easily under the blade of Doug's pocket knife. She had grabbed it while packing up her things. She had also looted a shed behind the hotel, taking several things she thought might be useful. One of those things was an old wooden baseball bat. She slipped it out of the duffel bag she had taken from their car, and gripped the taped handle. *Here goes everything.* She pushed the door open.

The front room was empty. She noted the wet smears on the floor and the broken furniture. Looking closer, she saw the bullet holes. Conscious of Caul's warning, she approached the door with care. The knob would not turn. *There are two ways to open a door.*

Hickory met hemlock. Hemlock held its own.

She glared at the door. *I need an axe.* "Okay. There're two ways to go through a wall." She had spent enough time with her contractor dad to know a thing or two about how walls were built. She tapped on it and smiled. *Drywall.* Swinging overhand, she plowed a furrow in the thin gypsum board. She hit again, lengthening the furrow, before stepping to the right and hitting over the next wall cavity. Once she had three furrows, she yanked on the ribbons of wall board between them. She changed her grip on the bat and jabbed at the backside of the board on the other side of the wall. It popped off easily, and she quickly punched a sizable hole into the next room.

"Hey, if you're in there...I will hurt you if you try anything stupid. You got that?"

Silence.

Bat first, she squeezed between two studs. She felt along the wall and flipped the light switch. She stood on a mattress on the floor. A kitchenette and tiny bathroom occupied one end of the room, which was otherwise featureless. *Where is she?*

She checked the shower stall—*empty*—and the window behind heavy blinds and curtains—*still nailed shut.* "Hey, Meeka's mom! Where are you?" Spying the base cabinet in the kitchenette, she pulled open the doors. A few forlorn pots and pans stared back at her. "Seriously, where are you?"

She turned and looked at the rest of the room. Along the other three walls were the mattress and box spring on the floor, a nightstand with a lamp, a spindly chair, and a wardrobe. *Uh, huh.*

Holding the bat ahead of her, she approached the tall cabinet. "I know you're in there. Come on out!" She stepped close enough to tap one of the doors with the bat. "Come out, now!" She hit the cabinet harder. "Now!"

The room was silent. She leaned closer, taking hold of the silver handle, and pulled.

23

Caul sped through town, his throbbing head distracting his thin attention from the road. The weight of his sleepless night was struggling with the war beat of adrenaline in his blood. The work of thirty years was coming to fruition, seemingly all because of Doug Sandow. *This is it!* He dialed the personal number for the director of Smithson Labs, Doctor Tate. She answered on the second ring.

"Sharon! It's Caul. I have confirmation. We need to go to delta status."

"More crabs?"

"No. Substantially more rewarding than my little crabs. I just fought three chotah. They're real."

Across the ether, he heard an indrawn breath. "Not that I doubt you, but you're bringing me evidence?"

"Photographs and a tissue sample. I would've brought the whole fish, but they're heavy."

"Tissue sample? How did you manage that?"

He hesitated. "I had to kill them."

Silence weighed heavily on the line until she cleared her throat. "That's...unfortunate. We finally have survived contact with a capital legacy organism and you destroy it?"

"It was necessary. They were about to kill me. However, where there's smoke..."

She heaved another heavy breath. "Fine, it's fine. I understand. That's great news! Were you able to communicate with them at all?"

"Uh, no. They only wheezed and tried to eat me."

"Lovely." She paused again. "Speaking of communication, when were you going to tell me about Meeka's genome?"

Caul's gut clenched. *Who leaked that information?* "Later. My apologies. I'm running on no sleep."

"So I was told." Again, silence filled the space between them. "Your feelings for her aren't going to affect your actions, are they?"

He tasted bitterness. "You know who my feelings are for. Please don't question my judgment."

"You know I had to ask."

"No, you didn't. Please just put everyone on delta notice. I'll be back in five minutes."

"It's done...and Caul?"

"Yes?"
"Good work."

The wardrobe held only clothes—Jillian wrinkled her nose at their shabbiness as she pushed them aside—and a few personal items, but no squid momma. Disappointed, Jillian opened the drawers on the left side of the cabinet—belts, underwear, socks. She got to the bottom drawer and frowned. It was full of wallets and purses. Her fingers released the bat, and she opened one of the wallets. No money, just a few cards and a driver's license of a bearded man named John Paul Taggart.

She set it aside and opened another: Sarah J. Smith. A third: Roy Raymond Baxter, Junior. A fourth: Evelyn Gilda Gulden. Jillian gasped and dropped the wallet. The image on the license started up at her like an accusation. Despite the longer hair and dated clothing, the woman in the picture was Meeka.

The wallet may as well have been a hot stove, but Jillian finally reached for it. The license was issued by the Commonwealth of Massachusetts, and expired thirty-two years earlier. "How?" She rifled through the rest of the wallet's contents, stopping when she came to a flimsy plastic case that held photographs. The top picture was of Evelyn, in the heights of 1970s fashion, embracing a young man with sandy brown hair and glasses.

"Hello, Caul Saunders."

She pulled out her phone and texted him.

Who's Evelyn?

Closing the wallet, she slipped it into her back pocket. She was reaching for another when her phone rang. "Hello?"

"How on earth do you know about Evelyn?"

"I found her wallet."

"That's impossible. Where?"

"Meeka's house."

A choking sound flooded the phone.

"I told you not to go there. You said you wouldn't."

"No, I said it would be foolish."

"Get out of there!"

"Relax. There's no one here. Who's Evelyn?"

"That creature—Meeka's mother—is there. Did she escape? Jillian, get out! She's dangerous."

"The door was still tied up and the windows nailed shut—only one pane broken out in the front, but the place is empty. She isn't here."

"You still need to get out of there and get somewhere safe! She's the one who abducted Doug. It happened early this morning, shortly after Meeka surrendered to the police. I just watched the recorded feed from the drone that monitored the hotel."

Jillian's heart stirred. "Where did she take him? Was he okay?"

"I don't know. The drone wasn't set to follow anyone, just remain on static duty, parked on the roof of a house across the street. Meeka got arrested, and then her mother showed up, climbed an arbor, and opened the bathroom window. She carried Doug out a few minutes later. He was unconscious."

"Which way did she go?"

"Toward the carriage house."

"So he might be here, somewhere!" She stood up and spun around. And screamed. Meeka was watching her through the hole in the wall.

"What are you doing here?" Meeka asked, scowling. "What have you done to my house?"

"Jillian!" Caul's voice squawked almost painfully through her phone. "What's happening?"

Hyperventilating, Jillian snatched the bat from the floor and thrust it in front of her. "Meeka's here."

"That's impossible. Are you sure it's her? Not her mother?"

"Appears fully human. No rotten egg smell. Why impossible?"

Meeka pushed through the gap, her face red and scowling. "What have you done to my house?"

"Stay back, you bitch. You seduced my husband and tried to kill me. I should kill you—"

"Jillian! Focus."

"Shut up, Caul."

"Listen to me. I'm looking at Meeka on live video feed, swimming in Frenchman Bay toward Bar Harbor."

"Hey! Hang up the phone and talk to me." Meeka's face darkened to purple, and she stomped across the bed and broken gypsum board.

"That's...you're looking at someone else, then, because she's right here in front of me." Jillian poked the bat at her.

"Oh, wow..." Caul said. "That would explain so much. Put Meeka on."

"I'm not giving her my phone."

"Then put your phone on speaker."

Jillian growled at him, but switched the phone over.

"Am I on?" Caul's voice squalled out of the tiny grille.

"Yes."

"Meeka!"

The woman shifted her attention from Jillian to the phone. "What? Did you have something to do with this?"

"With what?"

"Destroying my house," she yelled.

"Yes...a bit, anyway. Please listen! I know about your genetics...I know what you are." He swallowed audibly. "Are there more than one of you?"

Meeka's frown deepened. "How...why would you ask me that?"

"Just answer, please. How many of you are there?"

"I am many."

Laughter made the phone buzz in Jillian's hand. "I knew it! I knew it!"

"What? What does she mean she's many?"

"There's more than one of her. Don't you see? She's made! Think about her genome...it's full of non-human genes. Someone made Meeka...the Meekas."

"She still tried to kill me."

Meeka added a layer of guilt to her angry expression. "You're gonna hold that against me? I'm sorry, but Mother told me to. You still had no right to destroy my hou—"

"You seduced my husband and tried to kill me, you slut. Your stupid, trashy house is crap unimportant compared to my marriage or my life."

"Jillian!" Squawked the phone. She turned it off and stuck it in a pocket.

"Tell me why I shouldn't kick your butt?" Shaking and red-faced, Jillian stepped closer to Meeka.

"Because I'd win."

"The hell!" Jillian whipped the bat around, and Meeka slid down the wall, crying out.

Jillian stuck the bat in her face. "Fourteen years of softball, bitch! I think I can use one of these."

Her phone rang, but she ignored it.

"Why'd you seduce my husband? Why'd you try to kill me?"

Meeka rubbed her scalp. "Why the head? What is it with you two?"

"Tell me!" Jillian yelled.

"It wasn't my choice! Mother made me do it. I mean one of me. I—me—I personally never touched you or your husband. You have to believe me...I—all of us—never wanted to hurt either of you. It was Mother."

"But why? What'd we ever do to your mother?"

"Nothing. But Caul's right, I'm made. All of I are made, even the eldest me." She glared at Jillian. "But Mother wants new children. Better children, she says. And Douglas has the right smell. We need his seed."

Jillian trembled. "It's mine! He's mine! You've no right to take it...or him. Doug's children should only be my children."

Meeka bristled. "That's selfish."

What? "Are you for real?"

"I'm sorry. Mother makes me."

"That's a lousy excuse."

"But I want to be with him. I love him, and I've saved his life...several times. And paid the price. I don't—" She jerked and looked up. "Your life is in danger. You need to leave. Now!"

"Not until you tell me where—"

"You're no good to him dead. Run!"

The mattress and box spring, and Meeka on them, shook and were lifted from the floor by unseen hands. Jillian took off, bounding across the bed and through the hole in the wall. "You're coming with me!"

Eyes round, Meeka looked from Jillian down to the bed and back again. She followed.

"Ninety-three!" A voice grated as the mattress slammed against the wall.

They were almost out the front door when Meeka stumbled. Jillian turned to grab her, and Meeka whimpered and stiffened. *'Mother makes me,'* ran through Jillian's mind. "No!" She pulled Meeka from her crouch and slapped her. "Don't let Mother make you."

Meeka's eyes bugged. "Why'd...?"

"Because, if she's my enemy, then you're going to help me, not her."

Meeka nodded. "If I can."

They ran from the house, slamming the front door behind them.

In a locked and shielded room at Smithson Labs, Caul sat at a bank of flat screen monitors that perched on a long table, watching the live feeds and the digital recordings from the past day and a half. On another wall, a large screen TV displayed a map encompassing most of Mount Desert Island and Frenchman Bay, with tags denoting legacy creature interactions and employees lost in the field. As of five minutes ago, it also displayed Meeka sightings. Several technicians and a guest crowded into the small room with him.

"So I finally get invited to the inner sanctum...your little black box project. Do I get a cigar and a propeller beanie?" Sharon turned a lazy half circle in her chair and regarded Caul. "The board thinks this is a surveying project. Looking for natural resources."

"I heard about your budget cover story. I see you managed to get some elements of the truth in it." He kept his eyes on the screens. "As always, I'm pleased that you deal with the board, rather than I."

"Elements of truth." She snorted. "I've always suspected that this was nothing more than a high tech method for indulging your voyeuristic proclivities." She waved at all the images of Meeka on the screens. "My suspicions, borne out."

Caul struggled to keep the displeasure from his face. *How did everyone know?* "Meeka appears to be pivotal to our understanding of the phenomenon. You know that now, as well as I do."

A feral smile lit her face. "Yes, but I didn't fall in love with a pivot point."

His finger twitched, freezing the feed he was watching. He wished she would not behave like this in front of his subordinates. "I didn't invite you down here to indulge in speculation. Kindly refrain. Every aspect of this project supports the directives of the shadow charter."

She made another rotation in the chair. "I don't doubt that. However, you're simply too raw of a nerve to pass up rubbing. Imagine that...Meeka Saury a capital legacy organism, under our noses all this time." Her hands landed, palms down, on the narrow work surface beside him. "Now, where are those photographs you promised me?"

He pointed to an empty workstation, trying not to glare at her. *Meeka's a human woman, not some freakish sideshow display.* "I put them in your dropbox."

French polished nails clicked on keys. "Hmm. Violent. You did this?"

"Yes."

"I'm surprised at you, Caul. Killing something is a very passionate act. I didn't think you had it in you. What load?"

"Magnum. Jacketed hollow point."

"Impressive cavitation. It's .357?"

"You know what I carry." It had been Sharon's suggestion that he learn how to shoot. After the disappearances of several of their field personnel, everyone on staff had received security training. "Are you feeling all right?"

She froze. "Of course. Why do you ask?"

"You're not normally so...undiplomatic."

No reply was forthcoming. He glanced at her, staring at an image of a dead chotah. "They're soft bodied, it doesn't take much." He turned back to his monitors and allowed the frown to rise to the surface. "I didn't want to kill them. That's not my thing."

"I know." She cleared her throat. "Take a Taser next time. I'd like to have some of these alive. To play with…"

"I've instructed the technicians already. There's a full decon and containment team deploying."

She spun her chair around, and her gaze searched his face.

"Are you up to this?"

The muscles of his jaw tightened. He nodded.

"Good. Looks like they pack a nasty punch." She reached for the bandage on his head, but he flinched away.

"Don't, please. It hurts."

His text message pinged. It was Jillian.

Who's Evelyn?

"Impossible!" Hyperventilating, he dialed her number.

"Hello?" Jillian's voice.

"How on earth do you know about Evelyn?"

"I found her wallet."

"That's impossible. Where?"

"Meeka's house."

Panic choked him. "I told you not to go there. You said you wouldn't."

"No, I said it would be foolish."

"Get out of there!" He stood and glanced at the anxious faces of his coworkers.

"Relax. There's no one here. Who's Evelyn?"

"That creature—Meeka's mother—was there. Did she escape? Jillian, get out! She's dangerous."

"The door was still tied up and the windows nailed shut—only one pane broken out in the front, but the place is empty. She isn't here."

"You still need to get out of there and get somewhere safe. She's the one who abducted Doug. It happened early this morning, shortly after Meeka surrendered to the police. I just watched the recorded feed from the drone that monitored the hotel."

He heard a sharp intake of breath. "Where did she take him? Was he okay?"

"I don't know. The drone wasn't set to follow anyone, just remain on static duty, parked on the roof of a house across the street. Meeka got arrested, and then her mother showed up, climbed an arbor, and opened the bathroom window. She carried Doug out a few minutes later. He was unconscious."

"Which way did she go?"

"Toward the carriage house."

"So he might be here, somewhere!"

A scream pierced his ear. He pushed the phone from his head like it was trying to bite him. He heard faint, garbled speaking.

"Jillian! What's happening?"

"Meeka's here."

Caul flinched and looked up at the bank of monitors. Meeka was clearly swimming on one of the live feeds. The coordinates from the drone indicated that it was still over two thousand meters north of Bar Island. *That's been a heck of a swim.*

"That's impossible. Are you sure it's her...not her mother?" Caul glanced at one of his technicians and covered the microphone hole. "Get the team rolling."

Jillian was talking. "Appears fully human. No rotten egg smell. Why impossible?" A short pause. "Stay back, you bitch! You seduced my husband and tried to kill me. I should kill you—"

"Jillian! Focus."

"Shut up, Caul."

"Listen to me. I'm looking at Meeka on live video feed, swimming in Frenchman Bay toward Bar Harbor."

He heard faint shouting.

"That's..." Jillian said, "you're looking at someone else, then, because she's right here in front of me."

Looking at the monitor, Caul experienced a flash of insight. "Oh, wow...that would explain so much. Put Meeka on."

"I'm not giving her my phone."

"Then put your phone on speaker."

He heard Jillian growl. *You're being too emotional, Jillian.* She was trying his patience. "Am I on?"

"Yes." Jillian sounded like she was talking through a tube filled with ball bearings.

"Meeka!"

"What? Did you have something to do with this?"

Caul's brow wrinkled. "With what?"

"Destroying my house."

He felt a fleeting moment of guilt. "Yes...a bit, anyway. Please listen. I know about your genetics...I know what you are." He swallowed. "Are there more than one of you?"

Silence. "How...why would you ask me that?"

"Just answer, please. How many of you are there?"

"I am many."

Caul laughed and made eye contact with Sharon. "I knew it! I knew it!" She raised her hands, palms up, and scowled.

"What?" Jillian asked. "What does she mean she's many?"

"There's more than one of her. Don't you see? She's made! Think about her genome...it's full of non-human genes. Someone made Meeka...the Meekas."

"She still tried to kill me." Jillian's anger buzzed in his ear, unfiltered by the electronics.

"You're gonna hold that against me?" Meeka's voice. "I'm sorry, but Mother told me to. You still had no right to destroy my hou—"

"You seduced my husband and tried to kill me, you slut! Your stupid, trashy house is crap unimportant compared to my marriage or my life."

That is entirely unimportant at this moment. "Jillian!"

The phone disconnected.

"No! I told her not to go to Meeka's house." He dialed her number.

Sharon frowned. "We should have turned that dump over years ago."

"Legalities."

"Oh, and what you did today wasn't criminal in the extreme? Breaking and entering, destruction of property...murder." She sounded judgmental, but she was smiling.

"It's only murder if they're human. Chotah aren't human."

"Semantics."

He ignored her and pulled up the drone feed from Meeka's house on his bank of monitors. Jillian and Meeka came flying out the front door, slamming it shut behind them. "Put another drone on them. Keep them in sight at all times. Who was watching the house? Jameson? Didn't you see her go in?"

"Sorry, sir...I was distracted."

"Yes." He turned. "Sharon, the tissue sample is in Lab Four. One of us should go check on their progress." *In other words, get out!*

24

Darkness enveloped Doug. He woke with a start, his skin a sheet of smoldering flames. Dank air filled his nostrils, carrying the fetor of mildew and decay. Chill stone bit into his back. He tried to sit, but chains clattered, keeping his arms spread out. He raised his legs and felt the grip of chains around his ankles.

"Hello?" His voice was weak.

Plip.

Cold water dripped on him.

Plip.

He waited.

Plip.

"Meeka, come on."

Plip.

"Please? This isn't funny."

Plip.

"Meeka? I'm in pain.

Plip.

"And I'm hungry."

Plip.

"And I need to pee!"

Plip.

"And that dripping water isn't helping!"

Plip.

25

The women pelted down the long, curving driveway and onto a narrow side street. Jillian pulled up and scanned their surroundings. "Who was that, calling out, in the house? Was she calling to you?" She pulled Meeka toward West Street.

"Eldest, the first Meeka."

Jillian ground her teeth. "So, there really are a lot of you?"

"Yes."

"That's how you were able to be in all those restaurants? How you could be everywhere we were?" Jillian rubbed her neck. "This is freaking crazy. What're you, like triplets, quadruplets?"

"I number one hundred thirty."

Jillian's mouth hung agape. "Shut up!" She finally said. "No woman could give birth that many times."

The sole sound was the chirping song of a sparrow. Meeka turned away. "Mother is exceptional."

"Seriously, how can there be so many of you?"

"Mother made me."

"Oh, that clears up everything. Are you really all Meeka?"

She nodded.

"Don't you have a name for yourself? Like a personal name? You can't run around calling each other Meeka. That'd be confusing."

"No, it's not. I understand."

"Well, I don't."

Meeka pursed her lips. "Sometimes, Eldest Meeka calls me by my birth order."

"Is that why she said ninety-three? Was she calling you?"

Meeka nodded again. "I am the ninety-third Meeka born."

Jillian squeezed her eyes shut. *This is beyond bizarre.* "So help me, if you are lying, I will hurt you." She stood tall and pushed her finger into Meeka's chest. "Do you swear that you never touched my husband?"

Tears flowed onto Meeka's eyelashes. "I wanted to, but I never have. And I had nothing to do with your poisoning. Mother made Seventy do that."

Jillian glared at her. "What do you mean, you wanted to?"

"I—my sister, Thirty-nine, kissed your Douglas twelve years ago, and I knew he was the one." She swiped at her cheeks. "When I—

she—knew, I fell in love with him. It's what I was made to do." She looked at Jillian. "When I fell in love with him, all of I fell in love with him—I older and I yet born. All of I love Douglas."

"No! That's unacceptable."

Meeka flinched away from Jillian's outburst. "I'm sorry." She gazed down the street. "Really, though, did you have to wreck my house? I don't have much, and that was—"

Jillian poked her with the bat. "You tried to kill me."

"No, Mother tried to kill you. I have no control when she's in my head. But you hit me—twice! And so did Doug. You people are violent."

"Because you're—because he's my husband. Not yours." Jillian's hand clenched the bat. "Wait...why would Doug hit you? He's never done anything like that to a woman."

"Mother was trying to get him, to harvest. He hit me with a phone. My sister, anyway."

"Harvest?" Jillian shuddered. "That's disgusting."

"You're any different? I heard you saying you want a baby from him. You harvest his seed also."

"That's different. I love him! He's my husband!"

"I love him too."

Jillian menaced Meeka with the bat. "But you're a freak! You can't even have children."

Meeka flinched. "What?"

"Caul told me. It's impossible for you to have children with a normal human. You're sterile."

"That's not true. Tell me it's not true!"

"You're part fish and part lobster. You've got blue blood. I—well, how should I know? Caul's the scientist."

"Not all...she...she wouldn't lie to us...would she?" Meeka said to herself, and then walked away.

Jillian trotted after. "Hey! Where's my husband?"

Meeka's eyes were glossy with tears. "I don't know. I've been away all day. I need to immerse in me—my sisters, I mean. Then I'll know."

They had arrived at the Pequot Hotel. It looked less inviting to Jillian now. She scowled. *This trip is a horror story.*

"Great. Where do we find your sisters?"

Meeka hooked a thumb over her shoulder. Jillian looked back. "Where?"

"My house. But I doubt that will be a good place to be after today, now that Eldest knows you know about it. The secret is unveiled. The house is no good anymore."

"Okay, some other place? Call them?"

"I have phones, but not I. Besides, Eldest knows I'm with you. I'm compromised."

"So?"

"So you probably shouldn't stay around me."

Jillian's expression soured. "Nice try. You're not leaving my sight until I have Doug back."

"Okay...then we wait. I'll come to me."

They tried to sneak into the hotel, but Susan saw them as they went past the dining room.

"Meeka!" Her fingers smothered her mouth as she joined them in the hallway. "My goodness! Is it true?"

Jillian shushed her. "Is Troxell still here?"

"No, he left, right after you did."

"Good. I guess. Listen, Meeka may not be guilty, I mean not her, anyway. Oh, this is hard to explain." She patted Susan's shoulder. "We're going to go to my room. If you—if you see Meeka, send her up."

Susan's brows drew together. "I don't understand."

"Meeka has identical sisters."

"Really? That's—"

"Kind of! Susan, please...don't ask questions yet, just send her up to my room. And don't tell Troxell that she's here. It's important. Doug's life is at stake." *A little creative fiction, there, hopefully.*

A determined nod from Susan. "Okay."

The video feeds were on side-by-side monitors—Meeka with Jillian running down West Street and Meeka a few hundred meters from Bar Island. Caul pursed his lips. *Always Bar Island...why?*

Meeka was swimming like a dolphin, using her legs and undulating her body to move through the water. Flashes of reflected light on her wrists had clued him in as to why she swam this way. *Handcuffs.* Movement in the water beside her drew his attention. *Seals?* He leaned forward, peering at the screen.

"Are the boats close to her yet?"

"They're in position. Awaiting directions."

"Good, tell Rolly to..." On the monitor, one of the seals frolicking beside Meeka pulled the handcuffs free, while the other looked up at the drone. Its head, instead of being solid gray, had some black patterns, while its face, with a short, pale muzzle, was oddly familiar.

It raised its flippers in the air and turned them over, revealing small hands underneath.

One of the technicians sputtered. "Did that…did that seal just flip us off? How can it have hands?"

Caul goggled at the screen. *Selkies are real!* "Yes, it did." He rubbed his eyes and peered at the screen again. "Send the boats! Tell Rolly to get the seals too." He stood. "Is the decon team at Meeka's house yet?"

"Yes."

The door opened, and the director of Lab Four stepped into the room. Caul turned, surprised. "Aiden?"

"What's the idea, sending Sharon to haunt my techs?"

Caul clapped his fellow scientist on the arm. "A gift! And now, another. You're in charge. I'm going out."

Aiden sputtered as the door closed behind Caul. He made the M3 in record time and took an hour's worth of rubber off the tires just getting out of the parking lot. The drive through town was agonizingly slow. *Tourists!* His hands ached on the steering wheel by the time he reached Meeka's isolated house. The end of the driveway was blocked by a green Ford van, and a young technician in white, polyolefin overalls leaned against its hood. He jumped up as Caul approached.

"Doctor Saunders! I wasn't expecting you."

"Neither was I." He flinched at the pain in his thigh. "But, I can't stand sitting around any longer, watching life happen on a video monitor."

The tech nodded.

"Have you been in the house yet?"

The tech gestured over his shoulder. "They're getting ready to breach the door."

"Breach? Just open it. I picked the locks hours ago."

"It's locked again."

Caul tingled. Jillian and Meeka just left what was supposed to be an empty house. "I'll take care of it." He started around the van, but stopped. "Jonathon, right?"

"Yes, sir." The young tech smiled at the recognition.

"Where's your Taser?"

The smile evaporated. "Um, it's in the van, sir."

"Why?"

"I—I don't like guns."

"Great, great." Caul rubbed his bandaged head. "So if hostile hybrids come for you, you can scream like a little girl and die. How's that sound?"

Jonathon blanched. "I—I'll get my gun, sir."

"That's a good boy." Caul turned and continued to the house.

Another van was backed up beside the Oldsmobile, and three technicians in white overalls and two security officers in dark blue uniforms milled around the yard. One of the security personnel, a redhead whom Caul recognized but could not name, stood near the front window, cradling a large, black shotgun. The other security officer was preparing to hit the door with a burly steel ram.

"Hold on. I can pick the lock. We needn't leave a trail of destruction in our wake."

The man stepped back, allowing Caul access to the door.

"Sir!" The redhead had raised her weapon. "I have movement in the structure. Someone just closed the drapes."

"Steady, there. Who has tranq guns?"

Two of the technicians raised their weapons.

"I want those used as a first option, along with electroshock." He looked at the redhead. "Those are non-lethal rounds, yes?"

"Yes, sir. Rubber pellets."

"Good. They're soft-bodied legacy organisms, and we don't want them killed, just incapacitated. Watch their teeth, though." Holding the pick, he reached for the door knob, but the door opened a crack before he made contact. The car pressed against his back before he realized that he had even moved. Heat flowed to his cheeks.

"Careful." He cleared his throat. "Some of them have a ranged weapon. Only a meter or so, but still don't expose yourselves to it unnecessarily..." His voice trailed off.

The security officer glanced at him. "I suggest a flash-bang, sir."

"What?"

"A flash-bang grenade."

He looked at the officer. "I've, uh, already made a terrible amount of noise in this neighborhood today."

"They're not that noisy at a distance. And I was advised by Director Tate that the BHP have been notified of our activities."

Caul grimaced. *Sharon's calling in favors already.* "Fine. Do what you think is appropriate." He moved away from the house.

The male officer held up three fingers to the redhead. She nodded and took a black object from a pouch at her waist. She raised the object to her face, and then held it up. A silver tassel dangled from her teeth. He dropped his fingers one at a time. As the last finger went down, he kicked the door open and tossed the object inside. The female officer stuffed hers through the broken pane. Both turned away, so Caul decided he should also. After a few seconds, a whump jarred his teeth, and broken glass tinkled to the ground. The officer drew his Taser and looked at the white cloud pouring out of the house. He glanced at the female officer.

"I wanted flash-bang, not smoke." He shook his head and went through the smoky doorway. There was a faint pop, followed by a thud, and a hoarse cry. The female officer ran for the door. "Donny!" Pulling a compact light from her belt, she plunged into the house.

Caul drew his gun and skirted the Olds. One of the technicians stepped into his path. "Doctor Saunders?"

A shotgun blast made them all jump. Smoke wafted from the house. "Donny? Aw, no!" The female officer's voice spiked the air, followed by the staccato pops of a handgun. She backed up to the doorway, holding a semi-automatic pistol and the flashlight, the backs of her hands touching. She coughed. "Officer Thayer is down! These are not soft-bodied opponents!" She took a step backward, as she continued to fire. A giant, black claw thrust out of the smoke and closed around her, jerking her back into the house.

"Hey!" Caul charged toward the doorway. He went through the opening in a crouch and dropped to the right, getting beneath the fumes. Light speared the haze, making strange patterns. The semi-auto fired twice more, before clattering to the floor along with the flashlight.

"Doctor Saunders!" Someone called from outside.

He could see a little with the light. Thayer was on the floor, bleeding heavily from a head wound. Beyond him, gigantic legs of black chitin speared the floor. A wet gurgling sound filled Caul's ears, followed by the sight of the redhead falling through the smoke. Her eyes, open and fixed, stared at him in accusation.

"Dang it!" He raised his gun, to what he hoped was the correct height, and pulled the trigger four times in quick succession. A weird and violent hissing erupted, and the legs back pedaled until the thing hit a wall and fell over. He stared at the quixotically intelligent lobster face, shattered by at least two bullets, and wondered what nightmare he had fallen into.

26

Counting heartbeats, Doug finally heard sounds of movement at nearly two thousand. "Hey! Hello?" The stench of rotten eggs clawed its way into his nose.

"What do you want?" The voice was female, but rough and not one that he recognized.

"What's going on? Where are we? Let me go!"

A mirthless chuckle shook his ears. "How demanding you've become."

"Who are you?"

"Don't you recognize me, lover? I'm Meeka."

Meeka? "What's wrong with your voice?"

"Nothing's wrong with my voice."

"You don't sound like Meeka..." *More like Freeka.*

She made a dismissive sound.

He looked to where her voice was originating. "Could you turn on the lights, please."

Another chuckle. "The lights are on."

He opened his eyes wide and saw nothing. "The crab venom, it's messing with my eyes. I can't see."

Something scraped near his head, and he flinched as the voice, close to his ear, whispered. "As punishment for your obstinacy, I plucked out your eyes. They were delicious. I want you to be a part of me."

His heart skipped. "No." He blinked. "I can feel them."

Harsh laughter made him jump. "Happy delusion."

The chains thrashed as he sent questing fingers toward his face.

"Aw, what a pity. I made the chains so short. You can't do a thing."

"Why are you doing this?" He hated to hear the hysteria in his voice.

"Because, lover," a cold hand stroked him, making him jump, "I need something only you can make. In fact, it's time for another harvest."

"No! Get away from me. Help me! Meeka! *Mee-ka!*"

"Save your strength, I am Meeka."

"Liar!"

Wicked laughter pummeled his ears. "Oh, let me guess...you want *that* Meeka. Me as soft, innocent, young, *weak* Meeka. Well, sorry to disappoint." Something cold and leathery crossed over his chest and legs. "She's the bait." With too many legs, she straddled his hips. "I'm the trap."

27

Caul's phone would not stop ringing—Sharon calling, Chuck calling, the lab calling, the observation room calling, a reminder to meet Jillian at the hotel. He turned it off and stared at the carriage house. After the smoke had cleared, the two security officers had been rescued to waiting ambulances. Donny Thayer had received a head injury and was in stable condition. The other officer—*Kate... her name was Kate Ibarra*—had received crushing injuries to her abdomen and neck. She was dead from asphyxiation before the ambulance arrived. Chuck had called him—HIPAA be damned—about her wounds, wanting to know how she could have sustained such injuries. Caul had hung up on him.

Now, the yard was crawling with blue-uniformed security personnel and white-clad technicians, any curious passersby where being kept at bay by hastily erected plastic sheeting and the Bar Harbor Police. Chief Allen himself had met with Caul down by the road and assured him of the support of the police in this matter. "But please wrap this up quickly," had been the man's parting comment. The official word was that this was a HAZMAT clean up. Caul shook his head at the spin control and wondered what kind of deal Sharon had struck with Allen to get such largess.

The lobstrosity, as the technicians were calling it—apparently in homage to a local writer—had been wrapped in plastic, loaded into one of the vans, and transported to the Smithson campus. Caul did not care what they called it, so long as they worked quickly. The corpses of the chotah, from his first visit, were nowhere to be found, and Jillian had made no mention of them during her visit—a detail that troubled him. Based on what she had said, and not said, he fully expected to find a tunnel under the house. There was no other way all these creatures could be getting ingress and egress. *What comes up can, apparently, go down.*

As dusk approached, a heavily-armed team was preparing to breach the inner room. Bright floodlights inside the front room threw the team's shadows into stark silhouettes against the wall. Caul watched from several meters away. The Olds had been pushed aside, so he had a clear line of sight at the inner door as the lead officer bashed it open with one heave of a steel ram. He jumped clear as four officers with tactical shotguns covered the opening.

Nothing seemed to be happening. Everyone was looking up—for a lobstrosity, most likely—but Caul looked down. "On the floor!"

A carpet of living blackness poured out of the room.

The smart officers retreated. The unwise officer stood his ground and fired his shotgun at the mass, punching a hole through the boards and splattering the surrounding section of floor with crab paste. Before he could fire a third shot, the crabs covered his clothes and stung fiercely. He went down with a crash.

So that's what toxin number three does. "Water!" *If they can change strategy, then so can I.*

Two technicians opened up high-pressure nozzles on the crabs, blasting them across the floor and away from the downed officer. Another technician, wearing heavy rubber boots, ran in and dragged the officer clear of the house. Caul looked at the crabs scuttling across the sopping wet floor. *We could electrocute them. Too bad that isn't salt water.* The crabs rushed the front door again. And again the water blasted them back.

Caul grabbed a nearby technician. "Do we have some way of getting a hundred gallons of seawater up here in a hurry? No, never mind, just get a couple of pounds of salt. Also, some copper pipe or grounding rods, and a fifty foot, high amperage extension cord."

"I'll work on it!"

He returned his attention to the house. Someone walked up beside him, handing over a tall paper cup of coffee. "Pity we can't just back up a truck full of carbon dioxide and gas the lot of them. Just like our little rodent friends."

"Evening, Aiden," Caul said to the associate scientist, and gratefully accepted the hot caffeine. "Thank you, but I thought I left you in charge of observations."

"Well, thing is, I couldn't sit by and let you have this whole thrilling time to yourself. Besides which, you turned off your phone, so I couldn't give you updates. And, ah, Doctor Tate sort of got her knickers in a twist over that stunt. She likes a short leash, that one."

"How'd you know—"

"Eyes in the sky, mate." Aiden jacked a thumb upwards.

Of course. "Hmm, well, CO2 is a tenable solution, except I predict that there's a big hole in the floor. It would all drain into the ground."

"Not terribly discriminate, either. Well, I've news. Rolly's flotilla managed to not catch any of the Meekas, they all got away—"

Caul huffed out a sigh.

"—but, we did track them in the water, and we located the underwater cave that they all disappeared into."

"That's something, at—"

"We've got movement!" Someone shouted.

Inside the house, a heavy, wooden plank dropped across the inner doorway, forming a barrier nearly a meter high. Seconds later, a chotah raised its head above the blockade, followed by two finny arms and a pistol. *They have guns, too?* There was a moment of stunned silence, until the first shot caused the Smithson employees to scramble for cover. A tinkle of glass caused Caul to hesitate mid-stride. He drew his revolver and lined the sights up on the sloping silver forehead. In a mist of fish brains, the chotah dropped out of sight.

"They're shooting out the flood lights!"

Aiden hunkered behind an equipment trunk. "How'd they get a gun?"

"They probably stole it, like everything else. They've been stealing stuff for hundreds of years. Why not guns too?"

"Because it's not bloody fair, that's why!"

"Life's not fair."

"Sure, fine, but I'm still gettin' my thoughts around this fishman rubbish. And now they've guns as well? Bugger that!"

Another chotah rose and fired. Caul dispatched it too. *This clown party needs to end.* He grabbed the closest security officer.

"Nice shooting, Doctor Saunders."

"Uh, thanks—" *Miller? Michaels?* "—what have we got that will quietly clear that room?" *Too much shooting for a HAZMAT cover story.*

"CS."

Caul frowned. "Which is?"

"Tear gas."

"Mate!" Aiden, his face ashen, tugged at Caul's sleeve, pointing at the house.

Turning, Caul felt his knees tremble. "No, no, *no!*"

Meeka stood behind the barrier, pointing an antique pistol out the door. "I've been told I need to shoot you." She sobbed. "I don't want to."

"Tranq, now!" Caul whispered, his eyes never leaving Meeka's face. He dropped his revolver on the equipment trunk and raised his hands. "Meeka? Listen to me, you don't have to do anything you don't want to do, all right? Put down the gun and come out here. No one will harm you."

"I don't want to hurt you, Caul, but she's in my head. She's in my head and I can't make it stop. I can't make her stop!"

The barrel of her gun rose and thunder buffeted Caul's ears. Meeka twisted like grass in a stiff breeze, her shirt blooming a flower of dampness. Crumpling, she disappeared behind the barrier.

"No!"

Caul turned to find the security officer with his weapon thrust toward the empty space that used to hold Meeka.

"I said tranq!"

"She was posturing hostile, sir."

"You idiot! She wasn't in control of herself. Couldn't you hear her? Tranquilize all non-combatants and humans."

"Sir."

"Saints over us!" He ran for the house.

"Doctor Saunders." Someone tackled him, dropping him to the ground with a thud. The bandaged side of his head bounced off the hardscrabble lawn, inciting an explosion of pain.

"Get off me!"

"Sorry, but we can't let you go in there." Severage, the head of security, was pinning Caul to the ground.

"Get off! Get that barrier down and get her out here. She needs medical attention."

"Hostile!"

Guns barked, and Caul flattened himself as the bullets zipped like angry wasps over his head. A grating sound reached his ears, and he looked up in time to see a mass of crabs pour out of the darkened door. The hoses started, but shots broke the air, and one of the hoses went wild. The other hose shut off seconds later. Caul crawled, finally passing through the plastic sheeting and reaching the azaleas that Doug had crouched in three nights before.

Severage crawled up next to him. "Are you okay?"

"I'm not injured, but I'm not okay! We need to back off! People are dying. That was never my intent."

"Are you ordering a stand down, doctor? Because I'll need to clear that with Director Tate."

"You do that." Caul closed his eyes, soaking in the frustration and pain. *What a mess!*

28

The new room, number six, was not as nice as number four, not that either of them really noticed. Meeka sat in the solitary chair, while Jillian paced a hole in the floor. "So, how does that work, the 'You know what your sister knows' thing."

Meeka shook her head. "I've no clue. It's nothing I try to do, it just happens. When I—we get close, we overlap...we know everything about mys—ourself. We are pieces of a whole. The more pieces there are at one time, the more whole I am. Teacher calls me a hive mind."

"But ninety-three minds...ninety-three sets of memories...how do you do that? How do you hold each other's memories?"

"A hundred thirty. And I don't look at it like that. All memories are mine, regardless of which part of me collected them."

"But don't they get all jumbled up?"

"Oh! Not at all. Eldest keeps them straight. She's our memory keeper."

"Then can't we just ask her where Doug is?"

Meeka looked away. "I'll try."

"And who's Teach—?"

A light tapping vibrated the door.

"It's...you!" Jillian went to open it and found Susan in the hall, holding a tray of food. "I wasn't sure if either of you had eaten recently, so I brought you something." She pushed into the room and set the tray down. "So what's going on?"

Isn't that convenient, from altruism to gossip in two tenths of a second. Jillian frowned and shut the door. Taking one of the plates of what looked like chicken cacciatore, she ate while Meeka answered Susan's questions.

"Well, I need to get back downstairs—dinner rush and all. It's good to have you back."

"Thank you, Susan." Meeka glanced at Jillian. "There's no reason for you to wait up here. Maybe you should go downstairs too."

"Nice try...again." Jillian pushed the door closed with a thump. "Speaking of waiting, it's been two hours. Are you sure your sisters are going to bring us news?"

"I'm certain of it." Meeka frowned sadly, before looking down at her hands, squirming in her lap.

"When?"

"Um...now."

Cold fingers slithered over Jillian's mouth, and something sharp jabbed her in the neck. She struggled to escape, even as the corners of her vision faded. Meeka glanced at her. "I'm sorry. I tried to warn you."

Jack Jameson watched the three monitors that had been assigned to him, but he was having a difficult time not being distracted by the action on Dustin's monitors, which displayed the events at the carriage house from two angles and a view of the road out front. All Jack had was two parked drones watching the hotel and one airborne bird over the island, watching the spot offshore where one of the Meekas had swum down and disappeared into some cave. He flicked his eyes to his monitors occasionally, to check the fuel level on the in-the-air drone more than to actually watch the unchanging images. He could tolerate only so much boredom.

Dustin stretched. "Dude, if I'd known all that BEM crap was real, I'd've paid more attention during orientation and safety briefings. I just figured they were humoring dic-Tate-or."

Jack frowned at Dustin's outburst. "What's BEM crap?"

"Bug eyed monster, kid. Your momma never let you read science fiction? The Golden Age magazines were full of rocket ships, boy scouts on the moon, and BEMs. Great stuff."

Harvey glanced at both of them. "Stay on task." He was the most senior technician in the room and had been at Smithson longer than both Jack and Dustin combined. He had seen some eye-opening stuff in that time, including the lobstrosity that was cooling in a large walk-in cold room in the basement. "Try not to sound too ignorant all the time, Dustin."

"Huh? I knew what BEM meant."

"Knowing and believing are entirely different."

"Whatever, dude."

Harvey let the attitude slide—it had been a hard, over-long day. Movement on one of Jack's monitors caught his eye. "Jack, check your zones."

Jack's head snapped back to the screens before him. There was a hot spot extruding from the side of the hotel toward a cooler spot underneath. "Someone..." He switched over to the visible light camera, hoping for enough light, and zoomed in. "Holy...! That's a fishdude! And that's the Sandow lady, right?"

Dustin and Harvey crowded over his shoulders. "Yes."

"I...who do I call?"

"Don't bother the security team. They've got their hands full. Call the police."

"Okay, okay!" Jack rolled his chair over to the phone while keeping his eyes on the screens displaying the hotel. Dustin squinted at the grainy, low-contrast image before toggling back to thermal.

"Hey!" Jack dialed the police number. "Leave my drones alone!"

"The image sucked, dude."

On the screen, the bright shape—Sandow—fell, but the dim shape below—the fishman—caught her and laid her on the ground. Another bright shape came out of the window and dropped, followed by a fourth figure, another dim shape. "What's going on? Who's the second person? There's another fishman in the hotel, and it just pushed a second person out the window!"

"I saw that. Hold your panties, dude." Dustin switched back to the regular camera. "Oh, that image sucks."

Harvey pushed Dustin out of the way. "They're both Miss Saury." He toggled back to thermal. "One is as warm as Missus Sandow, but the other is cold, like the chotah. How can that be?"

"Hello?" Jack said to the police dispatcher. "Yeah, this is Jack Jameson at Smithson Labs—"

"Don't ever tell a cop your name!" Dustin rolled his eyes.

"—we have just observed Missus Sandow being abducted from her hotel room by a, uh, chotah and Miss Saury. What? Yes, I said a chotah. You know, the fishdudes? Oh? Officer Bass? Okay, all right, great. Thank you!" He hung up.

"Well?"

"They're sending an officer."

Dustin clapped his hands together. "This should be fun."

Harvey returned to his station. "Get back to work, Dustin."

Rolling back, Jack fired up one of the drones—a relatively quiet electric one—and got it airborne.

"Ha! Here comes the cop!"

They watched as the cruiser rolled up to the small group. The chotah carried Jillian, while the Meekas trotted alongside. The police car stopped, and the officer approached the group. The chotah and the bright Meeka went on, while the dim Meeka stood in front of the cop. "I wish these things had audio!"

"They do, but you're too far away to hear anything but the prop wash." Harvey kept glancing at Jack's screens.

"Okay...why is he just standing there talking to her? Is he blind? Did he really not see a six-foot-tall, walking fish?"

Dustin kicked him under the table. "Probably told him it was a costume and the chicky was drunk."

Jack was torn by what to do. He finally left the first drone to hover over the cop car, and launched the other drone to follow the group. The hotel would be left unsupervised. "Gotta," he said under his breath.

The group hustled down to Bridge Street and turned left. "They're going to Bar Island." On his other monitor, the cop and Meeka separated. "What is he doing? He's letting them get away. Where're our boats?"

Harvey glanced at him. "They're all put to harbor. Rolly and the others were reassigned, since there was nothing going on in the water and they're not going to dive on the cave until tomorrow. Why?"

"Because, they're crossing the bar. I'd bet money that they're headed to the cave."

The house was quiet. Caul was thankful for that, at least. No one on his team had been killed or seriously injured in the latest confrontation. The stung officer was rousing from his forced nap, one of the technicians with the hoses had been clipped in the arm by a bullet, and one of the vans had lost a windshield. Aiden stood nearby, talking on his phone.

Caul saw a flutter of white in the darkened doorway.

"Caul?"

Meeka! He was halfway to the house before arms grabbed him.

"Doctor Saunders! Stop, please."

He jerked out of the person's grasp. "No, this has gone on long enough. Meeka...come out where I can see you."

She stepped out onto the front stoop, a white rag drooping from her hand. Someone shone a light on them.

"Are you all right?" Caul examined her from head to foot. She wore different clothes from earlier. "You're not her...from earlier."

She shook her head.

"Is she...?" His throat closed before he could finish.

"Dead."

He winced. "I'm sorry."

"Me too." Meeka looked up, her eyes wet with tears. "I want this to end. I pleaded with Mother to stop. She says—she says you have to send these people away and tell them to leave us in peace."

Blood surged in his temples. "That's—that's unreasonable. She's the one who hasn't respected any sort of peace between us. The deaths, the disappearances, the thefts. She needs to reconsider her options." They stared at each other. "We've been preparing for this for years. I can't simply stop it now. Unless..." He leaned closer. "Where's Evelyn?"

"Please, don't force this. Please! Just send them away."

"I need to know." Years of questions with no answers filled his mouth. "What happened to Evelyn?"

"I'm sorry, Caul." Meeka looked away and shook. Her gaze returned, baleful. "Nice try, Saunders." The guttural voice he hated replaced Meeka's soft tones. "I have the advantage here. You'll do as I say."

"Am I speaking to Mother?"

"In a manner of speaking."

"Good. Are you behind all of this? You're more than just Meeka's mother, aren't you?"

"Obviously."

He nodded. *All of the strange stories and theories that Sharon has spouted for decades, could all of it be true?* "All right then, listen to me. We've been preparing for years to hunt you down and end your predatory behavior. We—"

"Yes, doctor, I know all about your silly corporation and its shadow charter. I was here long before it arrived, and I will endure long after it is gone."

How? "That's arrogant. Who are you?"

Meeka sneered. "Arrogant? Of course. Do you also think me ignorant? Do you think I haven't watched you as you've tried to watch me? This is hardly one sided. And you're doomed to always have the lesser vantage. I am certain of my children's loyalty. Are you certain of yours?"

He frowned. "What do you mean?"

"Send your people away, Saunders."

"Where's Evelyn?"

"Come with me and find out." She stepped back into the house.

Caul swallowed. "I don't think that's such a great idea."

"It wasn't a request." She glanced at the security officer who had followed Caul. "Loach, bring him."

"Yes, Mother." Loach turned and grabbed Caul, whose eyes bulged in disbelief.

"What are you doing?" He looked closely. The face, like Meeka's, was entirely human. "You passed a genetic screening! You're human! What are you doing?" Caul twisted. "Severage! We've been infiltrated!"

He reached for his revolver only to find it missing. The much larger Loach grappled with Caul, whose limbs flailed in unexperienced arcs, seeking his release, but striking with little effect. Ignoring the gnat, Loach resolutely dragged him into the house and kicked the door shut.

Aiden, in all ways a scientist despite his mandatory security training, stood blinking at the unexpected turn of events. Security officers pelted toward the house. "What, um…oh, blood hell! Get him out of the house."

"The door's locked."

One of the officers brought the ram back up and bashed the door. It gave way with a loud crack and swung inward. Crabs boiled out of the opening, driving the officers back. Technicians got the pressure washers working again, but seconds ticked by in the process. The officers, now clad in crab-proof rubber boots, entered the house, armed and angry—one of their own had betrayed them. Instead of exiting the house, the crabs now raced the officers into the back room, flowing into a large hole cut through the floor boards, and crawling into a hole in the ground below the house.

"Just as Doctor Saunders predicted," Severage said.

A recent recruit, Harker, peered into the pit. "Let's go down."

The hole was a twenty-foot vertical shaft that curved sharply, forming a ledge before continuing on at a descending angle. The rest of the passage was out of sight. The tops of ladders could be seen at the bottom of the shaft, protruding out of the passage.

Severage looked skeptical. "It's not safe. We need to get one of those ladders…maybe if we find a rope."

"We don't have time, sir. There are probably handholds in the rocks. I climb. I can make it." Harker stepped over the edge and started down.

"Probably?" Severage surveyed the wet rock face.

"Yes, there are holds. Cover me." Harker scrambled down quickly. "Okay, come on down. I'll cover you." He entered the passage.

Severage assessed the two remaining men. "Thomas, you're with me. Cooper, stay here and act as our relay." He turned to the pit. "You first, Thomas. If you slip, I don't want you falling on me."

"Sir."

Thomas climbed down, jumping the last five feet. "It's not that bad, actually. The surface is fairly rough. Lots of hand and foot holds."

"I have a better idea," Severage said. "Pick up one of those ladders and pass the end up to me."

Thomas looked down. "Oh, yeah. Good idea."

"That's why I'm in command."

With the ladder secure, he started down. "Hold the fort, Cooper."

"Yes, sir."

At the bottom, Severage joined Thomas and Harker, who had returned. He swung his shotgun off his back and activated his Picatinny-mount tactical light. "Gentlemen, let's go fishing."

Cooper watched as the passage swallowed them in its shadows and their voices grew faint. With the lack of activity, several other officers and a tech had nosed into the house. Cooper's mind wandered, listening to the chatter from the other room. Drake poked his head into the bedroom. "Nice hole." Cooper laughed and was starting to reply, when he saw movement near the base of the ladder. Thinking it was a tardy crab, he shone his light on it. A crack led from the wall of the shaft, across the ledge, and down the passage. As he watched, the crack grew larger.

He jerked his radio from its case. "Sir! Mister Severage! Evac! The tunnels are cracking. Repeat, the tunnels are cracking."

Darkness opened its greedy mouth and the ladder went tumbling away. Cooper grabbed at it, almost losing his footing. Drake snatched his belt and kept him from falling in.

He looked down. "My god! Are they down there?"

With a roar, the tunnel floor ceased to exist, falling away into blackness.

"What was that?" People pressed into the doorway.

Cooper and Drake froze. The lip of rock and dirt that formed the shaft below them was peeling away in layers, bottom to top. "Get out." Cooper came unstuck, turning for the door. "Get out!" He charged, pushing against the clot of bodies blocking the exit. The house groaned and lurched sideways. "Get out!" Tinkling explosions marked the windows shattering, and flying glass sparkled in the beam of his light as he gained the front room. The view out the door was disorienting. Everyone in the yard was leaning. He felt hands on his back, pressing forward, as he fought to stay upright. The house groaned like a wounded man, and the doorframe splintered as he leapt through it. He stumbled and rolled across the ground.

"Run!" Voices yelled. Curses fell like rain.

The ground beneath his hands shivered—a skittish, soil-colored colt. A ripping crash behind him motivated his legs to carry him forward. Someone grabbed him and pulled. "This way, this way!" The world lurched, throwing him and his savior off their feet. Cooper rolled over his shotgun, bruising his ribs, and came to rest against something heavy enough to stop him. In the glare of headlights, he turned his head and watched the jagged and broken profile of the carriage house roof drop out of sight.

29

Doug awoke with a jolt, feeling the ground pitch against his back. *Earthquake?*

"Doug?" asked a voice in the dark.

"Who's there?"

"It's me, Meeka."

Meeka's voice. "It's about time! Please get me out of here!"

"Shh. I don't have much time. Mother's busy, but she could check on us at any moment."

"My eyes. What happened to my eyes? I can't see."

She cleared her throat. "There are some things you mustn't ask me." Her voice sounded strained.

"What? Why not? Can you see them? Someone was here earlier. She said she'd eaten them!"

"That was me."

"It didn't sound like you!"

"Douglas, this is very important. You must obey me, no matter what I sound like, okay? I can't protect you unless you obey me."

Doug chuffed in disbelief. "Protect me? Protect me?" He rattled the chains. "What the hell do you call this? This isn't protection!"

Her fingers stroked his face, and he jerked his head away.

"I've kept you from being killed. A couple of times now. Please, Douglas. Don't fight me. Don't hate me."

"I don't, but you've got to let me go."

"I can't." Her fingers stroked down his chest. "I love you so much."

"Help me or leave me alone."

Her hand strayed lower, caressing him. "Of course I'll help you. I've died for you, my treasure."

She lay down on top of him. He squirmed, snakelike, and dislodged her. She crawled back on him, and he squirmed again. She held on this time, barely.

"Douglas, please! I want to be with you."

"To harvest?"

She was silent for several heartbeats. "The harvest will occur, whether you agree or not. Please don't give her reason to make this worse."

"You tried to kill my wife, you drugged me and chained me to the floor, and now you're trying to force me to have sex. How—"

"Don't you like sex with me?"

"If I consented, maybe," he said, sputtering the words. "But no one's asking, so no, I don't, especially with Freeka. She stinks! Seriously, how does it get worse than this?"

He smelled lilies. "Please don't ask," she whispered. He felt her lips on his, briefly. "I'm not happy that you hit me, but I'm not your enemy. I love you, Douglas."

30

Muddy shoe prints marked the deep mauve pile. Aiden turned and made another circuit, his thumb taking the brunt of his nervous stress, as he gnawed away the nail. "We'd need to move heavy equipment in, but the ground is too unstable for that. Allen forbade us from entering the sink hole. There's no chance of rescue. We had to evacuate the site."

"We lost..." Sharon seemed glazed.

"Apparently there's a cave system under that hillside. One of the caverns just let go and bloody well swallowed everything above it."

"Or they sabotaged it. Collapsed a cavern themselves."

"But that's their doorway!"

"Scorched earth, Doctor Wiltshire. Haven't you studied history?"

He ignored the taunt. "We have other problems."

"What?"

"We have infiltrators."

Sharon's face went rigid. "Explain."

"Loach, of the security division, was taking commands from the Saury woman. He's the one who dragged Caul into the house just before, well, it gave way."

"That's improbable. Everyone, and I do mean everyone, was genetically tested as a condition of employment. Even our janitors are certified human."

"Money?"

Her lips curled back from her teeth. "Please, Doctor Wiltshire. These creatures steal shoes from back porches. If they haven't got enough money to buy shoes, then they haven't got enough to bribe my employees."

"Right! Okay, then obviously we missed something, didn't we?" He drew blood on his thumb. "This is a sticky question, then. Obviously, we didn't know what we were looking for before. But, okay, we now know what a compromised genome looks like, thanks to Caul and his Meeka sequence. I'll just compare everyone to her and bingo!"

"Do it quietly. And use trusted people to help you with the analyses."

He stopped and pursed his lips. "How do I know that, exactly? How do you even know I'm trustworthy?" He laughed, high and breathy. "How do I know that you are a hundred percent human?"

Flinty gray eyes regarded him. "You will take my *word* for it." Her mouth formed a hard line. "Don't pander to sensational thinking."

"Right you are." He turned on a heel and left.

Sharon searched in a drawer for the prescription painkillers that she kept there. A swallow of gin shot the hydrocodone to a watery grave in her stomach. She looked at the hastily written field notes on her desk—the stories of a disaster she was only just beginning to understand. She pulled the papers to her and sorted through them.

List of destroyed capital equipment

List of injured personnel

List of known decedents/missing

She scanned down the list of ten names.

Saunders, Caul – Director, Science Division

She put her face in her hands. "Oh, Caul."

Plugging in parameters that would look for near identical sequences outside of known coding regions in Meeka's and Loach's genomes, Aiden clicked the Enter key on his computer and sat back to wait. His search used the consensus sequence of the Human Genome Project as the control. *Bloody well no fish in there.* He pulled a Rubik's Cube from a drawer, scrambled it, and then solved it. He was on the third run at solving it, when the screen displayed results.

Meeka and Loach shared three identical sequences, two on chromosome twelve and one on chromosome fifteen, that were not represented in the consensus sequence. "Lovely whomping gene clusters, masquerading as pseudogenes, hiding amongst the ITRs." He pulled up his own genome and BLASTed it against Loach's. This time, he refrained from the cube. Soon, the screen displayed the results. Aiden had none of the pseudogenes. "That's good to know!" He grinned. "I guess I'm human enough to run the rest of the checks."

Something rustled.

Aiden spun his seat around, his eyebrows shooting up like startled quail. One of the security staff was standing five meters away, a long, black flashlight in his hand.

"I—I didn't hear you come in."

"It's my job to be unobtrusive, doctor."

"Unobtrusive...yes, fantastic word, unobtrusive." Aiden's eyes narrowed. "Why're you standing behind me, in a dark, empty lab, in the middle of the night, holding a large, blunt object?"

"I was curious as to what you're doing there."

Aiden shifted his body to block the monitor. "I'm using the computer, looking at scientific stuff. Pretty boring, really." The man remained where he was. "Ahem, yes. Don't you have some doors to lock or something?" Aiden slipped his hands into his pockets.

"Not really. Did I see Officer Loach's genomic data there on the screen?"

"Uh, yeah." Aiden frowned. "How did you know what it was?"

The man waved his hand around. "We're in a genetics lab, and I'm not stupid." He shifted his weight, moving closer to Aiden. The big light rested on his shoulder now.

"Okay, well, I need to get back to work now, if you would..."

The guard took a half step closer. "Let's not play games. I see what you're doing there, with the genomes. In a few minutes, you'll likely pull up my file and run it and discover that I share a couple of genes with Loach. From there, you'll spend tedious minutes crapping small animals while you try to figure out who you can actually trust to send to arrest me." He smiled. "I decided to save you the stress and just cave the side of your head in. It's amazing how many head injuries are caused by wet floors and workbench edges."

Aiden swallowed nothing, his mouth drier than the floor he would supposedly slip on. "That's—that's pretty funny, officer...uh, what's your name?"

"Officer Gar, G-A-R, and it's not funny at all. I'm about to kill you. Nothing personal."

"Ah! Yeah, thanks for that. But what if I shoot you first?"

Gar smirked. "You carry a Taser in a holster on your belt in the middle of your back. With that lab coat on, you'd never clear it in time."

Aiden slipped the Taser out of his lab coat pocket and waved it at Gar. "Sod off, mate! Amazing what seeing people killed does for one's paranoia."

A long second stretched out before Gar threw himself forward, sweeping out with the flashlight aimed at Aiden's hand and the Taser. Without hesitation, Aiden fired the weapon, chanting, "Tasing, tasing, tasing," as he had been taught in class. The probes hit Gar on the chest and abdomen, bringing him crashing to the ground. He arched and strained as the high voltage lit up every neuromuscular junction in his body.

"Oh, it does suck to be you."

Aiden let up on the trigger and plucked Gar's handgun and Taser from his cop belt. "Anything else?" For a few seconds, he goosed Gar again, making him thrash. "Ahem, anything else?"

"Knock it off! Pepper spray...on my back."

"Got cuffs?"

Gar lunged. With a yelp, Aiden fell on his butt. Pulling the trigger, he sent Gar back into convulsions.

"You will not do that again! How many seconds would it take to drive your heart into ventricular fibrillation...thirty? Sixty?"

Gar writhed.

"This battery is new, so according to the specs, I can zap you for ten full minutes. How about that, eh?" Aiden released the trigger. "So much as twitch and I swear I'll make a banger out of you."

"Please don't do that again."

"Then stop being a damn fool!" He wiped the sweat out of his eyes, thinking. "Okay, um, when I tell you, you're going to stand up. Slowly!"

Gar pushed off the floor and stood.

"Good, now...get your cuffs."

Aiden secured Gar to a stout water pipe, and took his pepper spray and some other cylindrical objects from his belt, and the small gun that was holstered to the officer's ankle.

"Take the barbs out."

Aiden glanced at the man. "Right. Like I'm stupid. Those stay in until the police come take you away."

"Mmm. You trust the cops? How do you know they're not like me?" He chuckled. "Go ahead, call them."

"Shut it, mate." Aiden's hand hovered over the Taser for several seconds, before he resumed his work on the computer. This time, he pulled up every employee and ran the batch, filtering the results for only positive correlates. After several minutes, the screen displayed three results.

Dace, John

Gar, John

Loach, John

"John Dace," Aiden said under his breath. *John, John, and John...how unlikely is that?*

The handcuffs rattled. "Good luck finding him."

"Don't try psychology on me." Aiden turned to his captive. "How is it that you're all named John?"

Gar sneered. "Nothing's wrong with John. It's a better name than Aiden. Who the hell names their kid Aiden, anyway?"

Aiden frowned. "And why do you all have fish names? It's almost as if someone wanted us to catch you..." He turned back to the monitor and accessed the company server, pulling up their employee profiles.

Dace, John Isa
Age: 24
Division: Plant Services
Job Description: Maintenance, HVAC Specialist

Gar, John Isa
Age: 22
Division: Security
Job Description: Security Officer I

Loach, John Isa
Age: 25
Division: Security
Job Description: Security Officer II

Aiden clicked back to the genomic analysis software and ran all three of the men's genomes against each other. As the system was working, he fiddled with the Rubik's cube and stared at Gar's handgun. The screen displayed the results, and Aiden turned his head slowly. Tearing his gaze from the monitor, he stared in surprise at Gar. "Huh..." He dialed Sharon's office. "I think you need to come down to Lab Four and have a look at what I've found."

31

Doug awoke from drowsing to rough hands. *Not again!* He had never thought that there could be such a thing as too much sex. He had been wrong. The beastly woman grunted as she worked. *Every adolescent boy's fantasy...to be chained to the floor and used as a sex toy twenty times a day.* Doug had no idea how time was passing, but 'toy twenty times' was nicely alliterative and he was going insane.

"Get off me, Freeka!"

She slapped him—again. "Provide for me."

"I can't! You've taken everything. I'm worn out. I need to rest."

"You're useless to me unless I can harvest. Your wife and friends are busy trying to destroy everything I've done."

"Really?" A bitter laugh tumbled from his lips. "Good!" The odor of rotten eggs flooded the room. "Get away from me. You stink!"

She rolled off him, and then seized his left hand in both of hers. "I told you that most of you is unnecessary for my needs. If you won't cooperate, I'll punish you."

She pulled hard on his hand, pinning his elbow against the floor. He felt breath on his fingers, before something slimy caressed his pinky. He felt teeth clamp down on the second knuckle.

"Stop it!"

He pulled his hand, but could only twist it. Pain flared as she bit harder, tearing through his skin. Blindly, his fingers clawed at her face, but she bent them back until the tendons flared in complaint.

"Oww! Stop!"

She gnawed—her teeth ripping through his flesh.

"Stop!"

His muscles strained at the chains, trying to get leverage on his arm. "Please!"

He felt her teeth pushing into the joint, expanding it.

"Aaah!"

He heard a pop, and his hand exploded in white pain. He gulped air—a fish, dying in the brightness.

She released him, and his remaining fingers curled into a tight fist, his hand a mass of agony. Her breath caressed his ear. "Nine to go."

32

The shock of drowning snapped Jillian from her fugue. Lying on her back, water covered her face and the world was warped by it. She struggled to sit up, to swim, but she was everywhere immobilized by tight bands. Moonlight, dappled and refracted, found her, but the moon was moving away, becoming dim. Her eyes wheeled. Her ears hurt. She pushed against what held her. *Why isn't water running into my nose?*

A darkness hovered beside her and she flinched within the circle of her bonds. It drew closer, touching her shoulder, and she gasped, finding air, instead of water, at her lips. The dark shape came closer yet. With a jolt, she recognized it as Meeka, moonlight speckling her face. Jillian felt a sting on her shoulder, but could not pull away. Her thoughts grew confused and her eyes slipped shut.

Heavens, my head! Jillian rubbed her brow and opened her eyes to a drab, grayish darkness. "Huh?"

"Good morning."

She turned toward the sound. "Caul?"

"Ayup."

"Where are we? Why is it so dark?"

"We're in Mother Meeka's underground lair of despair, if you care."

Her eyebrows drew close. "Are you drunk?"

"Unfortunately, no."

Jillian rolled onto her side. "Is this rock?" She pushed against the floor, straining to see.

"Yes. We're in a pit, inside a dungeon, inside a cave. Like a turduckin only more, um, *foul*. I believe the correct term is an oubliette. The place you place people you wish to never see again. It's the place to be placed."

She sat up. "Yeah, I get your point. How'd we get here?" She rubbed her forehead. "I was at the hotel with Meeka...something poked the back of my neck—"

"You got necked by Meeka."

She glanced at the dark figure against the far wall. "What's the matter with you? Why aren't you being serious?"

"There comes a time when even my prodigious intellect is over-whelmed by the absurdity of my circumstances. Do you blame me if I devolve into a little silly behavior?"

"No, but I'll blame you if you suddenly become useless. Snap out of it!"

"I am snapped out of it! I watched one of my employees get crushed to death by a giant lobster, I watched Meeka shot to death, I blew half a dozen chotah to bits, I got stabbed in the head by Meeka's Mom the psycho squid monstrosity, yeah, I'm snapped out of it. I have been awake for over forty hours straight. This all has an absolute night-mare quality to it, thanks, but I am completely with it."

Jillian stood up, swaying. "Where's Doug?"

"How should I know?"

"You're the one with the prodigious intellect."

"Touché."

She looked up. A small circle of lighter grayness hinted at an exit.

"How high up do you think that is?"

"Four or five meters."

Yards. She took a big breath. "Hey!" Her yell echoed back to her.

"Ow! Please give some warning next time."

"Hey, up there!"

"Jillian! I've done that already." His fingertips tapped the floor. "They don't hang around. Why bother?"

She glared at him. "Because I want to find my husband and go home."

"None of us are going home for a while."

"Shut up! Just shut up! Don't you dare drag me down to your miser-able...miserable..."

"Pathos?"

"No...despondency." She wiped spittle from her lips. "If you're gon-na give up, then shut up. I don't want to hear it." She looked up. "I'm getting out of here."

He remained silent as she prowled around the dark space, feeling the floor and the smooth walls. The only feature was a small trickle of water that entered on one side, flowed through a trough cut into the floor, and exited via a hole on the other side of the room. The room was shaped like a cone, with the entrance at the apex. The method of escape was immediately obvious to her. "Okay, so we block the drain. As the room floods, it carries us up and we escape."

A slow clapping was Caul's answer. "I thought of that. Hours ago."

"Then why didn't you plug the drain?" Blood thudded in Jillian's neck.

"Because I'm a scientist, not a mystery writer. I measure things for a living, and at the rate that water is seeping into this room, it would take at least thirty-six hours for it to flood sufficiently to allow us to reach the lip of the exit. At least thirty plus of those hours you and I would have to be awake or we would drown. Are you prepared to stay awake for the next thirty six hours? I certainly am not." He watched her shadowy form slump against the wall. "Not to mention that the likelihood of them checking on us at a disadvantageous time is relatively high."

"I will get out of here."

"I don't doubt that. It's likely that both of us will get out of here, given the opportunity to think of an escape. At the moment, I am far too tired. You keep working." He settled onto his side, as best he could, and closed his eyes. His mind strayed.

"Why is this happening?" He roused to Jillian's voice. "Where are all these freaks coming from?"

He cleared his throat. "I'm afraid that's a bit my doing and Doug's doing. And a whole lot someone else's fault." He rolled onto his back. "These 'freaks' have been reported for hundreds of years. You probably saw all the sculptures of the chotah—the fishmen—around town. The Native Americans that lived in this region held beliefs of the chotah and other odd creatures, including a devil hag...an evil woman who bore the visage of a squid or a shark, depending on which tradition you hear. So great were the disturbances caused by these creatures, that the Indians abandoned Mount Desert Island save a few hearty souls who would venture over only during the summer months to harvest the food when it was plentiful. Come the fall, they retreated to the mainland."

"Why?"

"Food gets scarcer in the winter, and they didn't want to be eaten, I'm guessing. Human disappearances always peak in the winter months, even today, although some still go missing in the summer."

"What? Why doesn't someone do something about it?"

He snorted. "What do you think we've been doing? That's the secret reason why Smithson Labs exists. It was founded sixty years ago to uncover the mysteries of this area, the disturbances, the disappearances, the drownings, but especially the hybrids. Animals were discovered up here that didn't exist anywhere else in the world, and not just new species, but strange amalgams of existing species—like the Saunder's Crab."

"Saunder's Crab?"

"The little black crab that stung you. I discovered it, so I named it after myself."

"That's really geeky. And didn't I discover it?"

Caul ignored her barb. "Yes, well, geeky or not, this is an entirely new species, only it's not. It's built of genes from other animals as well as from crabs. Smithson makes transgenic rats as our cover business, but the real reason for all that genetics equipment and personnel is to hunt for hybrids—what we call legacy forms—and dismantle their genomes. This is like the Serengeti of freakish hybrid creatures in North America. Only Oregon is comparable—"

"Great. What's Doug got to do with this? I mean, I'm sure it has something to do with Meeka, but why Doug? She said that he smelled right, and when her sister kissed him, she imprinted on him like a freaking gosling and the whole flock of them fell in love right then."

Caul sat up. "Would you mind clarifying everything you just said?"

She sighed, but replayed her earlier conversation with Meeka, as best she could remember it.

"Fascinating. So, they all love him? Past and future? That's some potent mind control."

Jillian gasped. "What is that?" She whispered, a knife edge of fear in her voice.

He followed the dim silhouette of her pointing arm and looked up. Framed in the circle of dirty gray light that hung above them was a shape. It looked more like a sausage than a head, being grossly stretched out, extending over the opening on a thin stalk of a neck. Spindly arms reached, one at a time, through the opening and stretched down. Jillian pressed herself into the corner, her breathing ragged. "Spider!

"No, probably spider crab...and Meeka?"

The slender head nodded. "I heard you telling my story." The voice was exotic and breathy. "I am Twenty-seven." Metal pans clanked to the floor by Caul's feet. "Drink."

"What are you?" Jillian struggled to reconcile the voice of Meeka, no matter how distorted, coming from the throat of the abomination that hung above her.

"Meeka. I will be back."

The apparition retreated.

"What was that?"

Caul investigated the pans, which were empty. "It—she was apparently one of the hybrids I was telling you about, a more extreme hybrid of her than I have yet seen. This gets stranger by the hour. I wish I had my phone or something to write on. All the legacy creations are coming out now." He stuck one of the pans under the seep. "For sixty years, half of that time with me, Smithson has been searching for these creatures. We find them, occasionally, the small ones, and they find us, occasionally. The big ones. We've lost field agents to them over the years."

"But that was *Meeka*?"

"Yes, and crab." He chuckled. "Now who needs to snap out of it?"

"Shut up, Caul! Shut up and get me out of here!"

"Smithson has excellent security forces—aside from Loach. They will follow me and find us. We'll be rescued soon enough." He lay down again. "There's nothing we can do, at the moment, so I suggest you get some sleep."

Instead to taking his advice, Jillian huddled in the darkness, waiting for the monsters.

33

Click, snap. Sharon's shoes announced her presence well before she entered the lab. "All right, Doctor Wiltshire, please explain the emergency." She glanced at Officer Gar and frowned. "And explain this?"

"Doctor Wiltshire has gone insane, Director. Please uncuff me before he shocks me again."

"Ha! Nice try, mate. John Isa Gar there, late of our security force, tried to sneak up and stave in the side of my gourd."

"Proof?"

Aiden laughed in a stutter. "Look at his genomics data. There are three areas where he and Miss Saury vary against the consensus sequence, and their variation has a very high identity. Whatever those genes are, they do the same thing. Moreover, there are two other employees who share this genetic identity." He displayed the employee information screen. "See...John Isa Dace, John Isa Loach, and John Isa Gar, all the same first and middle name, like a sign post: John is a fish. All of them have fish-related names, even Miss Saury."

Across the room, Gar sat forward, listening.

Sharon examined the data on the screen. "Really? A saury is a fish?"

"Yes! It's like they're trying to tell us they're the enemy. Oh, and look at this. I ran their sequences against each other," he pulled up the screen, "they're identical, genetically. They're identical brothers."

Sharon's eyes narrowed. "But they don't look the same. Similar, yes, but not the same."

"Epigenetic programming, I'm guessing. Intrauterine reprogramming of the epigenome—manipulation of HOX genes—would cause variation in appearance, build, you name it. They're made clones, like Meeka. Who has the technology to do this?"

Her eyes narrowed further. She ignored his question. "Run their genome against Meeka's genome, only without the filters."

"Uh, sure." He assigned the appropriate files to the software. "What should we do with him?" Aiden gestured to Gar. "I was going to phone the police, but he brought up a good point about them. Can we trust them?"

"No. No police. Not ever. This is an internal matter. We dispose of him."

"Dispose?" He swallowed. "I'm not sure what you mean."

"Euthanize him."

"What? We can't do that!"

"You do it to rats quite regularly, do you not?"

Aiden's lips trembled slightly and his larynx rose and fell, as if he were speaking without words. At last, he choked. "You can't be serious? That's daft! He's human!"

"He's your enemy. He tried to kill you, and he would kill you, if given the opportunity."

"Still..."

The monitor displayed results. He tore his attention away from her, grimacing. "They're related." Aiden pointed at the screen. "See? They share the three gene clusters that I found, but they're also, what, fourth cousins or something. Or third cousins once removed, or second cous—"

"I get the picture, doctor. You may stop talking." She nudged him away from the computer, turning the screen toward herself, and assigned another file to be checked. Aiden frowned. She turned to Officer Gar and picked up the Taser. "I will give you one opportunity to redeem yourself. Is there anything you'd like to tell me?"

"About what?" His voice sounded different, deeper.

"About why you're doing this?"

Gar took a deep breath and spit on the floor. "You're cattle."

"No, we're human beings. What's the point in attacking us? All those people killed and missing. What's the point?"

"Mother prevails."

Sharon's expression became stone. "Not if I can help it." She pulled the trigger on the Taser and held it. As Gar thrashed, she turned away, staring out the dark window.

"If you leave that on too long, it'll kill him."

Her eyes never left the window. "I'm aware of what electroshock will do to the nervous system."

"Then you know you need to turn it off."

"I'm disposing of him, Doctor."

"But he's human!" Aiden's face intruded in her field of vision.

"So is cancer, but we still cut, burn, and poison it out of our bodies."

Gar became less vigorous and small, unarticulate noises escaped him.

"Director, please!" Aiden's voice was thin and strained.

She ignored him.

It seemed to go on forever, but when the screen updated three minutes later, she released the trigger and Gar collapsed. The odor of burnt meat hovered in the air. Aiden unclenched his fists and glanced at Gar's body.

"My God…" He tore his gaze away. "What gives you the right?"

"Doctor Wiltshire, you know a tiger by its stripes. You know it is a carnivore and it will kill you, if allowed. However, these—" she waved a hand toward Gar's corpse "—puppets look just like us. They behave just like us. Until they are controlled, until they become killers. There's no way to know when they'll be carnivores. They must be destroyed."

"But he was human!"

"No, he was an adulterated clone. He was made by the creatures that this institute has been hunting for over sixty years."

"Still—"

"Still, what? What do you propose we do with them?"

"Hold them, help them. We can figure out how to break the, what, control? They'd be absolutely normal if they couldn't be controlled."

"Grand! When you've solved that conundrum to my satisfaction, I'll stop euthanizing them. Until then, they present too great a liability." Glancing at Gar, a slight tremor shook her. "They've never gotten this close before."

"This has happened before?"

She cast a pitying glance at him. "Several times. It's not something we talk about during employee orientation, but it's why everyone who works here carries a weapon. However, they're getting far too clever with their deceptions. Will you be all right?"

"Yeah, I'm all right, I guess." With trembling hands, he turned the monitor back to himself. He noted the names on the screen, the name on the file that Sharon had loaded, noted the filial relationships, and a raw gasp escaped him. "You, um, you just killed your son."

With a click, she set the Taser down on the counter. "I know."

34

A whirlpool of pain existed in the dark, swirling Doug in circles like some macabre merry-go-round. His mind reeled with the realization that the foul woman had bitten his finger off. When he tried to touch his pinky with his other fingers, it simply was not there.

"Doug?"

"Meeka! Is she gone?" He heard a sniff. *Is she crying?*

"I'm sorry I ate your finger."

"What? Let me go! Let me go before she comes back."

"That was me…I bit your finger off."

What is she talking about? "Let me go!"

"I can't."

He thrashed, jerking and straining against the chains. "Take them off!"

"Douglas…I can't."

His finger throbbed.

"Your finger looks bad. I boiled some seawater to clean it up. It's cooling. Don't make me angry again, please. I don't like it when we hurt each other."

In Meeka's words, he heard echoes of Jillian's complaints about arguing. "I don't want to make anyone angry, but seriously, Meeka, listen. You've gotta take these chains off."

"I can't. Mother would be furious. Please stop. She'll want you hurt again. She might even kill you next time."

"Kill me? I thought she needed me, for the harvest."

Silence.

"She doesn't need *you* for the harvest." The sound of metal scraping on stone startled him. "The water's ready. Oh, your beautiful hand. This will probably hurt. A lot."

She was right. She plunged his hand into the still hot water and wiped it with a cloth—and jammed an icepick into the end of his finger, from the feel of it. With gritted teeth, he rode through the worst of it.

She dried his hand on a towel. There was a brief stinging, and then his pinky went numb. "What'd you do?"

"I sprayed some anesthetic on it."

He felt her wrapping something around his hand.

"Try to keep that dry."

"I'm not going anywhere. Honestly, please just unchain my arms."

"I can't." She took his hand in hers, and they sat in silence for a long time, just holding hands. It struck Doug that, despite everything they had experienced, this was probably the most intimate—truly intimate—time they had spent together.

"Meeka…"

A shuddering intake of breath startled him. "Brian wasn't meant to die."

"Huh?"

"The scorah was coming for you, following my scent trail through the water. Brian just got in the way. Scorah are pretty numb."

Doug's throat tightened. "What?"

"Numb…it means stupid."

"No, Brian! What are you saying about Brian?"

"He—he wasn't the target. You were."

"For harvest? Is he still alive?"

"No, Doug. Getting him was an accident. The scorah brought him all the way back to Mother before she realized that it had the wrong person. She killed it for its incompetence."

"Brian! What about Brian?"

She stroked his cheek. "I'm sorry. He drowned while he was being brought here. He struggled too much underwater and inhaled some."

Doug felt wetness on his face. "But why?"

"It was an accident. It was meant to be you."

He struggled to breathe. "You were trying to kill me?"

"No! I…" She sniffed again. "I was being obedient. I sampled you— that first night. Mother said you were right. She sent me for you, but you wouldn't swim with me. I found you the next day, but she also sent the scorah, just in case I—I failed, again. It all went wrong. And then you left. For forever, it seemed."

"But Brian was killed? For nothing?"

"His body fed Mother."

Doug choked. A final stone of misery toppled in his mind.

"She kept his ring, she thought it pretty. Mother loves pretty things. She thought you pretty—your smell. I thought you handsome. I still do. So does Mother. She never stopped looking for you. I tried to keep you safe. I blocked as much information as I dared; misdirected. Then you came back, and I love you. I was thrilled to see you, but—"

"Brian died for nothing. You murdered him!" Tears slid from his eyes.

"I'm sorry. Would you rather it had been you?"

"Yes! I'm the better swimmer. I could have fought it off."

She stopped stroking his cheek. "Did you? You faced it too."

The memory of the afternoon in Newport Cove welled up. "The squid in the cove?"

"That wasn't a squid. It was a scorah. You'd rebuked me, so Mother sent you the ring, hoping, I think, that you would return to the place you last saw its owner. And you did, you beautiful fool."

"But, you were there, on the trail. You wanted me to swim with you."

"Somewhere safe, Douglas! Not in the cove. Anywhere but the cove. I was trying to protect you. I jumped from the trail hoping you'd forget about the cove—be too busy rescuing me. But you're infuriatingly stubborn, and you swam in it anyway. Right to the island, right where she wanted you."

"I thought I might find you..."

"Hello? Coast Guard? It never occurred to you to call someone to rescue me?"

He flushed. *Why hadn't I?* "I—honestly, I thought you'd died. That Jillian would be blamed for your murder."

In the darkness, Meeka sighed. "You think too much."

"That'd be a first." He sniffed. "I need to wipe my nose. Please unchain me."

"No, it's time for a harvest."

"I can't!"

"Please...try."

35

Aiden peeled the nitrile gloves from his shaking hands as the door to the cold room closed with a thump. Touching the dead man had pushed him to extremes of revulsion. He was used to death, but dead rats were substantially different than the dead human he had dragged across his lab only seconds earlier.

"Is Mister Gar taken care of?" He turned to find Sharon and her personal security detail, Jordan and Lightfoot, standing in the doorway to the hall.

He nodded.

"Good. I think it best that you lock down this lab, and then go to the observation room and secure it."

"What are you going to do?" Aiden noticed that she had changed shoes, opting for flats instead of her usual stiletto heels.

"We are going to locate Mister Dace and neutralize him."

"He's back?" Aiden felt a flush of panic.

"Yes. Or, rather, he never left. What with the crisis this afternoon, we had many disturbances to our routines. We've isolated him, by his badge and the internal cameras, to the boiler building. I'll return soon." She was at the door when he went after her.

"Fancy having me along? I mean, the observation room is already locked down like a nun's knees, and that's," he waved toward the cold room, "just going to bugger the whole evening if I stay in here." He ran his fingers over his hair. "And I want to talk to you."

Her expression never warmed as she regarded him. "Fine, but bring Gar's weapons if you're coming. I don't want anyone along who can't defend himself."

"Oy! I did fair against Gar, didn't I?"

She raised an eyebrow before walking away.

"Sure...yeah...give me one second." Scooping the items into random pockets, he rushed to join her.

They were halfway to the boiler building by the time he finally felt organized enough to ask questions. "So why, may I ask, are there murderous clones walking our campus? Clones that—" he coughed "—appear to be related to you?"

With sure steps, she continued on her way, her face betraying no hint of her thoughts or emotions. At the verge of him asking again, she turned and speared him with a frosty gaze. "That's an unprofessional question, doctor."

"Sure, sure, and some dead man just threatened to play Hard Day's Night on my skull with a torch. Apologies if I'm not feeling terribly political at the moment, but I signed up to do science, not 007 meets Plan 9 from Outer Space."

She pursed her lips, unwilling to allow this impertinent young man too far into her history. "I hired you on Doctor Saunders's recommendation. Keep that in mind." She cleared her throat. "Many years ago, I think before you were even born, I lost my husband and my son to a boating accident. That was what the Coast Guard called it, anyway. The boat was found adrift, nothing out of place, they just weren't on it."

"My condolences."

She cast a look of disdain at him. "I'm telling you this not to engender sympathy, but to demonstrate the nature of the threat against us and the depths of your naiveté."

He heaved a silent sigh right before they entered an underground tunnel of unfinished concrete that led to the engineering buildings. Insulated steam pipes, water lines, and electrical busses filled floor-to-ceiling steel racks to their left. Overhead, fluorescent tubes glared down on them. Sharon slowed, allowing the security personnel to get farther ahead.

"Ten years after their disappearance, I saw my son in town, but not the nineteen-year-old man that he should have been. Rather, he was about the age he had been when he disappeared. I was stunned, frankly. It was as if my son had simply stepped, unchanged, from 1986 to 1996. I ran to him. Embraced him. I wept." She glanced at Aiden. "He behaved as if he did not know me. I took him home and called doctors. I demanded that they tell me what was wrong with my son—amnesia? Alien abduction? No one knew. He never spoke, even when I took him to his old room. On the second night that he was back, he tried to kill me—"

Aiden scoffed. "But he was just a child."

"A psychopathic child with a knife is no less frightening than a grown man with a knife, Doctor Wiltshire. Don't presume to draw fine distinctions based solely on your ample stores of ignorance in this matter."

Aiden tasted bitterness and contemplated simply turning away and leaving, such was his disgust at her tone. "You've no idea what I've faced in life."

She stopped walking. "Have you ever faced a knife-wielding person who's intent on harming you?"

"I was mugged in Chelsea by some bloke with a blade."

"Was he trying to kill you?"

"Well, no. He just ran off with my twenty quid."

"Then, you lack basis."

"Perhaps." They continued walking. "So, what happened?"

She looked away, her face wooden. "In the end, we subdued him, and I gave him a lethal overdose of etorphine, if you must know."

Aiden froze. "You murdered a child? Your own child?"

"He wasn't my child. My child loved me. The thing I found on the street that day was an abomination—"

"But he was a child! What gave you the right to take his life?"

She returned to where he stood. "Do you know what the police do to a dog that has bitten a person?"

"No, I don't. Something barbaric?"

"They shoot it. They deprive it of the opportunity to do further harm, to anyone."

"But that's a dog!"

With her fist, she jerked the sleeve of her blazer up her arm, revealing a faded, foot-long scar on the inside of her left forearm. Aiden blinked several times as he absorbed what he was seeing. "I have others." She pulled the sleeve back to her wrist and smoothed the fabric. "However, I don't show those to just anyone. The dog bit me, so I put it down before it could harm someone else."

"He was a human. He was your son!"

"It was a clone. An ersatz person, sent with the sole intention of killing me. And there were others, more assassins, sent over the years. Not clones of my son, or at least I thought not. Somehow, our enemies knew to alter the appearances of these clones—Gar and Dace and Loach. I review each individual applicant to this institution, looking at each photograph, and they slipped in anyway. Perhaps I should have had everyone screened against my own genome, but I value my privacy. Apparently, our enemies know that; know too much."

"I can't condone this—"

"It isn't your job to condone my decisions. Your job is to obey my directives and do your *job*. Will you do that, doctor, or should I consider this your resignation?"

The breath escaped him and he found it hard to get it back in. "Um, no." He choked out before getting some wind. "I'll just head back to the observation room."

He turned away.

"That is unacceptable. You wanted to come along, so I'm holding you to this."

Seconds ticked by as Aiden allowed air to seep into his lungs. *Control freak.* "I only wanted to talk with you about what's going on. I think I understand now, and, honestly, I don't agree with what you're doing. If that results in my dismissal from Smithson, then...so be it, consider me resigned. Good luck, Doctor Tate."

Sharon stared at his back, an expression of disgust marring her features. "You're here on a work visa, are you not?"

"Yes, so?"

"Walk away from me and I will see to it that you are deported within the week."

Aiden turned, walking backwards. "You do find ethical behavior challenging, don't you?"

Her nostrils flared. "On occasion, ethics conflict with survival. I prefer to survive. Good riddance, Doctor Wiltshire."

She pivoted and joined her security officers. They trod the remaining distance and used a badge to unlock the double doors at the tunnel's end. The space beyond was dark, save the pale green glow of the exit sign.

Sharon peered into the gloom. "Where are the lights?"

"Right here, ma'am." Jordan reached for the bank of switches.

"Wait!" Lightfoot grabbed him. "Do you smell that?"

"Smell what?" Sharon sniffed the air.

"Gas...there's a propane leak in here. This isn't safe. Even turning on the lights could detonate it."

"That's why they're off!" A voice shouted from the darkness. "You people need to get out of here. This space isn't safe."

Sharon bristled. "Come out and show yourself!"

"I'm busy!"

Light erupted as Lightfoot switched on a flashlight, revealing a figure in the khaki uniform of the plant services employees.

Jordan jumped. "Whoa! Didn't you say—"

"Low voltage. It doesn't spark." Lightfoot took a step forward, looking at the man in khaki pants and shirt. "You there, keep your hands where we can see them. Identify yourself."

"John Dace, maintenance. There's a gas leak in the building. All of you need to get out of here!"

Sharon scowled, marching forward. "The charade is over. I know who you are, Mister Dace."

His face twitched. "Sorry?"

Noise in the shadows drew everyone's attention. From the gloom, several chotah shuffled.

"Not yet!" Dace glared, walking toward them. The lead one lifted its hand, revealing a gun. "No!" Dace threw his arms in the air, just as the chotah fired.

There was a blinding flash, and then nothing.

36

S hh, he's waking up."

Waking up? Doug's eyes popped open. A gray ceiling curved over him. *I can see! She lied about my eyes.* He turned his head and found Meeka sitting on the floor beside him.

A gasp from near his feet. "He can see me! Didn't I spray his eyes? I can't remember." *That sounds like Meeka.*

He glanced at the speaker and someone ducked out of his view. He looked back to Meeka. "Who was that?"

She raised her hand to his face. A tiny slit on her wrist opened. He snapped his eyes shut, his face spinning away fast enough to make his neck hurt.

"No! Don't blind me again."

"It doesn't hurt."

"I don't care! I don't want to be blinded."

"But I think that you should be."

"Why?"

"I don't know. I didn't say."

"What?" *That made no sense.* "Can I look at you? Will you please not stab that needle in my eyes?"

"It's a spray. Yes, you may look."

"Promise you won't blind me."

"Yes, Douglas, I promise."

She looked haggard in the dim light.

"You've been crying."

"Of course. I don't like doing this to you."

Red tinged his vision. "Then why are you?"

She swallowed. "Mother." Only a faint whisper stirred the musty air.

"Seriously? Just say no!"

"You don't understand."

"No, I don't. I don't understand any of this. Please, please let me go."

"That would be defying Mother." She swallowed again, as a fresh wave of tears cascaded her cheeks. "I—I defied Mother, when I rescued you from the scorah two days ago. As punishment, she—she killed me."

That's...absurd. "You're not dead!"

"I'm not, but I am." She frowned. "Another me."

Another me? "Another Meeka?" *Oh!* "There's more than one of you? You're, like, identical twins or something? That's how you could be in more than one place at once."

She nodded. He heard a noise by his feet, and a Meeka look alike walked into view. She came and sat by Meeka. His gaze slid from one to the other and back, marveling. He could now see that the first was older, a woman of perhaps twenty-five, while the second was younger and looked like the Meeka he was used to seeing, in her late teens.

"Two!" He shook his head. "Listen, I'm sorry—"

They nodded. "Thank you," the younger one said. "Mother tells me that it is improper to mourn, but I still feel the pain of my death, the fear."

"So, you're triplets. Were, sorry. Okay, yeah, I'm sorry...but you've got to let me go."

"I cannot." They spoke in unison.

Okay, that's creepy. "Come on! Look, I'm sorry about hitting you. Which—which of you?" *Oops! Probably dead sister.*

"You hit me, but I am not here right now."

"Yeah, sorry about that, for your triplet."

"There are one hundred twenty-nine of me now. I seventy-two was killed earlier today."

"Say again?"

Meeka looked at the other Meeka. "Yes, I believe that's the problem." She gazed at his eyes. "Douglas, is your hand separate from you? Or your knee?"

"No."

"So I am a hand—" said the first Meeka.

"—and I a knee—" said the second Meeka.

"—but I am Meeka," they said in unison.

"You're both Meeka, I mean, all three of you were?"

"There are one hundred twenty-nine elements of Meeka, and I am but one."

He closed his eyes. "But—"

"When I am separate, I am many—"

"—but when I gather, I am one."

He shook his head. "Yeah, that's great, so, whatever. I don't want to lose anymore fingers. Let me go before that stinky beast comes back."

Both Meekas looked sad. "You mustn't talk about me like that."

"Stop! Stop being crazy." His left hand was wrapped in white cloth strips. "My hand hurts. Unchain it, please."

"No, Dou—"

"Will it cause problems?" The second Meeka looked at the first. "He's bound at three other limbs, I'm here, he's in the middle of the warren, and he's naked and shoeless. What's he going to do?"

"Mother—"

Doug jumped at hope. "Please! My back is killing me. I'd like to be able to roll on my side."

"See?" First Meeka said and scowled. "He pushes."

"Sister, do I love him?"

"Of course."

"Do I not see that he hurts?"

"Of course! I dressed his wound."

"Then let me relieve him of this pain too. Go and retrieve extra chain."

The first Meeka looked away. "I know not what I do." She stood and left.

The second Meeka smiled at Doug and bent down to unfasten the chain that bound his left wrist. "Will you thank me for this by allowing me to lie with you?"

Flickering lamplight dappled her skin. He inhaled, preparing to refuse, but stopped. He had no interest in sex with her, but she was a potential ally.

"I'm married."

A sad smile quirked her lips. "I know. I met your wife a few hours ago. She is looking for you. She—she loves you."

Doug's heart leapt. "She's okay? You didn't hurt her did you?"

Her hand strayed to his face. "I wouldn't do that. Please?"

"Your hand...it's warm."

"Yes. Will you?"

"You'll unchain me?"

"I promise."

She was gentle with him.

Afterward, she unlocked his left wrist and the chain hissed to the stone floor. He swung his arm around, stretching the shoulder joint, before rolling onto his right side. A groan of pleasure escaped his throat as the muscles and joints of his body stretched and realigned, and blood flow was unimpeded to his upper back and buttocks. Parts tingled and parts popped.

"Thank you," Meeka said.

Doug turned his head and looked at her. "You're welcome? Thanks for letting me move. What was so special about this time? You all have been harvesting for days."

"Not quite that long."

"It feels like it. How long *have* I been down here?"

"Only twenty-five hours."

"Only?" *I've gotta get out of here.*

With light footfalls, the other Meeka returned, carrying chains. She saw Doug and her eyes widened. "That is dangerous. I should do as I'm told." Her eyes widened even farther. "Why do I—why do I—you hide from my mind? Sister! What have I—you done?"

They faced each other with their heads down, twin scowls marring their features. He focused his attention on the bond on his right wrist. The chain was strong but relatively light, and it was formed into a loop around his wrist using a simple screw-gate link. Quietly, he turned the threaded section until the gate was just barely fastened.

"Yes, I see."

"Good. Help me to leave," ally Meeka said.

The Meekas stood and fled.

"Where are you going?" Doug unfastened the chain on his right hand. He sat up, chaffing his wrists, and looked around. He seemed to be in a cave. An old fashioned kerosene lantern hung from a hook in the ceiling. He reached for the chain on his right ankle, and became aware of the smell of spoiled eggs.

"No. *No!*"

He twisted the locking link, spinning it open.

"Oh, Sandow. You're a bad boy."

Adrenaline fueled him as he grabbed ahold of the chain that bound his left ankle and pulled it with both hands. The staple in the floor bent, shedding flakes of zinc, before one side pulled free with a *snap*. He stood up and froze.

37

Aiden entered the main building, the tunnel door slamming shut behind him. He felt a vibration through the soles of his shoes, and watched the framed art on the wall shiver. *Earthquake?* The doors groaned in their frames as a rumble shook the bones of his middle ear. *Outside!* He had lived through a few earthquakes during a postdoc in Berkley. He was on the stairwell and climbing, before he realized that the shaking had stopped. He opened the door to the ground floor and froze. Through the plate glass windows that overlooked the parking lot, the stark rectangle of the boiler building had been replaced by twisted metal, shattered masonry, and cavorting flames.

"Sharon!"

A second explosion flung bits of debris across the parking lot, cracking the already broken glass in front of him. Frantic banging drew his attention. A man was outside, trying to get in through a side door. Aiden badged the lock open and the man, a Bar Harbor Police officer, pushed the frameless sheet of glass out of his way.

"Do you work here?"

"Yes! We need to get a fire brigade out here. Director Tate and some of the security personnel were in that building."

"They're gone."

"No! They went to the basement level...they might not even be in the building itself. I need to go check the tunnel." He was turning away when the dancing firelight caught the officer's name badge: Bass. He did a double take, remembering what Gar had said about trusting the police. He walked away, trying to keep himself from running. At the stairs, he turned. Officer Bass was heading for the lobby.

"John!"

"Yeah?"

Aiden swallowed a billiard ball, his fears confirmed.

Bass's brow wrinkled. "Wait...how'd you know my name?"

"Security!" Aiden yelled at the ceiling, hoping the security cameras had microphones. "I need help!" He turned and ran down the stairs. Only seconds later, he heard the door bang off the wall, followed by pounding on the stairs above him. "Halt! I'm ordering you to halt!"

"Leave me alone!"

"How'd you know my name?"

Aiden reached the lower corridor and ran left, thinking about Sharon and the two security officers. The tunnel doors bowed inward and shimmered. At fifteen feet, they felt like standing beside a kiln. He could not go any farther. "Oh, Sharon...playing with fire..."

"Halt!"

He was trapped between the hot doors and Bass. "We need to call the fire brigade."

"How'd you know my name is John?"

Aiden felt a hitch in his throat. The weight of the day pressed down on him. "It was a lucky guess, mate." He bluffed and turned away from the doors. "We need to call the brigade..." *If you're a Gar clone, what are you going to try to do?* Thinking of Gar made him remember the dead man's gun, and he jammed his hands into his pockets.

"How'd you know my name?"

"Don't you have a job to do?"

"Depends." Bass stepped closer. "I have...friends who work here. Other Johns. I tried contacting them, but they don't answer. You're Wiltshire, right?"

Aiden nodded and thought of his lab upstairs and the corpse in the cold room. *If Sharon is gone, who's going to explain why there's a dead man in my cold room?*

Bass's voice dropped to bass register. "You know Officer Gar?"

Aiden's heart skipped up to jackhammer speed as sweat scuttled down his ribcage. "Uh, yeah."

The movement was subtle, but Aiden noticed when Bass's hand slipped a few inches along his belt, coming to rest on the butt of his pistol.

"Help me find him."

"I'd love to, but no, I've got to go help. With that." Aiden felt acid rise in his esophagus as he gestured toward the boiler building and took a step to go around Bass.

There was a scraping, of metal and leather, and Aiden found himself peering down a nine millimeter hole. "Bugger then." He backed up toward the hot doors, and felt himself begin to roast.

"John Dace. You know him?"

"Not exactly." Aiden licked his lips.

"He's a friend of mine." Bass stepped closer. "I was talking to him right before the explosion. He called me because he'd lost contact with Gar." Step. "And then, suddenly, Tate and armed guards showed up in the boiler building, the very same building where Dace was working. Coincidence?"

Aiden swallowed another billiard ball. "Must be, mate."

Bass smiled, revealing crooked teeth. "I don't think so. You knew Tate was in the boiler building, so you must be looking for us too. You must know where Gar is."

"I don't know!"

"You ever disjointed an animal?"

Blinking eyes betrayed Aiden's bafflement.

"The hip is an amazing joint." Bass lowered his gun, aiming it at Aiden's right flank. "But it's really fragile. How long do you think those fire doors are going to hold out?"

"What—what are you saying? You're going to shoot me and leave me down here to burn? You're a bloody police officer!"

"Depends..."

"Depends?" Aiden felt his heart fluttering. "Depends on what?"

"It's John, isn't it?"

Bass and Aiden looked at each other in surprise, and Bass turned to look over his shoulder. A short woman—she reached no higher than his badge—stood not five feet from him. With her white hair forming a ghostly halo around her head, she appeared almost insubstantial.

"Not you!" He snapped his attention back to Aiden and discovered a gun barrel pointing at his face. He froze. "I'm a cop! Are you stupid?"

"Depends, mate," Aiden said, mimicking Bass's earlier comment. "You pointed first. And my shot's fatal."

Bass's eye twitched. "Put your gun down. That's an order."

"Not bloody likely."

"Oh, you men and your masculine posturing."

Bass felt bony fingers jab him in the armpits and tickle. "Hey! Get off!" He struggled away from her, but she stayed on him like a terrier after a hedgehog.

"Put your silly pistol away. And that's an order." She laughed.

"I hate you! Leave us alone, you old hag." He lunged back against her, trying to send her sprawling. Instead, she climbed him, wrapping her legs around his waist and her arms around his neck and face, covering his eyes. She glanced at Aiden and smiled sweetly. "You should probably run now, dear."

Aiden ran.

Bass struggled, grabbing at her and trying to run her into the wall. He had the thought to shoot her off his back, but his gun was no longer in his hand. "Not again." He grabbed at her with both hands, instead.

"Shhhh." Her voice was like a spring breeze in his ear, drowning out the dark muttering that played constantly in his mind. She wrapped herself tighter around his head, resting her cheek on it. His movements calmed and tears wet his face. "That's right, relax. You're very tired, aren't you? I would be too, if I had to carry her around in my head all day. Come on, my dear, let it all go and sleep."

He collapsed, face first on the floor. She stroked his short hair, looked at the fire doors, and disappeared.

38

Hot bile pushed into Doug's mouth, and he spat. "You touched me? You had sex..." He shivered. "Oh, that's disgusting!"

She paused in the entrance to the small cave. "You can see me? Why? *How*?" She slid forward, her legs rippling. The lower half of her body was not even remotely human, being four muscular tentacles. The greenish-gray flesh continued to a mottled torso that lacked a navel and breasts. Her face was a disturbing parody of Meeka's, covered with long, writhing tentacles that protruded from around the vicious gash that passed for a mouth.

"Stay away from me." Doug dropped to a crouch and struggled with the chain at his ankle. The link opened and the chain came loose in his hands. Standing on shivering legs, he swung the chain like a weapon. "What *are* you?"

"I'm your wife, forever more. Now, lie down, lie still."

"The hell you are." He backed away from her.

"Where are you going, lover? Come to me."

His stomach roiled. "You're foul. You lied to me about my eyes. You bit off my finger. You..." He looked at the union of her tentacle legs and shuddered.

"You were disobedient. Disobedience must be punished."

"You're disgusting!" He spun the chain faster.

The odor of rotten eggs spiked, causing him to choke.

"Come to me, Sandow."

"When hell freezes! Stay back or I'll hit you." His eyes teared up from the odor.

"I'm also the only thing standing between you and death. Are you so eager to be food?"

"Liar! You need me...for semen."

She crept closer. "I already told you, I don't need very much of you for that. Come, make love with me, save your life."

He swung the chain, hitting her across the shoulder and neck. She screamed and grabbed the chain, yanking it from his grasp.

"You hit women far too often."

"You're no woman." He punched her in the face.

She reeled backwards and spun, smacking him with one of her leg tentacles. He felt as if a tree had fallen on him as he sailed into the wall.

"Ow!" She wiped at the clear fluid that flowed from her split lip. Grimacing, she slid closer. "Now, I'll just take you, and another finger, too. You'll learn, eventually."

"You won't touch me again." Seizing the lantern from its hook, he smashed the windshade on the cave wall.

"Broken glass? Will you cut me? Give me a little burn? I'm much stronger than that. You can't stop me."

He kept eye contact with her as he unscrewed the fuel reservoir cap and flung the lantern. "Here...catch!" It described a parabola between them, loosing a spray of kerosene at the apex. She screamed and raised her arms, batting it away at the last second and causing it to crash into the wall. He watched the liquid, waiting for it to burn.

She looked at him and a nervous laugh escaped her throat. "Apparently, the fuel needs a wick. You lose."

He had a vague memory that kerosene was difficult to ignite. Her wound of a mouth curled into some expression resembling a smile, and a gush of rotten egg stench flowed over him. She slithered toward him in the same moment that the little puddle of kerosene surrounding the broken lantern puffed up in flame.

Doug wanted to laugh, but he could only choke and strangle out a few words. "Apparently, you're wrong. You burn!"

The liquid and even the air seemed to explode in flames that raced across the floor, igniting the rivulets of kerosene that ran from her body. She screamed again and did not stop, slithering backwards and out of sight. He moved deeper into the cave, moving as far from the flames as possible, coughing from the stench and the greasy fumes. As soon as the fire began to sputter, he charged out of the alcove. The smoke from the kerosene mixed with cloying burnt flesh smells, caused him to choke and gag. In the passageway, screams echoed from the right, so he went left.

Eldest fled. The muscles of her tentacles flexed and rippled, but she still felt that she could not move fast enough. She panted, wishing for relief, trying not to scream again. Dark rings encroached the edges of her vision, and speckles of black danced in the air before her. She blinked, trying to clear her sight, and looked at herself as much as she could. Her skin was raw and weeping, or missing altogether in some places. She heard voices ahead and surged forward. Two inferior Meekas walked toward her in a passage.

"You! Bring Saunders and the Sandow woman to me. I will be in the Pool of Healing."

The two Meekas goggled as Eldest went past them. Their tears flowed as her pain and emotions bombarded their minds. Abandoning their previous plans, they ran straight to the dungeon.

Twenty-seven looked up when they entered. Their mental link was tenuous, overwhelmed by Eldest's distress. The older of the two, Ninety-nine, went straight to the jailor. "I need Caul and Jillian."

"It is not good to do this thing." Twenty-seven peered at them from her tall eyes. "She means to kill them."

The two young Meekas shared a guilty glance. "I saw, but what else can I do? Mother is angry and must be appeased. Shall *I* die again?"

Twenty-seven turned away. "Perhaps. However, you know what Teacher said, 'Violence begets violence.' Something large has shifted in the hive mind and I fear for my life and the lives of my brothers and sisters." She moved in her ponderous, stilt-legged gait, and retrieved a tall ladder. She gazed into the oubliette and lowered the ladder. "Ho! Awake my little birds."

Jillian and Caul cautiously climbed, their faces swiveling to assess the surroundings. Jillian, her mind visiting memories of Slenderman videos from the Internet, flinched away from the spindly woman.

Caul addressed her, tilting his head to see her face. "What are you going to do with us? I heard what you said."

"I mean to do nothing. My role is to maintain this prison and care for its inmates. I mete no punishments. It is not in my nature to hurt others."

Ninety-nine saw a glint of silver at Jillian's throat. She leaned closer and studied the medallion. "You are a Teacher too? Should I take her to Teacher, Twenty-seven?"

The spindly Meeka nodded.

"Come with me."

"Eldest has told me to bring them to her." One-hundred frowned.

"Yes, but she was burned. She will be in the pool for a while. We have time. Can you hear her mind quieting? What a relief!"

"I don't want to die again," One-hundred said.

"You must do this." Twenty-seven peered at the smaller Meekas. "She wears the medallion of a Teacher. I forbid you to take her to Eldest until she—they—have met with Teacher."

"Yes, sister."

They walked away, Jillian more than happy to put distance between herself and the slenderwoman.

Twenty-seven put a pincer-like hand on Caul's shoulder.

"Here." She held a shallow pan with his and Jillian's belongings. Caul looked in surprise at the large Taser that also rested in the pan. A green and silver sticker identified it as property of Smithson Labs. He glanced at her. "Why...?"

"I have much time to think, doing what I do, and I see much and hear more." She leaned close to his ear. "It is my belief that the eldest of us requires sleep, much sleep. A much needed and permanent sleep. Do you understand?"

He nodded.

"Good. Godspeed to your meeting with Teacher. She will be happy to see you."

"Thank you."

"I am but a humble servant."

The Meekas led the way out.

"What was that all about?" Jillian whispered.

"She gave these back." He passed along her possessions and put his own away in the appropriate pockets. Jillian frowned at her assassinated-by-salt-water phone. "And, I think she asked for a coup d'etat of Mother Meeka. She gave me a Taser."

"Really? Wow. Maybe Crabby wants to be queen."

"I didn't get that impression. See seemed more worried about the safety of her sisters."

Jillian nodded. "I can respect that." She frowned. "Not that I like them, or anything."

Caul regarded her and chuckled.

They walked through a succession of passageways, finally arriving at a low doorway. Even Jillian had to duck to enter the room, which was longer than it was wide. Mismatched chairs sat alongside crudely built tables, while a string of bare light bulbs ran the length of the room. At the far end of the room sat a woman with salt and pepper hair, talking to a group of dark-haired children of mixed ages.

Jillian grimaced. "They kidnapped children?"

"Sometimes, probably...but, I don't think any of these children were kidnapped."

"Why?"

"Look at them, Jillian. They're identical."

She squinted in the dim light. "Oh, my..." She felt her stomach clench. "They're Meeka. Little Meekas."

Ninety-nine and One-hundred went to the woman and talked to her. They all turned toward the door, and Jillian gasped. The woman was also identical to them, only years older.

"It's a freaking Meeka convention."

Caul stepped toward the woman like he was treading a minefield. He finally found his voice. "Evelyn? *Evelyn?*"

The woman's eyes grew huge. "Caul?"

"Evelyn!"

He went to her, unsure of himself after so many years of wanting; unsure of her. "Dearest! I've missed you." He raised his arms—the gesture tentative and tremulous—and she flew into them and shook in his embrace.

"I thought I'd never see you again," she whispered into his shoulder. "I always hoped you'd find me. The Meekas would tell me about you, so I knew you were looking. I sent you a secret message, through them. Did you understand? Did you understand their name?"

Caul was confused. "No."

"Me followed by the suffix ka. It makes the name a diminutive."

"Little Me?" Jillian grimaced. "You named them Little Me?"

"Yes. I was hoping you would see their faces, hear their name, and realize that I was still alive."

"No, I'm sorry. I didn't understand. I'm a geneticist, not a linguist."

Evelyn made a sad smile. "It's all right. You found me, eventually. Did you figure out the other name? I named the Johns as a warning."

His brow furrowed. "Honestly, I'm sorry, but I don't even know what you're talking about."

Jillian glanced around the room. "Listen, I hate to break up this lovely reunion, but I need to find Doug."

Evelyn shook her head. "I don't know any Doug."

Ninety-nine and One-hundred perked up. "I do!"

39

Doug ran.

He lost himself in the mindless motion, keeping only enough attention to not stumble on the slick stone of the dim passages. His thoughts burned for Jillian, and he saw her in his mind's eye. *She's looking for me.* The floor was colder and wetter, and the lanterns were so distant from each other that his eyes hurt as he came upon them. The next one was simply a pinpoint of light in the blackness. He ran toward it, feeling that the floor was sloping down. He sensed more than saw the low ceiling, but he could not duck in time. Pinwheels of light exploded in his vision, and he knew nothing more.

He woke to hands on his limbs, and fear seized his mind that Freeka had recaptured him. His lids snapped open, and silvery, upside down legs threatened his face. He blinked and raised his head. Fred's fishmen leered down at him with enormous walleyes. Four of them carried him by his arms and legs, suspending his body between them.

"Put me down!"

They sighed and gurgled.

"I said, put me down!"

They kept walking, their broken dishwasher chorus uninterrupted. He thrashed until one of them kicked him, its sharp toefins scratching his skin. "Ow! Can't you just leave me alone?" He let his head hang back and flinched every time the cut skin stretched. *So they're real. After Freeka, the fishmen were actually a letdown.*

They traveled through dim passages that seemed to cross and intertwine in no discernible way. *Even if I get free, I wouldn't know which way to go. Why is this happening?* He sensed that they had entered a larger space. The lights were completely absent here, but it did not seem to hamper his captors. They strode across the space until their footfalls told him the walls were getting closer again. One of them bubbled, and they all dropped him. His head bounced off the stone floor and a tiny constellation swam around in his vision. Metal squealed and clashed, and their footfalls receded.

He got up, his joints feeling oddly loose after the jostling carry. The squealing metal sound had come from a large gate that now completely blocked the only—and nearly invisible—means of leaving. He had thought that the cavernous space they had carried him through had been dark, but it now seemed well lit compared to the space in which they had confined him. He pushed against the bars, testing the gate's strength against his own. It flexed, but not far. *Not far enough.* He was working on the locking mechanism when he heard the sound behind him and froze. *I've heard that sound.* He closed his eyes and tapped his head against the gate. *What is that sound?* It was soggy leather on stone. *Just like—* He spun and his eyes popped open.

"Freeka!"

Scanning the darkness, he felt himself shrivel at the mere thought of her. *I really want some clothes.* Keeping his eyes on the nothingness, he slipped his left arm through the rusty bars and jiggled the latching mechanism. The noise came again. "If you ever come near me again, I will hit you and keep hitting you until one of us is dead! Do you understand? You're never touching me again."

He stood in pounding, sweat-drenched fear, but even after manipulating it for what seemed like an hour, the latch would not open and Freeka had not shown herself. He pulled his arm back through the bars, groaning as his shoulder rotated to its correct position. He slid down to the floor, the stone wall providing a sense of security that he knew was false. He was alone, exposed, and blind in this place. As he sat looking at everything and seeing nothing, a line from one of the horror novels in his grandfather's collection crawled, intact, from the ooze of his subconscious:

> **What need for light hath evil? For evil dwelleth in darkness; Evil is darkness.**

He shuddered.

Now, as if to taunt him for illicitly raiding the off-limits case in granddad's study, images of creatures foul and improbable capered and gibbered through his mind. The fishmen and squidwoman that he had seen were joined by reanimated corpses, cunning crabs, blobby and carnivorous jellyfishes, and vampiric eels with mouths the size of trash buckets. Without thought, his hands cupped protectively over his genitals. In a short time, fatigue overcame vigilance and sleep overthrew paranoia. His chin slipped down to his chest in a mockery of comfort, and his sleeping nightmares were no better than his waking nightmares.

40

Both Meekas jumped. "I know where Doug is."

"Good. Take us to him!" Jillian felt a thrill of hope.

The Meekas shared a glance. "You'll probably be mad."

"Why?"

"Mother's been harvesting."

Jillian flushed. "He—he wasn't willing, was he?"

"No. I had to chain him to the floor—"

"What?"

"—and he was so uncooperative that Eldest bit off one of his fingers to punish him."

Jillian felt the world rush up. Caul caught her just before she crashed into the rock floor. He glared at the Meekas. "She...bit his finger off?"

"Yeah." One of them held up her hand with the pinky bent at the second knuckle, to demonstrate.

Jillian gasped for air. "You're killing my husband."

"No! That's not true. I've been helping. Taking care of him. I—I died to save his life."

"It doesn't matter. Just take us to him. We'll sort the particulars out later." Caul pulled Jillian back to her feet. "You must be strong."

"I don't need a pep talk! I need to get these freaking crazies away from my husband."

Caul glanced at the Meekas, his brows rising. "She's a tad upset. Forgive her, um, language."

"It's fine. Just follow me." The Meekas turned for the door.

"Caul, please don't leave." Evelyn clung to his arm.

"I can't let Jillian go alone."

"Then I'll come with you." She looked to the Meekas. "Will one of you stay with the children?"

They left the classroom, Jillian, Caul, Evelyn, and Ninety-nine, and made their way through passages that became damper and less hospitable. "I don't understand, back there you have electric lights, but down here it is only scattered oil lamps. Why? And how do you get the electricity?"

Jillian tossed her hands in the air. "Caul! Can you please stop being a scientist?"

"I'm just curious—"

"I know, but I don't care. I just want to get Doug and get out of this freakshow. After that, you can spend the next five years asking about who cuts their hair and how they avoid rickets, okay?"

"Hmm, those are good questions, how—"

"Caul!"

They reached an intersection of tunnels and Meeka stopped, her feet sliding on the damp stone. "I sense..." She turned, looking in each direction. Lights burned distantly before and behind them, but no light could be seen to the left or right.

"What is it, Nina Nile?" Evelyn asked, using a pet name. Her hand hovered on the younger woman's arm.

Fear owned Meeka's face as she looked at them. "Me."

"You've been a bad girl, Ninety-nine."

Meeka spun to the right. "Eldest!"

"I've had so many bad boys and bad girls today." A barbed dart sailed out of the gloom and impaled Meeka's chest. She cried out and pulled it from her skin.

"Stop it, mon chou! She's only sixteen." Evelyn stalked into the darkened corridor.

"She's been bad, Teacher. She needs to be punished. Go back to your school. I will deal with...these three."

Chotah materialized out of the shadows, gurgling and shuffling, heading for them.

"Run!" Evelyn yelled.

Caul grabbed Jillian and Meeka and turned, but Meeka slipped from his grasp as she pulled back.

"Meeka!"

"Mother says no." A reddish-black stain was spreading across her shirt from where the dart had pierced her.

Caul blinked at the red blood, but the chotah would not allow him time to think. "I'm sorry, Evelyn!"

"Just run!"

They ran, blindly, into the black passageway. Caul fumbled with his phone, while the odd slap-scratch sound of running chotah goaded them forward. Light flared as he got the camera lamp turned on, and the pair ran much faster. After indeterminable minutes, the passage seemed to be rising and getting narrower. Caul stopped running.

"What are you doing?" Jillian tugged at him.

"Don't you feel that? The air is moving. This must be a way out."

The slap-scratch, which had been fading, began getting louder.

"Great! Can we go now?"

Their own footfalls drowned out the chotahs' as they leapt away. The passage narrowed further, making it impossible to run in tandem. Caul gave his phone to Jillian and pushed her ahead of him. "Oh, crap!" She stopped. The passage was interrupted by a cataract—a near-vertical shaft about twice as tall as they were.

"I'll boost you up. Come on."

"No!"

"Jillian—"

"I don't know what's up there, and I'm not leaving you behind."

"This may be our only chance to get help."

"You said your security team would be here. Where are they? Where *are* they?"

"Up, Jillian! Stop arguing with me." He knelt down and made a stirrup with his hands. "Turn around and step."

Jillian looked back down the passage. "Caul! They're coming."

"I know! Will you step in already?"

She faced the rock wall and put her foot in his hands. A squeak escaped her lips, and a grunt from his, as he hoisted her up. She gripped the ledge above her, surprised to find a handhold. She stuck the phone between her teeth and heaved herself up. The passage ahead was more of the same, and empty of fishmen, so she turned to give Caul some light.

As soon as Jillian was out of his hands, he turned and thrust the Taser in front of him. He activated the intimidation arc, but the lead chotah, wedged in the tight tunnel, was either unimpressed or too stupid to understand what it faced. Caul fired the first cartridge, hitting the fish squarely in the torso, and tased. The chotah bucked and flailed, and seemed to come apart as he watched. "Well, that was unexpected."

Before he could think too much about what had happened, a second chotah clawed its way over the first. Caul did not bother with the arc this time, but fired the second cartridge of the X3, and tased, to similar effect. The second chotah lasted a few seconds longer before it ripped itself apart.

"The chotah are soft. They're coming apart from the effects of the muscular tetany."

"Huh? Are they dead?"

"Oh, quite."

A third chotah was climbing over the twitching remains of the others. It seemed to hesitate when it saw the Taser. "Come on, work it out. If you boys are smart enough to shoot a gun, you should recognize that this will hurt you."

"You give them too much credit, Saunders."

Eldest! "Aw, nuts! Did you have to follow us?"

The chotah entered the gap a little too fast. Caul fired the final cartridge, almost regretting lighting this one up, and watched it shiver and explode. The passageway was now blocked with dead fish. He ejected the spent cartridges and slipped the Taser into his pocket. Turning, he hunted for hand and foot holds in the rock. There were not many, but he managed to make it to the top with help from Jillian.

"I'll catch you," Eldest yelled. "I hate fish!"

"You are a fish," Caul yelled back.

She growled, which he took as his cue to get Jillian moving. They went on for several minutes before Jillian slowed. "Seems like we're going down again."

"I know. Just keep moving." He heard grunting and swearing behind him. "I had hoped she'd give up."

The passage took a sudden dip downward into a dry basin full of rocks, branches, and leaves. A narrow crack ran across the floor and up the walls. Jillian shone the light upwards. The passage continued up, the end lost in the gloom, but a small tunnel mouth formed from the crack about thirty feet up the steep slope. It looked like a hard climb.

"This crack must go all the way to the surface. We should be able to get out."

The sounds of heavy breathing and leather scraping against stone reached them. Jillian, with the better view, shook her head. "No way. The passage goes completely vertical after that tunnel."

"All right then, the tunnel it is."

They climbed the sloping passage, making for the side tunnel. Caul had to take the phone about halfway up so Jillian could climb. He still arrived first, but waited for her and urged her into the opening ahead of him. At first, she was able to stand, hunched over, but within seconds she was forced to drop to all fours as the space became tight. The tunnel ended abruptly. She felt around, her fingers skimming over the rough stone, but there was no further opening, not even a crack.

"It's no good! We have to go back," she whispered.

"There is no going back. Let me see."

She pressed herself against the tunnel wall, making herself flat, as he shone the light past her.

"Nuts!"

Told you so. "Back up. Maybe there's another tunnel."

He looked over his shoulder as best he could. He could not see anything back there and he hesitated to shine the light for fear that it would be seen in the outside passage, but the prospect of blindly crawling backwards into Eldest was not a happy one. With nothing else to do, he turned the light and shuffled his hands and knees in the reverse direction.

The light diminished as Caul crawled away, leaving Jillian in the plunging gloom. The darkness and the rock pushed in on her, filling her eyes with nothingness. Her breath came in little gasps, and she backed up, no longer trusting the black void in front of her. The stone floor tore her knees and bruised her palms, but she sped up, heedless.

"Jillian! Slow down. You just kicked me."

"Go faster!" She was panting now, and the air tasted stale. Blood hammered in her neck. She felt Caul's hand on her bottom.

"Slow down!"

"Please, go faster." She could sense something moving in the shadows before her—getting closer. "Caul!"

Between her legs and arms, the light speared, turning menacing gray-black into empty sandy brown.

"What?"

She slowed, embarrassed by her panic. "Nothing. Sorry."

He resumed crawling, and the shadows returned. She swallowed and whispered, "There's nothing there...there's nothing there... there's nothing there." The walls pressed in, bearing her down with a thousand tons of rock.

Caul heaved a sigh when the tunnel widened enough for him to turn. Behind him, he heard nothing. "Jillian?" He looked and found her immobile in the tunnel. "Jillian, come on."

Jillian swallowed again. "I don't want to die down here."

"Then keep moving."

She nodded and slid a hand and a knee. Caul shielded the light within his fingers and pushed closer to the tunnel mouth. The passage outside was in darkness. Jillian shuffled up beside him.

"Are you okay?"

She stood up, the ceiling pressing against her scalp. "Yeah, I'm...no," she whispered, "no I'm not. This is crap! This whole thing is crap! I want my life back! I want my husband back! I want this horror show to end!" She took a deep breath and clasped the Saint Christopher's medal. "Okay...I'm okay."

Caul nodded. Shielding the light even more, he crept to the lip. The sense of space opened up around him as his breathing rasped in his ears. After the tightness of the tunnel, he felt that he hung over a great chasm. His fingers found the edge, and pushed a pebble over. He winced as it skipped and clattered to a rest.

"Boo!"

Caul choked and recoiled, unshielding the light as he scrambled away from the lip. Eldest's face seemed to hang in midair. "What silly little creatures you are." The coarse voice grated across his jangled nerves. "You cannot hi—"

Jillian threw the rock the instant she realized it was in her hand, and it hit Meeka's open mouth. She dropped from sight, sputtering. Jillian grabbed another rock and went to the lip, coughing from the reek of rotten eggs.

She peered into the gloom, unable to see anything. "Caul, some light, please?"

He joined her and shone the light downward. Eldest lay in a heap at the bottom of the steep slope.

Jillian blinked. "Is she dead?"

"I hope so." The odor rose over them, making their eyes water. "How did you do that? With the rock?"

Jillian glanced over at him—disheveled and dirty and hair sticking out in wild clumps—and laughed. The tumult of emotions in her heart was almost overwhelming. "This is unreal! My goodness... yeah, that was an okay throw, wasn't it?"

"Okay? *Okay*? That was an incredible shot!"

"Thanks. I played softball all through college." She laughed again, feeling giddy. "My nickname was Cannon, 'cause I'd always pound them in from the outfield. Doug thought that was pretty funny, that he'd fallen in love with a woman who could throw better than he could."

He smiled at her, elated by their small victory. "I'm glad you're on my side."

Choking drew their attention. Eldest Meeka rolled over and spit out the rock, some bluish blood, and a small handful of broken teeth. Her head swiveled around and she cast a baleful glare up at Jillian. "You will die." She stood, swaying like she stood on a boat and not the solid earth. "I will beat the life out of you and feed on your corpse." The odor grew stronger.

"You really need to work on your people skills. And feel free to come on up. I've got plenty of rocks." Jillian's mind felt barely attached to her body, like she was going to float away at any second. "Nothing can hurt me. I'm bullet proof!"

"Haven't you learned? You and your pathetic stones, your husband and his pathetic lantern. I cannot be stopped by stone or fire, Mother will heal me." She winced and threw herself at the rock face before her, as if it had insulted her, and hauled herself upward. She had not stayed long enough in the pool; she was not fully healed. But she had heard the treasonous thoughts of the lesser Meekas and had come.

"Fire?" Caul's brain ignited. "Hit her again. Make it count!"

He pulled the Taser from his pocket, as she lobbed an orange-sized rock at Eldest's head. There was a satisfying thud, but the creature clung to the wall, slipping only a little. Jillian was on the follow up pitch before Meeka even had time to growl. The next one connected with her brow, as she glanced up, and snapped her head back. She slipped and crashed in a pile of loose stones and curses.

"Your hair band!"

Jillian looked confused until Caul started reaching for her ponytail. "Oh!" She pulled the elastic ring out of her hair and gave it to him. He slipped it around the handle, over the trigger, making the Taser spark.

"You can't go down there. She'll kill you!"

Caul grinned again. "If I'm right, I won't have to. And if I'm wrong... we're going to die anyway." He leaned over the edge. "False Meeka! You're absurdly ugly and malodorously disgusting." He turned and whispered, "Throw more rocks."

Together, they barraged Eldest with insults and stones. Eldest screamed and thrashed and growled. When Caul's eyes burned from her fumes, and he could barely breathe, he dropped the Taser over the edge. "You'll want to get down, I hope." He wrapped his arm around Jillian and pulled her to the tunnel floor. She stared at sand grains, which jolted up toward her face. She saw sunshine, and she swore she felt it on her skin. A clamorous whooshing sound serenaded her, in concert with a penetrating, woofing boom. She clapped her hands over her ears, but it was already too late. Crack-fiend telephones assaulted her ears.

"What's happening?" She yelled, over the ringing sound.

The odors of sulfur and burned flesh scorched their noses.

"Crawl!" The sun got hotter and brighter. And then, it was over. Except the stench, which clung to them like wet cotton clothes.

"What was that?"

Caul fell on his side, the light making crazy shadows on his face, which was nearly maniacal. "Hydrogen sulfide."

"Thanks! That cleared up everything."

He smiled pure joy. "I'm very glad that worked."

"What happened?" She shook him.

"Eldest Meeka released hydrogen sulfide gas whenever she was emotional, but especially when she was angry. I imagine it was a chemical defense, it would be very effective at keeping others at bay, although she could have used it offensively. Wow, why didn't I think of all this earlier..."

"Caul!"

"Oh, yes, sorry. Hydrogen sulfide, aside from being obnoxiously vile and a deadly poison, is also a highly flammable and explosive gas when concentrated, such as the bottom of that passage. All it needed was a spark—don't tase me, doc!"

She laughed and choked. "You're a genius! I'm glad *you're* on my side."

They crawled back to the lip of the tunnel, but Jillian stopped. "Am I gonna want to see this?"

He grimaced and looked over, shining the phone light down. He turned away immediately. "Ugh. That's disgusting."

"I don't want to know! Please. I can't even look at a little cut."

"Oh! That's great!"

"Thanks."

"No, no, not your aversion to blood, I have bars." He texted a quick message to Sharon, Aiden, and Severage. "I'm telling them that we're down here and in need of rescue."

"Where is here, exactly."

"Under town, I imagine. I wasn't taken very far, or at least it seemed that way." He coughed. "Come on, let's get out of here."

They climbed down, Jillian keeping her face averted from Meeka's body. Their eyes watered and they coughed incessantly by the time they got to the bottom. "There's residual gas. We need to hurry."

Jillian nodded and, skirting the shallow pit, climbed the far passage. Caul stopped for a moment to gaze at the mass of wet and raw, bluish-white flesh at his feet. "You shouldn't have done this, Mother Meeka. You should have left us alone."

The sound of a rusty gate hinge issued from the tangle of tentacles. It took a few seconds for Caul to realize he was hearing laughter. He charged up the passage after Jillian, but not before he heard a few slurred words.

"I'm not Mother."

41

Aiden made the lobby in time to watch rigs from the Bar Harbor Fire Department, red lights strobing, roll into the parking lot between the buildings. Time seemed to stretch out as he watched the men and women rush to unroll hoses.

That was a heck of a roll...snake eyes...choosing to get fired saved my life... then choosing to be clever nearly cost it...wake up, Aiden!

"Doctor Wiltshire!"

He turned on his toe to find a blue-clad security woman behind him. He took her hand. "The world's exploding. Fancy a shag?"

"Sorry?"

"Yes, I meant the dance, not the, um, other thing."

"We're evacuating the building. You have to leave now." She pulled her hand away

He frowned. "What are you banging on about? The fire brigade is here. They'll have it out in a jiffy."

"The sprinklers have already activated in several zones in this building. You need to evacuate it, now."

"Well, if you insist." He started away, but stopped. "You are quite lovely. At least a drink?" *And maybe a shag?*

She pushed him towards the doors on the other side of the building from the fire. "Sounds like you've already had enough for both of us."

Aiden pouted. "I haven't had any." *Wake up, mate!*

He pushed out through the doors just as firefighters in turnouts were pushing their way in.

Shock...it's shock. Can't come that close to being killed three times in an hour and not have a little shock to the nog. He wandered across the parking lot to a knot of Smithson employees. *Wonder what the firemen will make of the corpse in my cooler?*

"Doctor Wiltshire? I'm glad to see you. We haven't been able to contact any managers, and I have an important update."

Aiden looked at the skinny boy in his baggy lab coat. "Jack." He read the boy's identification badge. "What can I do for you, Jackie?"

"Earlier, I was monitoring the drones and I saw Missus Sandow being abducted from her hotel by a chotah and two Miss Saurys."

"Sounds awful."

"Uh, yes, it was. Um, I called the police, and they sent an officer... Bass, and—"

"What? Repeat, Jackie!"

"Earlier, I was watching the drone feeds—"

"No, did you say Officer Bass, of the Bar Harbor Police?"

"Yes..."

"Bloody hell. Well, what's the rest?"

"He didn't do anything. He just talked to one of the Meekas, and then he drove away."

"Yeah, he drove over here." He started back toward the building, thinking he should find Bass and shoot him. *He's one of them.*

"Doctor?"

"Yeah?" He stopped.

"They took Missus Sandow to that cave we found, off the east end of Bar Island, and fed her to a squid."

"What?" He twisted. "Have you completely lost the plot?"

"I'd show you, but—" He waved at the firefighters filling the building.

"It's true." Harvey intruded on the conversation. "We tried to contact you and about a half-dozen other senior staff, but no one is answering their phones."

Aiden patted his pockets, locating his phone and Gar's gun. "Director Saunders is dead, you know that, I hope." They nodded. "And director Tate was in the boiler building."

"What? You're kidding?"

"'Fraid not, mate." He pulled out his phone. "Yeah, I got your message. What's this?" A recent message from Caul showed up in his text box. The screen illuminated his widening eyes. "He's not dead. Caul's not dead!"

The air moving past them carried the rank smells of charred skin and rotten eggs. They reached the cataract and found the floor and walls covered in pulverized fish. Jillian wrinkled her nose. "She must have been angry about the delay."

"Undoubtedly."

They worked their way carefully down the slippery rock face, cringing as the slimy fish flesh coated their hands and clothes. Pushing past the remains of the chotah, still wedged in the tunnel, they went single-file into the darkness. Caul led the way, toggling the back light of his phone periodically, trying to save battery life. The thought of being in these tunnels with absolutely no light made him queasy. Pressing against him, Jillian was hyperventilating as she thought of the dead creatures that filled the dark passage behind her. The way widened and they finally arrived back at the intersection.

"Welcome to Ambush Junction. Enjoy yer stay." Caul said in a drawl.

Jillian had a mad moment of disconnect. "Why are you behaving like Doug?"

"Pardon?"

"Ever since I got down here, you've been cracking jokes and making quirky comments, just like Doug does."

Caul grunted. "No idea. It's been a strange day, certainly. Perhaps this is what cockiness feels like?"

"Well stop, please. You make me miss him that much more."

His thoughts turned to Evelyn and the improbability of finding her after all these decades. He understood, better than Jillian could know.

"Which way?"

"Back to the school, I—" He turned his head.

"What is tha—"

"Shh!"

A tapping noise came to them from the passage that Meeka had been leading them to earlier.

"I think we should go now." Jillian's whisper made Caul jump.

He nodded and they ran. The damp floor made their feet slip, costing them seconds. Seconds added to minutes as the tapping became clacking. Caul dared a glance back. Lobstrosities—purple-black in the lamp light—charged up the slope, their sharp, chitinous feet scratching out traction on the rock.

"Go!" Caul said, panting and pushing her up the treacherous slope.

Hissing filled his ears as the clacking became staccato. "Go on! I'll hold them off."

"Don't be stupid. They'll kill you." She grabbed his hand and pulled.

They hit a drier patch and gained traction. The pounding and hissing lessened, but only fractionally. Patterns of light wobbled on the passage surface and a lantern smashed against the wall beside Jillian. "Aagh! Watch it, you jerks!" She spared a moment to look back, and screamed. Her legs pumped, and Caul watched her leave him behind.

"What are those? I thought chotah were chasing us."

"Some of my people called them lobstrosities." He puffed a few times, trying to catch her. "I haven't had a chance to study them."

They rounded a sweeping corner and Jillian nearly slid into the backs of chotah massed in the passage. She had sense enough not to scream again, but the chotah did not seem to have heard her. She turned and whispered. "We could use a door just about now."

"They can't hear you. Fish ears don't work well in air. Everything's on the inside of their heads, and they're used to living in water. Air is a lousy conductor of sound."

"Caul!" She pointed over his shoulder. "I don't need a lesson. We need to get around the fishguys. Now!"

The crustaceans drew closer.

Caul looked around, and then grabbed her shoulders, drawing her toward the inside of the curve. "Get down. Press yourself into the corner. Tight as you can."

The floor sloped toward a trough that ran down the opposite side of the tunnel. Caul reasoned that momentum would carry the giant lobsters down into the trough as they rounded the corner, and he hoped that he and Jillian would be overlooked in the dimness. The ground vibrated, and a few of the chotah turned their heads sideways to better peer into the darkness. Thundering and *snap-scraping* around the corner, the first crustacean lacked time to stop. Chotah spun away like bowling pins, one of them lofting and striking the lantern dangling from the ceiling. Shadow became night, and the darkness was filled with a cacophony of sounds. Jillian shivered on the ground, arms wrapped around her head, waiting to die.

Something heavy and sodden struck her back making her cry out. Caul's hand, she hoped it was, wrapped around her ankle. The sounds became terrible—rending and cracking noises and squeals of pain. More meat landed on her, making her squirm in disgust, but the eruption of gunfire caused a gasping terror to seize her. The hand on her ankle gripped harder, though, reminding her that Caul was still there, still with her. She tried to calm herself by squeezing her elbows to her chest and clamping her hands over her ears. The wall vibrated and a weight pressed down on her, forcing the air from her lungs in a strangled chuff. She drew a fresh breath with difficulty, using her belly more than her chest. More gunshots, but muffled now, as if at a distance. Thunder in the ground. And screams and screams and screams.

42

The flaming boiler building continued to paint the night sky a ghastly orange hue as Aiden stood a mile away on the Smithson Labs dock. Given their losses earlier, and the current crisis, only three security officers could be spared for the rescue mission. Taking advice from all quarters, he had formed a tentative plan to boat to the site of the Meekas' spectacular underwater escape. From there, he and the officers would dive down and follow whatever passage the Meekas had taken.

Their preparation efforts had been interrupted five minutes later by the arrival of Rolly and four of his environmental resources personnel. The large man, and his even larger assistant, Gere, had trotted down the dock, calling orders. The security staff had followed those orders without question, so Aiden had kept his peace.

They had loaded scuba gear and weapons, from Smithson's ample stores, onto three smallish launches, and were going aboard, when Rolly seemed to notice Aiden for the first time. "Thanks for the hand, but we won't be needing any lab techs on this trip. It's likely to be dangerous. Wouldn't want you to get hurt."

Aiden blinked. "I'm not staying behind."

Rolly smiled and turned away.

"Here, now, I'm no lab tech. I'm Doctor Aiden Wiltshire—"

"That's nice. Look," Rolly turned back, "I've got eight men to pull off a rescue against an almost certainly numerically superior enemy, on their turf. If I had all my ER guys and Severage and all his hard crew, I'd say, sure, let's babysit the limey lab geek, but I don't, okay? You'll just get in my way and be a liability."

"Seriously? Did you just call me a limey?"

Rolly frowned. "Don't cry. Be useful and throw us the mooring lines."

"I'm not staying beh—"

"I need men who can dive and shoot, not some spindly pipette jockey. Throw me the lines."

"Hello, big stupid man. I'm a marine biologist. I can dive."

The two men stood, glaring at each other, when a lobster boat hauled up from the dark.

"Ho, on the dock!"

Aiden broke the contest and glanced at the large vessel. Several men stood on the pitching deck. White hair seemed to be a theme among the mariners. "Yes?" Aiden said. "Can we help you?"

A man leaned over the gunwales. "Maybe we can help you." His grin was infectious. "I'm Fred Uhlebe. My mother said you might need a hand or two."

The view was magical. Despite his protest, Aiden had only dived with scuba a few times before—while on holiday in Mallorca—and never at night, so the current experience was captivating him. He lay on his back watching the shimmering bubble stack rise from his regulator, shimmying and pirouetting in the beam of his dive light. A thump on his arm made him rotate his head. Rolly, swimming beside him, poked two fingers at his eyes behind the mask, and then poked them forward. Aiden got the hint, executing a barrel roll so he could see where he was going. They approached the spot where Meeka and the seal-women had disappeared earlier.

Twenty feet under the light chop, Rolly played his light across the silt. He flicked the beam to the right and caught a glimpse of red wetsuit—one of the security officers, Cooper. He felt a tug on his own wetsuit and looked to the left. Gere was signaling for him to come. Rolly tapped Cooper's arm and made the same signal. They diverted left, and a low, rocky shelf came into view. Gere gestured underneath it, so Rolly looked, rising seconds later to give a thumbs-up sign. Aiden swam forward and pushed away some aquatic vegetation. A small cave was revealed, and he felt a thrill of excitement.

Rolly wrote a message on his slate:

> **Let's go in. I'll go first. Everyone stick with your dive buddy and follow the line.**

He passed the slate around so everyone could read it. When everyone had gathered, Rolly swam into the cave with Gere, scanning every surface with his light. The cave was actually a tunnel—wide, but not tall. The bottom was curiously free of silt, but he continued reeling out the strong, fluorescent-yellow mason's twine, just in case the water became murky. He swam for several minutes, periodically checking behind himself, before the rock above him receded. He kicked up and saw a surface reflecting light back at him. He broke it at low speed and shone his light around. A smallish grotto surmounted the pool that he floated in.

Gere broke the surface and spit out his regulator. "Air's breathable."

Rolly spit out his own and sucked in a lungful of air, laden with dank and funk. "That's good. I'd hate to have to drag your unconscious butt out of here."

The six-foot-seven, three-hundred-pound Gere chuckled.

Several more divers surfaced, forming a ring around Rolly and Gere. Aiden, enjoying being underwater, strayed away from the group. He noticed a series of cavities in the wall of the grotto and shone his light into the closest. *Something in there?* He swam closer and an explosion of tentacles and squid arms flew at his face. In less than a second, his mask and regulator were stripped away. He recoiled and thrust his head above the surface. "Squid!"

The longer tentacles pulled on him, yanking him below the surface again. He struggled with the creature, but he could not unwind the arms. It was dragging him toward the submerged hole. The water distorted his vision, but he could see well enough to recognize the clashing beak—big enough to take a chunk out his face—and the rasping radula beyond. *Stupid! Stupid!* He unclipped his dive knife and started slashing, just as strong hands jammed under his arms and lifted him.

He gasped in a breath. "Squid! Ah, that's absolute rubbish! That plonker could've chewed my face off."

"Get back, then." Gere dragged him through the water.

The entire team was active—half above the water and half below, armed with strong lights, knives, and spear guns—as more squid boiled out of the underwater cavities. The grim work was over in a few minutes. Several of the team sustained bites, and one of the Uhlebe brothers had inhaled water. He was hacking and red faced for several minutes.

When Rolly and Fred were convinced that the squid were all dead, they moved out across the pool to a rocky ledge with what appeared to be a low cave mouth beyond. They stripped off neoprene and left their scuba gear on the ledge, opening dry bags and trading out spear guns for the real thing. Aiden retrieved the gear that he had taken from Gar, including the semi-automatic, extra magazines, and a cylinder with a silver ring at one end. He caught Rolly looking him over.

"You know how to use that piece?"

Aiden frowned. *Oh, the gun!* "Of course." *Pointy end, trigger, bang!*

"Are you gonna use it, should things get violent?"

He thought of the chotahs' brutality, Gar's cold determination, and Bass's almost evil detachment. "Yes."

"Good, doctor. We'll make a man of you yet."

"Ugh! Come on, mate, you didn't really just spew that barmy mess, did you?"

Rolly raised his eyebrows and turned away. Aiden sent him off with a rude gesture. "Make a man of you yet," he said under his breath before making a face.

Cooper raised his hand for silence. "Gentlemen, if I may. The last thing that Mister Severage said, before he went into these god-forsaken tunnels, before these fishheads killed him and Thomas and Harker, was, 'Let's go fishing.' I don't know if they were successful, but let's do this in their memory, shall we? Let's exact vengeance for Severage, Harker, Ibarra, and Thomas!"

They entered the tunnel, with the Smithson employees leading. Aiden ended up between them and the Uhlebes. They walked for ten minutes before arriving at a gate with no visible lock. A space with multiple exits lay beyond the gate.

Cooper, on point, shook the gate. "That's surprising." He turned to Drake. "We got anything that will open this?"

"I left my plasma cutter at home."

"Haha." Cooper heard a sound behind him, almost like sandpaper on wood, and a jagged spike of metal erupted from his chest. Warm droplets struck Drake's face even as he was processing the point and Cooper's look of surprise. The object disappeared, leaving a sizable and bloody hole in the front of his shirt. Drake's shotgun rose even as Cooper's body fell, revealing a chotah clutching a spear. The gun roared as the spear flew. A cloud of chotah bits exploded through the air, while the spear struck the gate and went left, striking the wall and clattering to the floor.

Drake was surrounded by men, who rushed past him to Cooper.

"What happened?" Fred asked from down the tunnel.

"One of my men is down," Rolly yelled back, opening a medical kit.

"Jerry!" Fred called. "They need you in the front. There's a casualty." Aiden felt a tap on his side.

"Let me through, please, let me through. Country doctor. Let me through." The grizzled man pushed past, his hair flaring the color of new cotton in the lamp light. "Ho, coming through." He knelt beside Cooper, feeling his neck, while Rolly pushed a dressing against the hole in Cooper's chest. His fingers stood out, stark and pale, against the big wad of reddened gauze.

"You can stop doing that, son. He's dead. The spear severed the major vessels to the heart. He's already bled out. There's nothing we can do."

"Damn it!" Rolly stood up, scrubbing his hands on his pants. "This is a rescue mission, not a freaking stroll in the park. Any more of you ass-clowns do anything stupid on my watch and I'll fire you. Or bury you." He glared at the Smithson employees. "Drake, you gonna be okay?"

"Sir."

Rolly looked at Aiden, who was turning pale green. "Take Mister Cooper back to the boats while we get through the gate."

Aiden looked up, swallowing. "Why me?"

"'Cause you're the least valuable member of this team, frankly."

He felt a flutter in his chest. "I'll remind you that I'm a lab director, Mister...what? Cousins isn't it?"

Rolly smirked. "So?"

"So, I outrank you. I could have *you* fired."

A sour expression welled up on Rolly's face. When he spoke, his voice was quiet. "How many years have you worked at Smithson? How many years have you known Caul?"

"I don't know. One?"

"Twenty." Rolly raised his hand. "So kindly shut your holes." He glanced at one of his specialists. "Mitchell, if you would, seeing's how the doctor is too frail for such things. In the meantime, any ideas on how to get through this gate?"

Fred turned to his brothers. "Tim? Gabe? What'd we bring?"

They rummaged in their gear bags, and Tim held up a bright yellow and black cordless circular saw. "Sintered diamond rescue blade. Should cut through just fine." He went to the gate and applied the saw to one of the two crossbars. The blade shrieked and sprayed sparks. "They'll know we're here." He laughed.

Another chotah appeared just as the second crossbar gave way, and Fred shot it. Aiden flinched at the sound. The gate swung out of their way, struck the first chotah, and rebounded. "Shall we?" Tim asked and stowed his saw. Gathering in the room, they stood in a loose star shape and covered all the exits with lights and gun barrels.

"Any ideas about which way?" Gere glanced at the four possible routes.

Rolly turned to Fred and raised his eyebrows.

The old man pulled a compass from inside his shirt and glanced at it for a moment. "Well, judging by our progress and direction of travel, I'd say we're under the west end of the island." He pointed left. "That passage probably leads to Smithson, that passage—"

"Smithson? Why would there be a passage to the labs?"

Fred rubbed his chin. "You're trying to destroy them, are you not?"

"Not exactly...well, okay, yes."

"Don't you think they'd like to return the favor?" He held his tongue, letting his words sink in. "The enemy is at your gate, Rolly Cousins. Perhaps you should fight them instead of your own men." Fred caught Aiden's eye and winked.

"Sir?" Davis intruded on the silence.

"What?" Rolly glanced at the specialist.

"I can hear fighting down that passage." He gestured to the third tunnel opening.

"Where there's doughnuts, there's cops. Let's go." Rolly wrote a brief message on the wall with chalk and entered the tunnel with Davis.

Aiden squinted at the message. *Some kind of shorthand. Why did he think to bring chalk?*

They moved out, Drake falling in on one side of Aiden and Fred on the other. Fred's hand fell on Aiden's shoulder. "You were never in the military, were you?"

Here it goes again. Aiden glanced at the man. "No. Not really a family occupation, that. I went to university instead."

"Well, nothing wrong with that, but we do need a balance in this matter, by and large. Thucydides said it best, 'A nation that draws too broad a difference between its scholars and its warriors will have its thinking done by cowards and its fighting done by fools.'" He nudged Aiden with his elbow. "Don't ever forget that. In our imperfect republic, there are brave fools and smart cowards. I don't think you fall into the second category."

"Thanks." Aiden managed a half smile.

"All my family went into the military. My father—he's who I'm named after—served in the army in Europe. He made sure that all us boys knew it was a respectable act—serving your country. Naturally, I joined the army, too. I went to 'Nam—three tours. Tim, Peter, Josh, and Bart all went into the army. Jerry was the mold breaker. He joined the navy. Corpsman, of all things. Later, they taught him doctoring. He also led young Gabe astray. He ended up in the marines, go figure. Jarheads did well by him, though. Can't complain. He's a good kid."

There were scattered chuckles.

"Don't let him fool you. I just celebrated my fiftieth birthday and have more grandkids than Fred. And, I reached a higher rank than you did, old man."

Aiden turned in time to see the speaker, a man about his father's age. *Must be Gabe*, he thought. "How can you all be so light-hearted? A man was just killed." He glanced around, finally appreciating what he had gotten himself into. He felt a chill. "We may be next."

"Because," one of the brothers said, "we've all been in combat. We've all seen buddies killed. This is nothing."

"We're paying attention, doctor," Fred said. "But, none of us is going to wet his britches over a chotah. We've been fighting them too long."

"Besides, Fred's getting senile and can't remember to stop talking at inappropriate times."

The brothers laughed.

"You just earned yourself a lump of coal at Christmas, Peter." Fred shook his head, but he was grinning.

Aiden frowned. "Even so, why are any of you doing this? Joining us?"

The brothers' joviality frosted. "We have a score to settle. Mother said it was time."

"Great. Yeah. Clear as muck."

Fred spoke. "We go way back with the chotah and their queen. There's a lot of bad blood between our families."

"Queen?" Aiden was thinking of the conversations he and Caul had shared about the nature and behaviors of hive animals. He was struck by Fred's use of the word.

The old man nodded. "As Mother reckons it."

"In a literal sense? Like the Queen of England or a queen bee? Or are you just being poetic?"

"Queen bee."

"Oh."

The sound of running feet distracted his attention. Half a dozen lights and guns covered their back trail, revealing Mitchell pounding up the tunnel.

"That was fast," one of the brothers said.

"The lagoon was swarming with those damn crabs. I couldn't even get to my gear." He cleared his throat. "I had to leave Cooper in the tunnel. And the crabs started chasing me. They're not very fast, but they're coming."

The group ahead stopped abruptly, amid hushed discussion, followed by shouting and gunfire. "What's going on?" Fred called out.

"Hostiles ahead," Davis yelled in response.

"And hostiles behind."

43

Jillian? Jillian!"

A great crushing mass fell away from her, and sour air rushed into her lungs. "Help!" Her voice squeaked out. Light painted her eyelids, and she snapped them open. Bits of fish and other things fell through her limited field of view. She swiped at the wetness on her face, shoveling chunks of slimy gore onto the ground.

"Ugh! That's disgusting."

Strong hands grabbed hold of her and hauled her to her feet. More gore fell, a gruesome cascade of dismembered chotah piling up around her. The hands spun her, and arms embraced her—Caul, Evelyn, and Meeka.

Caul's unsober face filled her view. "I thought you were dead when I saw that a lobstrosity had fallen on you. The chotah bodies helped to protect you."

"What happened?"

Evelyn pulled Caul away to give him another hug, and Meeka grinned, watching them. "We were in a standoff with the chotah when we heard a disruption from way down the tunnel. The taucah and the chotah fought back here and died. I've never seen anything like it. They squabble, normally, but nothing like this."

"Taucah? Is that what you call the lobstrosities?" Caul leaned into the conversation.

Meeka nodded.

"I suspect they had our scent." Caul the scientist was back. "The lead...taucah probably became confused when it ran into a wall of fish-headed chotah instead of us. In the dark, they just reverted to instinct, and probably some of them panicked, and they tore each other apart."

Meeka nodded again. "Some of the chotah had guns, which is how they fought back against the taucah. They passed the guns back through their ranks." She shone her flashlight beam around. "Once the front didn't have guns, we attacked them. It was only a matter of time until the pinch between forces wiped out the chotah." A giggle escaped her pretty mouth.

"You don't feel any remorse? For the chotah?" Jillian asked.

Meeka wrinkled her nose. "No! Yuck! We hate the chotah. They're creepy and they stink. That's why we came down here, to eradicate them."

Jillian wondered at this new manifestation of hostility. "What happened to one big freaky family?"

Meeka's grin widened. "Eldest is no longer in our minds. It's incredible! I have my own thoughts and my sisters have their own thoughts… unrestrained." She shook her head, eyes closed, still smiling. "It's hard to explain. It was like having someone always hanging over your shoulder, whispering in your ear, listening to your thoughts, holding a dirty piece of glass over your eyes. That's all gone now. It's amazing! I want to go touch Douglas!" She winced and opened her eyes. "Sorry." She waved her hand. "Sorry. The imprinting is powerful. I know he's your husband, but I really want him."

Jillian's anger growled out of her throat. "You so much as lay a finger on him again and I will kill you. Got that? It goes for any of you freaks!"

Several Meekas surrounded and crowded her. "We respect your privileged position, Douglas's *wife*, but never forget that we loved him first and love him deeper, and when you are old and no longer feel the heat of your youth and your love for him withers, we will still love him this intensely, this passiona—"

Jillian slapped the speaking Meeka. "You've said more than enough!"

The Meekas menaced her. She heard Evelyn's voice calling, but it was Meeka's own voice, "Leave her be," that cut through the fray and made the other Meekas abandon their threatening postures and walk away. The spindly, nightmare Meeka—Twenty-seven—trudged down the passage, glaring at her departing sisters. "I apologize for their behavior. My hope remains that their conditioning will fade over time."

Jillian shivered, taking no comfort in the creature's words, nor her presence. "Don't you have a jail to run?"

"My gaol is emptied; I have set the prisoners free, just as Doctor Saunders has done for us." She gazed at the receding backs of the Meekas. "Unfortunately, some of my sisters are more resistant to freedom than I am, but then, I never lusted for your husband like so many of them did, nor was I as in thrall to Eldest. I am unique among the Meekas. Mother had so little of my crab DNA from which to work that she only made one of me." Her face, as much as it could, looked sad. "Come Doctor, Teacher, Wife…we have a war to win."

She set off down the tunnel, followed by several handsome men. They carried weapons in their hands and grim determination on their faces. One glanced at Jillian and nodded.

She watched them go before turning to Caul. "Who are they?"

Evelyn smiled. "Those are Johns. I started getting them in my nursery a few years after the first Meekas arrived. I still had help back then. Nettie was still alive, God rest her soul."

Jillian frowned. "Nettie? Why do I know that name?"

"Nettie Uhlebe. She's the lady who gave me my Saint Christopher's medal. She used to tell me, over and over again, how her best friend had given it to her when they were children."

Jillian's mouth moved up and down, flapping like a fish's jaw. "Ruth!"

Evelyn startled, bemused. "Yes, Ruth Tate. How did you—"

"Tate?" Caul felt unanchored. "This is just a big circle of interrelated madness. Are Sharon and this Ruth woman related?"

"Who's Sharon?"

"My boss."

"Caul!" The frantic voice of a Meeka echoed up the passage. They glanced at each other, before charging down the slope. Jillian was sick of traversing this tunnel. *Down, back, down again and it gets weirder every time.* The floor was littered with chotah carcasses, and occasionally, in the mess, a pair of dark eyes, dulled in death, stared up from a pretty face. She averted her eyes from the bodies of Meekas and Johns. *This isn't my fight. I just want my husband back.* Caul charged ahead, but Evelyn hesitated over each corpse, trembling and pale as rivulets of grief watered her face.

"Should you be here?" Jillian asked quietly.

Evelyn's wet, red gaze looked at nothing. "They're my babies. I raised all of them." Hesitant fingers closed eyes forever blind. "They finally gained their freedom and they're using it to fight her. And to save your husband. My heavens! Such a waste!"

"I'm grateful." Jillian spoke the words, but it crossed her mind that this was somehow justice for the Meekas' avowed fixation on Doug. *They hurt us. It's right that they suffer.* So said her mind, but her heart did not agree.

"Come on. This isn't the time to mourn."

Evelyn sniffed. "Child, I've been mourning since I was nineteen years old."

"I'm sorry."

"Teacher?" A Meeka approached them. "We need you to come. We can't guarantee your safety unless you're with the group."

They followed Meeka. Evelyn did not stop again, but at each fallen human they passed she faced and leaned toward them like a heliotrope tracking the sun. Finally, most of the human dead seemed to taper off, followed by the chotah dead. Thereafter, the tunnel was intermittently blocked by only dead and shattered submarine-bodied taucah and an occasional John. Regardless, the cloying musk of death clung to Jillian, maddening her. Escape, then, was joyous, and she fairly ran into the cavern where their party stood, wearing masks of anxiety.

Evelyn did not mince the issue. "What's the matter?"

With heavy eyes, Caul glanced at Jillian's feet. "The Meekas report that Doug isn't where they thought he'd be, where they left him. They're pretty sure they know where he is, but it's apparently not a great place."

One of the Meekas pushed forward. "I—actually not me, I mean my sister overheard a chotah talking about a prisoner found in the tunnels. They took him to her, to Mother. If he's with her, then she intends to do a terminal harvest."

Jillian felt her pulse thud and her face grow hot. "No!" She looked down, pinching her eyelids shut. "Wait, what do you mean terminal?"

"She intends to take his testicles—"

Jillian flinched. "What? That's—that's awful!"

"That will destroy the glands." Caul frowned. "They will die in a few hours and cease producing sperm cells."

Several of the Meekas shook their heads. "No, she can take them and transfer them to her own body, where they will survive and provide her with his seed, forever."

"She can't! Those are my babies in there! My children! She can't have them. She can't!"

Distantly, she heard Evelyn's voice. "That's what Mother did with my ovaries. She took them and made my Meekas, my little mes, my babies." She looked at Jillian.

A Meeka leaned close. "And, of course, she will eat him, afterwards."

Jillian's knees cracked on the stone floor with the sounds of ripe melons breaking open. "Where is he?" Jillian wobbled and rocked, knees throbbing, before Caul helped her to her feet. "We need to go. Now!"

"That way," several Meekas said and pointed.

She ran toward the opening, entirely enjoying pushing Meekas from her path, when she heard a familiar *click, clack*. Worried voices muttered around her, but she pressed forward. The clacking swelled, and several taucah barreled out of the passage, blocking their way.

"This is a problem," one of the Johns said to Caul. "We have no more bullets. The taucah are difficult to kill with bare hands."

Caul rubbed the back of his neck. "Then we retreat. Retreat!"

A roar, like fire, filled Jillian's ears. "No!" She wrenched an old rifle from the hands of a Meeka and pushed through the speechless others, running for the swarm of lobster monsters.

"Jillian!"

She ignored Caul and rushed the first creature, ducking under its claws and swinging the heavy gun barrel at its right legs. A crunch shot the air as chitin shattered, and the lobster fell sideways as its legs were swept outward. She swooped the barrel up and around and smacked the right arm, tearing through the pliable chitin of the joint. A vise clamped onto her thigh, making her cry out. She turned as far as she could and jammed the rifle barrel into the claw joint, trying to wedge it open. An axe-wielding John flew out of nowhere, severing the arm with a wild yell and a good swing.

"Thanks!"

She turned in time to bat away the other claw and hit the injured joint again. More chitin cracked. The lobster struggled to get its legs under itself, but it could not support its own weight on the right side. Instead, it paddled forward, its mouth parts clashing.

"Eyes!"

Jillian and John swung together striking both black bulges simultaneously. They ruptured with a viscous popping sound, making her face wrinkle in disgust. The creature scuttled away backwards. Jillian turned to find a new foe bearing down on her. She swung the gun, but this lobster was quicker than the first and evaded her stroke. The barrel struck the ground, throwing sparks, and the stock broke.

"Shit!"

She stooped for the barrel, as a claw drove toward her face. She fended it off with the shard of stock, but the other claw came low and she felt the world spin as she tumbled in the air. The stone floor rushed up and smacked her in the face. Skittering sounds and yelling merged and wove with the ringing in her ears. Shaking her head, she tried to push up, but her left wrist burst into flaring pain.

Hiss.

Something hard pinched around her waist, squeezing her through, side to side. The floor receded, as the pinch became an agony. A giant, black claw filled her sight. She blinked, as warm liquid ran into her left eye. The claw before her swelled and swelled again. *Bigger? Closer!* The lobster sought to make a pretty choker necklace for her, when her senses finally emerged from the fog. She arched backwards, raised her arms, and jammed the sharp wood into the pincer's joint. She gasped as the force of her thrust pushed her deeper into the claw that held her—scraping the skin from her sides.

The world lurched, and she fell, screaming.

Hands—human hands—took hold of her, and the crushing pressure ended. "Thank you," she whispered. The ground fell away again, but now arms carried her. She closed her eyes, but could not close her ears to the crunching and screaming.

She bounced, as her rescuer ran. "Lady, I need you to stand now," said a male voice in her ear.

"Why?"

"I need to return to the fight. If I put you down, you'll get stepped on." A hand swiped across her forehead, and she flinched. "Come, open your eyes," the voice said. "I'm setting you down."

She tilted and felt the ground beneath her feet. Like balking blinds, her eyelids crept upwards. The John who had carried her turned and left, but a white-haired wraith replaced him and hovered before her.

"Jillian!"

"Caul."

"We thought you'd been killed. Whatever possessed you to do that?"

"Doug."

"That's admirable, but you're no good to him dead."

She wiped her left eye, the fingers coming away red, and blinked. Twenty-seven and Evelyn stood close by, sheltering several injured Meekas. The crab-woman, with her long, skeletal limbs, leaned over the ring of defenders and plucked out the eyes of the attacking taucah. Her moves were lightning quick and precise.

Jillian grabbed Caul's arms. "Give me a weapon."

"I don't have one. We're trying to get out of here."

She glanced around, in the dim, chaotic lighting, and saw flashes of silver. "The chotah are coming." They poured into the cavern from every opening, and Jillian raised her hands in despair. "We're surrounded!"

44

Shots echoed in the tunnel, and Aiden was a child again, playing in the slough behind his Nana's house in Stoke Fleming, wellies squelching in the mud as he crouched at the end of a storm water culvert that ran beneath the A379. After discovering it, he had clapped and yelled into the pipe for nearly an hour, listening to the weird, warbling echoes. And sometimes sounds that he could not explain.

Odd memory. He pressed the foam plugs more firmly in his ears and glanced at the anxious, unfamiliar faces around him. *I don't want to be here after all.*

A barrage of gunfire pummeled his skull again and lit up the tunnel as if the sun were breaking through the stone.

"They're running!"

The mass of the vanguard trooped away, so the rest followed.

"Be careful of an ambush." Fred called.

They crossed over dead chotah and burst onto a ledge overlooking a cavern sown with chaos. Silvery chotah swirled among purple-black lobstrosities. "Oh, those are new," Josh said.

The creatures were ranged across the uneven floor of the cavern, facing into the center where a small group of Meekas and Johns clustered. Aiden saw a familiar face. "Caul!"

"Sssh, son." Fred smiled at him. "Tactical advantage—not letting the enemy know where you are. Course, those toothy trout appear to be deaf." He glanced back at his brothers. "Shooting fish in a barrel."

Fred raised his father's M1 carbine, casually took aim, and shattered the front of a lobster with a .30-06 full metal jacket round.

"Nice shot."

The brothers lined up on the ledge and fired methodically into the massed creatures. Rolly took note and arranged his men on the sloping ledge. "Do not fire on the people. Otherwise, fire at will."

Aiden, standing on the far side of the Uhlebes from Rolly, pointed his pistol at a milling group of fishmen and pulled the trigger. The gun bucked, flying back at his face.

"You have to anticipate the recoil," Gabe yelled over the din. "Use both hands for a steadier shot."

Aiden wrapped his left hand around the butt and took aim again. Before he knew what had happened, the gun stopped firing.

"You're out of ammo." Gabe said.

"Right." Aiden looked at the gun. "I have a bloody DSc, I should be able to figure this out." He pushed everything that looked like a button and was rewarded when a black rectangle fell out of the grip. He put one of the full ones in, pulled it back out, turned it, reinserted until it clicked, took aim, and pulled the trigger. Nothing happened.

"You have to cycle a round into the chamber," Gabe said.

Aiden stared at the gun.

"Release the slide lock."

Aiden stared at the gun.

Gabe reached over his shoulder, thumbed the slide lock, and watched the slide snap forward. "Now, shoot!" Aiden did.

At the other end of the ledge, Rolly watched the massed chotah reacting to the barrage of bullets. Many of them, along with the black lobsters, were rushing the bottom of the ramp up to their ledge. "We're about to have company."

He fired his shotgun until he ran out of shells, and then switched to his Colt 1911. The big bullets made nice holes in fish and lobster alike. He emptied his three magazines. "I'm out of ammo. How're you all doing?"

"I'm out, too."

"Look out!"

Several spears sailed from the shadows. One clattered against the cavern wall, but two found marks in the men. Gere yanked one out of his thigh, snapped the shaft asunder, and tossed it aside. Mitchell, though, stood with a bemused expression, looking at the shaft protruding from his abdomen.

"Shouldn't that hurt?" He looked up at Rolly.

"Jerry! I need your help down here."

They shifted Mitchell out of the way and shifted tactics, crouching and firing defensively now as more creatures attempted the ramp and several more spears were hurled at them. What appeared to be the last lobster plowed bodies from the ramp onto the chotah below. Gere fired his last round of buckshot into it, but still it came on.

"Trouble...trouble!"

Bart hustled over and his M14 cracked three times. The remaining chotah massed and ran out of the cavern, all down the same tunnel. "Huh! Look what I did...I scared 'em off." Bart's smile flashed white in the dim, foul air.

Leaving one of the Environmental Services men, Atwan, to wait with Mitchell, they carefully made their way down the ramp. Caul dispensed hearty handshakes to all the Smithson employees, while Fred pulled the three surviving Johns aside. "Is she gone?"

The men nodded.

"So, whose side are you on now?"

"Yours."

Fred smiled. "Good. Then I look forward to fighting alongside you, cousins, instead of against you."

Aiden was the last to reach the cavern floor and the last to shake Caul's hand. "It's good to see you again, old man."

"Psh! I don't feel old. I'm exhausted, though. I want a shower and three days of sleep."

"You need a shower, mate; you working for a cannery now?" Aiden surveyed the dead. "I'd just like to get out of here."

"We can't. We have one more person to rescue. Doug Sandow is still being held."

Twenty-seven rose from behind the three other Meekas who had sheltered her during the sniping. The newly arrived men responded by aiming guns.

"Put those down!" Evelyn stormed toward them. "She's one of us."

They reluctantly lowered their weapons.

"This has not gone well," Twenty-seven said. "The remaining cho-tah go to Mother's hall. I mourn my brothers and sisters, but I also mourn Douglas's fate if we do not hurry."

Red. Hmm?

Shuffle.

Doug straightened, his neck screaming in protest, and his eyelids popped open. *Light!* He was in a nearly circular room about forty feet in diameter. The wall he leaned against was not natural, but constructed of boulders and smaller rocks held together with some kind of gritty mortar. This barrier enclosed two-thirds of the space and rose to a height of about fifteen feet. The back wall was the native stone of the cavern, which rose perhaps sixty feet before curving overhead. A tall cave mouth led through the cavern wall opposite the gate, and it was in this arch that a light was bobbing and flickering.

He stood, trying to be silent. *One advantage to being naked, no clothes to rustle.* Still, he longed for at least a fig leaf or three. *Fighting in the nude may have been great for ancient Greeks, but I'm not happy about facing more weird crap with my flag flying.* He crept across the enclosed space, making for the cave mouth and the tunnel beyond. It bent away to the right, so Doug approached from that side and peered around the corner. He saw a flash of movement and lurched back as something stabbed him in the shoulder.

"Damn!"

The object felt slimy as he pulled it from his skin, flinching in pain.

"She didn't lie. You are quite the specimen."

No more...please, no more. Wishing for something to defend himself with, Doug thought of the Saint Christopher medal lying uselessly in his car. *God, I'm sorry I stopped believing in you!*

In silhouette, a figure glided into view, riding four thick tentacles.

"Stay away from me, Freeka, or I swear I'll kill you."

She did not hesitate, but flowed on, towering over Doug. "I'm not Bellah. I'm her mentor and mistress. And now, I must carry on her work, because she failed. I heard her death."

"Freeka's dead?" A sound, like a distant balloon popping, distracted him for a second. He looked back. "Who are you?"

"I am Ashrah. Leader of the chotah and lessers, and speaker for—"

A faint shout and more pops drew their attention through the gate to the cavern's far entrance.

"Your people come, fighting. I allow this. Once here, they will witness your conversion and suffer their deaths."

"I don't understand." His shoulder throbbed and tingled.

"Of course you don't, foolish man. My beloved Bellah refused to break you properly, so strong was her imprint on you. She loved you and did not want you harmed."

Freeka loved me?

"Taking a finger. Such a weak act." The heat of her gaze made him look away. "I would have taken your whole hand." She slithered closer. "Now, I will settle for nothing less than your legs. I will convert you. You will serve me."

He flinched. "No, I won't! Never again."

"You would fight me?" She pushed herself upward to her full height and surged forward.

His neck popped as he tilted his head back to look at her. "Yes."

"You would be so foolish?"

The cold metal of the gate pressed against his back. *How'd...?*

"You have nowhere to run."

"I'm not running—"

Her left hand lashed out and gripped his throat. Claw tips dug into the skin of his neck as she lifted him from his feet. His spine popped like a crackling string of fireworks. She leaned into his face. "Will you fight *me*? Make this sport? One pleasure instead of another?" She squeezed, turning his face red and causing his breaths to wheeze in and out. "It matters very little to me. You will either serve me—amuse me—or I will take your testicles to get what I need." Her slimy tongue lashed out, caressed his jaw, and slid across his lips. "And then eat you."

He flinched and wrapped his arms around her wrist, pulling himself up so he could breathe. "Put me down!" Her saliva dripped into his mouth. *Augh, yuck!*

There was more shouting, close by. The popping resolved into gunfire. "Capitulate!"

His left arm slipped off hers, too numb to control. "No! Just stop this. Leave me alone."

She pulled his face even closer to hers. "If a stud bull asked such a thing of you, what would you say?"

Meeka's words crashed into his mind, *'Mother loves pretty things. She thought you pretty...your smell.'*

Stud bull...I'm being bred for food? "Y—you want to eat my children?"

She threw him to the ground. "Amongst other things. You're useful animals to us."

He landed in a heap and felt a stab of pain in his right ankle. But it could not distract him from his rising gorge at the thought of her eating babies. *My babies!* "We're human beings."

"You're inferior. The strong always prey upon the weak."

With the shuffling-slap gait, the chotah burst into the cavern, and lights speared the gloom, casting demonic shadows on every surface. With one of her tentacles, she reached out and stroked Doug's thigh.

"Come...perform for me." She settled back on the ground.

He looked away, tasting bile in his mouth.

"Doug!"

He was on his feet, pressed against the cold iron, but it resisted his efforts to squeeze through. "Jillian!" He saw her, waving from among a group of men with rifles. He heard the sound of leather on stone.

"Doug! Behind you!"

He closed his eyes and did not turn. Ashrah's breath, when it came, was cool on his ear. "This is your last chance."

"No. I will not submit."

Cold fingers caressed the back of his neck. "Such a waste. Bellah spoke highly of your time together."

"Shut up!" He flinched away from her.

He smelled rotten eggs and choked, as she backed away from him.

"Mother comes," she said.

Clear as a struck bell, a note of disbelief filled his mind. *Mother comes?*

He turned and faced the cave, feeling wind on his cheeks. *As if a piston's sliding down a cylinder.* As Ashrah retrieved her lamp and returned to the enclosure, he noticed how smooth the walls of the tunnel were. *Like something's been rubbing them smooth...for years. Many, many years.* He glanced from Ashrah to the tunnel. *If she's ten-feet tall...* The cave mouth was at least three times higher.

Oh, shit.

45

The chotah fell back before the human onslaught. Caul could see through the hedge of Uhlebe men that the passage they were in opened up ahead of them. Heartened by the thought of space, they redoubled their attack.

"I'm out of ammo."

"We're nearly there." Ninety-nine called from behind them.

As if on cue, the chotah bolted. A cheer went up from the fighters as they surged into the cavern, only to die away as the chotah turned and formed a line across the space. Caul and Jillian pushed into the vast chamber, which was illuminated by sweeping beams of light.

"Doug!" Jillian jumped repeatedly when she saw her husband.

He jumped up and pressed himself against a black, metal gate, a look of wild desperation haunting his face. She stifled a scream as she saw Eldest rising up behind him. *She was lying down...what were they doing?*

Caul ran forward. "Doug! Behind you!" He swung a rifle butt at the chotah, looking at Eldest all the while. "I killed you." He pressed into the ranks of the chotah.

"Doctor, don't." Someone grabbed him from behind and pulled backwards. "You'll be flanked if you try that."

A gasp rose, and several Meekas called out in unison. "Mother comes."

Caul looked at the creature leaning down toward Doug's head and realized just how tall she was. "That's not Eldest." The final words of the burned and dying creature resonated in his mind, the dots connecting. "If you're not Eldest, you're Mother...shoot her! Someone shoot her! That's Mother."

Ninety-nine ran to him and touched his arm. "That's not Mother, that's Ashrah." She looked up and pointed. "That's Mother."

Caul raised his eyes. Above the stone wall, he could see the top of a cave mouth. At first, he thought the ceiling was collapsing, but then he understood what he was seeing. He understood. And felt fear.

Doug strained against the gate, pressing cruel lines into the skin of his back. *Break, break, break!* Something moved in the cave, and a wave of fetid air—a slaughterhouse stench—washed over him. He gagged. Bending, his stomach surrendered bile alone, and still the odor worsened. The sound of bellowing drew his eyes upward.

Wet and glistening, black tentacles stretched from a bloated greenish-black maggot's body, thirty feet tall. The surface of it shimmered, constantly moving, and a single, vast pool of glossy black gazed down on him. Stars did not live in that eye, only madness and death. It pushed out into the walled space, its massive body gliding on a layer of slime. Tentacles the size of trees quested toward him, filling his mind with the fumes of tumult. Images from his childhood—images spawned from reading Lovecraft and Derleth—paraded through his consciousness.

He was looking at Cthulhu.

The creature slid toward him, as he screamed and flailed, trying to get away. "Ashrah! Help me!"

"I won't. Mother says you must be harvested."

Mother...? That's Mother?

He regained his feet. Blithering filled his ears, as he wedged fingers and toes into the wall and climbed. He had to get out of the enclosure. Everything else was secondary—his sanity would support nothing else. He was halfway up the rough stones when a thick, rubbery limb found its way around his waist, and yanked him backwards. He flailed at it, bruising his hands and feet. Smaller tentacles coiled around his arms and legs, stilling his gross movements.

"Help me!"

Mother brought him close to her eye. The tentacles laid him back and pulled his legs wide. He felt small, feathery touches on his scrotum, making it shrink against his body. A thousand ants seemed to caress him, pulling the skin taut. Something cold, hard, and sharp touched him.

"No, please!"

Pain flared like white heat in his groin, and the cavern filled with the echoes of his anguish.

The giant eye regarded two oblong, pearly objects, held up by thin cords, before they were whisked away. A sonorous, undulating sound emerged from Mother. In a haze of pain, Doug felt himself moving downward. A sharp snap made him open his eyes, and a giant, black shell filled his vision. It lifted. Even in his agony, he understood that it was not a shell but a beak—a beak the size of a refrigerator. It crashed shut with another percussive shock, before opening again, as the tentacles drew him toward it. A surge of terror flashed through his mind, remembering what Jillian had said about squid beaks.

"Mother, no! Please don't," someone called.

Doug rolled his head, trying to see. "I don't want to die."

Mother warbled again, the sound vibrating in Doug's chest.

He looked up at the impassive eye above him. "Let me go." His voice erupted in tatters. A charnel house of odors washed over him from Mother's open mouth as she thrust his head inside her beak.

"Please don't do this."

He struggled against the tentacles, his body shaking from the effort, but her grip was unyielding, and he felt his muscles tear from the strain. Her rough, black tongue caressed the side of his head like a pillow of cold, slimy sandpaper—tasting him. The light grew dim.

"No! Oh please, no! No, no, no!"

He felt the pressure of the serrated beak against his neck, and hot urine mingled with the blood on his legs.

All was dark.

"Please!"

More pressure—unbearable, crushing.

"No!"

His nose and mouth filled with her saliva, and he choked.

He felt a blinding flash of pain.

And Mother swallowed.

Jillian watched in horror as a moving wall of evil emerged from the cave mouth. She closed her eyes and prayed. She prayed as she had not prayed in years. Doug's pleas had made her clamp her eyes shut. His screams made her prayers erupt from her throat.

Caul was working the group. "I need one bullet. Someone has to have one bullet left."

People searched, some willfully turning away from the horror before them, but found nothing. Others ignored him, plunging into the ranks of the chotah, working out the frustration of powerlessness. Several empty guns were hurled, but fell short of the beast or bounced off, harmlessly.

"Wait!" Aiden grabbed his arm. "I have this. I forgot I'd stuck in my pocket." He held up the cylinder he had taken off of Gar. "Here."

Caul took it, his eyes widening. He recognized the cylinder from security training, and it was even better than a bullet.

"Jillian! Jillian!" Running to her, he shook her. "Take this. It's a flash-bang grenade. Throw it at the eye. Throw just like you did the rocks with Eldest Meeka."

She looked down, surprised. *Smaller than a softball.* Doug's muffled scream yanked her attention back to the present. The evil thing was killing her husband. She trembled, nearly falling, but managed to pull herself together and stand up straight.

"Jillian! Now." As he had seen the officers do, Caul pulled the pin on the grenade. He wrapped her hands around it. "Just throw. At the eye."

She tore her gaze away from the arching, bloodied body of her husband and fixated on the glossy dome above. "Right." She pulled back her arm—an act she had done ten thousand times—an action purely imprinted in her muscles—and snapped the grenade in a fast, flat arc. It sailed through the air, tumbling slightly. Several dozen pairs of eyes watched its dark flight. Caul remembered at the last second to look away. He embraced Jillian and pulled her face to his chest.

The fuse burned down as the parabola diminished. Four feet from Mother's eye, the grenade detonated with a stunning burst of light and pressure, and then struck her eyeball with a resounding smack. She bellowed and her tentacles flailed outward. A membrane slid over her injured oculus, as she retreated back into the tunnel, swallowing against the injury to her auditory organs.

Doug's body, thrown by Mother's frantic reaction, tumbled loose-limbed through the air, and landed on the row of chotah, smashing several of them to the ground. Caul and Jerry raced to him, afraid of what they would find. To their relief, his head was still attached, but jagged lacerations marred each side of his neck. He was covered in scratches, and blood flowed freely from his violated scrotum. They worked to stabilize and bandage him as best they could, oblivious to the mayhem of chotah slaughter going on around them.

"Is he going to be okay?"

Caul looked up to find Jillian, tear-streaked, hovering beside him. He grabbed her hand and squeezed. "You saved his life. One second longer, and he'd have lost his head."

She strangled out a sobbing laugh. "That sounds like something he would say."

Jerry drew a breath. "He's as stable as I can make him, but we need to get him to a hospital."

Looking around, Caul saw that there were no standing chotah. "What happened to them?"

Jillian shrugged and reached for Doug. "Who cares?"

They constructed a sling out of gear bags and belts, and got Doug loaded up. A Meeka approached Jillian just as they were preparing to set out.

"Here, I found this, in there." She pointed to the enclosure beyond the now opened gate. She held out her hand—an oblong object, pearly and a bit bigger than a large grape, nestled within.

"It's his."

Once a team had retrieved Mitchell and Atwan, several of the Meekas volunteered to lead the rescuers out to another of their houses, this one near the hospital. After assuring Jillian that he would join her soon, Caul watched them go. Aiden and Rolly stepped up beside him.

"Is he going to make it?"

Caul shrugged. "Come on, guys, how many times do I have to say this? I'm a biologist, not a physician." He glanced at their expectant faces. "However, I think he'll pull through."

"Was that his wife? With the grenade?" Aiden asked.

"Yes. She saved his life."

Rolly smirked. "That was a heck of a throw. Think we can recruit her for the softball team?"

"I doubt it. I imagine they're going to want to move to Kansas or Wyoming or somewhere else far from the ocean." Caul's brow furrowed. "What happened, anyway, with the chotah?"

Rolly rubbed his lips, wishing he had a toothpick. "Don't know. That grenade went off and a few seconds later they just fell apart. Started wandering away, fighting each other, you name it."

"They must have been telepathically linked to Mother." Caul shuddered. "When she got the smack in the eye, the link must have been disrupted. Speaking of her, she's our problem now, you know?"

The men cautiously approached the enclosure. After assuring that the gate was blocked open, they went inside.

"Is this safe?" Aiden peered at the cave.

Rolly scoffed. "Safe enough, doc. What are you worried about? That thing moved about three feet a year."

Aiden keep his light on the tunnel, which curved away into darkness.

"Oh! And then that happened." Rolly went to the left and dropped to a knee to examine a squid-faced corpse pressed into the rocks. "Those tentacles were murderous. They flattened her."

"That was Ashrah."

They turned to find a Meeka watching them.

"Ashrah?"

"She was like Eldest, only older. More powerful and dreadful; less human. She hated us, almost as much as Eldest hated us. She hated the chotah and the taucah, too. Both of them were full of hatred. So much hatred."

Insight sparked in Caul's mind. "You said that when Eldest died, you were freed. Is that what happened to the chotah? Was she controlling them?"

Meeka nodded. "We should leave. Mother is horribly upset, and I hear her moving down there."

"Yes." Caul gazed down the tunnel into the gloom. "That's a battle for another day."

46

Doug woke in a wholly different place than where he had lost consciousness. Instead of darkness, there was light. Instead of the stench of rotting meat, there was a scent of pine cleanser. Instead of slime on his scalp, there was a soft pillow. He moved his head and immediately regretted it.

"Mister Sandow? You're in the recovery room. Try not to move, okay?"

He cracked his eyelids and blinked against the fluorescent lights. "I'm not dead."

Laughter. "No, not today."

He sighed and let his lids slip closed. *I'm not dead.*

Doug woke a second time to voices. "I'm still not dead."

The voices stilled, his world lurched, and then Jillian's voice pummeled his ears. "Doug! Oh, I'm so glad to hear you speak."

Lips, frantic and eager, mashed his. His neck hurt, but he did not care. The lips kissed his nose, his forehead, and his jaw. He opened his eyes and beheld Jillian inches from him. She began to shimmer and run, like a watercolor painting in a rainstorm.

"Doug? What's the matter? Are you in pain?"

He gasped. "No...I mean, yes, but—" he swallowed "—it's not important. I just thought that..."

She gazed at him. "Thought what, sweetie?"

"I thought you hated me?"

Jillian's eyes filled, too. "No! No, never. I'm sorry! I hated what you did, but I love you. I always will."

He wrapped her in his arms and did not let go for a long time.

Hands clasped on the white, cotton blanket. "The surgeon was able to put your boy bits back together. He thinks you'll make a full recovery of function, even if you are missing a testicle." Jillian rubbed his arm, her expression filled with hope.

"Good, I was already kinda half nuts before—"

"Douglas!" She rolled her eyes.

He chuckled, but it felt forced. "We'll make that baby yet."

"You already have!"

They looked at the door in time to see Ruth roll through in her wheelchair, pushed by Fred. "Are you taking visitors?"

"Yes!" Jillian jumped up and hugged the old woman. "Fred." She hugged him too.

"When are you two going to believe me?"

Jillian put her hands on her belly and rubbed. "I believe you, Ruth. I can feel it."

"Good!" She turned her gaze to the bed. "And you, young man. Why was your Saint Christopher medal in your car? You could have saved everyone so much grief if you'd simply worn it." She reached into her purse and pulled out another medal. "Here. Put this on, and don't take it off. Angels were watching over you, but you're dangerous. You need all the help you can get."

"Yes, ma'am."

Jillian took the medal and put it in Douglas's hand.

"His neck is still too injured to put it on."

"Well, make sure you put it on just as soon as you can."

A knock distracted all of them. "Hello? Is it a party?" Caul, Evelyn, and Aiden entered, and one of the Meekas poked her head into the room. Douglas felt pain at the sight of her.

Caul grinned. "Are we interrupting?"

"No," Jillian said, "but I'm not sure we're supposed to have this many people in the room." She was not pleased to see Meeka either.

Evelyn smiled. "Nina Sest and I wanted to get some coffee, so we'll just step out."

Caul embraced her and pecked her on the cheek. "I'll miss you."

He turned and shook Fred's hand. "Good to see you. And you Miss Ruth. Jillian—" he turned toward the bed "—and, my favorite cretin. You're a little worse for wear, Doug."

"Douglas."

"Hmm?"

Jillian smiled. "He's decided that nearly having his head snipped off is a substantial life event and should be marked as such by," she glanced at him, "growing up? Isn't that what you said?"

He nodded.

"Of course, he was strung out on morphine when he said it, but apparently it's stuck. He wants to be called Douglas now."

"More power to you, Douglas," Caul said. "Perhaps we should all do that. Fredrick? Aidenick?"

Douglas chuckled. "Sure dude, I dub thee Colander. Your head is porous enough."

Caul looked askance at him. "Get thee to a punnery, young man."

They all found chairs and talked about the past week with subdued enthusiasm. The subject of the lab came up and Caul became somber. "Sharon's remains haven't been recovered from the boiler building, but the board has already appointed me interim general director. And, along with all the county and state people poking their noses into what's been happening, we had some visitors from the federal government today, including some military brass."

Aiden sat up, wanting to ask a question that had been bothering him for days. "Missus Uhlebe, how was I able to see you, the night of the fire? You..." He waved at her legs.

"I sometimes go walking, outside this body. That night, I had many relatives in distress—Sharon, John Gar, John Dace, and John Bass. They all needed help."

"You were related to them?"

Caul tilted his head at Aiden. "Forgive his ignorance, Ruth. He comes by it naturally, having grown up in the wrong country."

Aiden frowned.

"Oh, Caul. Stop teasing everyone." She turned to Aiden. "Yes, I'm related. The Tate and Uhlebe and Smithson families go way back on Mount Desert Island. My maiden name is Tate, and Sharon is— was—my second cousin, once removed."

"But how could I see you? Talk to you?"

A shadow crossed Ruth's face and she looked away for a moment. "What I say here stays here, all right?"

"Certainly, yes."

"We three families—Tates, Uhlebes, and Smithsons—our families have always been, well, different. Possessing the abilities to see distantly, hear each other's thoughts at times, and walk outside of our bodies during dreams, sometimes. We were labeled as witches in Massachusetts. That's why the families moved up to Maine, to get away from persecution. We've been in each other's back pockets ever since.

"Of course, nearly as soon as we got here, those blasted chotah have been haunting us. I was the first dream walker to actually see the mother monster...to understand what it is...what it can do. My dreams, and the reports of them, inspired the founding of Smithson Labs. The shadow charter portion, anyway."

Jillian frowned. "Shadow charter?"

"Caul? Do you mind?"

"No, not at all." He glanced at Jillian and Douglas. "Again, this isn't for general knowledge. The shadow charter is a document drawn up by the patriarchs of the three families several years before the lab was established. It basically outlined the goals and governance of an organization dedicated to studying and eliminating the threat presented by the chotah and the many other hybrid organisms—they called them legacy organisms—that were harming the families and other citizens of the area."

"But you're not related? To the families?"

Caul chuckled. "No, I'm not. Not at all."

Ruth shifted in her wheelchair. "However, Evelyn is."

"Yes." Caul's expression saddened. "Evelyn and I were sweethearts in high school down in Weymouth, outside of Boston. In '79, I was up here doing a summer internship at Smithson, and Evelyn came up for a visit with me and her cousins. She and Sharon and some other young Tates and Smithsons went out for a swim and some boulder crawling and Evelyn disappeared. We searched for days. Eventually, I had to return to the university, but I never forgot about her. She was my one true love. I dated other women over the years, but I never forgot Evelyn."

Nudging aside glasses, he wiped his eyes. "After graduate school, Jack Tate offered me a position at the lab. I accepted, obviously. But being back up here raised ghosts. The first time I saw Meeka—" he sniffed "—I couldn't believe my eyes. There was my Evelyn, back from the dead. But, she wasn't, obviously. Meeka consented to a date, we went out, we kissed, and I got the cold shoulder. Imagine that, will you? Your fiancé, back from the dead, only she isn't your fiancé, just a clever doppelganger."

"That's so sad." Jillian wiped her own tears.

"So, picture my surprise a few months later when you show up, Douglas, and she lights up like a klieg lamp. I was only a little angry." Caul's grin was wry. "But, by the saints, if you didn't start the mess that brought my Evelyn back to me."

Douglas felt heat on his cheeks, but returned the grin. "See? I'm the hombre in the white hat."

"Be glad you still have a head to wear that hat," Aiden said.

There was a patter of laughter, but the room chilled, regardless.

"Yeah, on that subject, what's going to happen to Mother?" Jillian's expression was murderous. "Extermination? Dynamite?"

Caul cleared his throat. "Absolutely not. We've got her contained. We'll be studying her and regulating her offspring."

"She deserves to be destroyed, after all the misery she's caused."

"I don't disagree," Caul said, "but killing her would be reckless. Very reckless. She's a singularity and so unlike anything we've ever seen. She changes almost everything that we understand about biology."

"Still."

Caul nodded. "Still."

She sighed and focused on Ruth and Fred. "I don't understand why she had such a fascination with your family."

"Ah, well, like I said, there's something different about us. Something in our blood, perhaps. We were witches once."

"She certainly coveted your genes," Caul said to Douglas.

He shifted uncomfortably on the bed. "Right. Which leaves the pink elephant question. What's so special about me? Why'd she want my, um, swimmers?"

Gazes shifted and shoulders shrugged.

Caul removed his glasses and polished them, as he looked back at Douglas from under heavy brows. "We may never know."

47

The silvery bell over the door of The Kindest Slice tinkled a greeting to the couple as they entered the pizzeria. They looked around until they saw waving hands and familiar faces.

"Jillian! You look fabulous."

Caul greeted her with a shoulder clasp and kiss to the cheek, as she rose from her seat. He reached over and shook Douglas's proffered hand. "Good to see you again."

Caul helped Evelyn into her chair, and then helped himself to the seat beside hers. "And who is this handsome young man?" He peered into the infant carrier resting on the table.

"This is Doug. Well, Doug Junior, but we usually just call him Doug or Little Doug." Jillian smiled as she gazed at her tow-headed, six-month-old son.

Douglas thought about how Jillian used to use that aphorism and grimaced. Life had changed.

"Wonderful!" Caul beamed at them. "And you're still going by Douglas, then?"

"Heh, Doug*less*, most of the time." He held up his three-fingered hand and thought of his half-empty pouch. The surgeons had added a prosthetic testicle during the final reconstructive surgery, but he could tell the difference; he was less of a man than he used to be.

The laughter around the table felt strained.

"That's not terribly funny," Caul said. "It's remarkable that you can joke about such things."

He pasted on a fake smile. "It's gallows humor, and gallows humor isn't funny unless a body swings."

Caul frowned. "Quite."

A blonde woman with a baby passed their table.

"Is everything else going well?" Evelyn asked, ignoring the men.

Jillian smirked. "As well as can be expected. Slugger here is back in the game." She thumped Douglas's arm.

"Jillie!"

"Oh, stop acting embarrassed. They both know what happened." She leaned close, lowering her voice. "We're trying to get pregnant again."

"So soon?" Evelyn asked, surprised but without judgment.

Douglas sighed and picked at a spot on the table. "We're not *trying* exactly. Rather, we're not not trying."

Silence settled on the group for several seconds, before Caul and Evelyn nodded. "I think I understood that."

"We're letting nature take its course." Jillian reached over and rubbed Douglas's arm. "I'm just thankful that everything came out as well as it did."

Doug Junior cooed, and they stilled for a moment as they stared at the chubby little man smiling up at them.

"We were surprised when you called. We've been pretty good lately. We've mostly blocked out..." Douglas grimaced.

"I am sorry. We didn't come to reopen wounds for you."

"I didn't think so, but why are you here? Why now?"

Caul put both hands flat on the table. "Well, mostly we wanted to see you because it's been so long since the wedding—"

"A whole year." Jillian grinned. "I can't believe it. How are you doing?"

Evelyn blushed. "Settling into a happy routine. He adopted all my underage ladies."

"Seriously?" Grimacing, Douglas rubbed his finger stump.

"That must make for interesting mornings!" Jillian said. "How are they? How many are there now?"

Caul leaned across the table and smirked. "We have twenty-nine still living with us—all human. We're at the residential facility the Army built at Smithson. Nina Nina, Oni Hunter, and Hunter Won just turned eighteen, so they have moved into separate government housing with the older Meekas, several of whom are helping us at the lab and at the home. And they're helping us make a lot of progress in our understanding of Mother."

A waitress stepped up to their table to take their order. Caul noticed that Douglas would not make eye contact with the woman. "Still tough, huh?"

Douglas glanced up. "Yeah, a bit. Still lots of triggers."

"I ran into Fred Uhlebe in town the other day. Said he's been down to visit."

"All of them have, even Ruth. They've been helping me with the nightmares. Still lots of those, too." He rubbed his face. "One or two of the Uhlebe clan comes down once a week. They rotate. Fred brings Ruth, if she's up for travel. She likes our church."

"Yes," Jillian said, cutting in, "she's such a sweetheart. She asked us the last time she was down what we had learned from the experience. I told her I had learned how to forgive. To fully forgive." She gazed at Douglas.

"And you?" Evelyn asked.

"Who, me?" Douglas asked and flushed. "Um, I told her I'd learned to never vacation in Maine."

The laughter was unforced this time.

"I'm not kidding!" Douglas said, his face etched with lines. "And, I still can't go into the fish section of the supermarket."

Jillian shuddered. "Oh, shut up, please. The first time I saw the lobster tank, I almost came unglued."

"Yes." Caul glanced at Evelyn. "We haven't had much of an appetite for seafood, either." He returned his attention to Douglas. "Is the military still visiting you?"

"No, they haven't been around in over a year, like two weeks before the wedding."

"That's good."

The waitress brought their drinks, and Caul took a long sip from his water glass. "They've been mostly hands off with us, after the initial flurry of activity, that is. There are inspectors still, but mostly just government scientists who work alongside us."

"You're still interim director?" Jillian asked.

"No!" Evelyn took Caul's hand and squeezed. "He was made permanent director. He's now a full government employee. We all are."

"Congratulations."

"Thank you, but it's really not such a big deal. The lab needed a director, and I'm the most qualified. Besides, it's easier for them to keep us under their thumb this way—we all had to take secrecy oaths and get government security clearances. Sharon would have been ecstatic. She always loved the secret agent aspects of the shadow charter, much more than I ever did."

Jillian frowned. "So...should you be here, talking about this, with us? I mean, won't you get in trouble?"

"Yes and no." Caul laughed. "It's fine. You two have something of *de facto* clearance, because you were there. I'm not really at liberty to disclose anything new, mind you." He glanced at Evelyn, who nodded and placed a reassuring hand on his shoulder. "Except for one small thing."

He pulled out his phone and typed for a few seconds, before slipping it back in a pocket. "So, Jillian, tell us about your photography business. Everyone raves over our wedding photos."

"Hold on. What were you just doing?"

Caul's grin was nervous. "I—I want you to meet someone."

"Who?"

"Just be patient." He raised placating hands. "And please keep open minds, all right?"

Douglas pushed back from the table, his face awash in conflicting emotions, and he struggled to control his breathing as Meeka walked up to the table carrying a small bundle. "Why are you here?"

"Douglas, please." Caul took the bundle from her. "This is Nina Fore. She helps us."

Nina Fore waved, before walking away to sit at another table.

"Why did you bring her?" Jillian glared at Caul. "I specifically said that we never wanted—"

"Jillian, please let go of the past." His expression entreated. "They've changed. They've moved on. Several of the older Meekas are dating, one couple is talking of marriage. Whatever influence Mother had over them is gone."

Jillian fumed and looked away, thinking of Meeka and Douglas together. She had forgiven Douglas, but Meeka was still an open question—an open wound. Talking about the younger versions was one thing, but seeing a grown woman Meeka in the flesh was entirely another. Time had healed only a little of that hurt.

Douglas, though, was watching the bundle in Caul's arms. It moved. "What is that?"

The older man smiled. "This...is yours." He held out the bundle, and Douglas could see a small face, eyes closed, nestled into the folds of a blanket. "Someone who Doug Junior needs to meet."

Douglas swallowed.

Caul laid the bundle in Douglas's arms. "This is Daneka."

"Daneka...?"

Glancing around, Caul spoke quietly. "Mother started producing them about four months ago."

Douglas looked up, panic on his brow. "Them?"

"Thirty five to date," Caul said.

"Why? What are they?"

Evelyn reached over and stroked the baby through the blanket. "This is your daughter, Douglas. Well, really, our daughter."

Douglas dropped the bundle on the table. "That isn't funny!"

Jillian flinched as the baby fell a few inches and hit. "Douglas!"

Evelyn snatched up the now crying infant. "It's not a joke!" She soothed the baby, who looked around in dark-eyed disbelief. "For whatever reason, Mother is making girl children based on our DNA."

The idea hit Douglas like a fist, and he gaped at this old-woman version of Meeka. Meeka—the memory of whose body still woke him in the night, turgid and drenched in sweat. He had pondered life with Meeka, and imagined what their children would look like. Now here, in front of him, was one of those inky-eyed daughters.

"Hey, please no more of that talk." Despite her protest, Jillian held out her arms for Daneka.

"What are you doing?" Douglas watched her with mounting worry.

"Hush, you. It's not her fault. She's just a baby." Jillian peeled back a corner of blanket. "Oh, and what a cute baby you are too." She looked up at Caul. "Did you say thirty five?"

"And more coming, as far as we can tell."

She stroked Daneka's cheek. "I'm keeping her."

Douglas flinched. "Jillian!"

"Hush. This is your flesh. And Little Doug's half-sister."

Caul leaned forward. "I'm sorry, but they're all wards of the federal government, at the moment. I had to make special arrangements to even bring her down here."

Slowly, Jillian's lower lip pushed out and her eyes grew wide. "But, she's so cute!"

Caul and Evelyn both laughed. "I'll see what I can do. It would be good to get some of these children fostered out, and you've got a better claim on them than anyone." He glanced at his wife. "Except you, of course."

Daneka's cries were making Doug fussy, so Jillian handed her back to Evelyn and lifted Doug from his carrier. As she was preparing to nurse him, Meeka came to the table.

"I'll take her. She's due for a diaper change anyway."

"Sure. Thank you, Meeka," Evelyn said.

They watched her walk away.

"How is Mother doing that?" Douglas was not sure he really wanted the answer, but he felt compelled to ask the question regardless.

"Mother's interesting. She's like a gigantic, living gene manipulation laboratory. We still don't understand most of what she can do inside her body, but it is apparent that she can take the DNA of different organisms and make new combinations, make new organisms. Meeka, well, the Meekas, are one of those organisms."

"What is Mother? Where did she come from?"

"That, we don't know. Bellah and Ashrah were the only two surviving squidheads—apparently there were five Bellah or Eldest Meekas, but they fought, right after birth, and Bellah killed her sisters, making herself Eldest Meeka, regardless of her birth order. The next Meeka was Six, and so on, but no subsequent Meeka was born a squidhead."

Douglas scrunched up his face at the mention of Bellah.

"She killed them? As babies?" Jillian shuddered. "Why?"

"Because they were special. Based on our studies, they had a large percentage of Mother's DNA. They had many of what we're calling Mother's control genes—the genes that allowed her to exert her will over the Meekas, Johns, chotah, and all the other beasts she created. Apparently, she needed a filter and a repeater, though, so she created the squidheads first. She could link, telepathically, directly to them, and they, in turn, communicated and controlled their siblings. However, there could be only one leader Meeka, and Mother wanted the strongest of the bunch."

"How barbaric! And how do you know this?" Jillian asked.

Caul looked around. "Hmm. I just realized this is new information and you probably shouldn't be hearing it. I'm so much more the scientist and lecturer than I am a government agent or secret keeper. But, I don't think it will hurt to tell you. Twenty-seven can communicate with Mother. She has a language—based on polyphones and rhythms, more like music than language—but, she can speak to Twenty-seven."

He glanced at Jillian. "I know you had some issues with her, but that lady is amazing and has been invaluable to us. We've made strides in our understanding thanks to her, but there are some things that Mother refuses to talk about. The hows, the whys, and where she came from get no answer."

Jillian shuddered. "It's all like a bad dream now." She switched sides with Doug just as the waitress brought bread sticks and salads.

"Oh, bad timing." Evelyn looked on with sympathy and a trace of envy.

Douglas chuckled. "Nah! We have a system down for this. She feeds Doug and I feed her. It's all good." Jillian kicked him under the table. "Um, when she needs me to, that is."

"Well, good." Caul smiled at everyone. "Shall we?"

"I'll say the blessing. Then we shall." Douglas gave thanks for their food and company then looked up and grabbed a salad fork. "Yeah, bad dreams. It's funny that we went to Maine looking for a blessing and nearly got killed in the process."

"But we did get our blessing." Jillian stroked Doug's downy hair.

"And we got ours." Evelyn raised her hand, wrapped around Caul's. "If not for your return to Maine, I doubt that I ever would have escaped the tunnels."

"Yes, I grudgingly admit that you did a good thing," Caul said to Douglas. "It was messy, but your actions brought the light back to my life." He kissed Evelyn's hand. "So, thank you."

"All's weird that ends weird!" Douglas lifted his glass, and they clinked all around. "Cheers!"

"Cheers!"

He gazed into Jillian's blue eyes and smiled. "Cheers."

48

Nina Fore stepped out of the ladies room and surveyed the dinner party from afar. The four friends seemed to be having a good time, and she was out of sight and mind, so she thought it was best that she stayed that way. As she stood, a voice spoke to her.

"She's beautiful. May I hold her?"

She glanced down at the blonde woman in dark glasses.

"Certainly. And this is this your son?" Nina gazed at the baby, wrapped in a fuzzy blue blanket, lying on the seat beside the woman.

Nina sat, and the women exchanged babies. Nina pulled back the blanket from the boy's face. "He's so handsome."

"Just like his father."

The women sat in apparent silence, looking at each other's faces. Finally, the other tilted her head, her fringes of blonde hair joining to cover a frown. "So few survived…"

"Unfortunately. But this worked." Nina smiled and bounced the little boy, who gurgled. She felt a longing in her own womb.

"Yes." The blonde looked up. "Now it's time to find out if it will again. I hear that slugger is back in the game. So I—*you*—you and the other red-blooded sisters need to come down here."

"We're working on a plan."

"Good." The blonde paused. "I've missed you so much."

"We've missed you, too, Nina Tree."

"It's Nan Trenchard, now. I thought it best to blend in better."

Nina Fore nodded. "Nan. I like it. And I like your hair."

"Thanks." Nan's expression became tight. "It's been hard to…adapt, without me—*you*. How long can you stay?"

"Until they're done eating and talking. Probably an hour or more."

"Good. Let me just look at you then. It's been so long." Nan smiled and leaned across the table. She removed her dark glasses, revealing inky eyes—deep as the ocean. "Yes, it's good to you again. To see me."

The Story Continues...

Life has finally settled down for Douglas Sandow, seemingly almost to a new normal.

But peace is never meant to last. Not for long, anyway.

The ALEWIFE
Sins *of the* Mother

The Sins are coming...

7.10.2017

Epilogue

Everything about *The Alewife* is fiction—distilled straight from my head—or is used fictitiously; Bar Harbor and Mount Desert Island are real places, but they exist in a parallel dimension to those places in this work. Likewise, the folklore of *The Alewife* is an amalgam of historical sources and my own created pantheon. Several readers have asked about the creatures in the book, wondering if I would tell them more. So, without giving away spoilers, I'll provide a short bio on each.

Chotah (KO-tuh): These are all mine, although they are loosely based on some of Lovecraft's creatures, as noted in the text. These walleyed pikers are some of Mother's oldest minions.

Danekas: I'll explain these girls in *Sins of the Mother*.

Havasrå: Straight out of Scandinavian folklore; an aquatic succubus.

Huldra: Also straight out of Scandinavian folklore; a sylvan succubus, with a cow or fox tail.

Jillian: Yes, I realize that she is human, but given the hate mail she has received in the past two years—from men and women alike—I strongly suspect that many readers find her more monsterous than Meeka.

John: One of Mother's successful humanoid creations.

Meeka (ME-kuh): Mother's most successful creation to date.

Mother, aka Cthulhu: Certainly not the Cthulhu of Lovecraft fame, Doug can nevertheless be forgiven for drawing this conclusion based on the appearance of what he can see of it.

Taucah (TAU-caah): These are all mine, especially the size and relative intelligence, although they are compared to the lobstrosities from Stephen King's The Dark Tower series by some of the Smithson Labs technicians. As the chotah are Mother's infantry, I wanted a creature akin to lightly armored cavalry, and what better candidate than a lobster?

Scorah (SOH-ruh, S as in *scene*): All mine, and logical secondary creature characters given Mother's apparent genetic background.

Squidheads, aka Bellah and Ashrah: All mine, although drawing inspiration from Lovecraft.

Selkies: These are creatures found in Scottish folklore. They are seals that could remove their skin and become human women.

Sirens: Mythological women of Greek folklore who would sing and lure sailors into the water and to their deaths.

Saunders crab: All mine. These cute little guys can work together in groups, numbering in the thousands.

About the Author

Jason T. Graves

Writer, editor, illustrator, educator—Jason is most at home making things or teaching. He takes his coffee black and his beer blacker. You'll find him most days doing the former while consuming the latter. Oh, and he was once punched, a single time and very lightly, by Muhammad Ali.